STORM IN THE BLOOD

R!

r

I

A STORM IN THE BLOOD

Jon S. Fink

Cutting Edge Press
London

This edition Copyright © Cutting Edge Press 2010

Jon Stephen Fink has asserted his moral rights to be
identified as the author of this work under the
1988 Copyright, Design and Patents Act.

Set in ITC Baskerville
by Keyboard Services, Luton
keyboardserv@sky.com

Printed in Great Britain by
JF Print, Sparkford

Distributed by Turnaround Publishing Services, Unit 3,
Olympia Trading Estate, Coburg Road, London N22 6TZ

ISBN 978-0-9565445-1-3

To Lisa, from beginning to end

Be it Russian or Pole, Lithuanian or Jew
I care not but take it for granted,
That the island of Britain can readily do
With the notice: 'No Alien Wanted'.

— 'Will Workman' writing in *The People*, 1909

Those who live and labor in the great East End feel hot and angry at the sight of faces so un-English and the sound of speech so foreign. In face, instinct, language and character their children are aliens, and still exiles.

— from a Whitechapel clergyman's letter, 1906

Who are these fiends in human shape, who do not hesitate to turn their weapons on innocent little boys and harmless women?

— article in *The Daily Mirror*, 1909

I

INHUMAN CRIMINALS

One

In their village the Bermansfelt family had a *reputation*. Mordechai's branch of the Bermansfelt line was crazy in its own way, but everyone agreed that the whole squabbling lot of them, going back generations, was crazy in the blood. And so it was, one autumn midnight, that no neighbour in Sasmacken over the age of seven was surprised when certain events on the Talsen Road turned Mordechai Bermansfelt from a clockmaker into a condemned man and his teenage daughter Rivka into a fugitive.

In a locality that took a hard attitude towards Jews, the Bermansfelt family's reputation for unpredictable behaviour had one advantage: it shielded them by obscuring their motives beneath a fuzz of gossip. Once, a young Russian army private approached the Bermansfelts' youngest daughter in the street. 'Miss, please,' he said, a few steps in front of her, bashful in a way that hinted things might turn nasty if shyness didn't get him what he was after. That night, a lifetime ago, he was after fifteen-year-old Rivka. 'Miss? My friends — they're laughing at me. They say I'm a coward if I don't talk to you. Will you stop for a minute?'

Rivka smiled, offered him a trace of her own shyness and kept her pretty mouth closed. She didn't look down. She didn't look side to side for help. This encouraged the trooper to beg, soulfully, 'Please, Miss, tell me your name.' From a restaurant doorway his uniformed pals egged him on with cat calls, gestures, insults to his

3

manhood. Rivka stepped back into the street, holding her smile. When the Russian private made a move to follow her she flashed him the flat of her hand at the end of her stiff arm. And then she started to sing.

Her eyes playful and ferocious, a disconnected smile below, she sang: '*Nokh eyn tants, beyt ikh itst bay dir... Libster her, ikh bay dir shenk zhe mir nokh eyn tants mir... Ikh hob dik gezukht mayn gants lebn lang ... Ists farlir ikh dikh tut mir azoy bang... Bist gekummen tsu shpeyt in meyn glik... Iz shoyn oys, libster her...*'

> One dance more, I beg of you,
> Dearest Sir, I beg you grant me
> One dance more...
> I searched for you all my life,
> Now I'm losing you and I'm so sad.
> My joy lasted only an hour.
> You came too late,
> It's over, dearest sir...

Balodis the grocer, who did regular business with the garrison, kept an eye on things from the doorway of his store. For everyone's sake he stepped in to salvage the teenage soldier's dignity. In Russian Balodis advised him, 'Don't get your hands dirty for nothing,' Balodis advised him in Russian, 'She's crazier than the limp prick who dribbled her out.' There were times when slobbering prejudice worked in the family's favour.

Another memory of village life would survive in Rivka like an ancient catfish in murky river water – the face of Sasmacken's local garrison commander, Colonel Y.M. Orlov, a minor aristocrat who showed genuine creativity when it came to malice and abuse. In this he proudly swaggered in the footsteps of Peter the Great, who had kicked the Swedes out of Latvia a hundred years before and flooded the country with Russian colonists. Where they couldn't outbreed the natives, the Russians stripped them of their language, laws and social freedoms. When the Letts objected, they were killed in their thousands, cut down in the streets, chased into freezing rivers, slung into prisons, exiled. Latvian Jews received all this, with the added benefit of not having to leave their houses.

Normally it was beneath the dignity of a Russian officer to pay Jews on time or the agreed price for their work. Or at all. It was a principle of authority and Orlov was a tower of principle. Unless you could dodge his summons with an attack of hysterical blindness, the smart choice was to accept the offer that glowed like a hot coal inside it.

Too flustered to fake blindness, Rivka's father accepted Colonel Orlov's commission to build him a mantel clock, in the Louis Quatorze style, as a decoration for his master bedroom. For five months Mordechai dedicated himself to the job night and day. The finished clock married use to beauty in a stately ceremony of glass, enamel, brass and wood. He delivered it himself, trudging miles out to the manor house for the satisfaction — the physical proof — that he had, thank God, made it to the end in one piece. His payment? That night Orlov burst in on the Bermansfelts' dinner, swinging the clock in a burlap bag, like a litter of kittens he was going to beat to death. On the floor in front of them he took his rifle butt to the gilded wood and the enamel face and smashed Mordechai's work to splinters because 'This pile of junk ticks so loud it even keeps the maid awake.'

Helpless, ashamed, unhinged, Mordechai retreated to the woodshed after Orlov thundered away on his horse. He stayed there for the rest of the night and late into the next day. After enduring the Russian's assault he needed solitude to remember who he was, to give him strength for the next onslaught. When he finally came inside, his wife, Rebekah set a cup of tea on the table for him. He sipped some through a sugar cube and asked for a piece of dry toast. After another cup of tea, his family keenly silent around him at the table, Mordechai spoke. The words, like solid things, had formed in his mouth overnight. Out they tumbled: 'I know what to do.'

That was all, and Rebekah let the remark go. She was delighted that her husband wasn't lying dead in the street or in a jail cell in Riga with his back flayed to raw strips. Her suspicious daughter, though, tried every trick she knew to get him to tell her more — to tell her his plans. Mordechai answered Rivka the same way each time, by touching his finger to his lips. A little tilt of his head, a sour frown that said, *What you see – that's what I'm doing*.

Then, one dinnertime, Mordechai wasn't in his chair at the table. He wasn't contemplating the cobwebs in the woodshed, either.

The minute they knew he was gone, a cry went up and the Bermansfelts fanned out across Sasmacken. The five sons scoured the streets; Rebekah and Sara knocked on neighbours' doors. Rivka searched farther afield, outside the town limits. She looked up into the clear cold sky, its distance and darkness threaded into the world with shadows of tree branches. Some ghostly hand must have touched her shoulder, guiding her along the dark road. It could have been Mordechai's spirit hand reaching out to her from his hiding place.

Rivka bunched her skirts in a determined fist and ran down the Talsen road. Half a mile from Orlov's manor house, out of breath, she found her father hunkered by the roadside. 'Papa?'

He ducked behind the nettles and slipped down into a pool of shadows. 'Ssh!'

'If I can see you hiding there, anybody can.'

'Shush! Watch your voice! What can you see if you're on a horse? I could be a wild animal in here,' Mordechai whispered. 'A big dog. I'm telling you.' He levered himself up again over the lip of the ditch, he put it to her: 'You can help me,' he told her. 'Good.'

Mordechai crossed to the other side of the road, crouched behind the whitewashed nub of the Talsen milestone. Unafraid, in a subversively normal tone of voice, Rivka said, 'Whatever you're doing, Papa, it doesn't look like a good idea.'

'They don't expect us to complain. Not in their own language.'

As she sat and watched, her father looped a coil of thick rope around the stone and anchored it. Then, shuffling sideways he stepped around her, letting the rope's length sag and flatten on the road. He kicked earth over it as he crabbed back to the ditch.

'If you don't want to help me, do you mind going home? Stay out of the way.'

'Papa, one minute you were with us in the kitchen, and the next minute — *pssht*, gone. For all we knew they dropped you down a hole.'

'That's the thing we're facing,' he said.

'Come back with me, will you, Papa?'

'As usual, I'm the only one with a calm brain. Riveleh, if you're not going home you have to hide in the ditch. Or go behind those trees.'

'So you'll ambush the Russian army. Yes, all right...' Rivka said, getting the picture. 'Then what?'

'Not all of them. One or two.' Mordechai picked up a rock the size of an orange and dropped it into his coat pocket.

'One or two?'

'If I'm lucky.'

'Then what?'

'God knows.'

A dose of reality. 'I'll find you in Riga Prison, or the morgue.'

'Quiet, please, darling. Here they come.'

Her freckled fingers scraped back the edge of her shawl. She held still and listened for vibrations in the air. A rhythm of hoofbeats carried down the road. She knew that quick, potent, earth-muffled rhythm. It was how the cavalry rode. Her father leaned up to see the single horse and rider cantering towards him from the town.

Now the argument turned into a wrenching tug-of-war. Rivka sank her heels into the spongy earth of the ditch bank and leaned her body backwards, using her weight to force the rope out of her father's hands. Mordechai, a fish on a line, caught and struggling, hissed at her to *let go* and move out of the way. If her hands could work as quickly as her brain, she still had precious seconds to get her father away from there with no one the wiser. Rivka ran to the milestone and pulled at the knotted rope knuckled around it. She scrabbled at the granite for a hand hold. Her fingernails tore; the rope might as well have been carved into the rock. Still seconds, still ...

Rivka stepped into the road before the thought to do it formed in her head, waving her shawl as a warning. She walked forwards, in front of the rope, away from her father's hideout.

Maybe the rider was drunk; or maybe he took the figure waving at him in the road for the shadow of windblown branches as he galloped past. In the same moment that Rivka jumped to safety, Mordechai sprang

8

his trap. The rope snapped up from the ground and caught the animal knee-high, snagged its forelegs and tipped him over, headfirst.

The big chestnut Don rolled to its feet; the Russian officer did not. He lay on his stomach, blood trickling out of a gash in his forehead. Rivka and Mordechai stood over him. 'Don't let him see you, Papa. Go home!' She daubed the wound with the sleeve of her dress.

'Did I kill him?'

'Thank God, no. He's waking up. Will you *go*?'

Mordechai paced in a small circle, momentarily off-course in a wilderness of his own. The Russian had enough strength in him to raise the upper part of his body. He sat splay-legged in the middle of the road. A faint sign of relief flickered across his face, scratched and bruised as it was, when he realized he wasn't there alone. 'What a tumble I took. Is Kolya hurt very bad?'

'Your horse?' Rivka asked, one eye on her father, purging the shakiness from her voice.

'Kolya. His hoof needs a shoe.'

'Kolya's fine. He's by the tree, behind you. See him?' She brushed more of the sweat, dirt, and blood out of his eyes.

'He's grazing?' Rivka supported his shoulders as the Russian arched his neck to look. 'Kolya's like me. Eating, always eating.'

But the Russian couldn't focus very well on his horse or the tree. And he didn't see the rock that flashed white-gray when Mordechai pitched it at his head. That spasm of violence shook a yelp out of Rivka and a groan from the Russian, who collapsed sideways on the ground. 'What...?' he said to no one, to himself, smearing wet blood out of his eyes with his tunic sleeve. 'What happened to me?' He unholstered his revolver, but his aim was wild. The first shot went up into the trees. His second bullet hit the ground an inch from Mordechai's shoes, splashing chips of rock into the air.

Rivka was sure the noise of gunfire could travel on the night air all the way to Sasmacken. 'Run,' she begged her father, pulled at his arm, dragged him backwards away from there.

The rest of the Russian's troop must only have been two minutes behind on the Talsen road. In a blink they were there: Four riders, five — Rivka couldn't count how many, were circling them, shouting questions, and answers too. 'What are you doing out here?' 'What's your name?' 'Your *name*, cunt!' 'You're a terrorist.' 'Is that what you are?' 'Who's the slut?' 'Where do you live?' 'I know him. That's the Jew clockmaker...' 'Didn't Colonel Orlov finish with you?' '... from Sasmacken.'

At the centre of a carousel of hooves and boots, flanks and faces, whipping tails, jangling reins, Mordechai snapped out of his trance. He grabbed Rivka's shoulders and hugged her close to him. His whisper had desperation in it, and sudden strength. 'Get away from here.'

'Not by myself.'

'Do what I'm telling you. Don't go home — you have to get to Talsen. It'll be all right. Go to Jankel. He'll know what to do for you.' Then, to the riders, his arms waving above his head, Mordechai announced, 'Yes, yes! I'm Bermansfelt! You and your monkey colonel can go crap in your hats!'

Rivka felt a shove in her back, and she stumbled through a gap that curtained shut behind her as the whole gang of them fell upon her father. Then she ran. Into the ditch and along it, across the corner of a field, to the pine woods beyond. Two soldiers on horseback chased her, shouting to each other, maddened, laughing,

10

firing their guns up, down, sideways. Wild shots smashed the branches and tree trunks on every side. Charging through the tangled shadows, they couldn't see what they were shooting at.

In the forest, hours later, only a mile from home, Rivka ducked down and tucked in, then slept in the dirt, more lost than hidden.

Two

For most of the next day Rivka tore through the forest, slipping on pine needles, dodging from tree to tree at the sound of circling Cossack horse hooves. And when she could think, she thought: *Here's the inescapable reality – men shatter the world and women run for cover.* By oratory and legislation, by custom and impulse, by inborn nature, men lay out choices in the raw for women – just as Rivka's father did for her on that terrifying night early in October 1910.

Clothes torn, running in circles, she made it out of the woods with cuts on her face and arms, a mangled knee, a sprained wrist. At the first farmhouse Rivka struck lucky. Jews lived there. She was allowed to shelter in a chicken coop for one night. But this was just the first step of ten thousand, and worse luck was on its way.

Bad luck sat eating potatoes cooked in pig fat, in the squalor of the ramshackle hut she happened across on her second day of hiding. It occupied a corner of a beet field that belonged to two bachelor brothers, farm labourers, Letts, who fed her a bowl of soup and listened, sad-faced, nodding, to her story. 'Terrible, terrible,' one brother said. The other agreed. 'Terrible. You're a little girl. You tried to stop him. Maybe by now the police know everything and it's not so bad. There's one sure sign: If they put up a reward to catch you.' Brother Number Two barely disguised what he was thinking. He said, 'One of us can go find out.'

Rivka knew no Yiddish song would work any magic on

those boys and — even as old as they were — she figured, two against one weren't the best odds if she ended up fighting her way to the door. So she went at it another way. 'Oh, *thank you*,' she cooed. 'Can you go soon? *Now*?' She wrung a fold of her skirt in her twitching hands, in their debt, at their mercy, offering them her frailty and fear, which she didn't need to work very hard to muster. As soon as Brother Number Two left for town, Rivka sneaked out the window. She was on the run again and didn't stop until she reached Talsen, where her cousin Jankel had a print shop. When he opened the door, she fainted into his thick arms.

For a few oblivious hours she was free. Then she woke up in bed and remembered where she was and why. She sobbed so heavily that Jankel expected to find her tears on his shirt front pink from blood. And, with that, the storm was over.

Now, just as she had faced down the Russian soldier in the street, as she had faced her demented father on the Talsen road, Rivka faced her situation. She told Jankel the news of Mordechai's one-man uprising against the Tsar of Russia. All of this he knew already, but he wanted to hear Rivka tell it.

'I don't know if he's alive or dead,' she told her cousin, her voice losing its steadiness.

'Somebody will know,' said Jankel.

Her first question, the only one she asked him was, 'How soon can I go home?'

'Sleep now. Stay inside. I'll visit Rebekah.'

Jankel returned from Sasmacken with hard information. Mordechai was, yes, in prison, and Rivka — his Accomplice in the Attempted Murder of a Russian Cavalry Officer — was sought by the police for questioning. All it had taken was a quarter of an hour one night, a single misbegotten act, to transform her into an enemy of the state.

Plain as he could, Jankel told her, 'You have to get out of the country.'

Travel vouchers, permission to travel, passport, steamship ticket: Jankel forged them all. He was a master at it. His underground connections, his network of political friends, spread from the northern borders of Courland down to Riga and beyond. Many of them were members of Liesma, The Flame, a revolutionary gang dedicated, *consecrated*, to acts of political terror, mainly armed robberies, 'exes' — expropriations, from banks, businesses, private and public wealth. Latvians among them, nationalists, communists, some Jews, it was true, but they spoke a language foreign in every other way to young uprooted Rivka.

The underground moved her from village to village, safe house to safe house. She travelled by foot and horse cart. Sometimes she had help avoiding the patrols of Russian gendarmerie and Cossacks, other times she was left to make her way to Riga alone. To comfort herself, she thought of her mother's eyes, cherishing Rivka across the kitchen or from the bedroom doorway. They were a spiritual blue, and they looked out on the suffering world the same way Rivka's did. Particles of the deep and clear, unreachable, high atmosphere were embedded in her face.

In three days those eyes were looking out, for the first time, on England.

The seventy souls who travelled with Rivka in the hold of the *Comet* dissolved into the crowd on the quay. People moved in no direction, in all directions, a jumbled mass with no centre. Rivka was shoved along in a dirty sluggish

15

flow of the destitute, all struggling with baggage, bundles, children, thirst, hunger, fatigue. In front of her, calling out surnames behind waving hands and scavenging eyes, washing through and past the streams of newcomers in a counter-tide, were the Londoners. For a minute Rivka let the jostling panorama pour in through her high blue eyes.

Jankel had guaranteed that an escort would be there to meet her, but she suddenly doubted that the yellow tablecloth she carried, the bright bundle of donated skirts, blouses and food put into her hands by her last contact in Riga, would be enough of a marker to single her out.

She stood scanning the dockside for her escort's unfamiliar face. Quick as a squirrel, a young boy, shoeless, dipped out of the horde and made a grab for the bundle at her feet. His fingers hooked the rope that secured it; he avoided her glance, his bead on the kill. He spoke to Rivka in Yiddish. 'I'll take you to Whitechapel, Miss. Free lodging. Cheap food, Miss.'

Then, out of the same bulge in the crowd a man's hand flew down and slapped at him so hard that the boy's flat cap jumped from his head. The man spoke to her. 'You need to watch out for lads like that one. Even Jews rob Jews. His father, I know him. Birnbaum. He's a crook, the worst kind. If you give him an inch he'll steal everything you own then push you out in the street. Please. My name is Marks.' Marks pointed at the badge on his lapel, which Rivka couldn't read. He tapped the badge and said, 'Hebrew Ladies' Protective Society. You arrived alone? On her own, a woman...'

'Someone is meeting me here,' she said.

'Is he?' Marks looked around, friendly and sceptical. He'd seen women abandoned by husbands, brothers,

16

even fathers on this disorderly dock. Marks gave a nod towards the danger prowling around her, the men lounging at the door of the gin shop. He raised an eyebrow at the shouts slashing across the wharf.

'*Move that load of shit!*'

'*Shit-arsed Russos. Landin' fee. Landin' fee, get me? No money, you row your arses back to the boat!*'

'What can happen you don't want to imagine. We have to look out for each other twenty-five hours a day.' Rivka was aware of a tall man standing nearby, listening closely, making Marks' point for him. 'If you need a place to sleep I'll take you to the Temporary Shelter in Leman Street,' Marks went on. 'I took some others from Latvia last night. Which boat brought you out?' he asked, carefully polite and cheerful under pressure, offering small talk as part of the service, as he reached to take her luggage. 'You have everything? This way,' Marks said to her.

'*Crimp.*' A curse, in English. Behind it, the tall man stepped clumsily into Marks's way, blocking him with his body and brute intention. 'Give me the bag.'

'So you can steal it? No!' Marks answered back with a sharp look up. He only came up to the tall man's chest. 'This lady is under my protection. The safety... She's under the safety of the Hebrew Ladies' Protective Society.'

'I can get twenty badges from the same place you got yours.'

The insult lit red fires in the patches of skin above Marks's beard. The tall ruffian kept at it, looked Rivka in the face and said, 'Stay away from this *shundiknik*. He'll knock you on the head and sell you to men for two shillings a time.'

'You see? *This* is what I'm telling you,' Marks cried out, runty arms flung up, indignant, exasperated. 'They

17

swarm in, men like him. Prowlers. To rob you. They steal from other Jews. It's repulsive. I know the Chief Rabbi,' he shouted to keep his attacker off. 'I'm an *official*.' But when Marks bent over to pick up Rivka's luggage a savage kick in the ribs spilled him onto the ground.

'He didn't deserve that, did he?' Rivka demanded an answer.

'He must have,' said the man, meaning, *yes of course he did, it was what happened to him.* His eyes were mild when he spoke to her, and possessive. His message was simple: Rivka's business, from here on, was his business. 'Look for the yellow,' he said to her and stooped to grab a hold of the eye-catching bundle. He turned to Marks, with a warning: 'She has friends here.'

He delivered a vicious slap to Marks's face. 'Liesma. You understand?'

Three

Behind his back, friends and strangers alike called her escort 'The Limper'. Joseph Sokoloff, nicknamed Yoska. The crippled right thigh, the pits and sores on his skin, the black and broken teeth, the thick waist and legs, the extra weight he himself called his 'cow belly,' whatever his body did to attract his attention, Yoska ignored it. Or else, too conscious of his impression on strangers (especially attractive strangers like Rivka), he haemorrhaged conversation to take the spotlight off of his flaws.

Rivka's guide through Cable Street kept ahead of her even with his wide-gaited limp. His torso swivelled with each step he took; left foot planted, right foot dragging behind, so that he seemed to be forcing himself permanently uphill. To make up for it, he set a quicker pace, swerving through the buyers and sellers, cornering around the stalls, through the Yiddish and Cockney hurly-burly of market voices. The first time Rivka heard the English language it reached her ears as a cascade of exotic confusion.

Wot's yer game, eh?

... no bloomin' good.

'No bloomy good,' Rivka mimicked. 'What does it mean?'

'Very bad.' Yoska gave the bundle a shake, craned it out at the end of his long arm and tested the weight. 'You didn't leave with much, did you?'

'Not even my own clothes,' she said. 'My father is in prison, did Jankel tell you that?'

Sympathy and concentration pursed Yoska's lips. 'I don't know any Jankel.' His smile turned that lie into an intimate joke. 'Did he tell you about me? My name?'

'My cousin told me the name of the boat. That's the only one he told me.'

'I'm Yoska,' he said without looking at her. 'I can fix you up with anything here. Anything you want.'

'How soon can I go home?' she asked him.

'I'm like you. Always I'm thinking about the future.'

She was here and her father was there, everybody she knew was there, those were the facts. So Rivka gave in to a more useful worry. 'What can I do? I have to work.'

'What did you do at home? For money, straight pay.'

'Bakery.'

'We know a good place. A restaurant. All of us go there.'

'I can carry plates.'

The first broad street Yoska navigated, Rivka in tow, could have been lifted from a town in Latvia and set down across the North Sea. Shops announced their existence and purpose with black and white signs in English and Hebrew letters. A fried fish shop, a rag-and-bone yard, a cabinet maker, a coffee house, and more than one hole-in-the-wall restaurant, each with its own advertising scent hovering around the door. Hot oil, mildew, sawdust, frying onions, crusty toast, smoked herring. They walked past spreads of fruit and vegetables that topped the wooden market stalls with colour and aproned the sooty brick of the buildings. Among them too, white chickens dangled by their feet, pink meat leaked blood, gutters clogged with slops and dribbled with ooze that spread to the street, where it clung to passing boots and shoes.

Down those close dogleg turns Rivka had the feeling of

descending into Whitechapel. The streets felt close with human noise. Shouts for food, shouts of buying and selling goods and labour, shouts to the wild children from women who sat in chairs on the street, the sharp rattle of high wheels on the cobblestones when carriages and carts hauled by, all of it stole her attention. Occasionally, Yoska would break off from something he was saying to point out a landmark important for finding your way around the crooked turnings and hive of courtyards. The blind sprawl groped in a hundred different directions, with no guiding hand except necessity.

Whitechapel's buildings rose out of the pavement, darkly. A rind of soot held them together. In places they grew out of each other, the way ancient trees throw down branches that somehow take root. Bridges connected floors across alleys, built with scraps of wood, zigzagging sideways, upward, into a tower of corners. Filth, two feet thick, caked into a sediment on the slanted tin roofs. Garbage slopped from upper windows, from the upper storeys, piled up in layers of fish and meat bones, rags, old boots, broken plates, God-knows-what. She looked up, through the shambles. Above her Rivka could only see squares of anaemic cloud. Any brightness that wasn't stopped by the roof tops thinned to nothing at ground level, where the bone-coloured light was soaked up by shadows that webbed every entrance and exit. Her new world.

Sensitive to Rivka's mood, Yoska said, 'Keep your eyes open. Plenty of opportunities here.' It was good advice; her *comrade* was eager to help her because her exploit commanded respect. A Cossack killer! She was a friend from the first minute, and with a friendly eye Yoska stole glimpses of her walnut brown hair, her freckled hands and throat, the slow, soft contours of her face. And to top

21

it off – Yoska believed Jankel on this score – she was a scrapper, a fugitive, ambusher of Russians. Over here, he was the protector, she the protected. Who'd say it was bragging to reassure Rivka that she was in the care of a seasoned revolutionary?

'It's been quiet in London,' he said. 'I like it better that way. What I do, I use my brains.'

'You can write down the address of the restaurant?'

'Sure, of course. Shinebloom's. We call it Shinebloom's. I'll introduce you to the manager tomorrow morning.'

Their hour-long walk from Tilbury brought them to a wall at Commercial Road. The onrush of motor traffic stopped them as hard as if they'd come to the bank of a wild river. Held off by an unbroken, unbreakable stir of hansom cabs, coaches, motor-omnibuses and motor cars, they watched for a chance to cross. A block away, the flow thickened and pooled. Pedestrians colonised the pavement, passengers climbed down from the omnibuses and out of the flapping square doors of coaches and automobiles, their heads and hats bobbing in the crush. From where Rivka stood, it all resembled a stretch of bubbling black water disturbed by the wind.

This was not the stunned scramble of refugees who landed with Rivka at Tilbury Docks. Here, the crush there moved with the purpose of the city. Perched on the kerb she watched Englishmen parade along Commercial Road – tight-mouthed passengers behind the upright windows of broughams, distantly distracted pedestrians, frock coated *gents* whose habits maintained the nation. Look how the English move. Steady steps. No fear in their faces, and less than a mile from where their steamships arrive and depart, is the underworld.

Yoska took her hand and stepped out into traffic. In his dusty brown overcoat he stretched his arm and flipped his free hand upward, broad and pale, assertive. The drooping green snout of a motor-taxi dipped as the driver braked and gave them time to cross.

At least here I'll see no Cossacks or Russian officers, Rivka reminded herself. She was living in this place now, her feet stood planted in Great Britain. A momentum just starting to build had conveyed her here. Look behind, Rivka thought, and you'd see the life that this driving pulse had outrun. Latvia was expunged. Sasmacken. Riga. Zalenieku. Druza. Tirzas. Libau. The kerb stones beneath her feet were London kerb stones. The overcast sky, English sky.

Four

Under a canalside stretch of the Parisian sky and shadowed by the same pale gray weather that comforted Rivka on her walk across the East End, Peter Piatkow sat on a borrowed café chair with his half-eaten lunch, a bowl of potato soup, going cold in his lap. A rocky motion, the watery bump and shove he felt in his organs, told Peter he was drifting into a crisis.

He focused his eyes on the canal with keen purpose, as he fought himself at the same time to forget what the purpose was. His mind quieted. In disturbed patches, the dull green water was flecked, fish-scaled, with daylight. Just then the thought occurred to him: this is how an animal or insect sees it, liberated from ideas, a liberation you don't need violence to win for yourself. In fact, in that slipping space of time, Peter won it with the opposite of violence.

A moment at rest. Beside this water with its chaotic reflections, he felt himself floating free of morality, accomplishment, history, comradeship, the good fight, every one of civilization's hall-of-mirrors illusions, with nothing required of him any more except to be present for this blank ecstasy. Now *here's* a revolutionary hope, such democratic purity; any pair of eyes can watch the glimmering water in the Canal St Martin at lunchtime on an overcast day and partake of the same single truth about the world. Start again from there.

Our substance is all particles and vibrations; that's how the world is, always was, its changeless natural shape.

Who lays it bare and tells us, *dares us*, to open our eyes and *look*? Who is the epoch's authentic genius of material existence, the visionary who sees through the confusion of human interference down to the heart of things?

Peter settled the matter in a whisper to himself. 'Brother Claude.' Monet before them all, he decided, silently completing the argument, Where Monet is, movement comes to rest.

A memory of one of the artist's Waterloo Bridge paintings swirled through Peter's thoughts. Blue factories in the distance huffing out blue and brown smoke, haze everywhere you look, the unifying world-haze, people and the things they make embedded in it. The haze connects everybody and everything. There they are, crossing the bridge in daily migration, the caravanserai of human traffic reflected on the surface of the Thames, while the river, its dumb nature and substance, sloughs underneath. Monet framed it on his canvas, the hidden fact of London — or Paris or Riga or Moscow — movement you can't boil down to a political slogan. *If I stood on the embankment of the Thames*, Peter went on thinking, *wherever Brother Claude had set up his easel, I'd see exactly what he saw.*

Peter's mental freedom was a fast-fading sensation; to take stock of his trouble he had to clear his head, and think, think, think. Was that, after all, the reason he quit Marseilles and came back to Paris? For a holiday from agitation? From informers? Maybe there was nothing he could do about it; his calmness attracted agitators from every direction. Even so, at times here, when he was blandly employed, Peter missed the activity, or noticed its sharp absence... One thought one minute contradicted by the next in the next! Never troubled by doubt before, now he felt it arrive every morning when he woke up, with a plunge of ice water in his stomach. And after he slumped out of bed to get dressed, the fit of his clothes was wrong, the trim of his beard, the name he went by. Today he forgot he disliked potato soup, it usually reminded him of the paste he used to hang wallpaper.

Along with everything else in the world-haze, somewhere, *something* had to be solid and certain. In London just a couple of years ago, in Jubilee Street, in the smoky air of the Anarchist Club. To the police it was a heathen temple, rat's nest, alien outpost, turbulent mosque. Peter's crowd. But he dodged the thundering proclamations, kept out of the debate. Those *spielers* with the lung power and lack of inhibition who promised to deliver a new world minus the imperialism ... which meant minus the imperialists, their friends, allies and beneficiaries ... which meant the ruling class, merchant class and counter-revolutionaries among the working class on every continent, anywhere those sickening bedbugs could be flushed from cover, denounced, eradicated!

Oh, yes?

What about booting the Russians out of his homeland? If it took revolution in Russia to free Latvia, then Peter swam with the revolutionaries, his heart swollen with joy. Many times a special guest at the Anarchist Club, his purpose was just as clear: to paint backdrops for the occasional skits and plays they put on and, while he was there, to demonstrate how to manufacture, plant and detonate a nitro-glycerine bomb. Anarchist entertainments.

Among the comrades, those scrappers, one man recognised who Peter was, separate from what he'd done. A friend. He was still in London, calling himself Gardstein now, George Gardstein. 'Karl,' Peter said out loud.

'Monsieur?' Looking at him slouched there by the canal, M. Brassaud the *patron* of the corner café and rightful owner of the chair underneath Peter, softened his voice but not his irritation. What satisfaction would arm-swirling rage get him from this slumped heap of surrender? Besides which, the gloss of sweat on Peter's forehead in the cool air made the *patron* wonder if the man was ill. 'Monsieur, the chair. Give it back to me.'

Peter hauled himself to his feet and picked up his tool bag. It rattled with his collection of brushes and tins of turpentine.

Behind him Peter heard Brassaud grab up the chair and grumble, 'Next time maybe you'll order an *aperitif* so I can retire.'

Only half a block away, in Rue des Vinaigrieres, waited the afternoon's job, repainting the door of a dress shop. The owner hired Peter on recommendation, not as a survivor of torture or escapee of Russian jails, not in honour of a veteran in the revolutionary underground, the dressmaker was no sympathiser. She hired him on a Frenchman's good word. Peter's last employer, a tailor in Montparnasse, had high praise for his talents with brush and paint, especially Peter's skill at outlining street numbers in a second colour. 'Oh, he's intelligent,' the tailor said of him, 'but he's a good worker.'

On the money he was earning Peter could afford to maintain just one address, so his habit was to eat in different bistros in different quarters of the city. He always waited for an aisle seat close to the door. If, passing the bread, anybody haphazardly asked personal questions, or came at him snuffling like a pig after truffles, in each place Peter gave them a different story. His table-mates believed they were enjoying the company of 'Alois' or 'Paul,' a plasterer from Alsace-Lorraine or

28

vaguely 'the South,' not a foreign radical in the cross-hairs of the secret police. With the limbs of a runner and a labourer's muscles, he could still run fast if he had to, though lately a thickening at his belly and hips had become noticeable, and not only to Peter. At twenty-seven, could he already be a middle-aged man?

Peter kept his table talk brief and common in these neighbourhood restaurants. He spoke a smooth French, barely accented, solid Russian, convincing German and Yiddish, clear English. In Le Barricou D'Or he was known as a native of Marseilles, and in Chez L'Ami he was Thomas Peter, a Swiss-German chemistry teacher. Around the Marais, where shopkeepers and waiters knew him by the names Paul Pavloff or Peter Schtern, he passed as a Jew.

And it was to the Marais that Peter strolled for his dinner after he finished work in Rue des Vinaigriers. Stepping from the street into La Roulante des Rosiers he always imagined entering the hold of a barge. Eight or ten tables with their pairs of benches crammed the narrow room as if leaving space for full-grown customers was an afterthought. By early evening La Roulante's ancient tile floor wore a layer of tobacco ash glued to it here and there by precious sloppings of soup or wine.

You'd think by looking at the couple dozen men and women eating and drinking that they were there together at some celebration, singing at the table on the right, loud conversation on the left. Across the narrow gangway two old men growled through a folk song about English knights — *Chevaliers de la Table Ronde, goutons voir si le vin est bon* ... an old woman with a bandaged foot dragged herself from friend to acquaintance to stranger begging a loan of twenty-five centimes to get her coat out of hock ... a red-headed Italian girl leaked tears as she finished reciting a poem about suicide ... at the end of Peter's table a quarrel had broken out between a bricklayer and a carpenter over whose work is harder on a man's health. At Peter's elbow a pair of prostitutes resigned themselves to their luck, advising each other not to expect any trade within ten streets of des Rosiers, it being the start of the working week; all the men with money to throw at pleasure were in better neighbourhoods, where anyway the competition between streetwalkers was cutthroat...

Tumult all around, communication with the kitchen reduced to gestures and glances, intricately understood by everyone — *Another pitcher of wine here! Plate of chops!* The pool of human noise ringed Peter like a moat and he sat placidly in the middle of it. These things, he thought, the human body's burdens and pleasures, aren't touched by revolution...

Meals at La Roulante had another advantage: His vegetarian diet didn't rouse any real curiosity. The waiters assumed that Peter avoided meat on account of nearly empty pockets; when he found work, the five francs a day had to stretch to cover rent, food, clothes (and his laundry, postage and sometimes travel), common costs to workers like him. One difference between him and the others was that they bought the minimum of food to buy the maximum of drink.

The truth was his plate of cooked carrots and parsnips, beet soup, bread and cheese satisfied Peter in a way not much else did these days. He ate, head down, not entirely in self-defence, every now and then glancing slowly at the people around him. One glance, the seat opposite was vacant: at the next it was filled by a young man in cheap but laundered clothes and a black peaked cap, slouched *à la mode* on one side of his blond head. Peter had noticed him earlier, hovering at the door with an eager appetite. Between bites, Peter made the mistake of looking Black Cap in the face, which gave the — what was he? a student? — an opening to ask if there was anything on the menu that the cook didn't ruin.

Peter said, 'The beet soup is good.'

'It looks good. You recommend it?'

'If you like the taste of beets.' Peter said, and leaned down further over his soup bowl.

But Black Cap went on, 'Looks like more of a vegetable stew,' he said, to no reply. He tried again. 'What about the chops? Are they lamb or pork?'

'Haven't tried them.'

Black cap rose halfway out of his seat to get Madame's attention and said, 'They're probably horse.' He signalled his order to her, wiped his forehead with the back of his hand and regretted ordering the meat. 'She serves everything burned, looks like. Your soup and, what have you got there — carrots? That's smart.'

Peter threw a glance toward the door. 'Meat's no good for my stomach.'

'No? You don't eat it?'

'No.'

'Only vegetables, that's interesting. And fruit?'

'That's right.'

'Vegetables and fruit. Clean food, good for the stomach. You can trust her not to burn the carrots, anyway.'

'They're boiled.'

'Does she fish them out in time?' He ignored Peter's silence and plunged ahead. 'You're right, meat's heavy on your insides. I should have ordered the beet soup.'

'It's the best thing she makes,' Peter said.

'You can look forward to healthy years on that kind of

food.' The room noise swamped him so Black Cap repeated the point.

'Yes.'

'Good food, good life. Bad food... Maybe it's better not to be born at all.' He abandoned the thought behind an apologetic wave. 'Sorry. No politics in here.'

'That's not politics. It's philosophy.' Peter reached down the table for the loaf of bread and accidentally knocked the arm of the working girl sitting next to him. 'Pardon me.'

She returned his smile, with genuine sweetness. 'I'm no peach. A little tap won't bruise me.'

As his plate of chops was passed along to him, Black Cap picked up his conversation with Peter again. 'No, I'll order the soup and carrots next time, if it's as good as you say. Does she ever make it with cabbage and sour cream, *à la russe?*'

Maybe the boy was lonely. His accent wasn't Parisian. His stab at sociability struck Peter as forced and clumsy. Maybe Black Cap was slumming. Or was he a police informer? Callow, open, curious, harmless, the kind of personality that's attractive to the Sûreté, not to mention the Okhrana: Russian secret policemen, even more than French ones, fall head over heels for appealing characters like him, and they pay better ... that is, when they can't blackmail or threaten the family at home. Either way, the Okhrana can turn callow boys into poisonous rats overnight. Peter offered him a smile, lifting his glass, taking a last sip of wine. Is Black Cap trawling for radicals, he wondered, or is he sitting here because I'm here?

Peter leaned close to the girl, whispered to her, 'Can you come with me?' Then he abandoned his spoon in the half empty soup bowl and got up to pay.

'What,' said Black Cap, 'can't trust the cooking after all?'

'You have it.'

The cashier was Madame's baby-faced grey-skinned older sister, who also kept a droll eye on the regulars.

'They get what they want here, don't they?' he observed.

She shrugged. 'Everybody comes back.'

'You're lucky. You hear the voice of the people.'

She agreed. 'One franc, twenty centimes.'

Outside in the street the girl told Peter her name was Claudette.

'Is it?' Peter said.

'If you want to ask for me next time.'

She took his hand and started to lead him around the corner. He told her his name was Paul, offering his arm to lead her back the other way. 'No,' she said and dug in her heels. 'My room is over here.'

'I want to get out of the Marais.' *Camouflaged with you on my arm*, he could have told her, *as a strolling couple in the boulevard crowd*.

Under her reddish curls the girl gave him a sly look. 'How long will you take?'

'You should come home with me,' Peter bargained. 'I want you for the whole night.'

'I'm your extravagance, is that it?'

'If you've got the money it's no extravagance. Come home with me.'

'Where?'

'Montparnasse.'

'Too far, too long. No. I work here. It's near my room and I don't have to pay for the Metro.'

'I'll buy your ticket. And one for the return.'

'But my hotel's so close.'

33

'Your pimp, too, I'll bet.'

'I work for myself,' she lied.

'You can decide, then. How much would you earn on a Monday?'

'If I go somewhere else tonight how will I know?'

'Whatever it is, you can make just as much, more even, in Montmartre, around there, Montparnasse. My neighbourhood.'

'I don't think so. Why?'

'You're much, much prettier than the girls I see walking the Marché every day. You know who I mean, the ones at the fountain. Something shines out of your face, believe me. You could be an artist's model.'

She stood back from him and gave Peter the kind of look she got from men a hundred times a day. His workman's clothes (hectically stained), his clunking tool bag, his fingers flecked, dirtied, with white, green, black, and guessed Peter's angle. 'You want me to work for you!'

'No!'

'Are you Arab,' she kidded him, 'or Corsican?' Peter jerked his face away from her hand. He shook his head, a signal for her to read: he'd stop talking until she stopped clowning. 'You can take those lightning bolts out of your eyes,' she said.

'I'm not angry at anybody.'

'Good.' She slipped her hand back into the crook of his arm.

'You've got artists for friends, then?'

'Yes.'

'Famous ones?'

'Notorious.'

'Who? Who'd pay me? How much?'

'Two or three francs for a couple of hours. I think that's

the going rate. With food and drink thrown in. Drink, for sure.'

'I can make the same here,' she said. The slight wobble in her voice made Peter doubt that was true.

'Can you keep it? Some? Any? How much?' He made his proposal with earnest charm, 'What you might earn tonight in the Marais, gamble it against what you might make tomorrow in Montparnasse, for work that won't make you an old woman before you're thirty.'

'I won't be an old woman.'

'A face in a painting doesn't age,' Peter suggested gently. Then he replaced pretty persuasion with ironclad facts. 'Anyway, it won't stop you from making money however you want.'

'Are you an artist, Paul? You talk like one.'

'Yes. I paint.'

Five

With the pavement of Montparnasse under his boots, Peter's tension drained out of him. It trickled down from his neck, through his arms and from his hands. Up the steps of the Métro, Peter's walk slowed with a looseness in his limbs. He didn't say a word to the girl for the whole ride from Saint-Paul to Pigalle, but not because the judder and rattle of the carriage would have forced him to shout; at each stop Peter silently watched the ones who got on board, where they sat or stood. Between stations he kept his head down.

Once they had turned the corner of Rue Danville he livened up. He was this woman's escort and scout, pointing out local characters by the nicknames he'd given them — 'Treasure Trove,' an old woman who trawled the gutters for lost jewelry... 'The Flies,' a trio of young women, gaily drunk, usually singing, none of them ever spotted on her own... 'The Monument,' an ex-army officer in his frayed uniform, medals on display, who planted himself outside the cemetery in the morning and in the Café Sebastopol at night, delivering patriotic speeches and entertaining the clientele with his own lewd verses of the national anthem... They were all out on the street tonight, The Pygmy, Didier's Egg, Madame Aubergine...

'No sign of The Amorous Pinhead,' Peter said, turning his key in the door. 'Maybe we'll see him at breakfast.'

Even with the light from the landing she couldn't see very far into his small room, and disobeyed him when he

37

told her to wait outside until he switched on the bedside
lamp. Her foot made contact with something that
collapsed when she kicked it. A splash of electric
lamplight showed her she'd knocked over a stack of
unframed water colours. Stepping over them she said, not
exactly surprised, 'You didn't lie to me.'

Except for the brushes soaking in jars and a collection
of tins and little boxes, Peter kept his place tidy. Her eyes
slid onto a panel of freshly hung wallpaper next to the
bed, the same brown floral pattern that covered the
other walls.

'It was shabby. If I can fix something, I don't stand on
ceremony,' Peter said. 'I'm working my way around the
room.' He picked up one of his paintings to show her, a
small still life of flowers in a blue and white vase. Daisies,
buttercups, scarlet poppies, the air of summer.

Peter's girl admired it with a musical hum. Each one he
handed to her won the same reply – his street scenes,
landscapes, one of a pond and water lilies, which he told
her outright was his amateur copy. 'Don't ask me,' she
shrugged. 'Art should be pretty. Your paintings are pretty,
so they're good.'

'You think so, Claudette? They're 'pretty'?'

In the teeth of a lecture on the beaux arts she
unbuttoned her short jacket and then her blouse. Her
bare shoulders had gentle power in them; the curve of
her thighs, the youth of her skin, the rude tufts of hair in
her armpits, acted on Peter. He caught the sharp scent of
her when she raised her arms to untie her hair.

A roughhouse shove tipped Peter backward across the
bed. The girl bent to untie his shoes, slipped them off his
feet, then lay next to him. Before he could frame a
correct thought about fair wages for streetwalkers,
modelling for artists or anything else, her mouth was on

his, his hands on her hips. The moment sank into its physical purity, the same stuff as the shimmer of light on the canal, slipping past him as fast as Peter could grope for a hold on it. From the taste of her mouth his attention slid to the sight of her wide shoulders and small breasts, the soft angles of her face, until his pleasure took solid form as she arched her back and pushed herself against him and stayed there a while, long enough to grind the spinning wheel of his senses into a fixed memory.

As if a shade had rolled down on daylight and raised on night, after a sleep that could only have lasted ten minutes, Peter opened his eyes on the settled state of things. Paris went on without any need for him to be there. The girl stood near the bed pulling her blouse on but she left it unbuttoned. She grabbed a rag off the floor, one Peter used for his water colour brushes, and asked if she could use it to wash herself.

'There's a cleaner one somewhere. On the other table, the round one, right side of the door.'

But she'd already poured water from the jug into the bowl on the wash stand and dropped the rag in. She wrang it out and squatted to rinse between her legs. She said, 'I have to ask you for money, *cheri*.'

Peter switched on the light. Her face looked rougher than it did half an hour before. Drained, lined. He wondered how he'd paint her if he had the talent for portraits. If anything, his paintings were a record of his limitations. 'On the dresser there's a porcelain dish.'

He heard her fingers tickle through the coins. 'You don't have enough here,' she said over her shoulder.

'Try the drawer.' A foraging animal rummaged through his things. She picked over the useless bits and pieces, his keys, pocket knife, cuff links, collar buttons, a scatter of centimes. 'Come back to bed,' he said. His hope was that she'd heard it as a cosy invitation not a plea. His hope quickly guttered.

'I can't tonight, *mon cheri*, no,' still digging for loose change. 'You said you'd give me my fare, too.'

For the Metro home to the Marais. Peter turned over in bed, his back to her. 'Take whatever you want.' Then he turned around again to say, 'You can take all the money you can find.'

She told him straight, 'I'm not staying.'

'Who knows who you could meet tomorrow? Delaunay has his studio a few streets from here.'

She spelled out what should have been obvious to Peter all along. 'I don't want to be a model. I can't sit still. See?' And she was up again, doing up her buttons and hunting Peter's room like a child on a scavenger hunt.

'Please yourself.' He shrugged, retreating.

If it was a game the girl concentrated on it with a seriousness that narrowed her eyes. She riffled his coat and trouser pockets, clutched a few more coins. A single uncomplicated idea guided her from one likely cache to the next. He wanted her to leave.

Her haul couldn't have added up to more than a few francs. After she'd counted it she said, 'I lied. There's a man. His name is Jojo. He'll hurt me if I stay away.' It was a practical worry, not a moral one. She gave him the information without complaint or appeal in her voice.

Peter didn't say another word to her. He rolled onto his side, kept his back to her and switched off the light. When he heard her footsteps tap their way down the stairs he got up and locked his door.

A few weeks later he saw the girl on the corner near La Roulante. By the look of her friend standing with her, the way he gripped her wrist, Peter figured he wasn't a customer. Jojo, her protector. Across the street she recognised Peter but gave him no friendly sign. Instead she pointed him out to Jojo as Peter headed for, then avoided, the restaurant.

He told himself he had nothing to repent, he didn't lie to her that night, no, he would have done his best to find a Montmartre artist for the lady to charm. Even so, I'm a hypocrite, a dolt, Peter thought, for trying to tantalise her. Shiny blandishments. Isn't that *their* tactic, the favourite argument of the comrades he hated? A beautiful future is waiting for us if we survive a little hardship, some mutilation maybe, or the occasional unspeakable atrocity. So it turned out a street whore's realism was stronger than his.

Peter roasted himself under his breath. 'You *child*.' And he thought back to himself as a boy adventuring up and down the Talsen meadows, watching patrols of Russian soldiers march by. In childhood he was as innocent of the persecution, kidnappings, public hangings and routine savagery as he was of the armed resistance he'd lead against them. His robberies, murders and jail breaks hovered in the future along with Russian reprisals — pliers taken to his fingernails, the freezing cell, starvation, beatings, the shattering echo of firing squads, endured for the rumour of a golden tomorrow scheduled to dawn on the first day of revolution in Russia.

So there it was, the cloudy turbulence Peter felt inside his skull: firm ideas crumbling to powder. To find a solid foothold, start again from the fundamentals, like a child, begin with childish questions.

When does the future start? Where does the sky?

Six

With the élan of a stage magician Charles Perelman swirled his black sombrero and matching cloak onto the coat rack, singing a sweet air of apology to Rivka. He'd meant to be there at the docks to meet her, he would have been out and home again in five minutes, never mind, it could wait, God's truth, nothing was more of a pleasure than being there to welcome Yoska's friend himself the minute she arrived. Yoska wasn't with her? 'Good, good.' Because this man wanted her to himself, Rivka supposed, sniffing a rivalry there.

'Mrs Perelman made me a cup of tea.'

'As she should.' Charles Perelman's healthy brown hair defied age, his wide-set Spanish looking eyes, black as a doe's, defeated suspicion. Even when he said the most innocent things with a conspiratorial wink, like a man who expected his words to convey double or triple meanings.

In the tiny entry way of his Wellesley Street terraced house, Perelman squeezed around the heap of coats and shoes and formally presented himself to Rivka, bestowing kisses on her cheek, left, right, left again. For a few seconds, a trace of eau de cologne hung like a velvet drape around them.

'Deborah!' Perelman shouted up the stairs. 'Deborah! Come down and visit!' But his wife remained an irritated, answering voice in some distant part of the house. His children, though, roamed down the stairs and out of other rooms in ones and twos. A tribe of six, evenly divided between boys and girls. In the middle of directing the brewing of more tea, slicing of bread, ordering pots of jam and honey, Perelman conducted her along the hallway.

Rivka felt a touch on her shoulder and Perelman lowered his voice. Its sound was as warm as a cello thrumming directly into her ear. 'You came to us from Russia?'

'My family, they're in Sasmacken.'

'Courland. I know Libau,' he nodded, registered Rivka's answer, carried on. 'Where you bagged your Cossack.'

'Is that what I did? All I did was run away.'

Perleman studied Rivka's face. 'Yoska's friends, you've met them?'

'Not yet.'

'Not yet. You will. The Gardsteins have a lot of friends from Courland. Wonderful people, the best.' He paused. He spoke. 'Rivka, I work in my own way. Special Branch know me. Sometimes they post men in the street outside. If they want to, they can pack me in a crate and ship me to Russia. They'll hang me for 'crimes' — can you believe it? — socialist *crimes* back there.'

Delusion, bravado, half-truth, justified fear, a mixture — whatever the deeper reality, Perelman took pains to display himself as a man in the thick of anti-government struggle.

'You don't have to tell me your business.'

'Be aware of things while you're living with us. That's all I'm saying. A small piece of information in the wrong ear, it's not so healthy.' The gentle advice somehow also carried (was she hearing clearly?) a not so gentle threat. Followed by a smile, followed by a friendly squeeze of Rivka's shoulder, followed by a bow delivered with a maître d's sincerity.

Perelman showed Rivka to the room he rented out at the rear of his ground floor. It was a stuffy place, narrow as a rowing boat, windowless and cramped by wooden packing crates. Under Perelman's energetic direction Rivka slid them against the walls and cleared enough floor space for him to lay down a single horsehair mattress. With eyes closed, how much space does a body need?

'Do you enjoy looking at art?' Whether she did or didn't wasn't going to make a difference. Her landlord slid a canvas out of the space behind the table that occupied most of the room. 'What do you think?' He held the work of art at chest height for Rivka to appreciate.

The painting, his visionary work, was hideous. A collision of ferocious colours and slabs of hellish night. About three dozen terrified Jews ran wildly from houses, all at the mercy of Cossack marauders. Splintered furniture, heaved out of windows, lay piled in the streets. Another dozen Jewish victims hung by their necks from lampposts.

'Does it have a title?' Rivka's eyes moved from lynching to bonfire, Cossack devil to wind-splayed trees while she stretched her mind to imagine what artistic name you'd give to an orgiastic eruption of inhumanity.

Perelman announced it to her, and to posterity: '*Pogrom in Minsk*. You see how the colours...?'

'The red and yellow. They're very expressive.'

'Exactly, *exactly*,' he said and lowered his broad behind onto the bottom corner of the mattress. 'A touch of Turner. Painting's a holiday from my photography.' He waved behind him at the source of the chemical odours hanging in the air. 'I wouldn't give the name 'portrait'. They're just records I make of people's faces.'

Perelman crossed his legs and steadied the painting

between his knees. 'The Rothschilds bought one of mine, exactly the same.' His account of the Rothschild family's personal crusade to rescue him from the Tsarist torture cells kept Rivka awake for another hour. Then he kindly left her to sleep.

The noise of Perelman's children playing and squabbling leaked in through the walls, with Perelman's voice and heavy footsteps retreating upstairs.

'Deborah? Deborah! I'm going out at six o'clock,' Perelman said.

Deborah replied, 'To photograph?'

'Yes. No. Yes. Why?'

'Because are you eating?'

'How can I eat with this noise?'

'You can't live without eating.'

'Why do you think I'm going *out*?'

Shut in her rented room, in exile from the happy racket of home life, Rivka listened to the children's voices, a dozen feet scuffing the floor, dishes, pots, pans clattering, taps running, doors slamming. The same noises she left in Sasmacken. The picture formed in her mind, of her sisters and brothers collected around the table, her mother ladling soup and dumplings into seven bowls, not the usual nine. Minus hers and minus Mordechai's.

Another picture crowded in: her father in his prison cell, where he squatted on wet straw, sleepless, beyond avail, ripped from the heart of his family. The daughter ached the father's ache. He must be suffering over the misfortune he'd delivered her into; he sat awake, tortured by the thought of his brave Riveleh curled under a thin blanket in a filthy room somewhere out of reach, out of his sight, all because of the trouble he stirred up. She longed to comfort him as much as he must have been longing to reach across the North Sea to find her and comfort her, slumped against the wall of his cell, the world shrunken to the worry of whether his next stop was going to be the hangman or the firing squad.

Beside the bare mattress, Rivka shimmied down through four layers of skirts to relieve herself into the chamber pot Perelman's boy had bashfully ferried to her from another part of the house. No one told her where to go to empty it. As she stared down at the clear warm human smelling soup, Perelman's son Carlusha bustled in through the door, his father's miniature and emissary as master-of-the-house. He balanced a pitcher of warm water in a cracked china bowl and told Rivka she could use them for washing. On the cane chair he dropped a folded cloth and the remains of a bar of soap. Either Carlusha didn't hear her ask about the sanitation arrangements or he was too shy to answer the question, and in the next second, eyes averted, he was gone.

By yellow gaslight Rivka scrubbed her face, brushed her hair. To make herself attractive in London the same way she did at home.

Seven

True to his word, Yoska collected Rivka at Perelman's house next morning. 'We'll stop before Shinebloom's restaurant. Five minutes, that's all.'

Together they must have been a sight: the Limper, six-foot-four-inches of him, with five-foot-two-inch Rivka in tow, strolling across Whitechapel to Karl's flat in Gold Street.

'Nina will feed you, don't worry,' Yoska prepared her. 'Then she'll tell you to wipe your mouth. A real *babushka*, I'm telling you. A ball breaker into the bargain. Karl loves her from here to the moon.' Yoska shrugged off this fact of life, and chuckled at its craziness. He waved a wise finger. 'But he hasn't married her.'

Nina Vassilleva didn't speak a word, not *hello*, not *come in out of the cold*, not a syllable of welcome. A limp gesture, ushering Rivka and Yoska indoors with a closed hand.

'They're coming in,' Nina announced, in Russian, to a figure standing in front of the dead fireplace. To his landlord he was P. Morin. Closer to the truth, Mourrewitz. Or Mourremitz. Murontzeff or Mourem-tzoff. In London, George Gastin, H.A. Gartner. Sometimes, Grunberg. More often, George Gardstein. To his London circle, Karl. He travelled on passports bearing the names Schafsh and Khan and Yanis Karlowich Stenzel. Shrewd, refined, persuasive, just twenty-four years old, he'd stepped into the leadership after the Liesma gang's most catastrophic year.

Karl was the type of young man who kept all the tumult

screened off behind a soft voice. Every confidential
sentence came out crafted in the tones of a drawing room
intellectual, an impression bolstered by stacks of books
and pamphlets on his floor, desk, table and sideboard,
not to mention the labelled bottles of chemicals and odd
pieces of laboratory equipment installed around the front
room.

Karl's smooth features gave away two intimate facts: he
was at ease with the kind of attention physical beauty
brought him, and he could use his handsome looks or
override them any time he wanted. In one of the formal
photos of him, his neat, dark hair, straight and fine, thickly
brushed back at the sides, sloped up into a gentle wave
away from his forehead. The hair of his moustache was
sparse, a soft fringe that dipped around the corners of his
mouth, and worked against the assertion of masculine
maturity that rested firmly in the centre of him. His
flowing tie (usually burgundy or plum) and his genteel suit
came close to a theatrical flair, and on its own gave him the
natty air of an actor-manager. His athletic physique was on
display, even covered by his woollen jacket and waistcoat,
and Karl carried it with the absolute right to ask questions
on any subject, to any depth.

His fingertips strayed over a rack of test tubes. 'You can
bring me another distilling tube can't you, Yoska? One
with a brass frame.' Karl's wide-set eyes held none of
Yoska's mildness: to Rivka they did not seem unfriendly,
but they had the watchfulness, the formal and glancing
suspicion, of a border guard.

Karl ignored Yoska, finished with him for the moment.
Eyes lowered, he rearranged bottles of chemicals in a
drawer, handling them like chess pieces. He picked up a
copy of *Mutual Aid* and pencilled a note in the margin in
his minute, scientific handwriting, a spontaneous

objection or agreement in his silent tutorial with Kropotkin.

Then he turned to Rivka, 'I wanted to meet you,' he said. A nod at Nina. 'She didn't.'

Rivka said, 'Thank you, Mr Gardstein. For getting me out of Riga. Your help. My cousin Jankel didn't tell me if...'

'Call me Karl.'

'Call him Poolka,' Yoska teased.

'There's a grocer two streets away who lets you buy on credit,' Nina said to Rivka.

'Near here? I don't remember the street where I'm staying, but the landlord's name is Perelman.'

'We know where you're staying. We used to rent from Perelman. You can trust him, he runs with us.' Nina was a small woman, exactly Rivka's height, her waist slightly thicker, shoulders slightly plumper. Nina handled her with some caginess. 'The grocer is Hindmann, he's in Cable Street. Max Hindmann.'

'Where Yoska took me. From the boat.'

'Maybe you walked by his shop.'

'But he doesn't know me. He'd give me credit?'

'He knows *us*. He'll do it.' A boast of blunt influence. And that concluded Nina's business with Rivka. The scrolled lips, the businesslike frown — Rivka had seen expressions like Nina's before, privately public messages on the faces of clerks and minor officials whose job it was to handle her. Russians, usually. Nina was Russian, with Slavic seriousness brooding in her eye sockets, giving the bark-brown eyes their depth and darkness. Swirling slowly in that depth was alertness too, Rivka could tell. Intelligence and a pledge to strive. A passerby looking in through the window anyone would might even have suspected a family resemblance between Nina and Rivka,

51

might have mistaken them for sisters. Both had the same dense hair, carried the same way, piled up on the wide, round head. But where Rivka's face seemed to search you out, every angle of Nina's face focused ahead, past you — her straight nose mounted over her flat, jokeless mouth, her chin so intense that all by itself it warded off any casual or friendly approach.

It was only by rocking his hips to the edge of the settee that Yoska could haul his large, unstable body to its feet. He asked Karl, 'Are you going?'

'For a few weeks.'

'Then I can stay here.'

'Yes, why not.' Karl brushed crumbs from the blanket, fluffed and turned the pillow, took off his jacket and lay down on the bed. 'One of us has to come home with a prize.' Put that way this was a direct question, drenched with tired distraction. 'I'm going to visit my family. They're in Courland, like yours.'

Karl answered the question Rivka didn't ask. 'We're scattered everywhere.' She understood the message here: Karl was inviting her into his confidence: he understood homesickness and exile, injury and recovery, the singing nerves of life on the run.

He communicated all of this to Rivka in the handshake he gave her at the door. 'Nina's going to take you to Hindmann's. Can you find your way back to your room?'

'I think so.'

'Nina can send you in the right direction,' Karl assured her. 'Yoska needs to stay with me for a while.'

There were rumours, always, in the jewellery trade and as usual, Yoska Sokoloff had the inside track on two or three at a time. It helped that he was a watchmaker, natural and nimble with intricate mechanisms, which required sharp attention to very small details. But he needed to visit the Houndsditch jewelry shop again, investigate it as a target, look for possible traps, estimate for himself the size of the treasure inside, base it on observation, not rumours. It was too early to congest Karl's mind with the ins and outs of a burglary; wasn't that what he counted on Yoska for, to line up robberies worth the risk?

A nap on the settee was a daily habit with Karl: now, as Yoska watched, he dropped off to sleep in less than a minute. Noiselessly as he could, the tall man dragged his heavy right foot behind him, shut the door and directed himself to go out and bring back a prize.

Eight

While Rivka poured coffee and tea, served plates of fried fish or fried liver and bowls of potatoes at Shinebloom's restaurant, three men, engaged in entirely different business, were setting the stage for her future. Shinebloom's occupied a good-sized, squareish ground floor room in Sclater Street. There was no time of day when the restaurant wasn't congested with diners and assorted fumes. From the kitchen, steam; from the clientele, tobacco smoke and the gases of political argument, grumble and mudslinging. Rivka reckoned it was as noisy in there as the street outside, at all hours, too. The clatter of horses' hooves, high wheels and growling motor cars was replaced by the din of scraping knives, forks, spoons, clattering plates, platters, bowls and mugs, the shouts of 'More soup here!' over 'Look, girl!' above 'Hey, Miss!' mainly in Yiddish, Russian and fractured, practical English. The voices wrestled for her attention — to fetch and carry, to attend to every one of them first. It rose like dust from a busy road, the laughing and squabbling noise.

First, in Shinebloom's through luncheon and dinner, then without stop until she'd clocked up four late hours at a scruffier coffee house a few doors away, Rivka faced an audience of men. In both dining rooms, the same reminder: as a waitress and as a woman she was an aside. She lived in their country — men's — invisible as a breeze circling around their serious business. Or maybe not quite that imperceptible; they noticed her function, which was to bring them their food. 'More of the same, Miss!'

At home in Sasmacken, Rivka was a frowning bystander as her fifteen- and sixteen-year-old friends buckled under men the way a frail body succumbs to typhoid. Not Rivka, not to those patriarchs-in-the-making, who from first breath to last salivated at the sight of a woman's plump breast. No, she refused to be the woman that a man saw with his appetites.

Rivka offered up a yielding smile to some customers, but she kept its reverse meaning to herself. She served borscht and pierógis, cleared away dirty plates, moved in her dark blue apron, sweating under her light blue linen head scarf, from kitchen to table, this corner to that corner, ferrying bread and margarine, bowls of soup, jugs of water, glass pitchers of milk, pots of tea and coffee, to tables of men bent over their plates, snuffling into their meals.

Somewhere in that thick ruckus Rivka's ears caught the ideas of those times. Radical opinions floated on conversations in the smoky, stuffy restaurant whose every inch she trooped hour upon hour, day upon day. Underground groups, official and outlaw, made plans, drafted manifestos, debated fine points. An age of violent collision, in London, an empire city of nothing but possibility, the old order harpooned, hot-headed idealism on the rise. She couldn't have missed seeing Leon Beron open for business at his regular table. Beron usually held court in the Warsaw from midday to midnight, reliable as an undertaker, on hand to fence the stolen property that funded every revolutionary group he could name. Tonight he graced Shinebloom's 'to avoid an appointment' — with a pickpocket or a policeman he didn't say.

As he waited patiently for Rivka to walk over and take his lunch order, Beron appeared to her the very portrait of respectable English prosperity. The winged collar and tie, expensive woollen coat garnished with astrakhan, the £5 gold coin that adorned his watch chain, each detail naturally arranged and easily worn. Something of a pasha, she thought, swivelling his dark head in the restaurant's stew of ferocious arguments and passionate agreements over race horses and police activity (subjects that interested Beron) and over Russia and socialist revolution (subjects that did not).

Rivka recognised the wide back, heavy arms and sprawled legs of the man who shared Beron's table. It was Yoska. He didn't see her, though, but leaned away, absorbed in discussion, negotiating along these lines. 'I'm telling you, Leon, I felt the *heat* go from that brooch right through my clothes. Soon as it was safe in my pocket.'

'Twelve pounds, four shillings and sixpence, the lot.' Beron's appraisal came unclouded by any interest in Yoska's mystical experience of housebreaking and burglary. Down here with the anarchists or up there with the plutocrats, Beron knew, a piece of jewellery sparked the identical desire — to command wealth. Loot was loot; there was no mystery on a dealer's side about brute beauty. 'The chains are eighteen carat. The watches, eighteen. The necklace, the brooch . . . My estimate . . . I'd say the silver will be worth something. These stones: no.'

'No?'

'Definitely no.'

'But it's just your estimate.'

'Tonight you can have my final figure.'

'Twelve pounds isn't final,' Yoska flatly summed up the situation, shoulders drooped under Beron's oppression. 'It might be twelve, ten or what, you can't be more exact?'

57

'Yoska, no, come back tonight. I'll talk to Ruby Michaels. If you want to push me for it, at the moment I'm in a position to say your items to me are worth something less than the amount I can get from Ruby.'

The lull in their conversation allowed Rivka to break in. 'Can I bring you something, gentlemen?'

'I'm a *gentleman* now!' Yoska said to her, touching Rivka's elbow, affectionate, familiar. All his attention went to her. 'This is Rivka,' he said to Beron. 'She's very good-looking, isn't she?'

She smiled at Yoska and replied, 'The brisket is good today.'

'Rivka, here you have Leon Beron. An ugly crook.'

Beron glanced away from the menu to return a small beaded sewing kit to Yoska. Ignoring Rivka, he said, 'What made you take this?'

Yoska said nothing, covered the item with his big hand and swept it into his coat pocket. Beron got down to the business of ordering. Smiling, acknowledging each of his instructions with a sharp nod, Rivka memorised the long list — yes to the brisket but no gravy, gravy to be served in a gravy boat, boiled potatoes not overcooked, brought to the table hot, and bread without margarine on a separate plate, and to drink... As she contemplated the list of food Beron wanted and how he wanted it cooked and served to him, Rivka tried to picture Mrs Beron. What kind of woman would be the mate of this sturdy black-market trader? Round and motherly, silvering hair piled up, only out of her apron to put on her dressing gown, provider of a secure and comfortable home. Mrs Beron's skin would be doughy, her thighs heavy, her waist thick. Her husband was her horizon. She cooked for him, warmed his bed, lied to the police for him. She knew what he did, where it came from, every penny of the trading, the buying and selling, honest profit from his bent clientele, never mind, the money supported hearth, home and brood, it was all for them.

'No brisket for me,' Yoska was saying. 'No borscht. Gravy and potatoes.'

Rivka stopped short of recommending the meat. Maybe Yoska couldn't afford the brisket. Didn't he have a wife or lover who'd force him to eat better food? She'd have to be a tolerant woman, Rivka guessed. To kiss his mouth and comfort his eager eyes. To make him wash, or not to notice Yoska's odours of sweat, stale skin, rotten teeth, exertion, need.

'Thank you, gentlemen.' As she squeezed around the next table, stopping to clear the plates, Rivka heard a voice behind her.

Nine

'You can be more generous with him,' the voice was saying.

Rivka glanced over her shoulder. The young man sitting behind Yoska hadn't read her mind; he was addressing Leon Beron. His steady, slightly Mongol eyes and hedgy brows hinted at a Jewish intensity; his tumultuous hair, haphazardly parted, was a storm cloud above the intellectual force concentrated below. A sharp scent of the disciplinarian hung around him too. On his broad face his flattened nose was on show, a blunt caution to anyone thinking of excluding him from any conversation going. A big game trophy might decorate a wall with the same expression on its face.

'Should I?' Beron replied, without giving the heckler the courtesy of a glance. 'Maybe I should turn my business into a charity.'

'Why not?' Another heckle.

Yoska said, 'After an exe, Leon, you know what this fellow does? He sends his share to Russia.' Yoska tilted his head, gave a brotherly nod in the direction of the heckler, whose name was Jacob Peters. 'Nobody knows how he feeds himself.'

Until the noise near the kitchen drowned it out, Jacob's voice streaked across the room. It was there again, cranked up to full volume, when Rivka returned with Yoska's gravy and potatoes, Beron's meat and borscht.

'... or which Social-Revolutionaries you could trust, which ones were probably Okhrana agents, which Social

61

Democrats were weak Marxists.' Jacob watched Rivka
serve the food, rearrange the plates and glassware; he
rode out the distraction until Beron made the mistake of
assuming Jacob would show some manners and let him
eat in peace. 'Class slavery! The Zionist future!
Legitimate targets of political mass terror, Lettish
nationalism versus socialist solidarity, our Party, their
party, the whole Anarchist Club circus, it's entertainment,
that's all. Nothing gets done in London.'

'Big ideas, confusing everybody,' Beron noted, then
belched.

'I'll tell you what confuses everybody,' Jacob started to
say.

'Please don't,' said Beron, heartfelt, heartburned.

A voice from the other end of the restaurant chimed in.
'Moscow is on a knife edge! London is rubber, everything
bounces off the English...'

From another diner: '*Mishigas! Mishigas!*'

A giant toy balloon could have bounced from table to
table the same way, but no matter where the subject
landed it was always swatted back to Jacob. 'Crazy?
The King of England is crazy. Revolution is an act of
sanity.'

'I'm eating my lunch in hell,' Beron moaned to nobody.

Rivka sympathised. 'Try to concentrate on your
borscht.'

To enlighten her or include her — either way, Rivka felt
a mild jolt when Jacob spoke to her directly. 'Scientific
Illegalists over there, Marxists and Social Democrats
there. That one's a Russian anarchist. There's a German
communist. Those there, those three are Polish anarcho-
communists. Christian Socialists there, Individualists
over there, Socialist Revolutionaries in the corner,
pooling their money to buy one pot of coffee.'

With the flammable exception of Jacob, none of the little commissars she served at Shinebloom's was as considerable a personality as Karl. They yapped about revolt and freedom in the same agitated voice they ordered her to bring borscht and pierógis. Oh, but when he addressed her he paid Rivka Bermansfelt the compliment of understanding that her freedom had one concrete meaning — her own money from her own work. He was clear: he saw what to do, then he arranged things. It staggered her to open her mind to a feeling that trembled in her legs for days, and warmed her stomach: he existed, he wasn't imaginary at all. Karl was a man she could love with a wife's devotion.

Yet Karl was with Nina, that was the situation, so Nina must be who he wanted. In a fair competition, Rivka told herself, he might have chosen me. At nineteen she was years younger than Nina, as much as five or six. In looks, size, form, nearly identical. In spirit, calmer; in movement, more graceful; in public, more amiable; in private (a sudden flash told her) more passionate. Yet Nina Vassilleva stood in front of her like a full length mirror and showed Rivka the green immigrant, a country girl, clumsy and ignorant among the English. Back and forth she went, measuring Nina's qualities against hers. Attractive was not how Rivka felt carrying food from the kitchen to Leon Beron's table.

With one sweep she delivered another bowl of potatoes, the next sweep cleared away the empty plates and the gravy boat. 'Leon sits at the same table every time he comes here,' Rivka heard Jacob complain, 'and to his ears it's one big meaningless argument.'

Beron appealed to Yoska, scornfully, 'Believe me, I try not to listen.'

'Now I'm going to tell you what you don't want to hear.'

Up went Jacob's scarred finger to separate right from wrong.

Yoska sniggered. He wiped the back of his hand across his mouth. A slick of spit and small pieces of potato, garbage dropped from the stern of a boat, spread from wrist to knuckles. 'What do you think, Rivka, who's going to win?'

Her detached smile, unreadable to Yoska, said, *Not you.* 'Let me take the rest of these plates away.'

Jacob didn't stop haranguing poor Leon Beron. 'Everybody in this restaurant hates your guts.'

'Don't listen to him,' Yoska advised. 'Rivka, you don't hate Leon, do you?'

'No, he's...' she stumbled into embarrassment.

Yoska egged her on. 'He's what?'

'Very fatherly,' Rivka decided.

Beron laughed off the whole business. 'No, no. It doesn't matter. Nothing Jacob Peters says makes any sense, everybody here knows it.'

'Conflict, Leon. Permanent conflict — between what's now and what's coming next!' Jacob rose out of his seat with the intensity of a fist in flight. 'Holy God, the prize that's going to come out of this.' His arm flung out and knocked Rivka's tray. Plates and glasses crashed to the floor, a percussion orchestra splashing through the restaurant noise.

'The Pistol!' Yoska, laughing, let Rivka know. 'See why we call him the Pistol?'

The manager hurried over. Red-faced, jaw tensed, totting up the loss shard by shard, the soup bowls, the plates, the glasses. 'Second time today,' he said, loudly. 'Twice in one day!' Theatrically stern, holding his head, moaning, '*Oy gevalt,*' mostly for show.

Before Jacob fled the scene he had a prophecy for

them all. 'A coup d'état is starting in this room.' Then he was gone.

On her knees, head down, Rivka got busy cleaning the mess. She gathered the fragments one by one onto the tray. Yoska's pity rose sadly above her, a fleshy cratered moon. He watched her sop up the mess with her apron.

'Here's a rag,' the manager said. 'Don't use your apron.' No anger but a cockeyed glimmer of pleasure. 'Wait. Stand up. If you had any money, I'd fine you. Since you don't...'

'What do you want me to do?'

'What *can* you do?'

Rivka stood without complaint, shoulders stiff, staring over the half-turned heads of the men. She sang, '*Nokh eyn tants...*' Rivka's singing voice was angelic. Her pure soprano had the charm and strength to quiet every diner, bury every shouted pledge, rupture every political argument. '*Beyt ikh itst bay dir, libster her, ikh bay dir shenk zhe mir nokh eye tants mir...*' It was the voice some of the men carried home with them through the damp streets, the sweet plea of a young woman unafraid to ask a beau for one more dance. Rivka's song asked each one of them.

Yoska led the applause, the first to raise his arms over his head in praise. He slapped his huge square hands together, lips curled above his red gums, grinning, baring his black teeth, a man who couldn't be prouder if he'd married Rivka five minutes before and she was singing to him at their wedding feast.

Ten

The clean brown paper he'd found on the pavement, blown flat as a sign against the wall of a Brick Lane coffee stand; for Yoska, dragging himself along to Rivka's place of work, it certainly was some kind of omen. Only a narrow fringe of one of the edges was stained by crud and damp. In the wake of the deal he struck with Leon Beron, to stumble across exactly what he needed — paper attractive enough to wrap Rivka's gift — was proof that his luck was in. Wasn't it miraculous that anything as delicate as paper, abandoned in the street for hours, days even, could remain so clean? For a ribbon, Yoska unpicked a strand of twine he stole off the end of a barrow.

Clark's coffeehouse at that late hour was as busy with workingmen on their way home as it was early in the morning, with the same hammered faces. A few doors away at the King's Arms they drank themselves stupid, the Exploited Proletariat. Yoska counted himself a member of this class, in good and prominent standing, in spite of one well-known detail: when he worked for straight pay it was in the polished surroundings of a jewellery store he would end up robbing, not in any salt mine of a sweatshop or factory. At the table just inside the door he found an empty seat. Yoska awkwardly steered his bulk around the two men sitting there. Neither one looked up at the disturbance. Crumbs, sauce stains, grease smears, particles of boiled eggs and fried fish littered the bare wooden table top. As if he was crushing ants he poked at the stray bits with the pad of his thumb, brought his thumb to his lips and nibbled, absently calming his nerves.

Rivka shuffled between from the till to the kitchen and tables in her bespattered apron, sweat glowing on her forehead, at the end of a late shift, pacing the trail of demands between cook and customers. Yoska watched her take thruppence for a pot of tea from a slouching young man, scan the room for a vacancy and send him to the table next to his. Yoska waved his big square hand, but Rivka didn't see him — or perhaps it was the rule there ... yes, that was it: she had to ignore him. No Personal Business Conducted On The Premises. To ignore him so ostentatiously was her coded welcome.

The two men sharing Yoska's table weren't talking. They scooped forkfuls of grub from plate to mouth, mechanically, swallowing without chewing or tasting. By the look of the brown muck on their plates, a wise move. Noises from their throats, noses, flapping lips, summed up, for Yoska, the kind of people Rivka stooped to serve.

From the end of the room she finally returned Yoska's wave with a beleaguered smile. Rivka mimed bringing a cup of tea to her lips. He nodded, held up his penny, but with the same gesture she saw Yoska use to stop traffic in Commercial Road, she had him stay where he sat.

'Only another thirty minutes of this,' she said when she brought his tea over.

He looked at the cloudy brown water in the metal cup. 'It'll take me that long to gargle this down. For my reward, I'll walk you over to Perelman's.'

Rivka didn't hear what he said. Her face was turned away to catch an order from the kitchen. 'Sorry. They boil it to mush.' Then, confidentially, 'This morning, first serving, it was stewed too. They brew it in one big pot, Yoska, it's a witch's cauldron.'

Yoska sipped, clowned a disgusted face. 'No, it's very good. Good temperature.'

From the kitchen the manager shouted her name. Rivka sped off in his direction, balancing a heavy tray of dirty plates and mugs. Yoska winced. All right, Beron, we need money for food and a roof, shirts, skirts and shoes, so we work. But not to serve, Leon, not to *serve*. Here, Rivka served. Here, she got bossed from pillar to post, swatted by customer to cook, cook to customer.

The old man sitting next to Yoska finished his eggs, wiped his mouth on his coat sleeve, missed a curd of yolk on his chin. Here they are, the men who order Rivka around. If they look at her at all do they see a workingwoman performing a task? No, to them she's nothing *but* the task No one looks her in the face, unless it's to ogle her like they ogle the whores in Spitalfields. They think of Rivka's soft legs under her skirt, her naked breasts, her arms reaching around their backs, hands squeezing, breath from her mouth huffing against their cheek. Yoska felt disgusted for her. He knew her for the woman she was, the fighter. Those legs stood up to a Russian soldier, those arms brought him down, and here she was, waiting on pigs.

They walked in silence from Sclater Street, but at the top of Brick Lane Yoska said to her, 'You have to get used to the English weather.'

Rivka bunched her shawl's edge under her chin. 'If I stay.'

'If I know anything I know the Russian police. They won't forget about you,' he promised her, 'you and your dead Cossack.'

'He didn't die.'

'Worse for you.'
'Worse for me.'

A cold wind tattered the dark air. Cold as it was outside, though, conditions were worse in most of the rooms along Brick Lane, as crowded as the cargo hold of a Chinese junk. The street crawled with as much human life at midnight as it did at noon. Gangs of children ran on bare feet up one side-street and down another, in and out of places where the gaslights shed their powdery green light. A family huddled in a doorway; the woman used a knife to trim the frayed strips of the rags she wore; her husband's head lolled on her lap, his trousers caked with gutter mud. Two children unconscious on the step, were they breathing? The dirty pity of the sight burrowed into Rivka.

When a cart stopped short in front of them, Yoska performed a dance step — slide the left foot, drag the right — to avoid colliding with it. 'Maybe if we walked on the pavement?' Rivka ventured.

'It's better to stay in the street. Safer.'

To walk beside Yoska, Rivka thought, was to walk in the sheltering shadow of a folk- tale giant, a limping Golem. As if he'd caught that flickering notion, her protector smiled down at her, benignly, baring his black teeth. It was the soot on the walls, the dust on the kerb, the grime on her own second-hand clothes. Rivka had left Riga with only the odds and ends Jankel found for her: four crumpled skirts and blouses, one petticoat and an odd number of stockings. Wearing them made her feel she'd donned a disguise. At least twice a day — climbing out of bed at six in the morning, climbing in again at eleven-thirty at night — she wondered, *Is it always going to be like this?*

From the mouth of an alleyway a man staggered into

Rivka, drunk or wounded. In a flare of violence that rose up and took charge of him for one hot instant, Yoska gripped the man's lapels and shoved him away. Rivka's assailant fell backwards on the pavement, and rolled unconscious into the gutter.

'Did he hurt you anywhere? Touch you?' Yoska's voice was loud, furious.

Rivka shook her head. 'It's worse in the restaurant at lunch time.'

This tripped a laugh out of him. 'Wait,' he said. He dragged his foot and the clodhopping rest of him to an archway in the middle of the block where a pocket of quiet sank away from Brick Lane's noise. He was still puffing when he stopped, Rivka thought Yoska wanted to catch his breath.

'This is for you,' he said, pressing a package into her hand.

'What's this?' Rivka said.

'Open it and you'll see.'

She untied the string, undid the paper. The beaded case sparkled under the gaslight. The beads were as tiny as barley grains, worked into a decoration of flowers, dog roses, pink blossoms twined by green leaves.

Yoska nudged her again to open it. 'The best quality. You see there? Scissors, needles...'

No more favours, Rivka was thinking, *no more debt.* 'What's it for?' She said.

'For sewing. See? One of the thimbles, there, that one...' He flicked it with his fingertip. 'That one's gold. I think so.'

'Sewing and what else?'

In innocence, Yoska missed the point. 'Just sewing.'

'It's a beautiful thing,' she had to tell him, and tried with a gentle frown to refuse it.

He ignored the frown. 'Did you look at the bead work? It's fancy French.'

A shake of her head. 'It's too rich for me.'

'No, but that's ... London is so ...' The right word wasn't in his head, one word for the degrading desperation, the unrewarded sweat, freedom you could mistake for punishment. 'Dirty. So,' Yoska said, 'I want it for you.'

If he hadn't said that, she might have gone home with the wee satin case out of kindness. The note in his voice hovered between a plea and a boast, delivering Yoska's real message: I want Good Things for you, the Best of Things, a Better Life. That was less than the whole story. This is the rest: I want you to want this From Me.

'No,' she said. 'No, Yoska.'

'You don't care for it?' Maybe its fineness was the problem: maybe this Cossack killer was more communist than he. 'It belonged to the wife of a bank manager.It was liberated during a Liesma exe last night. Karl was happy enough with the pot,' he lied. 'Instead of putting this in with the rest I kept it back. For you.'

'I'm sorry if you did that.'

To quiet any doubt Yoska showed off the scissors' sharp blades by snipping bits from the end of the string. Rivka took the sterling silver tool from him, as Yoska thought, to get a feel of the quality. She slipped the scissors inside, closed the lid, buttoned the mother-of-pearl button in its loop of satin thread, then pressed the sewing case into his hand, wrapping and all. 'You should save this for someone special.'

'Who's more special than you?' Gambling everything, he bent down to kiss Rivka's mouth.

Her arms hung at her sides. She twisted her head away. 'You have to stop now.'

'Is it something about me?'

'No.'

'You have another man?'

Here was a quick way out and Rivka took it. 'His name's Benjamin.'

'Benjamin.'

'He's in Riga. He plays concert violin. Yiddish songs sometimes, too. In his own band.'

Yoska nodded, conceding, 'Benjamin's the leader. He's coming to be with you?'

'No. He wants peace and quiet so he can play his violin. Anyway, being with me right now is dangerous. Benjamin's waiting for when I can come back.'

'Benjamin's an unusual type. Sounds like he is, to me.'

His heart stormy and rocking in his chest, Yoska limped away from Rivka's refusal, wrapping the satin box again in its clean brown paper.

Yoska you unfaithful dog! You let a pretty face tangle your emotions and humiliation is what it gets you every time!

Another warm room waited for Yoska half a mile away. On his way there his shiver of embarrassment disappeared beneath a shiver of cold. As he walked he rehearsed what he'd say to the woman who waited for him there, as he put the paper-wrapped gift in her hand. 'Here's the start of a better time for us, Betsy.'

Betsy Gershon appreciated his ways. She knew the ropes, shared the same spirit. Take what's here to take, have what you can have now. Betsy knew the ropes. Five years ago hadn't her husband packed up and left her, to plant himself in the Crimea? A flock of pigeons or English weather you can count on better than people.

Here's the start of a better time for us, Betsy. Every word of it the truth, too, there and then. Three weeks since he lay down in her arms. Tonight she'll bring him upstairs, lead him by his hand through the door, where the first thing he'll see is her green-painted iron bed, the heavy blankets opened like the peel of a piece of fruit. Betsy will undress him, button by button. She'll want him to kiss her face and throat, her mouth, her brown nipples. Down in his trousers Yoska felt her effect on him as he thumped the soft edge of his fist on Betsy's door, shuffling on the cold pavement outside 100 Sidney Street.

Eleven

Peter's uncle, a colonel in Tsar Nicholas's army, had made a promise to the twenty-six-year- old jailbird two years before, in '08, 'Money doesn't have to be one of your problems,' he said, 'you can have all you need from me.'

'If...?'

'Is that a question?' The older man sipped his coffee and tilted back his head to be drenched by the Marseilles sun.

'It's a hundred questions. If I go back home? If I 'settle down?' If I'm a good little boy and stop hating the Russians...'

'You don't have to like them, just stop shooting at them.'

'Yes, and...?'

'And see different friends. Those rag-tags you go around with, Peter. They're troublemakers. It's simple: they're nobodies, lowlifes, just people who don't want to knuckle under.'

'Revolutionaries.' Peter set the record straight. 'Why should people hold still while the Russian Empire rapes them?'

The sloganeering, or the idea that he was hearing it from his nephew's mouth, jerked a sharp laugh out of the Colonel. 'That bunch couldn't overthrow a grocery store. They got *caught* and dragged you into court and prison with them.'

'That's not how it happened.'

'I don't care. You want more of the same? Should I mention the wreck it made of your mother?'

'You don't have to worry about her.'

'Oh, *you're* going to? With your father in the ground? Well, you don't have to worry what *he* thinks anymore, either, do you?'

'No.' Peter looked away.

His uncle's voice, and intention, softened. 'I apologise, Peter.' With his uniformed arm, he clasped his misguided nephew's shoulder: his sympathy belonged with his kin, even if his accommodation had to be with the forces of order. 'Listen to my offer.'

'If.'

Uncle-Colonel refused to take the bait. 'I'll give you an allowance, a good one, every month, so you can attend classes at the university in Paris. Study anything you want. Any subject except politics.'

'Politics is the only subject there is.'

'You mean it's the only one you're interested in.'

'Everything interests me,' Peter said honestly.

'Good.' His uncle got the impression they were finally making progress. 'What about economics? A baccalaureate in such a serious field and you've got a civil service job for life. And after you have your degree, well' — a generous puff of his cheeks — 'stay in Paris if you don't want a career in Riga.'

'Economics is politics,' Peter said flatly.

'Geography, then. What about studying maps and terrains, that kind of thing? You like to draw, don't you? Learning about the Hottentots?'

He counted on his fingers as if they were the undeniable realities themselves: 'Colonies, countries, borders, populations, resources — what's geography if it isn't politics?'

'You'll say engineering is politics, too.'

'Yes! I design a bridge, so some foundry owner can hire

workers to manufacture the iron for it, so he can sell it to the city, so the city can hire labourers to build it so people can walk across it to their jobs to earn their rotten wages. So tell me please, how can I study anything that isn't politics?'

Uncle Colonel struggled to muffle his neck-reddening fury and embarrassment as the head waiter stopped to refill Peter's wine glass...

That was two years ago and the event still rattled around in Peter's head. 'Money won't be your problem,' he reminded himself out loud. He drew the edge of his straight razor downward along a brown stalk in the centre of the wallpaper panel he'd hung the week he moved in to the flat. A puff of plaster dust floated in the lamplight when he pried the slit edges apart. Then, with his forefinger, Peter nudged a sealed envelope out of its hiding place. Apart from that clutch of bank notes and forged identity papers the only thing he took from Rue Danville was his painting of the lily pond, unstapled from its stretchers and rolled in his suit jacket pocket.

Ten hours later he stood on the deck of a mail boat, lightly flicking cigarette ash into the English Channel.

It was the right time and reason to travel to London. Since he'd quit Marseilles in the dead month of January, prickly questions and pricklier answers ran him in circles. Peter had to talk with somebody besides himself. No one in Paris, no one in Marseilles. In London, at least, there was Karl. He and Peter had survived the same years. Side by side they had done the same violence and suffered the same wicked reprisals.

A year ago, Peter had read reports and editorials in English newspapers about the outrage in Tottenham — the last masterwork of Christian Salnish. A bungled robbery, a running gun fight in the streets, a cowering little boy slaughtered by a bullet through the mouth, a policeman killed outright, a sick old man shot in the throat, both of Salnish's men hunted down and shot dead, all in bright daylight. Brutality and havoc with nothing to show for it except five corpses and a backlash of loud encouragement for the Russian vendetta against political thugs who terrorise and torment the innocent.

As far as Peter knew, Karl had no plans to launch any such armed assault on London He wondered if the reason for a year's quiet in London was that Karl, too, had been slowed down too by dizzying doubts.

France drifted somewhere in the murk behind him with no sight yet of England over the boat's ploughing bow. Around him Peter saw only gray water and blanched air, not even another ship. Salt mist hung low overhead; he felt he was afloat in it.

'Not afraid of catching cold out here?' someone said.

Peter smelled the cigar smoke before he turned to see who was smoking it: a middle-aged Englishman pacing toward him, a man of about Peter's height, bulkier, with a heavy moustache balancing chubby red cheeks, under a bowler hat and a long coat with a broad astrakhan collar, only the lower button done up. One hand pocketed, he approached Peter with the confidence of a banker or a detective.

'Are you heading home or getting away?'

Peter made a helpless gesture of apology, fluffing the air with open hands, and muttered in a German accent, 'Not English speak, mister.'

The man's face tightened. 'You better bloody learn English. It happens to be what we speak in England.'

Good and proper warning delivered, he marched back toward the cabin, leaving Peter alone to stare into the fog that soon enfolded the boat, billows of the world-haze connecting him to London, to his comrade Karl, in the swirling vastness Peter's only living friend.

Twelve

Rivka couldn't afford to be tugged off balance, pulled backward by memories of her family. So, for sixteen hours a day six days a week, she was grateful, for something besides the £1.4s.6d she earned at the two restaurants. The Bermansfelts were out of reach in Sasmacken; that was the hard fact. Her life was in London, beginning with the geography of the district — the synagogues, schools and social clubs, strangers' faces and local street life, prices in the market, opening and closing times of the shops, where Yiddish ended and the city's native language took over.

Rivka was an eager learner, especially of spoken English. Her best teachers were the girls who worked alongside her at Clark's coffee house. As a mimic, she was practically clairvoyant. A scrap of local slang might drift above the din into Rivka's ear and right away she'd parrot it, Cockney accent and all, usually without understanding a syllable. Next thing, she'd buttonhole one of the other waitresses for a translation.

Thus it was Rivka swooned over the lyric beauty of the language. 'Bewitch a pot of boiling water with some tea.' Clear water *bewitched* into a beverage the colour of tree bark! What poetry! Could you say sugar bewitched it sweet? And this sassiness tickled her: 'I know one thing and that ain't two!' Meaning: here's something I know *without a doubt*. Rivka laughed out loud at the brassy comedy of it and went around repeating the phrase all day. That night, when she trudged in the door close to

81

midnight, her landlord asked her if she was too tired to sit up for a while and talk to him. Eyelids closing under their own weight, Rivka disappointed him: 'I know one thing and that ain't two...'

Without trying, she became a favourite at Shinebloom's. One October afternoon, the sky dripping gloom outside, a Cockney grandmother had wandered in and shuffled to the till. Rivka looked at the old blanket she used for a shawl; from under its muddy fringe, a knotted hand poked out, clutching a penny. 'Can you let me 'ave somethin' for this? Anythin'. I'm that faint.' She repeated the plea, this time addressing Rivka as 'daughter.' Rivka dropped the penny into the till, then prepared a plate for her — boiled potatoes, a little corned beef, a thick slice of bread and margarine, a mug of sweet tea — and walked her to a chair in a corner of the room where the old woman could eat her meal without embarrassment.

When Rivka turned around she saw the manager himself manning the abandoned till. The slant of his head told her he'd witnessed the whole transaction. Before Rivka had a chance to apologise and explain — she had already taken enough from her own change purse to make up the difference — the manager stopped her with an open hand.

'I don't want your money,' he said. 'You'll pay a forfeit. Stand here, next to me.' Rivka obeyed. He banged an empty pot with a spoon until every face in the restaurant turned. 'Rivka is going to show you she's sorry for breaking the rules,' he announced.

After a curtsey, theatrically contrite, she said, in English, 'I am *most* sorry.'

The manager gently shook her by the arm. 'And?'

Rivka paused a moment. The she opened her mouth

and a song came out. '*Nokh eyn tants, beyt ikh itst bay dir...*
Libster her, ikh bay dir shenk zhe mir nokh eye tants mir...'

A rolling wave of applause washed away her mis-
demeanour.

Between the two places she worked in Sclater Street,
Shinebloom's and the more English Clark's, Rivka held
Shinebloom's a notch or two higher in her affections. Before
long she'd forged a straightman-comic working relationship
with the manager, who bragged about the nickname she'd
given him: The Mayor. The palaver in Shinebloom's rattled
on like the hubbub of a village, especially on Sundays, and
the small wide man who presided there kept up with the
wants and needs of staff and clientele alike as though he'd
been elected to satisfy them. The Mayor saved his special
concern, though, for George Gardstein, the softspoken man
Rivka knew as Karl. There was always a table available for
him and Nina and whatever combination of the Liesma
crowd roamed in with them.

A second salvation, this job at Shinebloom's. Rivka
didn't need anybody to tell her, though that's what
Charles Perelman did as he'd celebrated her news with a
warm hug. Congratulations laced with a few Old
Whiskery Uncle words of care: *be on guard around
Gardstein's gang*. Perelman said he knew them inside and
out, the way a smart landlord knows the people he rents
to: Fritz Svaars, body too big for his brain, a strongman
for Karl once upon a time, gone soft now. Fritz's woman,
Luba, a 'dizzy idiot' for her married lover... Fritz's cousin
Jacob Peters, just a hothead, a bigmouth. Karl himself, a
'raving beauty' with a sledgehammer behind his back.
Nina, with a little anvil where her heart should be. And
Yoska Sokoloff: in Perelman's opinion, a jellyfish who
'finagles this so he can finagle that.' Keep your distance,
he advised Rivka, and see what you see.

Whether alone or together, they didn't look like gang members, criminals, idiots, hotheads or jellyfish — at least not to Rivka. They were people like herself, washed on oily waves to Tilbury and straight from the docks into Shinebloom's, glad to find their lemon tea and *lockshen* pudding waiting for them, and a woman with an accent from home to serve their food. When she looked she saw their differences — different manners and moods, which ones looked at her when she took their order and which ones did not, which of them could see in her eyes the splinter of absence she saw in theirs — and all this kept her looking.

This Sunday noontime, six of them occupied two tables at the front of the room. Seeing them together, close as a bunch of grapes, on the street or in Shinebloom's, you would conclude that the main activity of revolutionaries in London was *kibbitzing*. Debating and condemning, falling in and out with each other while they filled and emptied their plates. Beyond those activities, as far as Rivka could tell, what occupied Nina, Karl and the rest was the same business of day-to-day survival that busied her.

Karl sat back from the table to give Rivka room to serve his whitefish and potatoes. 'Did you talk to the new neighbours?' Rivka heard him ask Nina.

'Who?' Nina glanced up, distracted by Rivka setting a quarter loaf of black bread next to the water jug.

'The new people on top of us. Did you talk to them?'

'Not very much.'

'How many times?'

A sideways wave of her hand swished the irrelevant question out of Nina's way. 'You eat too fast. It's why you get pains.'

'What pains?'

'You don't taste your food.'

'Because everything's white. Fish, potatoes, cauliflower.'

'I need money for the laundry. And your shoes, they're still at Bondarchuk's.'

'They're ready?'

'Since Friday.'

'Why didn't you get them then?'

'I need two shillings.'

'You didn't ask me for it on Friday.'

'When I thought of it you and Peter were busy talking,' Nina reminded Karl. 'On Friday Bondarchuk closes early.'

'Remind me to find some money for you later. Back at the flat.'

Digging up two shillings for shoe repairs seemed a long way from toppling the Tsar, the Kaiser and the King of England, but who knew for sure what kind of secret activity Karl and Nina hosted behind their drawn curtains? Nobody outside their circle could say with confidence, so stories about them trailed around in their wake:

Rosie Trassjonsky, small, hunchbacked, trails around with Karl because she is pathetically in love with him . . .

Nina takes advantage of Rosie's weakness, keeps the crippled girl under her thumb . . .

'George Gardstein' was once a circus acrobat and he used his skills to escape over the wall of Riga Central Prison . . . He lets his friends call him Karl because it was his father's name . . .

Nina is the truest Socialist of the group because she practises free love with every one of the Liesma men . . .

Karl openly approves but underneath harbours agonising jealousy . . .

From what she saw at Shinebloom's, Rivka found each of these rumours as believable as the next.

Revolutionists, 'Liesma,' her rescuers — who were they? Behind the locked doors and curtained windows, they could be moon men, for all she knew.

'Hey, Fritz! Lend me some money!' Jacob hailed his fair-haired cousin two tables away. He gave a broad, jokey wave to the young woman with Fritz, who wore a winter coat despite the restaurant's oppressive heat. 'Luba! Give him some money so he can lend it to me!'

Luba's overburdened, donkeyish face drooped another inch, and Fritz scooted his chair around so that his back was facing Jacob. Then, huddled over, he asked Luba, 'What about it?'

'He embarrasses you in public,' Luba tutted.

'It's your fault.'

'Mine? How?'

'You don't give me enough money. It makes me look bad.'

'With you there *is* no enough.'

'You see me buying fancy clothes? I *eat*. I buy *coal*. I always come home to you.'

'Yes, for more money.'

'Maybe tonight I won't come home.'

'Then I won't be there either.'

Fritz growled, stood up and almost knocked the tray of food out of Rivka's arms. Luba reached up, touched Fritz's broad hand, tugged him back into his chair. 'Are those our pierógis?' he asked Rivka, savouring the smell rising from the plate.

At the end of the table closest to the door, Jacob tossed his shaggy head in wild agreement with something whispered to him by a man Rivka had never seen before. He paid Rivka for his meal and Jacob's, thanked her in Yiddish without meeting her eye. As he looked away from her, she noticed his fine brown hair, brushed back off his

86

brow to reveal a complexion any woman would have been glad to own, a feature that made his beard and moustache even more memorable.

'Peter, tell me how you're enjoying life with Fritz and Luba.' Jacob said, loud enough for Fritz and his young mistress to hear, two tables away. Luba tucked herself against his cousin's chest like a menaced animal sheltering under a boulder.

Peter lit a cigarette, drew in the smoke and exhaled before he answered. 'They gave me the front room.'

'Mine.'

'Luba cleaned it for me. It took her a whole day,' he kidded Jacob, horribly serious. 'She did a good job.'

Jacob lowered his voice a little. 'God gave cows more self-respect. Fritz talks to her about his wife, tells Luba everything. Even how they're emigrating to Australia in January. I don't care. They can go to hell.' Volume raised again, half facing Fritz, 'With the rest of the anarchists, who believe in *nothing*.'

As Rivka cleared away their plates Karl leaned towards Peter to offer him the last piece of black bread. His friend took it, slipped it into his coat pocket, then dipped his head closer for privacy, and through the threads and blur of Peter's cigarette smoke Karl gave him his exclusive attention.

Behind them, trouble loafed in through the front door. They'd been hanging around outside for a quarter of an hour, the Cockney lads, joshing each other, whistling through their teeth at the Jewish girls who walked by. They were regulars at Clark's and if she'd been looking through the window and not ferrying plates back to the kitchen, Rivka would have recognised the one who tried to charm Fanny Perelman with a cheeky wink as a troublemaker called Arthur.

87

The boy was sympathetic to other outsiders who scrabbled to make a living under the cosh of marauding police, and that sympathy made him cocky in the company of Jews. He singled out Fanny because aside from her slender neck, fair hair and her father's Spanish eyes, but also because he knew she spoke English. 'I went into the Sugar Loaf and I learned a lesson. Want to know what?'

Fanny's eyes snapped away from him, looking to Nina to give her a lead. Nina stared directly into his Cockney face, a look of dry disbelief and challenge. 'We know what you learn in a boozer.'

He laughed with his mates at Nina's pronunciation. 'I use the Hanbury m'self. That's a Englishman's *boosa*. Thing I seen fer true in comparison is the English, they drink, and the Jews talk.'

Fanny said, 'We don't want to talk to you, please.'

'Yer talkin', though, aren't you?' He crabbed toward her between the ledge of the windowsill and the back of Nina's chair. He bent over the table. 'A little bird told me your real name's Fenia.' Carelessly, no disrespect meant, his elbow pushed in front of Karl's face. It was shoved away. The boy's, 'Excuse me,' came out in a puff of sarcastic courtesy. 'Do you want to say somethin' to me?'

By this time Fritz was standing at the open door with Luba, and the stir at Karl's table stopped him in place. Fritz's heavy shoulders were hunched forward in weariness; his pale gray eyes anticipated nothing; what was in front of him to do, he did. Now he gently shunted Luba outside, then with the same big-knuckled hand he touched the lad's shoulder. Fritz said, 'Go away. Nothing for you in here.'

And the lad landed a roundhouse punch on the side of Fritz's head.

88

The surprise of it threw Fritz off balance. He stumbled backward into an empty table, sent a chair skittering, and dropped to the floor. Rivka looked over to see Jacob spring out of his seat and shove his pistol into the lad's armpit.

'Not in here,' Karl said to Jacob.

Half a dozen plates slipped from Rivka's grip. The noise of their crash and shattering pulled The Mayor out of the kitchen, and the first thing he saw was Rivka standing in the middle of hundreds of white china fragments. He missed seeing the Cockney's terrified surrender and hearing George Gardstein say: 'Put your hands down, you idiot.' He didn't see what Rivka saw: Jacob pocketing his gun before he vanished out the door. The Mayor clapped his hands for attention. 'Rivka has something to tell you,' he announced.

'I broke five plates,' she confessed.

Up on his toes to accentuate the point, The Mayor corrected her. 'I count six.'

'Six!' Rivka shouted out her shame, a plucky smile before and after, triggering a round of high-spirited applause.

Rivka nodded, accepting her fate, and in a few seconds quiet, if not calm, spread through the whole restaurant. She sang, *Dayne oygn shvarts un groys, Makh itst tsu bay mir in shoys, Shmeykhist, heylst mayn vund... Papa dayner vogelt um, Tog un nakht keyn brekl ru, Alts far undz mayn kind...*

> *Close your big black eyes*
> *As you curl up in my lap,*
> *Your smile heals my wound.*
> *Papa is wandering*
> *Day and night without rest*
> *All for us, my child...*

Peter sat as still as the rest of Rivka's audience. Her singing voice, its persuasive purity, dug channels into them as they listened, transported and helpless. To Peter's ears, it was the melody of this girl's struggling pride. And for him alone the flat drawled vowels of her Talsin accent, tenderly familiar, carried more force than Jacob's gun.

Thirteen

Luba kept her gaze on Fritz, who stood on the improvised stage at the other end of the rehearsal hall. Head lowered, shoulders slumped, he concentrated on new instructions from the director. As he took in the critique of his performance Fritz wore the look of a scolded schoolboy. 'Fritz has been back here ten months,' she said to Peter. 'Since January. Karl said he wasn't so shaky before.'

Peter looked up from the scenery he was painting. 'Before when?'

'That Russian prison.' Luba watched the director arrange Fritz in a pose: right arm curved over his head, brandishing a wooden sword; left arm crooked, thrust out, triumphant fist to the fore. He threw his whole being into his role in the play, a socialist drama called *Girts Wilks*. It was a part nobody else wanted, in the story of a young revolutionary on the run. Our hero persuades a farmboy to hide him, but a prowling rat of an informer bribes the boy with a stolen watch and chain, and, tragically, the rebel is betrayed. Disgusted by his son's low morals, the farmer shoots the boy dead.

Luba said, 'Karl says since he's back he looks smaller.'

Abandoned, thought Peter. *Not reliable.* Now Fritz controls what he can control – this controllable girl Luba Milstein, who abides. She abides him denying her a key to the Grove Street flat, abides his sulks and then his wild bouts of heels-in-the-air elation, abides his treatment of her – speaking Lettish with his friends to keep her from

91

eavesdropping, the same thing as Fritz shutting a door in her face. He did that too. *Where's my dinner? Come to bed.* Or sometimes Peter heard him tell her, 'Go to bed', as if nineteen-year-old Luba were an irritating child. *Keep me company. Go away. Come back.*

Peter glanced up from his work, painting a backdrop for the play. 'I'd say he's heavier in the face.'

'Fritz looks all right by me,' Luba said. 'He's starting again. We should be quiet.'

Peter saw the borders of Luba's life marked there, in her choice to stop talking and fasten her eyes on Fritz. He watched her, slyly, as he added green brush strokes to a tree that looked like a tree, and once again he felt the failure of his talent to paint faces. What made that knowledge harder to take was his power to see beyond a face to its character, and the cold fact that his hands didn't move with the talent to make its portrait. Luba's face turned three-quarters in the dirty light of the rehearsal hall, the dull glow of her skin — yes, Peter had no difficulty imagining how an artist of, say, Cézanne's skill and vision would capture these minutes in Luba's life, and her life in these minutes...

Nothing hidden in her expression, no rage there for her to bury... A narrow face with no insistence in it recedes behind a nose that belongs on a Middle Eastern face... She watches her lover and thinks she's lucky to be protected by a man like him... Her womanliness gathers in her heavy-lidded, credulous blue eyes, full, high breasts and a mouth that depending on her mood can look either comically large or voluptuous... The black silk that neatly decorates the rim of her straw hat she sewed there herself, a remnant she brought home from her work finishing skirts at her brother's sweatshop in Whitechapel... Small people become either fearsome or fearful and this Luba is the kind who scrambles for safety...

Luba's round of applause greeted Fritz's bow. For her he encored his dramatic line: 'I am Gamba and you are a traitor!'

'Doesn't he mind playing a policeman?' Peter asked Luba.

A shake of her head. 'The story has a happy ending.'

'I'm Gamba and you are under arrest!'

'Good, good!' the director cheered Fritz on. 'Now *show* him.'

Fritz struck the statuesque pose he'd rehearsed, sword arm up, fist thrust out. Close observation of Russian police attitudes towards socialist heroes gave his interpretation a fanatical authenticity. Not just Russian, either; Fritz was wanted by the authorities in five countries. The Russians had merely been the last ones to get hold of him. For eleven days in Riga the Okhrana hardmen had pummelled his face and head so brutally, and with such relentless glee, that he lay unconscious in his cell for three days. They beat his bones and crushed his spirit for good. That's one change a man can't disguise.

'I am Gamba!'

'Yes, Fritz, that's it! An iron fist! Showmanship!'

'I am *Gam*-ba!'

'He's Gamba, already. He won't get any better!' The shout bounced in from the side of the hall. Another director, who was through waiting with his troupe of speciality acts for a fair crack on the boards.

But the director of *Girts Wilks* was a perfectionist. He ignored the barracking and told Fritz to expect more of the same when he was onstage. 'You're good or bad, they'll yell at you anyway.'

'Why?'

'Why? Because they're jealous.' He showed no sign of ending the day's rehearsal. 'Now...'

The other director hurried over. 'Now what? Now *stop*. Three o'clock is the Pavilion's time.'

'Then why don't you go rehearse in your big theatre and stop annoying us?'

'What do you care? We paid as much as you did to be in here. And you're using the time we paid for.'

Fritz's director looked over his rival's shoulder at his assembled troupe and capitulated. 'You probably need it more than we do.'

He shrugged.

'We're taking this stage.' He turned and waved over one of his acts, a slim man carrying three Indian clubs and a unicycle.

Wooden sword waving, fist shaking, Fritz jumped in to rally the counterattack. 'I am Gamba! Go fuck yourself!'

The director from the Pavilion, who was called Harry, counted Peter Piatkow a friend. Now he appealed to Peter across the empty space of the hall, beleaguered and desperate. Peter shrugged the reply that in this battle Harry was on his own.

Fritz refused to budge. 'Crazy as he ever was,' Peter said. 'Big and crazy.'

Luba called to him, and Fritz's sword and fist dropped to his side, like the arms of a puppet whose strings were cut. 'If he told me at noon it was midnight, I'd believe him,' she whispered.

As Fritz walked across to them Peter recognised the fractured look on his face. My comrade. *Mon frère*. Maybe it spread like an infection, this shaky discontent, through the ranks to every fighter who sabotaged telephone lines, raided a bank, murdered a policemen, and was jailed, tortured, went on the run only to find himself spurred on to other necessary actions, robberies, burglaries, assaults, shoot-outs, by the shining promise, always closer, of the last revolution this world will ever see. Necessary for whom? Maybe it was a good time to let Fritz hear that someone else felt the same strangeness he did. Peter looked at his friend's neatly parted and oiled hair, his excited eyes, his soft-featured face, and behind the jaunty moustache saw the hellcat Fritz used to be. No, there was no useful talk Peter could have with him.

'On the same day you took me in the rowing boat,' Luba told Fritz, sprucing up his lapel with her hand, 'Peter was in a boat, too. Coming to London.'

'Think of that,' Peter said.

'Don't want to think any more,' Fritz said. 'Thinking's a trap.'

Luba said, 'I'll compare your horoscopes.'

Fritz kissed the top of Luba's head. 'An idiot lives inside there.'

She hooked her arm through his and took him out into the dust and traffic of Spitalfields. Back to the odour of rotten things — fruit and vegetables, fresh meat hacked in the kosher butchers, trickles of blood collected between the pavement stones. The odours of prison.

Peter stayed on, finishing his backdrop for *Girts Wilks* and enjoying a private show of Harry's acts. For his finale, the unicycling juggler was joined by two dancing girls who led him off stage. A skinny man in tweed plus-fours impersonated the calls of about a dozen different birds; then two fat comics acted out the hilarious effects of laxative pills accidentally baked into a cake.

The next act, however, got Peter to stop painting. He looked and listened.

'I'm not bloody Marie Lloyd, am I?' The girl's screechy protest went unanswered at first.

At last Harry had to admit, 'No. No, you're not Marie Lloyd. You're no star name yet, darling, that's right, you're not *established*.'

'Am I 'er?'

'No.'

'So I want t'sing *me own* song!'

'We haven't got a song for you, Katie. Max is trying to write one.'

'Fer me signature.'

'That's right,' he said. 'For today let's just hear the one you've been practising at home.'

' "The Boy I Love is Up in the Gallery".'

'Can you sing it without the piano?'

'Well, it's how I done it at home.'

'When you're ready, then, Katie, all right?'

She stood for a moment in quiet thought, a beautiful girl, beautiful the way an English girl can be. Apple beauty. Every curve and soft colour brought to life in the English summer, burnished by the English autumn. That's what this pink fleshed and blond ringleted dollop of honey urged a man to romanticise, even a man like Peter, infected and ailing with every strain of doubt.

And she sang —

> *I'm a young girl, and have just come over,*
> *Over from the country where they do things big,*
> *And amongst the boys I've got a lover,*
> *And since I've got a lover,*
> *Why I don't care a fig...*

The awfulness of her voice clanged in Peter's ears. The girl didn't sing, she yowled, she belted out a tin-eared bray that washed over everybody in the rehearsal hall like the stink from an open sewer. Harry gave Peter another one of his trademark surrenders: *Look at her – what am I supposed to do?* But Harry couldn't look at her. Peter couldn't *stop* looking at the brassy collision of heaven and hell. As the final jagged notes of her song tore free from her throat, Harry mimed playing a trombone — *The orchestra can drown her out!* — and Peter went back to his painting.

The landscape he created for *Girts Wilks* was a road in the countryside. Peter had improvised the details — a milestone in the foreground, an old manor house in the distance — and when he stood back to survey his workmanship and be disappointed by it, he realized with a swell of tenderness in his chest that he'd added the homely features of the Talsen road.

Fourteen

Where was the best place to approach Shinebloom's singing waitress? And could he say (and be believed) that the beautiful English hiccoughing donkey in the rehearsal hall last night laid him low by polluting every note of music she breathed, while Rivka's singing, bumpkin accent and all, held out a realistic hope of purity in the roaring world?

Peter was no strategist, he was an improviser. For good or ill he left strategic thinking to men gifted with more organised minds than his, for instance Lenin and Karl. Against a challenge Peter trusted his instincts, even when they were vague, as they had been lately. The most obvious answer was Shinebloom's, where she worked. Possible complications? Difficult for them to talk over the noise, also she'd take any attempt to get her alone to hear out his proposition as a masher's cheap ploy.

He would deal with these obstacles and any others that might come up there and then, Peter decided, as he stepped inside Shinebloom's from the already darkening November afternoon. For an hour he sat at a table by the door drinking tea with lemon, slowly eating his barley soup, and didn't say much more to Rivka than, 'Can you bring me the salt, please?' He studied the situation. There *was* a glossy cheapness to it on the surface: *How would you like to audition as a singer? My friend hires acts at the Pavilion Theatre and when I heard you sing the other day.* He couldn't costume the words to sound like anything except bait in a scheme to get her alone.

The slap and clutch of a large hand on his shoulder broke Peter's concentration. A reflex tightened his muscles, twisted him half out of his chair. 'Karl's worried about you,' Yoska said. He used his grasp on Peter to pivot around the end of the table, supporting his bad leg, and dropped heavily into the vacant chair.

'Why?'

'He didn't say,' Yoska said, then briskly moved on to a more important piece of business. 'Look here.' From two pockets he clawed out his haul — over nine pounds in cash and a gold watch and chain. 'Feel it,' he said, holding out the timepiece. 'It's still warm. Lifted it on the way over.' Peter admired it with a nod. 'I thought Leon could be in here since he's gone from the Warsaw. Have you seen him? Beron?'

'No.'

Rivka was serving a few tables away. Yoska caught her attention with a fond salute, and she returned the greeting with a tilt of her head toward her armful of plates, an apology for having to keep her mind strictly on her work. He turned back to notice Peter also looking Rivka's way with a particular intention. 'You're wasting your time with her,' counselled Yoska.

'What do you know about it?'

'Rivka's got a man. Not here. At home.'

'How do you know?'

'She told me.'

'Why did she do that?' Peter asked, lightly.

'She's pretty, all right?' Yoska fumbled with his silverware. 'So I tried, why not?'

'To lift her.'

'That's right!' He took the joke and wasn't insulted. Far from it. 'She's some Benjamin's prize.'

'Benjamin who?'

'Rivka's man. Aren't you listening? Home in Sasmacken.'

'Doesn't matter to me,' Peter said. 'What else do you know about her?'

Yoska rubbed his face with both wide hands to stimulate his memory and passed on to Peter the story of Rivka Bermansfelt that everybody in Liesma knew by now. How she and her father ambushed a detachment of Russian cavalrymen on the road between Talsen and Sasmacken, that her father was captured but Rivka went on the run, how a cousin of hers in Talsen, Jankel Somebody, forged her papers and slipped her out of the country, and Karl brought her to London, even fixed her up with the job at Shinebloom's. 'After that...' Yoska brushed his palms together and held up Karl's clean hands.

'You know better ways to help her?' Peter said in Karl's defence.

'I asked him, no, I said,' Yoska stammered. 'What I asked him is why can't he use her, for *something*, you know?'

'You mean, for an action?'

'Why not? A face the police don't know here.'

'What did Karl say?'

Yoska shook his head. 'My opinion, it's Nina talking.'

Peter sipped another spoonful of barley soup. 'Doing anything besides stealing gold watches?'

'Cooking.'

'Cooking? Something for Karl?'

'You don't want me to talk about an action here.' He leaned close. The pits in Yoska's cheeks, his clotted complexion loomed toward Peter like a flank of the moon. He went on, 'I can't give you any details. It's a big job, a rich one. After we send Salnish his percentage we'll still have enough left over to keep us alive for half a year. Talk to Karl if you want to help.'

In the few weeks Peter had been in London, one thing after another had stopped him from having a satisfactory talk with Karl. Peter could wait a little longer, take advantage of the next opportunity to catch Karl on his own, away from Nina. Meanwhile he could occupy himself with Rivka. 'Introduce me to her,' he finally said to Yoska.

'You're fearless, Peter. Right now?'

Peter glanced over and noticed an elderly Orthodox Jew rise from his table to help his wife with her coat. 'Wait till she clears the table behind you.'

'What name should I tell her?'

He weighed the question for second. Then, firmly, he said, 'Peter.'

When the time came, Peter tucked his hand into the small of his back, a nod to formality without the stiff neck, and courteously stood to speak Rivka's name. She spoke his in polite reply. They traded half-sentences of small talk, then left each other's company with no promise to meet again.

Between then and the late hour Peter saw Rivka (from a doorway across the street) finish work and start homeward, he mulled over the single question he'd returned to ask her. He phrased it every way imaginable: dryly, as a business opportunity. Casually, as a suggestion that just happened to spring to mind. Stirringly, as a rare chance to make a great change in her life. Benevolently, as a favour he might do for a friend, not to mention for his friend Harry at the Pavilion Theatre. Yet, no matter how Peter formulated his side of the offer, his motive remained slippery to his own touch.

So Peter's thoughts went on troubling his stomach as he shadowed Rivka at a careful distance along Brick Lane. Her footsteps clicked across pavement slimy with refuse. She appeared ahead of Peter in a ring of lamplight, then disappeared into the next pool of darkness. She walked in short, confident strides around and through the night-time business of those streets, where market stalls now wheeled off their pitches were replaced by fist-fights, shouting matches, the pigeon cooing of prostitutes and the grunts of their alleyway customers.

Peter followed Rivka close enough to hear a man brag or lament, '... wiv a few *shillins* in me trouseys!' before the drunkard toppled into her and slurred, 'Beg pardon,' as his fingers curled around Rivka's upper arm. 'Pardon me, darlin'.'

Rivka's smile was sweet-natured, but not even a drunk could mistake her meaning. She twisted out of Trouseys' grip and wagged her finger in his face. Behind him his friends raised cheers and insults. No revolution in England, Peter thought as he waded through them, not for this numb underclass, and then the sight of Rivka in the lamplight at the turning into Whitechapel Road shook politics out of his head.

He passed by shops with notices in Hebrew covering the windows, Hebrew scrawlings chalked on the brick walls, Hebrew advertisements. In the busy road, mixed in with the Yiddish laughter, Russian arguments, German and Polish dealmaking, were the English, too, muttering: 'T'isnt always six ounces.' 'T'isnt, no. An often you can't hardly eat it. An' they cheat you out of yer fair money.' Rivka pushed through, face front. *No one knows her around here*, Peter thought and watched her cross the boulevard. He looked at Rivka and saw a foreign pedestrian like him, dodging high carriage wheels and swampy heaps of horse manure.

Where Sidney Street met Stepney Way a policeman touched the brim of his helmet when Rivka walked by. '*Gutn-ovnt. A sheyn ponem!*' She returned the constable's compliment with the same calm smile she used to warn off the drunk on Brick Lane. Now they have police trying out their Yiddish on innocent citizens! Doll's face or not, it's a matter of privacy and none of the constabulary's business.

The PC said nothing to Peter as he went on pacing his beat, and Peter nonchalantly glanced away. Gatekeepers, that was Salnish's name for the police. This constable let Peter and Rivka deeper into Little Jerusalem, to cross over from the upper world. Jewish workers slogged home, Jewish dossers slept in muddy yards, Jewish rag-pickers sorted their hauls, Jewish thieves fled like smoke into the brick tenements, fur-hatted rabbis patrolled their congregations, Jewish gamblers rolled dice and dealt cards, Jewish babies cried for food and warmth. The same as everywhere else in the East End, kerb stones dissolved, it seemed, under mounds of wet filth, grinding man-made roadworks back into soil, but unlike truly *English* streets, occupied by English residents, in these rows of windows you could see Sabbath candles, just smears of light, miniscule flames of unremarkable devotion.

In Wellesley Street, without slowing, Rivka's walk relaxed. She had a '*gutn-ovnt*' for a few people on her way. Neighbours, Peter supposed. One of these, a man of about his age, greeted him, too. '*Gut-yontev,*' he said. Peter replied, '*Gutn-shabes.*' Peter as an immigrant Jew; this false identity, out of his half-dozen, felt the most natural fit. A Jew in London. Hidden and conspicuous at the same time. Their language is a blanket pulled over their heads, outside the English but lodged in England, accepted without belonging. This gives a man secret freedom.

104

He felt a surge of that freedom as he ambled closer to Rivka. He would have to speak to her now, before she reached her front door. 'Rivka?' He stood in the lamplight on purpose, to keep from frightening her.

'Hello?'

'My name is Peter.' He took a step closer. 'Yoska's friend.'

'Peter. I remember you.'

'Yes. Good.'

Their voices brought Charles Perelman to the front door. He opened it a crack to see who Rivka's companion was, then quietly squeezed the door shut again. From the front window, shielded behind an edge of the curtain, he could get a better view. Later on he'd ask Rivka how she met the man and whether she had any inkling of what Peter the Painter was doing in London. By his watch he observed them in conversation together for seventeen minutes. If Perelman had been able to eavesdrop or if he'd been a lip reader, he would have jotted down but not made out the meaning of this exchange:

Rivka Bermansfelt: 'I only sing when I'm in trouble.'

Peter Piatkow: 'Can you sing if somebody pays you for it?'

Fifteen

Up on the balls of his feet, The Mayor shook both his fists at her, pure vaudeville tantrum, before generously allowing Rivka two half-days off work — Thursday for her first excursion in to the West End, Friday for her audition at the Pavilion Theatre.

'Harry wants you at his theatre tomorrow afternoon at one o'clock. Did I tell you that?'

'You told me,' Rivka said.

On the omnibus's upper deck as it rounded Piccadilly Circus and the boulevard rolled open in front of them, Rivka almost swooned from the rush of light and space. Prosperity's steady work carved out the rosy brick and polished granite buildings that stretched ahead, majestic as a canyon, and prosperity's English children moved through the street below, human affairs like a deep river. Men with ivory-topped walking sticks, fine hats and broad collared overcoats, the women's black or chocolate brown dresses trimmed with burgundy, bottle-green, plum silk, flashes of colour under coats and wraps that could make a woman look like she was being molested by a bear. Civilization shined out of Piccadilly's windows, from dress shops, wine shops, food shops, nameless marble-clad buildings Rivka thought could as easily be banks as hotels.

Just as remarkable to her was Peter's ease amongst it all. His tweed suit, his confident bearing, not blasé but unawed, made him indistinguishable — to Rivka, anyway — from an Englishman. When he told her where their long ride from Stepney was taking them, she half expected a lantern lecture from him to caption the passing scenery, some commentary or revolutionist's critique of the immoral wealth on parade, the manifesto of his Liesma brotherhood, but she got very little conversation out of Peter.

He watched for their stop. 'And you know where it is, how you get there?'

'Oh. I thought... No – yes, I can find out.'

'I can't be there,' Peter said. 'I have to see Karl.'

'I'll find it all right.'

'If Harry likes you enough maybe he'll let you sing in one of his Yiddish operas.'

'Good.'

Peter cocked his head. 'You don't know what an opera is, do you.'

'It's singing. With a dance to it.'

'No. With a story. It's a play, and everybody in it sings. Usually while they suffer and die.'

'In Yiddish this is no surprise to me.'

'Harry also puts on Gilbert and Sullivan in Yiddish.' He waited for a glint of recognition from her. 'Gilbert and Sullivan?' The omnibus stopped at the kerb and spared Rivka another embarrassing display of her backwoods greenness. Peter nodded for her to get up. 'We'll walk from here.'

From the bus stop at Green Park, Peter forged their way across Piccadilly, one step ahead of Rivka for safety's sake, keeping clear of the motor and carriage traffic. Once they reached the *chic* side street he hung back to walk beside her, but didn't take her arm. His mind was on higher things, or at least things that waited ahead, and whatever they were, the closer Peter got to them the more excitement they kindled. His mouth tightened, his skin, smoothly opaque as a bar of soap, bloomed with a pinkish blush in his cheeks and throat.

At the entrance to the Grafton Galleries his crisp manners weren't forgotten in any rush to get inside. As he held the door open to usher Rivka in, she thought she heard him say in a low whisper, edged with reverence, perhaps not even meaning her to hear, 'This is the real revolution.' Then they stood in the first room. 'Look', Peter invited her, as if the painting in front of them was a creation of his own.

The painting emerged from the full wall it occupied with the insistence of a living presence. Almost eye to eye in front of her, when onlookers strayed off to view the other art works, Rivka had clear sight of a red-haired woman of about her own age serving at an elegant marble bar. It wasn't pierógis and borscht she was serving, either, but champagne, oranges, cognac. Reflected in the huge mirror behind her, the roomful of chandelier-lit gaiety whirled in the far distance, regardless of the girl, it seemed, and the dulled absence in her face, her inhibited silence, reflected back the same distance and disregard.

Peter translated its title for Rivka. '*A schenk bei Follies-Bergère*, it's called.'

'Why didn't he, didn't the painter—'

'Manet. Edouard.'

'Why didn't he call it by her name, that girl's?'

'He did.'

Rivka looked again, at the serving girl's dark velvet dress, nipped waist, her rose-white flesh, then at the bottles displayed on the bar, their bodies a green that was almost black, their necks wrapped in pale pink foil. 'He made her look like a bottle of champagne.'

'She *is* the Follies-Bergère. You see it?'

'I get to feel that way sometimes,' Rivka said. 'Not usually at Shinebloom's. At Clark's. I stop looking at their faces. I pretend I'm someplace else.'

'Where?'

She glanced upward to catch the memory. 'Back in Shinebloom's.'

Other rooms stored more treasures. Peter plunged in to the Cézanne landscapes, still lifes and portraits, canvases by Matisse, Signac, van Gogh, Picasso, even some African pottery, and Rivka worked to stay with him. With half a sentence trailing behind him, more than once, he disappeared through the tight spaces between the well-dressed men and women who crowded the rooms. Whenever she got the chance, she asked him questions. About the colours and subjects. Were these painters the most famous in France? Did they live on what they sold? She asked about the places in the landscapes, the patchwork of shades in this one, the wildly blurred shapes in that one.

At the Seurat he ran out of answers for her. A drizzle of dabs that was wind in the high trees at the same time it was sunlight across a tiled roof at the same time it was fields in summer at the same time it was the shadow of a wall, gripped him there in silence. Particles of coloured light shimmering in space. Here it was again, the world as it really existed, the world-haze. He didn't say to Rivka: They dissolve everything out of the fixed, concrete and fated, these *seers* who look at people, their trappings and belongings, and see *constant motion*... Around him the blind babblers hammered spikes into Peter's ears. 'Are these Frenchies *at large*?' 'In some asylum, I shouldn't wonder.' 'Not worth my while, or my wife's, neither.' 'Get the police! There's been a horrible accident — with paint!' Each one aimed a shot to outdo the other's droll

110

superiority. It was a sickening thought: threads of that same world-haze connected him to this pool of know-nothings. And by the laws of valence in a vapour, them to him. Brittle tinkling laughter and smug ridicule reached Peter wherever he stood in the gallery.

'Childish dribbles!' 'Indecent!' 'Pornographic!' 'Raw anarchism!' They flung these slogans over Rivka's head, at the Gauguins. Women's voices, mightily offended, loud enough to make sure their husbands knew what they thought. Rivka looked at the same picture and didn't see the lewdness, only a young Tahitian family at peace in the evening beside their canoe.

'What do you see?' Peter asked her, politely eager to hear.

She told him: the husband was at rest, home from his day's work, so he was naked, shorn of his work clothes. In the bowl he drank from was something sweet made by his wife. She was the woman relaxing on the far side of the canoe, combing her hair, unworried. Their little boy, naked like his father, played by the canoe. He wasn't old enough yet to go out and help his father catch fish. They looked like the first family on earth, loved by God as much as they loved each other.

Peter listened, thoughtfully, then said, 'Why do you bring God into it?'

'The way they love each other,' she said. Then, because Peter showed he was still listening, Rivka found more to say. 'That's God talking to people.'

'No it isn't.'

'What is it to you, Peter?'

'Father, mother, son, everyone's lost in their own business. But *together*.'

He pushed through the burgomasters and lazy bohemians with glances over his shoulder to make sure

111

Rivka was still following him — out of the gallery now. But in the middle of the room Peter stopped. For a parting look, she thought, at a Cézanne portrait, the one of his wife Hortense seated in a big red armchair. (Earlier he'd asked Rivka what she thought of it. 'Hortense doesn't love him in that one,' was her opinion. Yet in its blood-reds, jewel-blues and -yellows, the scene was aglow with the fragile heat of one human being's memory: this woman in her Sunday skirt and blouse, her prim coiffeur and unquiet obedience, the armchair, wallpaper and sunlight fused in her husband's eye.) Rivka felt a coldness sift through her when she realized it wasn't the picture he'd stopped to look at but the man bent double in front of it, in a spasm of laughter, having a hard time catching his breath.

'She's a farmer's wife! No beauty, is she!?' Another man patted the cackler's back to help his breathing, or else to congratulate him on a fair point well made. 'An artist ought to make the ugly ones look pretty, shouldn't he?' Oh, he was too smart to let any French bugger play a joke like that on him and get away with it. 'Whole game's a damn' swindle,' he coughed.

For a second or two Peter was nervous — until he realised that the rumble inside him was really revulsion, a poison mash in his belly he had to disgorge, or it would choke him. He stood at the Cackler's elbow and asked the man, in English, 'You get a shock from this? Good. I say *good*, you can have a shock!'

Assaulted by the Frenchy art — and now, to top it off, assaulted by a French madman! '*What's* this now?'

Peter waved his arm at the Cézanne, at the whole gallery. '*His* painting of her, Paul Cézanne's picture. Not yours, *not yours!*'

'He's raving, coming in here! Raving at me!' The

Cackler looked to friends for help. 'Some jumped up Frenchy!'

One of the Cackler's friends made a grab at Peter's arm and threatened to hold him till a policeman could be brought. 'You can't go 'round disturbing the peace any time you want to! What do you think of that?'

Peter's outburst shook Rivka. It broke like a flash flood or lightning storm, with the force of some natural disaster. Her sudden fear was for him, because the silence that dammed him up for twenty minutes afterward, under the blush that heated his face, told her that he couldn't help himself. For the whole length of their walk to Piccadilly Circus, no touch on his arm, nothing Rivka tried to tell him, penetrated deep enough to draw a response. Finally, as they searched the traffic in half a dozen directions for the right omnibus to take them home, Peter said, a little mysteriously, 'A bomb blows up.'

'What are you talking about?'

His breath smelled sharp to her, metallic. He seemed to concentrate on each word he said to her, as if he were working out the ideas as he spoke them. 'People oppose you.'

'What are you talking about, Peter, a bomb?'

'The bomb or gun isn't the terrifying thing. Why was that idiot laughing? I'll tell you: he's protecting himself.' He paused a moment, looking for words. 'The paintings don't scare him. He's scared about what they'll make him think after he looks at them. A bomb blows up a tram car, or a policeman's brains get splashed on the ground, or a friend's blood. Then you know something for sure — there are people alive who want to break you into pieces. Your suffering is their reward. They are unreasonable men. Nothing you can do will ever make them stop. They

113

won't stop until you're gone. Someday in the future. When they are up and you are down.'

'Are you one of those men?' Rivka asked, fearing his honest answer.

Peter glanced across to Shaftsbury Avenue and thought, *these were the old arguments*. He spoke them out loud to test their strength, on Rivka and on himself.

'That one's ours, on the other side,' he said, pointing to a bus. 'If we miss it I don't know how long we'll be waiting here.'

Sixteen

Without looking up from his newspaper, the assistant stage manager directed her to the wings, stage left, where she should wait to hear her name called.

Remarkable. On the other side of the world from Sasmacken, in the Pavilion Theatre, she felt at home. More here than she did as a waitress in Shinebloom's, a lodger with the Perelmans or as a Jew shopping for a loaf of pumpernickel in Whitechapel Road. She rested her hand on the dull, cooling edge of the curtain's lead counterweights, then gripped the tendon of the rope they swung from, romantic as a hawser of a tall ship, and the tarry wooden floor muffled her footsteps over to a rack of costumes stowed behind the safety curtain. The fineness of the dressmaking, striped silk skirts, a rabbit-fur stole, and the tailoring of men's clothes — Orthodox hats and black coats among them — seemed to hint at the treasures this life had stored up for Rivka, this 'theatre life.'

Unimaginable.

No, the shuddering didn't seize Rivka's stomach until later, after she'd finished singing for Harry and returned to the sheltering dark backstage. Her bones vibrated like piano strings, a hummingbird fluttered in her chest, her head floated in a ring of cloud. How much could she earn from one performance? *So* much? First performance, one song, tomorrow night. A part in an opera? Maybe yes, Maybe no, but her name would be on the Pavilion's next playbill, Rivka Bermansfelt's debut as a singer of Yiddish songs.

And what *about* her name? It was all right for the East End, but not up West. 'Can you sing English songs?' On the first time through, with piano accompaniment, she learned the melody; by the third time, tutored from the third row by Harry, she was singing 'The Boy I Love is Up in the Gallery' with the stretched vowels and brass hard consonants of your actual Cockney miss. 'Think of an English name for yourself,' he instructed her. 'I'm going to tell my friend at the Tivoli all about you, hm? How would you like to sing in a music hall in the Strand?' And support herself on her singing, and buy a dress that came decorated with burgundy ribbons.

Either the bus conductor misheard Rivka's Cockney-Yiddish pronunciation of *Tivoli* and *Strand* or the bell-ringing and engine noise garbled it completely — or else in Mile End she'd climbed on to the wrong bus altogether. Instead of being set down in front of a first peek of her music hall future, Rivka stood lost on a corner of Parliament Square. From a painted tea tray in Clark's, she recognised the House of Commons, which she thought was called Big Ben, and pointed it out to a nearby Police Constable.

'Walk or ride?' he quickly asked her.

'Please?'

'Sorry, I can't help you,' he muttered, impatiently, and hurried to join other policemen crossing the street towards the Commons gates.

With a better grasp of the English language, Rivka would have been able to read the messages on the placards brandished by small bunches of women who, in pairs and sixes and dozens, were pooling in the square. DEEDS NOT WORDS, VOTES FOR WOMEN, OUR

CAUSE IS NOBLE, JUSTICE. As the women walked by, men on the surrounding pavement snarled curses at them for their own entertainment; laughing and ugly the bullies kicked out at passing ankles and feinted blows with their fists. As gravely imposing as the Palace of Westminster's stone walls, the policemen watched for mischief and stood their ground. Tall, strong men, gold stripes of rank on their sleeves, in their long black coats they overshadowed the bully boys just by *talking* to them. *English police*, Rivka thought, *serious and honourable*. Look how many they sent to protect these women.

The front room in Gold Street was a box of cold air. Two days ago, when the coalman drove by in his cart, Karl wasn't home: Nina was, but she forgot to flag him down. Against the chill they boiled pots of Russian tea on the stove. Peter surrounded the heavy mug with his fingers and palms. As he raised it to his lips he heard Nina say, 'Do you want me to bring a piece of fish?'

Karl looked up, but not at her. 'From?'

'By Perelman's. I have to go comfort Fenia. Her father hit her again. In the *face*.' Nina tucked herself into her coat, tugged its seams neat and walked back to the table where Peter sat. She filled the half-empty mug that sat in front of him with fresh tea. 'He choked her, too, that dog. I saw the marks on Fenia's neck.'

'She can't stay here,' Karl said. 'I don't want it.'

From the door, ready to set off, Nina said, 'Do you want fish or not?'

'For lunch or dinner?'

'Dinner.'

A quick exchange of glances across the table with Peter was the beginning and end of any discussion. Karl decided, 'No. We'll eat at the Warsaw.'

To Peter (and to himself) Karl airily described his

ménage as 'the London arrangement.' He had shared his days and nights with Nina Vassilleva for more than a year; their bedsitting room had the atmosphere of a burrow they'd dug for themselves with freely given confidences. What would this man and woman be to each other away from the political turbulence constantly pounding at their door? Any visitor to Gold Street would see what Peter saw — a beautiful young couple, a man of persuasive charm and a woman of sure-footed moral determination, both of them intelligent and capable, fond partners in the struggle for money, safety and a place where they could belong.

Nina's footsteps trickled down the outer hallway, pursuing Fanny Perelman's domestic drama. Karl waited until he heard the street door shut before he relaxed back into his conversation with Peter. 'Charles Perelman should watch out. There's a force in her. Nina gets it from her father.'

'Does she?'

'Indrik Gristis.' Peter shook his head; ignorance of the name caused him no worry. Karl repeated, 'Indrik Gristis? No?'

'Gristis? No. That's his only name?'

The hero of Nina's life, Karl explained. One of the early converts from servitude to rebellion. Indrik was a chef in one of the Tsar's palaces, then when the '05 revolution came, Brother Gristis commander of a squad of riflemen. 'Gritsis and thirteen other men on horseback against an artillery battery that was bombarding a village near Kiev. The Russians had a Gattling gun. Indrik led them in. He was the only one who survived it.'

'Unlucky. For the thirteen, I mean.'

'We don't live in a magic world,' Karl observed.

'Anyway, they killed those bastard gunners first and Indrik took their gun.'

'No, I never heard that story.'

'Nina told it to me.' Karl gave a sympathetic smile. 'She's her father's daughter.'

'And what did you get from *your* father?' Peter asked him.

Karl took the question seriously, then delivered an answer. 'My hair.'

'It's beautiful hair.'

They laughed together, Karl easily and warmly, enjoying the companionship of an equal. He said, 'There's nobody to talk to here.'

'Paris, either. Not counting police informers.'

'Somebody after you?'

'Of course!' Peter said lightly, with honesty. 'It's been quiet in London, since that craziness last year.'

'Yes, I was going to come find you. I tried.'

'Did you? When?'

'Summer. July,' he said. 'I thought of you. Were you in France?'

'Yes.'

'Paris?'

'No. You came to Paris?'

'No. I tried, though. To sniff you out.' Karl sipped at his tea. 'If anybody could find you...'

Peter flattered him and meant it. 'You'd've been a welcome sight. I wanted to talk with you, too, and have this conversation. You thought of me?'

'London finally settled down in the summer. After Tottenham. *Peter's got the ideas*, I thought. *Talk to him. He's the only one who can help you.* Peter. Let's work on a plan together. Collaborate on an action. An exe.'

He asked, flatly, 'Why?'

119

'Same as always. To raise money and make a splash.'

'I don't have any ideas, Karl. No clear ones.'

'Good, that's all right. Neither do I. My mind's been a lumpy stew for months. Let's get on our feet again.'

'I'm on my feet,' Peter said. 'Can't see straight, but...'

Peter's mulishness annoyed Karl. 'You wanted to talk, you said. About this.'

'Exes? No.' Peter laughed. 'I was thinking about you. I wanted to find out,' Peter said, 'if you were going to repeat Salnish's mistakes.'

'Only my own.' Karl lit Peter's cigarette, refused the offer of one for himself. 'Don't blame Salnish for that bloody mess in Tottenham. He was a good leader, he planned it all right. The men he got to do it, though... They were undependable. You can't predict, sometimes.'

'Men are the worst danger, don't you think? If you can count on them or not.'

A frown, a slight shrug. 'There was nothing wrong with the Tottenham plan.'

'Except it ended up in a massacre.'

'Don't exaggerate.'

'Four dead? A little boy. One policeman. Two of Salnish's men. Is that progress?' Peter asked, for information. 'Have you made *any* progress you can measure since last year?'

'Pressure is building up.'

'In the boiler.'

'Yes.'

'The one in Russia or England?'

'History's boiler,' Karl suggested. 'Guaranteed, Liesma's still the flame underneath it — last year, this year, next year.'

'No recruitment speech, please, Karl.'

Peter had become a student of history, specialising in

lives of the revolutionaries over the last decade. Latvian freedom from Russian occupation was the first cause of the armed robberies, assassinations, minor atrocities and public outrages calculated to be warnings to authority and shocks to complacent lackeys. Throw them out and fill their vacant places with liberty, fraternity, equality. These actions weren't crimes done by criminals, but acts of self-defence carried out by and for human beings against talking apes whose habits and ideas proved that they didn't deserve the consideration one human gives to another. Imperialist pigs. Tsarist sheep. Russian cattle. Born for the slaughterhouse. Were the others born to be slaughtermen? Peter's conscience ached, not over the killed (they were gone), but for the rip in the world's fabric their killing left to be repaired. He held a strange picture in his mind of a mantrap laid in the future that catches men today.

'New ideas are breaking in on me,' he said to his friend. 'In the middle of the day I was sitting by a canal, looking at the water. I didn't see it. The water or the canal, whatever was there, I couldn't hold anything in focus. I got dizzy and felt sick.' Peter dragged on his cigarette, then let the smoke seep out through his nostrils. 'When I try to remember... *this* happened because I did *that*... I'm *here now* because I was *there then*... everything's a smudge.'

'Yes,' Karl said.

'Yes?'

'You can't say *here's success*' he said, opening his right hand, '*and here's failure*,' opening his left.

'Sure, yes. Maybe. I get a dizzy spell when I think about how we've gone on for ten years.'

Karl said, 'After Salnish got out of London and went back to Russia my head was spinning, too. Then I thought

121

about it. *What's troubling my thinking? Why can't I tell a clear thought from the other kind? Where did these ideas come from?*

'Where?' Peter tensed to hear.

'Boredom. For me. For you maybe it's something else. A mood. You cave in to a mood and,' Karl slapped his hand down on the table in flat defeat, 'You can't move forward.'

The vibration of Karl's slap on the table passed into Peter's chest. 'No. Not a mood. It's... whatever I do or I've done, seems...' The hand with the cigarette in it made a little circle in front of him. He stopped short of uttering the word *useless*.

Karl heard it, though. Brother Peter needed him to bolster a flagging heart, so Liesma's commander launched in to a demonstration of faith. 'The cause is Liesma, Liesma is the cause. Peter, it hasn't been quiet here since last year. From France you can't see what's going on in London. I'll tell you the daily business I do that Salnish never had to. I settle arguments between Fritz and Jacob, between Jacob and Yoska, squabbles between Luba and Fritz. I push Leon Beron for better rates and push everybody else to keep going, everybody together, in the same direction. The ones who can't steal to save their lives have to work in sweatshops ten hours every day. Then they come to me so I can tell them the one certainty I know about our business: we get money to buy guns in Russia to make a revolution.'

'Does anybody — Fritz or Jacob, Yoska, any of them — ask you if you've heard how soon it's coming?'

'When we're ready to move forward,' I tell them. 'Right now, we have to stay put.'

Karl was thinking of the day when news of the idiotic mess in Tottenham reached him — the bungled robbery and the injuries, the murders and suicides that had followed. Afterward, his instinct, like Salnish's, was to get out of London. That next morning, as he lay in bed, Nina came to him. The coal fire she'd made while he slept warmed the room and milky daylight strained in through the dust on the window. She tucked herself under his arm, kissed its smooth muscle. Karl's eyes were open, reading the cracks in the ceiling. One of Nina's hands clasped his; the other stroked his thick brown hair, gently grooming a tumbled wave of it back from his forehead. She spoke of valour and steadiness. He vowed never to work under Salnish's command. 'History rules us,' she replied.

If that were true, he said, they should follow Salnish, and leave London.

'He's already gone,' she said, 'I'm sure of it. Who will lead Liesma, then? Jacob Peters? You have to stay.' She kissed him on his mouth, his face, his naked chest. In an existence brittle and fragile as a windowpane, here, in this bed, lay the only softness real enough for him to touch. By the afternoon, Karl saw the situation Nina's way.

'You know what you are, Peter? A dangerous provocateur. It's dangerous for me to associate with you,' Karl joked. 'You'll get me in trouble with Nina.'

'She's more important to you than Liesma.'

'No,' he said. 'They're the same.'

'But you want to be with her. If you had to choose?'

'Easier to trust her than a gang of men.'

'Because you can look ahead without making a plan.'

'"Look ahead." What does that mean for any of us?'

'Buying a piece of fish for dinner.'

'That's right. That's all,' Karl said. He tried to end the conversation there. Then he added reflectively, 'Nina needs to be with somebody who stays in the fight.'

123

'Not against *her*, though.'

'Her opinions keep me honest.'

'You care about what happens to her, too.'

This was the tenderest subject and its inspection rattled Karl more than he'd expected. Peter's questions sliced down hard into thickly armoured nerves. 'Let's go for a walk,' he said, 'I want to see Fritz.'

'Luba's working today, so he'll want some company.'

'Good. And no women hanging around to pester us.'

Rivka searched for a route on foot to the Strand and landed on the wrong side of Parliament Square. She ducked her head and obeyed the stiff instructions of the policeman who blocked her path and pointed her back into the slowly churning commotion. One by one as the placard- waving, banner-furling women folded in among their sisters, men waited on the pavement nearby, tearing the placards and banners out of their hands, shredded, smashed, stamped on each message. DOWN WITH THE PREMIER'S VETO. THERE'S TIME IF THEY'VE THE WILL.

'Go home!' a skinny young rough shouted, So close in front of Rivka that she smelled his sour breath.

'Give us the vote and we'll go home!' a voice shouted from somewhere over Rivka's shoulder.

The rough's replied by barking at her like a chained dog.

Something more than a physical force gathered at Rivka's back and pushed her along. The square was turning into a pen, a bear pit, with hundreds of women caught inside and as many men ringed around them. Older men, young ones, flat caps and top hats, workmen's jackets and frock coats. The choice English

124

obscenities were lost on Rivka, but not the menace that heated the faces of the circling men, packs of sourly smiling tormentors whose bellies were warmed by the satisfaction of beating down, so easily, a weak and contemptible enemy. A chilly shock tightened Rivka's skin; the next few steps she took were nervous and felt uncontrolled as she realized the policemen weren't there to defend these women, their job was to stop them.

They were men in uniform who sided with men in plain clothes.

As Rivka sidestepped and wrestled her way through the crush, she saw a police constable yank an elderly woman by her arm with such strength that he twirled her off balance and on to the ground; she sprawled on the grass, her gloved hands over her face. With his knee, the policeman pressed his whole weight on her chest. Left and right, in front and behind Rivka, women stood captured by roughs who squeezed the breath out of them. Some of the women fainted and were left where they fell; others, limp and crying, found themselves tossed into the welcoming arms of policemen.

The violent tide shoved Rivka backward, to the very edge of the square. Some of the women fought back and made for the street to reach St Stephen's Gate. Two steps away from her a girl no older than Rivka calmly opened her handbag, pulled out a belt, swung it over her head and slashed the buckle down a policeman's face. It drew blood but the attack didn't slow him down. He lunged at her, lost his footing, and she bolted into the road.

In ones and twos the women broke out of the square and dashed through the traffic of horse carriages and motor cars. One of them got to the iron railings on the other side and started to climb. Her skirts tangled underneath her. Two men hauled her onto the pavement but she twisted free, got up and ran a few feet, then fell, tackled by a constable who watched while both men kicked her till she lay quiet.

Still they rushed towards the Commons entrance. 'It's my intention to speak to Mr Asquith or die trying,' insisted a woman in a dark blue dress.

'Die, then.' The policeman's truncheon cracked the side of her head. He clubbed her again when she tried to sit up. She looked to be about the age of Rivka's mother.

Crazy as Cossacks, a dozen or more police charged the square and swept the women, Rivka included, toward the Abbey. For a fraction of a second she saw an opening and ran for it. In the next half second it was gone, closed off by the broad chest of a PC who'd lost his helmet and taken a wound to his face. The blood from it dried in a jagged fork on his cheek. He looked directly at Rivka. 'That's the one gave me this!' he called to his sergeant.

She stumbled around them and ran; another broken dash like her chase through the woods by the Talsen road. A hundred yards ahead, Rivka could saw an open street. She didn't look behind her but heard the chase of footsteps, the rasping breath and shouts of the policemen and, closer, the other women they were hunting. Her shoes slipped and skidded on the pavement.

First Rivka felt a blow land on the back of her neck. Then a web of dull pain spread over her skull before she dropped to the ground. She didn't see the boot that kicked her in the ribs, or if it was the same boot or another one that pounded her even harder in the stomach. She couldn't breathe, she couldn't move without sending shards of pain to every organ in her body.

A cry broke over her head. A man's cry. Rivka felt a pair of hands under her arms lift her to her feet. She saw the soft blond hair, tangled and damp with sweat, framing a middle-aged face. Its mouth said, 'Winston's ordered police from Whitechapel to come down here and deal with us. The ones who're used to rough work. Can you run?'

'Please... To go home back for Wellesley Street... Brick Lane, Brick Lane...' Her English gone now, hounded out of her.

The woman pulled Rivka along the flank of the Abbey. 'This way. Quick. You understand?'

Rivka understood she had to keep running. She followed as close as the pain in her chest and stomach let her, but fell behind. Her friend rounded the corner of the side-street, which gave Rivka a clear view of an omnibus just pulling up to the kerb. Then she heard a shriek, a woman's cry this time. A man grabbed a fistful of this good woman's blond hair and twisted it till he'd forced her onto her knees, then his other fist cracked her in the face. He raised it again, bloodied.

Rivka stumbled past him, past the alarm of his shouts, in sight of the bus, in reach of it, she thought. The sharp blow across her shoulders knocked her down. Another one lashed her lower back. On the ground on all fours she was a rabbit savaged by dogs. The next kick to her stomach rolled her into a black pit deeper and farther from waking than any sleep.

'A piece of carrot,' Karl said without pointing. 'It's stuck to your beard. No, above your chin.' His satisfaction was complete when Peter raked the orange crumb away and spooned another helping of the root vegetable casserole from the serving bowl onto his plate. Six o'clock was an early hour for dinner at the Warsaw, several of the tables waited for evening customers. 'I don't recognise anybody in here,' he said. 'Except Beron.'

Karl, a refined eater himself, touched the corners of his mouth with the border of his napkin. His whitefish, dumplings and boiled cabbage held more interest for him than the possibility of unknown informers infiltrating the Warsaw. Leon Beron, doing business with Steinie Morrison at his regular table, wasn't worth a glance. 'Leon only says hello when he knows we've got merchandise for him. There's nothing from us lately, not even Yoska, so he ignores me.'

'Can you afford to pay for this dinner?'

'The owner owes me a favour,' Karl said. 'Favours. More than one. How much can your carrots and potatoes cost?'

Most of their meal passed in silence. The pleasure of eating was a simple appreciation the friends shared, and the Warsaw served good food. Eastern odours — steam and onions, fatty meat broiling, fish frying in oil, dumplings boiling in chicken broth — turned England, for an hour or two, into more of an idea than a place on the other side of the Warsaw's door.

Relaxed by the comforts of the place, and Peter's friendship, or from the aftertaste of tea on his tongue, Karl thought back to his earliest interest in chemistry. 'Lemon juice. Fourteen years old, in love with Natalia. I wrote out my heart, in lemon juice on a piece of paper. Very passionate and secret. At the very top of the page, I also wrote out for her, 'hold the letter over a candle flame, the invisible will be visible.' So Natalia's father read it.' Karl cocked his head at the memory. 'Our secret messages are different now, isn't that right? Now there's less at stake.'

Peter had suspected, even hoped, to find that Karl shared a melancholy like his own, laced with the same doubts about the value of bloody revolution. To get him to admit as much, that was another thing. Karl waved off doubts as if shooing off the waiter who kept returning to refill their tea pot.

Karl spoke to Peter confidentially, in Lettish. 'Seen Rocker yet?'

'Does he know I'm in London?'

Ah, Karl thought. So Peter's relationship with the German anarchist godfather has changed. 'No, I don't think.he does.'

'What, is Rudolph trying to get the Anarchist Club started again?'

Karl flicked the question aside with his cigarette ash. 'He told me something last week, very disturbing.'

'So you want to disturb me with it,' Peter said. 'All right.'

'Last summer two boys came to him for a helping hand. These were young kids, seventeen, eighteen. They asked Rudolph to help them with an action.'

'If they knew him, didn't they know Rudolph wouldn't —'

'He'd never met them before. Malatesta told us where to find you . . .' Karl buzzed his lips at the thought. 'They were Russians, both of them. This was their idea: to plant a bomb at the Lord Mayor's show. Blow up the Lord Mayor of London. And bystanders. As many as they could kill.'

'Citizens? Visiting the show?'

'This is something new, Peter. A new kind of action. They decide on their own what's a legitimate target. Rocker was furious. But he was also clever. He didn't throw them out, he discussed it with them. Assassinate the Lord Mayor, all right, one in the eye. But how could they justify murdering innocent citizens?'

'What did they say to that?'

'Oh, those Russian boys were clever, too. 'If people come there worshiping the Lord Mayor then they aren't innocent.' There's an argument that can't lose! The bombers decide who's innocent.'

'Well, I didn't read anything about it in the newspapers. So the Lord Mayor must still be in good health.'

'Rocker made them give up the idea,' Karl summed up, but as he smoothed the ends of his moustache it was plain his mind was stuck on a different angle of the problem. 'We think they were Okhrana. Or Okhrana was running them. Look at the sense it makes: they send foreigners to commit such an atrocity, blowing up the Lord Mayor and a hundred Londoners. The Okhrana hands over two Russian anarchist bombers to Special Branch and says, "You think that's something? In Russia this happens seven days a week!" The only solution, they tell the English, is to close your borders to political refugees.' He gave Peter a few seconds to absorb the point. 'This is the conspiracy against us.'

'Jacob talks like those boys,' Peter said. 'Russians. Zeal on the outside, wildness in.'

'Give Jacob the chance he'd build a bomb factory in your bedroom and put Fritz to work,' Karl had to agree. 'It'd be another Tottenham every day.'

'Onward, *onward*,' Peter's bitter joke.

'The organisation was looser over there,' Karl allowed. 'An action was an action. We had to *advance*, right?'

'Yes. Why not?'

'Salnish was a hero to everyone in Riga Prison.'

'All right.' Karl stopped eating, showed he was listening.

Peter held his voice low but tapped the table to mark each point. 'The Salnish who organised Tottenham was

130

the same Salnish who organised that prison raid, too. He broke in and pulled Fritz out, and how many other men? The action had to be done. He led his men in and, no one wounded or lost, got away from there clean.'

'He out-thought them. Out-fought them, too, twenty to one.'

'Didn't he?'

'But that's not what you're talking about.'

Urgency brightened Peter's fine eyes. 'Something besides Salnish's judgment is different now.'

Karl said, 'It was a while ago.'

'Four years, that's all.'

'Half a decade. Almost.'

'Before our customs house,' Peter reminded him.

At night, four of them against three guards. One night watchman and two police guards. Peter held them against the wall, his gun at their backs, while Karl and the others went for the strongboxes. The night watchman swore up and down he didn't have the keys.

Karl guessed why Peter had dragged this into the conversation. 'You want to, what, make some example, talk about the old man who wet himself . . .'

'You think he prized his job? Guarding the Tsar's money?'

'He prized saving his skin,' Karl said. 'With the barrel of your gun in his mouth.'

A few feet away, in the lightless back room of the customs house, Peter listened to the police guards talking back and forth in half sentences. The first one wondered what the 'gangsters' were going to do with them. It didn't make a difference, the second one said: either the Lettish bastards were going to shoot them on principle . . . The first guard finished the thought – or the Tsar's officers were going to arrest them for not resisting and shoot them anyway. So what's to lose?

131

'They ran, didn't they? Not for the door, no, at *me*. To save the box of money, you think?' Peter answered his own question. 'For themselves.'

'And you shot them, Peter. You rescued the action.'

'I want to hear it from you. Karl, tell me the reason you keep going.' Peter stubbed out his cigarette and grasped his friend's forearm. 'To accomplish something or keep something worse from happening? Or is it just what you do with your time?'

Karl didn't answer until Peter let go of him and settled again in his chair. 'You can't be emotional about it.'

'What's wrong with *that*?' His voice rose louder than he'd meant it to. 'We aren't supermen. I'm not, you're not, we're men, that's all, aren't we?'

Coolly wary of going any further down that line Karl said, 'Keep emotions out of our plans. That's all I'm saying.'

'And I'm saying no action *has* meaning without emotions.' It was a plea, not a philosophy. 'We don't live in history.'

Lightness returned to Karl's voice, the sound of a man who'd avoided falling into a trap. 'Not yet.'

Across the table Peter offered his hand. Karl grasped it in his. Then smiling, one with sympathy, the other with acceptance, the two friends shook hands.

Every one of the demonstrators arrested in Parliament Square on the Friday was released, cases dismissed, at Bow Street Magistrates Court the next day. Of the more than one hundred brought before the magistrate, Rivka Bermansfelt alone was remanded in custody to answer charges of obstruction, malicious damage and assaulting the police. In her patchwork English she was able to communicate to the desk sergeant at Canon Row her name, age, the address of her lodgings and the name of her landlord.

'What's her language? Any of you know it?'

'She might be Polish. Or just a Yid.'

The sergeant cooed to her, 'Are you a proper Yid, my dear?'

Rivka's freckled arms and hands caused a small stir. One of the constables won a round of laughs speculating, 'By the looks of 'er could be she's half Paddy.'

By now her stomach and chest were racked with pain, and she tried hard to get her jailers to hear her complaints. A nurse swabbed Rivka's bruises with a cold soapy sponge; a doctor passed her fit to be questioned. In his attendance notes for the warden he advised, 'The chaps from Special Branch ought to arrive equipped with a Russian-Yiddish interpreter.'

The voices Rivka heard — stone hard, echoing somewhere outside her cell — sounded Russian. Dimly, as her senses returned she understood the reality of the prison cell, its metal door, damp stone walls, the uniform she wore, rough as burlap, a green serge dress and blue checked apron, which didn't hide the broad black arrows printed against the green. Was she in a Russian prison? Her life in London — was that all a memory or a dream? Could it be that she'd never escaped from the Cossacks or from Latvia? That she was locked in Colonel Orlov's prison?

The metal door swung back and a wardress came in, carrying a tray.

'Eat some food, will you, Fourteen eighteen?'

A crustless cube of bread smeared with margarine sat on the tray; beside it were a pint of cocoa and a bowl of thin soup. Rivka raised her head in time to see the door swing closed. A narrow horizontal slot in it framed the matron's eyes and eyebrows for a moment, then only the dim corridor light. Rivka turned her back to it and sipped at the soup. She swallowed a mouthful and felt it trickle into her stomach. It didn't make her feel worse and for these injuries her mother would have tended to her with the same remedy. *Eat*, ketzel. *Some barley soup. A little more, try*. Rivka attempted a bite of bread. The margarine didn't take away the dryness; it only added a dose of oil to the pasty mixture coating her tongue and teeth. She swallowed some of it, then retched air and watery spit. Rivka's arms were barely strong enough to hold her face off the floor. The vomit rushed out of her three times, choking streams that splashed her bed and the walls with milk and bread, thin soup, juices of her body, Rivka's saliva, mucus, bile, blood.

Two wardresses, each holding one of Rivka's arms, ushered her along a corridor between cells that somewhere became a corridor between ordinary rooms. Plunked into a stiff-backed chair in one of these comfortless rooms, behind a locked door, she waited alone for half an hour. There was no other furniture in there except a small metal trolley. Where the white enamel was cracked and flakes of it missing, blooms of rust dirtied it. A single electric bulb shed waxy light from the ceiling. Soon Rivka wasn't alone in there. The prison matron unlocked the door and stood aside to make room for two nurses, a doctor, the warden and two other men, one middle-aged and fair-haired, the other younger and dark.

They took up places around her at distances decided by their importance, Rivka guessed. The warden stood closest to her and said, 'Hunger strikes won't be tolerated at Holloway, no matter what you've heard from other women.'

It seemed to Rivka he was calling on her to speak. To defend herself. In English, she said, 'I have in my stomach ill. Sick, sir.'

'You refuse to eat.' He made a gesture toward his open mouth, his fingers clutched together, as if feeding himself a morsel.

'It's mean, mm, she doesn't see —'

'Miss Simms, you mean?' pointing toward the matron. 'She didn't see what?'

'She doesn't see, mm, ill in my ... here.'

The fair-haired man spoke to Rivka without moving from where he leaned against the wall to her side. He spoke in English. Immediately, the younger man spoke for him in Yiddish. 'You struck a policeman with a belt. It's a very terrible crime.'

She replied in English. 'No. He stand behind of me. To hit me down.'

Again, the question in English first, then in Yiddish. 'Where are you from? What country?'

A subtle signal from the young man, the swirl of a finger, advised Rivka to answer in Yiddish. She followed him in this, but spoke to the fair-haired man, saying she used to live in Sasmacken, in East Courland, in Latvia.

'What's a Lett doing at a WSPU demonstration? Are you a member of the WSPU?'

Above and beyond translating Yiddish to English and vice versa, the young man made a note of Rivka's answers in the kind of pocketbook she'd seen policemen use. She told her story of the journey to the Strand that took her so far off course. She didn't know what the people around Big Ben were doing there. She'd never heard of suffragettes before, she didn't know what the initials WSPU meant, and when its meaning was spelled out for her Rivka shook her head.

'The Strand's quite a distance from Parliament Square.'
She knew that now.

'Do you believe women should have the vote?'

If the men said so.

To the young man his superior said, 'Write "no response".' He took a step closer, showed Rivka his face, his stance. 'You believe women have advanced? The educated native also tells us that he's advancing, pulling up level with the white man.' For a second time he instructed the interpreter to enter 'no response' as Rivka's reply. 'Tell me where you live.'

They had this information already. The young man urged her to repeat it. Wellesley Street, she told them. A room.

'What's your landlord's name? Who takes your rent money?'

Charles Perelman, she told him.

'Did anybody arrange the accommodation? Did somebody find the room at Perelman's for you?'

She said, 'He inwited me live dere.'

The three men spoke together, the warden included in the whispered conference. Then Rivka was asked, 'How do you get your money? Seamstress?'

She works in a restaurant, she told them. Two restaurants.

'Which ones? Where?'

Shinebloom's and Clark's. Both in Sclater Street.

'Are you friendly with any particular customers at Shinebloom's? Men, say? Other Letts? Jews?'

She tried to be friendly with everyone she served.

'How did you come to London?'

By steamer.

'Under your own steam?' As the mild laughter drained out of the room, he asked, 'By yourself, I mean. No one helped you — with money, papers, that sort of thing.'

I'm a refugee. Cossacks attacked my family. I came here to be safe.

'Why did they do that, I wonder, those filthy Cossacks?' The young man didn't interpret that remark. 'Are you an anarchist?'

Before Rivka could think how to answer, the warden cut in. 'Obviously she's a radical.'

She caught the change of tone, threatening enough for her to use English, directed at them all. 'Everything what I say ... no bloomy good.'

'Are you an anarchist? Do you have anarchist friends?'

'No! Friends of me. Helping. Only! Only!'

'I don't believe you.' He clutched Rivka's mouth.

'I am singer. Please, sir...' Crying now, shaking her head free. 'You hurt me dere. Den I am not sing.'

'*Can't*. You mean you 'can't' sing.'

'No, please. I am *singer* only! No troublemaker!'

Rivka told the young man, and asked him to write in his pocket-book that it wasn't possible for her to be an anarchist, she didn't know what an anarchist did.

The chap from Special Branch repeated his round of questions twice more. Rivka could only give him the same answers in the same words. She was a match for his patience, but not his stamina. Without fanfare the fair-haired man and his interpreter put their hats back on, signalling to Rivka and the warden that they'd finished with her. She had no idea what had finally satisfied them that they'd got enough, or all they were likely to get, from her. The warden opened the door to let them out, Rivka heard the warden call the older man Mr Whitfield and the younger one Mr Wagner.

Rivka waited for the wardresses to take her back to her cell. But they didn't lift her from her chair: instead, they tied her to it. Cloth straps around her ankles fastened

Rivka to the chair legs. As a wardress on each side of her pinioned her arms, the warden leaned close to Rivka and said, 'You think we've never seen that trick before, Fourteen Eighteen? You pretend you're eating the good food that staff provide, then force yourself to expel it in a sickening mess on the floor.'

'I want go ... to home.'

'I'm sure that you do,' he said, not unkindly. 'Should've thought of that before you hurt the policeman yesterday.'

He nodded to the doctor, a short thin man, ungentle and expressionless, who ordered Rivka to open her mouth. She shook her head, clamped her jaws. 'Usually,' said the doctor, 'this is done where other prisoners can watch. Do you want us to do that? Take you out to the reception room?'

The nurse's hands caught Rivka's head in a strong grip — one at her forehead, the other at her chin — pressing down with her whole weight to force open the lower jaw. Rivka twisted away and felt a crisp slap on her cheek. She let out a breath — of anger, outrage, animal ferocity — creating enough of an opening for the doctor to push a metal wedge between her teeth, preventing her from closing her mouth. Bracing a bony knee on her thigh, the doctor fed a length of rubber tube into her throat. On its way down the flexing rubber scraped raw flesh; another taste of metal, the flavour of her blood as she choked it up.

'Hold her, keep her steady!'

'Yes, Doctor. I'm trying to.'

Another pair of hands pinned Rivka's shoulders against the back of the chair. She fought for air, a single breath to keep her body alive, resisting, every gasp plugged by the fattening rubber tube gorged with the mash of bread and milk now being sloshed into the funnel above Rivka's head. Quick as it slopped into her stomach it churned there, rushed back up her throat and splashed froth from her slack mouth.

Someone had neatly replaced the Bible, prayer book, hymn book and two pamphlets — *Fresh Air and Cleanliness* and *The Narrow Way* — on Rivka's bed. The vomit from hours before lay uncleaned and freshly slicked with more; patches of it glistened on the cell floor under the electric light. Rivka's thoughts sailed to her father, carried skyward on her weak, sympathetic breath. Poor Mordechai, a Lettish man degraded by the Russians, as a Lettish Jew, made the Russians' special toy, his tolerance and caution broken. 'I'm your daughter here,' Rivka whispered to the air. 'I'm your good daughter.' She rolled onto her side and sang to the wall, '*Nokh eyn tants, beyt ikh itst bay dir . . .*'

For a third time Karl woke to Saturday's dim overcast morning, ticked into its last hour now. The bedsheets' body warmth kept him drowsy and submissive to sleep. Awake, dressed, busy, Nina had already been out on homely errands and returned with fresh rolls, a jar of English jam, even, somehow, a scuttle full of coal. The room swelled with heat from the fireplace. From his bed Karl could see tea steaming in the blue china pot on the table. He crooked one arm behind his head.

Nina said, 'You're ready to eat?'

He nodded. 'Yes, Nina. Please.'

'You'll be glad to hear Perelman apologised to Fenia for hitting her.' Nina ladled a small mound of jam on to a plate, sliced the roll in half, poured a cup of tea, sugared and stirred it.

'He wouldn't have. You had to shame him into it.'

'That's him.' Nina raised one shoulder, half a shrug, all

139

the effort Perelman deserved. 'Some men don't bend to shame. He does. He cares what we think of him.'

Karl held a spoonful of jam on his tongue and slowly breathed out. He sniffed summer air. 'English strawberries.'

'Fanny didn't accept so quick. She's making him suffer a little.'

'Yes? How?'

'A new hat. Not only. He's a bully, Perelman, you know why? Because his wife goes with those men.'

'What men?'

'Other men. Younger men. He flattered himself with Deborah. Is he twenty years older than she is? More?'

'Thirty. He was bragging, for sure.'

'What does he expect from someone who has to put up with his crazy running around...'

At that moment Karl felt lulled into a cloud of sensual pleasure: the sweet fruit of the jam, the sound of Nina's voice. He listened to her report of her mission to the Perelmans — the treaty she negotiated between father and daughter, Nina's successful mothering, her acid observations of home life *chez* Perelman — but his attention flickered and faded. He huddled into himself. Whispery half-thoughts tugged him backwards in time to the unsettling conversation he'd had with Peter the night before, and further still...

Lemon juice is invisible ink, he reminisced. *Chemistry is change made visible. Alter one fact, thought Karl, you make an experiment with history. If this, then that.* If he gave up the leadership of Liesma, then someone else — Jacob Peters, for instance — would step in. *All right. Let Lenin's quartermasters get along without my help, let the great revolution arrive or not arrive in my absence. Take Russia out of my life's arrangements and what's left? Mornings like this one, with Nina.*

140

Karl's contemplation ran in this direction:

A man needs a livelihood; that's enough of a reason to act. What career would I have? Where? Not in England. Not Latvia or Russia, I've put those places behind me. France, Germany, Poland, where I'm a wanted man? Australia? America? Karl had never visited America. Fritz had, the year before. 'Karl, it's a green country,' he said. He meant naïve. The job there would be to make himself over with an American name. Jack. Jack Martin. Fritz told him about Pennsylvania. Penn-sylvan-ia. Sylvan, wooded. Penn's woods. He imagined living in a house outside the city near the woods — from P. Morin of Gold Street, London to J. Martin of Pennsylvania, USA — finding a situation as a chemical engineer, eating his breakfast there, not here.

Early sunlight washes in to the kitchen from windows on two sides. Even on autumn days, the room is warm and airy. Their Pennsylvania house has four other rooms, two downstairs, two bedrooms upstairs with a bathroom between them. Stands of plane trees, chestnut, oak and maple line the low hills. This time of year, the middle of November, their leaves are still scarlet, orange, yellow, waiting for the cold nights to prune them. Nina hasn't made tea for her Jack. Americans drink coffee in the morning. After his second cup he leaves Nina who cooks at the stove – pork chops, fried potatoes and celery for his lunch. Outside, from the road, a man calls Karl's name. 'Jack! It's Albert and Bill!'

Saturday, yes. His neighbours, father and son, promised to come over to help him finish erecting the long wooden fence he's building to protect his garden from the dangers of passing motor cars. He'd sunk the posts himself; shaving the ends of the rails and laying them in is a job for two men, and with young Bill, they're three. Together they finish the whole thing in a couple of hours and the three men go inside to drink Nina's coffee and eat slices of her apple strudel.

'See, that's good lumber you bought, Jack,' Albert says.

'Not so good for my hands,' says his son, showing off blisters on every one of his fingers.

'I'll knit you some gloves,' Nina promises Bill.

'It'll stand up to the weather,' Albert says of the fence. He asks Jack, 'Made any breakthroughs at the chemical plant?'

Karl leans back in his chair. 'Nothing I can talk about.'

'To the peasants,' Albert kids him. 'Your free labour!' He scoops another bite of strudel into his mouth.

'Free neighbour,' corrects Jack.

He means this freedom, his. To choose what he makes his responsibility. A house, a fence, a debt. The historical causes that landed him here are a thousand human generations and his only consequence is the first of the next thousand.

I'll live another fifty years and die in my Pennsylvania bed when I'm seventy-four. In 1960. Who knows? Perhaps by then the revolution will come meet me in America. History and a man's history, one in the other. You can leave that to men with the head for it, men like Salnish, Lenin and Jacob.

Karl's mental experiment unsettled him less than he expected. He might even talk it over with Peter that afternoon, he thought. Karl drifted back from his daydream of a pastoral future and said to Nina: 'Let's go away from London tomorrow.'

'Where?' she asked, reaching for his empty plate.

'The countryside.'

Nina covered her mouth with her hand and laughed. Then, 'Karl, you're lost any place outside the city. When we went to visit Jan Kernow at the seaside, every five minutes you wanted to know what time it was.'

'The seaside's not the countryside. I'm talking about trees and meadows,' said Karl, 'not cold wind in your ears and wet feet. And no Kernow, either.'

'We don't have train fare.'

'It's cheaper to live in the countryside.'

'In that case we'd scrape for train fare to get to London.' Nina brushed the crumbs from Karl's plate into a wash basin. She heard a knock on the street door, two taps, followed by three. It reminded her: 'I met Yoska by the Perelmans. Him and Max Smoller. He said he wants to talk to you today.'

'Smoller?'

'Yoska.'

'Not with Smoller.'

'I told him: just you. And not until later because Karl's resting.'

'What time is it?'

'Twelve.'

The knock came again. Karl said, 'All right. Let him in.'

Yoska's raw knuckles attacked the door with another gleeful melody of knocks. As an optimist he felt justified: as a comrade, vindicated. He was one of the few reliable ones, a plain fact Karl was obliged to appreciate.

That security was the secret inside Yoska's good-dog grin when Nina brought him inside. One look at him and Karl was sure it was the sight of fresh food on the table that kindled the joy heating Yoska's cheeks.

Karl finished dressing by the fireplace. Nina helped him button his shirt collar. 'Have you eaten anything today, Yoska?'

'I can always eat,' was the reply. He limped to the nearest chair, lowered his thick body down in to it. 'What is it? Strawberries?'

'Strawberry.'

'From Reuben,' Nina said. 'Same as they sell in the West End.'

Yoska said to Karl, 'I have something for you, too.' He retrieved a small square of paper from the inside pocket of his overcoat. Karl and Nina watched him open it out and smooth it on the table. It was a sketch in pencil of the layout of a building. Nothing was labelled. Yoska waited for Karl to speak.

Nina obliged him, frowning. 'What is it?'

'A prize,' Yoska answered. His broad index finger stabbed at the bottom end of the T-shaped line drawing. 'Houndsditch,' he said. 'Number 119.'

He had come to Karl with a story about a jeweller's shop on the premises called H.S. Harris, doing brisk business for the last six or seven months. Savvy about jewellery trade gossip, Yoska mentioned — but brushed aside — rumours of Romanov necklaces, brooches, even a Fabergé egg entrusted to Mr Harris's firm for repair. The significant fact was that shop was a success, patronised by a wealthy clientele, gentlemen who worked in the City and other princely types. For four hours on Friday, Yoska had watched them arrive and depart. His conservative estimate of the contents of the Harris safe: lengths of gold chain, rings, watches, earrings, and, if they were lucky, a small amount of gold and silver bullion. The haul could bring them — 'Two hundred pounds? Three hundred? You'd need somebody besides Leon Beron to move it on.'

Karl made a closer study of the layout. 'From this it looks like you can see the safe from the street.'

'You can't go in through the front,' Yoska concurred.

'What's behind the shop? Here. These are connected rooms?'

'Flats behind. In Exchange Buildings. Number 9, 10 in the middle, 11. Nine and eleven,' — he pointed to the boxes that formed the two ends of the T's crossbar — 'they're for rent.'

Any robbery is a set of practical problems, some

general, others particular to the target. Karl quickly became absorbed in the task of identifying the obstacles to the forced entry of the long, narrow jewellery shop at 119 Houndsditch. He concentrated on Yoska's sketch, marked its margins with a red crayon, asked for missing pieces of information, applied his intelligence to the concrete difficulties of a concealed break-in, safe cracking and escape.

Yoska dredged up a host of details, and they tumbled like lock cylinders into Karl's calculations. The Exchange Buildings occupied a cul-de-sac ... a narrow yard accommodating the toilets separated the back wall of the flats from the back wall of the jewellery shop... the shops in the area close for business around seven o'clock. He thought ahead to the necessity of raising finance — to rent the flats, to purchase tools, chemicals and cutting equipment. To face off danger from citizens and police, to take the prize, to prevail: it all depended on choosing the right men.

As little as she thought of Yoska, Nina's silent geisha withdrawal from the two men's company conveyed something more to Karl. Her half-smile and gently narrowed peat-brown eyes lifted her man on a wave of the confidence she placed in his virtue. Faith was not too rhapsodic a word for it. Nina stepped out of the room and into the chilly hallway, closing the door behind her without a disruptive sound, her part in the male ceremony of serious work.

Yoska left Gold Street elated; he would have clicked his heels if his lame leg had allowed it. After he'd gone, Karl undressed and slid back in to the voluptuous daytime comfort of bed. His thinking was reflective and clear. *A house to share with Nina in the American countryside is not a thing in this world. A robbery that hasn't been pulled off yet is not a thing in this world. Both exist in the same place, an ideal future – that's to say an undecided one.*

He measured and weighed the two propositions, dissected them side by side and extracted the difference between a scheme and a fantasy. Karl pulled the blankets up to his chin, shut his eyes, and from the skinny bones of Yoska's sketch began constructing a plan to break through two brick walls, cut through an iron safe and rob H.S. Harris's Jewellers of all the wealth it possessed.

Seventeen

In clothes that were not hers, in a part of London she didn't know, Rivka re-entered the world as an ex-inmate of HM Prison Holloway. Where were her plain black dress and half-jacket, underclothes, stockings and shoes? Scattered. Tossed into boxes and reception room heaps. Perhaps covering another released prisoner released ahead of her. 'Better than yours,' was the wardress's judgment of the dark blue jacket she handed to Rivka. 'You had an awful tear down the sleeve, the one you come in with. I remember it.'

What Rivka remembered was that they'd incarcerated her for two days and nights, and did worse than that to her, besides. They — the policemen in Parliament Square who chased her down, beat, kicked and arrested her, the one in Canon Row who charged her, the magistrate at Bow Street who sentenced her, the plainclothesmen who interrogated her, the prison doctor who obscenely brutalized her, the wardresses who clamped her to the chair — planted a rock in Rivka's gut. Each step she took jarred this dead weight until its toothed edges clawed her stomach. Blindly, she explored its hardness, roughness, nauseating bulk, and the cost of cradling inside her something so alien as bewildered fury.

Her clothes on an unknown stranger; a stranger's blue jacket and chocolate brown skirt on her. Also shoes from somebody whose feet were a size larger than Rivka's. If she had to run in them she'd break both her ankles. The blouse they gave her was another disaster, yellow sweat stains under the arms, too tight in the bust, a button missing. A clownish costume altogether. As she stood waiting for Charles Perelman to materialize from the thin stream of faces passing through the station entrance Rivka was worried by the thought that he wouldn't recognise her; she'd have to approach him and watch him recoil from this vagrant come to pester him for a handout. 'It's me. Rivka,' she'd have to say, and watch his disgust break into pity.

Along with the second-hand clothes, the wardress had handed her a message written in English and Yiddish on an official HMP form. It instructed Rivka to meet her landlord at Caledonian Road Underground Station. How Perelman found out so quickly where she was and the date and hour of her release was a mystery. A gentleman had bestirred himself to fetch her home; to know that satisfied her well enough.

In a minute here he was, unmistakeable in his cape and wide hat, with his mountaineer's stride. Perelman reached to touch Rivka's hand. His compassionate, courtly greeting disastrously failed to camouflage the grim surprise that tightened his mouth and weighed down his eyelids.

'How else would you find your way back? Ask a policeman?' A step ahead of her, Perelman thought, with his explanation.

Rivka walked slowly toward the platform, Perelman led her by the arm. 'I could do it,' she said.

'You could, I'm sure,' he said. 'Now I'm here and you don't have to.'

'It's a long way to come. It is, isn't it?'

'On the train it's not so far.' He escorted Rivka into the carriage. With his gloved hand, Perelman brushed the seat clean before letting her sit down. 'Any way you cut the pumpernickel, *toybele*, you're my responsibility.' He'd used his sincerest tone, but — beholden? humiliated? — her cheeks reddened and Rivka quickly turned her face away. Perelman explained. 'You didn't come home so I went looking. Then the police came to talk to me.'

'I'm sorry. Mr Perelman, I'm sorry, you shouldn't have trouble from me.'

'They're the ones with the trouble!' He said, wickedly, 'My good friends in the London constabulary told me you hit one of them with your belt.'

'I don't remember. I'm not sure if I did or didn't.'

A gloomy frown. 'Every time they breathe on you it's a lie. You didn't come home so I demanded, I protested. You know they wanted to keep you in for six more days? I protested. How you're a good girl. You work hard, pay your rent and keep away from bad types. They made some mistake, I told them. I made a solid case, it convinced them.' Perelman sang this from the crest of a wave of eager sympathy, as though he doubted he'd be believed.

Though, sincerely, Perelman felt bound to the girl by kinship. She'd just taken her first steps in the foothills; he was the veteran climber, stood high above at the summit of the same mountain of entanglements. It's a blessing she hasn't got the Okhrana also on her back, he thought, only lesser demons, those low-voiced, mannerly gentlemen of Special Branch. Because she's the object of police attention, they can cover her with dirt. Any time, on a suspicion, a whim. There's no end to the varieties of damnation they can rain down on Rivka's head. Sickening rumours about her. Prison again. Deportation. From this depredation, Perelman told himself, he had the power to defend her. To fix things through his contacts in the Metropolitan Police so that Rivka could stay in

149

England unmolested. Beat coppers at Leman Street, plainclothes at Old Jewry, higher-ups at Scotland Yard. Strings dangled to be pulled.

The train bumped on the track and jostled Perelman's shoulder against Rivka's. He pressed her hand. 'Pardon me,' he said and heard his apology swallowed up by the rushing, clacking noise that filled the carriage like tatters of paper in a windstorm. One more assault to add to the intrusion of random stares from passengers clustered around them. Eyeing up what perversity? A swaggering old satyr repulsively, publicly parading his enjoyment, his tender prey, a blemishless, blameless child, the old goat's pleasure, the rosebud under his hoof trampled and damned... An outward show Perelman can't help, which, as usual, contradicts the finer truth of it.

He felt pleasure, yes, from Rivka's physical closeness. Warm and unashamed, close as family, especially here among this travelling congregation of their English hosts. Closer than his family, even. This unspoiled young woman, whose name two months ago he didn't know, was singled out by circumstances that bring her to him. All things considered, wasn't *closeness* the natural feeling? The trace of warmth his arm felt when it bumped against hers reflected back to Rivka, and connected them. Affectionately, naturally, decently.

And he thought, *She's as fresh as my girls were in the beginning, how all daughters are at first. Until they change into children who flaunt their disrespect and wives who cheat in the open, in the street, in closets and offices.* He looked at Rivka, who sat beside him with eyes lowered, and saw the child she was half her lifetime ago. That little girl was visible to him, frank enough for him to photograph. *Rivka is comfortable with me; living in my house she's unafraid.* Perelman pressed Rivka's hand again. She patted his forearm, then pulled back her hands, made two prim fists of them and curled them in her lap.

So it happens again, back again like a curse! Misunderstood, he thought, brought into the light, his secret intentions never fail to look vulgar.

From the Aldgate Underground station they walked home in a light rain. Rivka clomped along in her oversized shoes, clumsy as a dray horse, but quieted by the brick walls of terraced houses that were not the brick walls of Holloway Prison, as the wet pavement of Commercial Road was not the wet floor of her cell. Outside those walls, the fundamental dignity of possessing a name was returned to her. With forced cheer, he asked Rivka if she wanted to eat something when they got back. Instead of a direct answer, which would have been simple enough, she told him how the English had treated her, capture to release.

His reply, as he opened the front door, was, 'I made up a bed for you in Fanny's room.'

With a daybed next to Fenia's green bedstead, the narrow room was cramped. Fenia had arranged a little table next to Rivka's bed set with a candle, pitcher and wash basin. 'Can I sleep?'

'You don't want to eat some soup first? Deborah put some on the stove,' he said.

'Tell Mrs Perelman thank you. I need the bed more.'

'It's terrible trouble you had,' he agreed. 'You need to look out for yourself and know who protects you. I'm your friend saying this.'

Rivka let her shoes fall off her feet. 'I won't go to Big Ben anymore.'

'Tell me, that's what I want you to do. If people — Karl

151

and Nina or anybody else — try to talk you into trouble, just tell me' He gave her a clipped nod and shut the door.

Anybody else? Did he mean someone she knew or strangers? The police? The Letts, other Jews? Their faces — the constable who grabbed her, the doctor, the warden, the Questioner, the Yiddisher — broke apart and reappeared with Karl's fine brushed hair, Peter's tall brow and artist's beard, Perelman's Spanish doe's eyes, Yoska's pocked cheeks. Then the mob of them stood together in the Underground train, in the guttering light and slashes of tunnel darkness, a circle of nine men yelling nonsense at her. Voice tangled with voice, their lip-flap noise electrifying Rivka's solitude while her body travelled on ahead of her, sleepbound.

Her transformation was not a dream, it was her dream's substance. As she dipped her head to drink from a moonlit pool Rivka saw the reflection of her half-human features. The blue eyes of her mother, unmistakeable, their colour leeched from the high atmosphere, blinked back from a silver-furred face, and above it feline ears that stood sharply erect. The hands that supported Rivka at the pool's edge, tucked close under her chest, were paw-like. No matter how much water she lapped, dryness still crusted her lips and tongue. The thought flared in her mind: *This is me reborn, my new life, a nocturnal animal scavenging in the forest.*

That midnight blackness covered Rivka as she awoke, though it was not the middle of the night but early evening. And a knock on the door told her it wasn't a forest, either. Fanny Perelman's voice, asking if she wanted to eat, reached her from a rectangle of light.

'Some water,' Rivka said. 'Please, Fenia. What time is it?'

'After six.

'At night?'

'You slept all day. We thought it was better to let you.'

'What day?'

'Monday.'

Fanny disappeared again through the rectangle of light and came back with a pitcher of cold water. The liquid burned Rivka's throat on its way down; still she drank two glassfuls, then floated into a light sleep. At around seven-thirty Fanny returned with a visitor for the convalescing patient. The version of the story that roused Nina Vassilleva reached her by way of Fanny, who'd got a vividly indignant second-hand chronology from her father. The Perelman tribe, each in his own way, was agitated by the barbarity and injustice suffered by Rivka.

Then Nina swept in to Wellesley Street and it felt as though a berobed judge had arrived on an undertaking to confirm the damage, dole out blame and seek fair settlement. Little Carlusha pushed his sisters and brothers aside for a prime place in the bedroom doorway, while his father bobbed behind Nina and Fanny, recounting what he'd done for Rivka from that morning in Holloway to five minutes before, when he told Deborah to heat some soup. Still agitated he waited to hear from Nina, from anyone, what else needed to be done for Rivka's comfort and recuperation.

Nettie, the ten-year-old, edged in for a closer look at the purple bruises on Rivka's cheek. 'Does your face hurt?'

'A little,' Rivka said.

'Did you fall on the floor?'

'Yes.'

'How did you?'

'A man pushed me down.'

'You got up and ran away.'

'Not fast enough.'

153

'I think you're brave,' Nettie told her.

'Are you brave?'

'I'm *quite* brave.'

With her fingertips Rivka touched the perfect pink-white skin of the little girl's cheek.

'You can take the children out of this room,' Nina said to Perelman. 'And you go out, too.'

Perelman broke off from shooing Carlusha into the hallway, 'No, I'm staying. You don't tell me where I can go in my house.'

'I'm staying, too,' Carlusha announced.

'No.' Nina dropped her hands onto the little boy's shoulders and marched him out the door.

'Try that with me,' Perelman dared her with a cocky smile.

'Throw a jug of water on him,' Nina joked to Fanny, for her father's benefit.

'I'm no tomcat,' he responded, playfully.

'No, you're a bad little dog, Charles. Go out, now,' Nina told him firmly. 'Your bark-bark-bark's hurting Rivka's ears. And mine, too.'

'And mine,' cheekily, from his daughter.

'And Nettie's. We don't need a chaperone.'

Perelman disagreed, over his shoulder. 'It's exactly what you do need. All the time, day and night.' Halfway into the hallway he grouched to Fanny, 'Later you'll tell me what the three of you were talking about in my house.'

'I will, Papa,' she said to him, and after she shut the door, to Nina she said, 'I won't.'

Nina greeted Rivka silently, with irony, apology, head-shaking amazement, lips pinched together to pronounce sympathy for her and contempt for her attackers. She pulled a cane chair close to the bed, where she quietly sat in her hat and coat. 'Did you eat today?'

'My throat,' Rivka said. 'No good.'

Without turning away from Rivka, Nina said, 'Fenia? Make some tea for me. Will you?'

'There's a pot brewed downstairs,' Fanny replied, but didn't move from where she stood.

'Make it fresh. Please, Fenia. And a plate of something.'

'For you?'

'For me, yes. You can bring soup for Rivka. Not too hot or salty.'

Nina's message to Fanny finally got through; she wanted a little while to speak alone with Rivka. When Fanny left the room, Nina unpinned her hat and laid it on the floor. She sloughed her coat off and let it fall from her shoulders onto the back of the chair. She leaned closer. 'Show me,' Nina said. 'What they did.' She attended to Rivka with a doctor's intimate concern. 'Can you sit up?'

'My neck hurts. My back, and here.' She wiped her fingers across her rib cage, then, on one hard breath, propped herself on her elbows. With Nina supporting her arm, Rivka bent forward. Her hair had survived the recent ordeals roughly tamed, enough of it upswept, bunched and pinned to leave her neck bare.

'It's a rotten bruise he gave you here.' Very lightly Nina drew the tip of her finger in a line above Rivka's shoulders. 'It's a wonder he didn't break your neck. You can wear your hair lower until this heals. I know how to fix it.' From Fanny's bedside table Nina borrowed a hairbrush.

Rivka felt the hairpins plucked from the nest of her hair and the nest fall apart. 'Maybe the policeman did it, at Big Ben. Or the doctor. I don't know which one.'

'This will cover it over,' Nina said, 'and be *soigné*. Tell me if I'm brushing too hard.' The slow strokes were as

155

determined as they were gentle. 'What else did the stupid barbarians do to you?'

As carefully as her memory allowed, Rivka repeated the history of each wound. Her hoarseness and sore mouth were from the rubber tube, the boot kicks to her chest. There were other souvenirs she couldn't explain, red abrasions around her wrists, scratches on her neck and scrapes on her knuckles. 'Why did they jump on me? I didn't do anything against them.'

'You insulted them.'

'No. I don't remember. Not to the policeman.' Rivka thought for a second. 'The doctor. Maybe him.' She shook her head; numb memory, another punishment.

'You do it by living here,' Nina said. 'Did you speak English to them, the police or the ones in prison?'

'First I tried. They didn't want it.'

'They hate you more when you try and fall on your face. Your ugly foreign accent reminds them how strong they are.'

'Over *me*,' Rivka said, for Nina to confirm the absurdity of it.

'No, all of us. To them each of us is all of us.' A jet of pain flashed a wince across Rivka's face, and Nina winced in sympathy. 'Let me look.' The hem of Rivka's nightshirt had bunched around her waist. Slowly and with great delicacy Nina raised it over Rivka's breast and held it there. Her other hand moved over Rivka's ribs, only the lightest breath of pressure from her fingertips. 'Did they touch you here? On your breasts?'

Did they? Rivka couldn't remember any lewd assault. 'For sure not while I was awake.'

'They threatened you? In your cell?'

What a remarkable thing. Rivka remembered so clearly a welter of ringing details: the prison corridors, how they

echoed and smelled, her cell, the side room, the cruelties
done to her there and before, while any recollection of
what she did to defend herself remained foggy and
beyond her reach. Didn't she put up a fight? How was she
with them? Obedient and weak? A timid girl begging on
her knees? Where was Rivka Bermansfelt when they
threw her onto the vomit-slicked floor or pinned her to a
chair and pushed a rubber tube down her throat?

The cold shock that she had done nothing but squirm
and scream and take the blows trembled through Rivka's
chest and arms, its ice sank through her legs, preparing
her body for the paralysing fear that the nineteen years of
her life were gone. Time only flows in one direction and
it has carried Riveleh away, far enough now so she could
see her life as it was just days before becoming an unreal
abandoned shadow figure in the distance. Dragged
downstream, between there and nowhere, dragged
under. This river knocks the breath out of you the same.
Rivka covered her eyes to keep hold of herself, to stay in
one place, inside her skin, but she was going, she was lost.

Tears leaked through her fingers. 'I think God made us
good. He's better than men are, a better man. And men
want to do good and be like him, for God's favour. Jews,
Russians, English, they're the same. Like that, anyway.'

Nina gently pried Rivka's hand free, uncovered her
eyes. She didn't let go of it. 'You want an answer? They
think everything they do is good because they're doing it.
You want to wait for them to make apologies for what
they did? You'll wait a long time. Not just those men. All
of them are romantics.'

'Your man is?'

'Karl? He's the worst kind. Dedicated.'

*She knows men. Nina knows the men she knows. She stays
close to her Karl, cleaning, writing letters, while he spends*

157

hours in bed. Him and his entertaining thoughts. He entertains himself with elaborate delusions. Sometimes in bed with Nina he describes them to her, calmly and earnestly. She knows the Nina-Lena-Minna he sees in bed, haloed in romance, is different from the Nina-Lena-Minna he watches pile lumps of coal into the grate. In bed, languid as a cat, earnest as a young priest, Karl twines his limbs around hers and strains to hold on to a passionate vision of her, her face aglimmer on a silver icon, until his eyelids flicker, his whiteness splashes out, he breathes her name. Then, quickly, the physical world spins back into place and takes over. Karl faces what's necessary. Daydreaming a different world in bed is another necessity to him, so it doesn't worry her.

She knows Yoska. A man who found his talent and trusts it. His confidence makes you trust it. This good thief makes me laugh, every time I see him, *Nina reminds herself.* He stuffs more into his pockets than he gives Karl to send to Russia. *'All right,' he said last time, 'I'm guilty. You want me to go?' Protesting, dragging his poor leg around the room, behind puffs of romantic honesty. For the hundredth time he flung his reason against their smiles – he fights his battle against the smug collaborators of empire... Imperialists teach their citizens how to act – cold-blooded and greedy. Yoska is their chastiser, loss of property their comeuppance.* Stay here, Yoska, sit down, eat some more.

She knows Fritz. He suffers like a saint and his mauled spirit skewers Nina's heart. He can thank his Russian torturers for turning him into such a romantic anarchist. They drove him deep into himself. He's no patriot anymore, no country can claim Fritz's affections. Why should he fight? He's already free. He has the power to make promises to his wife and lie to his mistress, for Freedom's sake. *I should detest him,* thinks Nina, *but my heart won't let me.*

She knows Peter. Be suspicious about paintings and men who put their value so high. Later she'd find a better moment, Nina decided, to pass along some sisterly advice to Rivka: If you're smart you'll protect yourself from someone who makes paintings of landscapes so beautiful and welcoming; it's because he yearns to live in them. *Unreal places. No, Peter's eccentric fascination with colour smeared on canvass wasn't romantic, and it wasn't his most annoying trait, either. Nina bristled when she thought of his pathetic delusion – the romance of refusal: he wasn't a man trussed to the consequences of past deeds, he wasn't bound to his own history, his passion had been sapped. A comrade, Peter the Painter? He reminded her more of an exhausted roué.*

The men Nina knows are moons circling close to her in wobbling orbits. Except for Indrik. Her father is a planet, a burning sun, enormous, steady and solitary in black space. He travelled the farthest of them all: Father made a revolution of his own. By the strength of his two arms and two legs he crawled out from under the Tsar. He traded his warm dry quarters in the Winter Palace for a bivouac in a field of mud and snow. He was the only undeluded man Nina ever knew, one who didn't look for romance in the battles he fought, or in the fighting, win or lose.

In the low lamplight Nina's eyes deepened. Rivka noticed they were wet, and briefly, before Nina brushed it away, the wetness glossed her cheeks. 'Karl is good to you. Anyone can see it,' Rivka said. Nina tucked her chin, gave a nod.

Oh, this intimacy undid Rivka. As it emptied her out it left her as close as a sister to Nina, both of them daughters of men savaged by the jaws of the same fate. Gulp after gulp of air stopped in Rivka's throat, her lungs ached, she cried out, but no sound reached her mouth. Nina's hands rubbed her back. Nina embraced her to quiet Rivka's panicked shaking and then kissed her forehead. 'What? Tell me. That's right, that's right...'

Fanny clicked the door and, food-laden tray in hand, lightly kicked it open. Nina shouted at her, 'Not now, Fenia. We're all right.' To Fanny none of it looked all right. Not Rivka's uncontrollable, choking cries or Nina's helplessness to comfort her.

Rivka's failures and misfortunes drubbed her head, they cascaded down from heaven. She caught her breath enough to say, 'Because of me ... my father...'

'That's right, tell me. What?'

'Because of what I did, my father ... because I didn't help him. Now he's dead. I know it,' Rivka said. 'I'm alive because of him and he's dead because of me.'

'You don't know. Did your cousin write you?'

'They've killed Papa in jail in Riga. Because nothing stops them. Policemen beat him to death, I know they did.'

'Maybe.' Sober-voiced, unsparing, Nina showed her how to face down the horror of reality. 'You don't know for sure. We haven't heard anything from there.'

Rivka, for now buried, unreachable. 'They caught him because I'm not so good. My family hates me. *They should.* God hates me.'

'Don't talk like that, Rivka! Who is God?' A trace of a smile tickled the corners of Nina's mouth. 'Up above God's a policeman, and on earth, a policeman's God. London, Riga, St Petersburg, Kiev, Talsen, anywhere.'

Though she was calmer now, Rivka wouldn't be consoled. 'Yes, because I hate the soldiers and I want to go back and beat them to death. They put this hate in me. I want to break their bones and cut their faces with a knife. I hate them for making me want to hurt them. Now I'm somebody God hates.'

'Who do you think God is? Your big friend on a gold chair in the sky watching over you? He protected you, Rivka?'

'Yes. Before what happened on the Talsen road.'

'So yesterday he was your friend but not today.'

'Because I want to hurt those men. The ones who hurt my father. God turned his back on me because I was a weakling. I didn't help. What's good in me anymore? Nothing, not a drop of good anywhere.'

'I think God stopped watching over that Cossack you killed.'

Before the whole story poured out of her, Rivka shook Nina with a confession that on the Talsen road that night she tried to save the Cossack's life, not help her father take it. Back she went, to the months Mordechai devoted to building the Louis Quatorze clock, his intricate and beautiful work, Colonel Orlov's rampage, the grim hopelessness (and worse) that infected the Bermansfelts because of it. By the end of it Rivka was leaking tears again, her shoulders shaking under Nina's hands. The roadside melee with the Russians dreamily folded into the Parliament Square riot and she wept, 'What did I do there? What did I do?'

'They decided for you what a woman does,' Nina said. Whether she meant Russians or Englishmen, fathers or lovers, she made it clear to her new little sister, 'From now on, we'll decide. Won't we, Rivka?'

'Yes.'

'Won't we?'

'Yes'

This one was not a cowering woman like Rosie or a man-pleaser like Luba or a butterfly like Fenia. Nina could bring Rivka home to Karl the very next morning — yes, in the shape she was in and *still* a better class of prize, halfway to a comrade.

Toward the end of the next afternoon, Karl slipped in through the stage door of the Pavilion Theatre. He knew

161

he'd find The Painter there installing his *Girts Wilks* backdrop and the bits and pieces of scenery Harry hired him to produce. As Peter added dabs of green paint here and there to a tree in the foreground, streaks of golden brown to the distant bend of country road, Karl stood at his back, softly blasting away at the crimes committed by police, law court and prison against Rivka's body, mind and spirit.

Backstage was the ideal spot for Karl to do his seductive turn. Alone with his friend among the shadows, crawl spaces and hidden machinery, he levelled his shoulders and bore down on another man's heart. 'They made sure the woman they let out of there on Monday wasn't the same one they locked up on Friday.'

'How bad is she?' Peter controlled his worry, at least kept Karl from hearing it. 'You saw her?'

'This morning she came to us. Nina doesn't want the girl to go back to Perelman's.' A shrug that said it was all the same to him. 'She took Rivka to find some clothes. Holloway Prison zookeepers stole hers.'

'Which one has money for new clothes? Nina or Rivka?'

Karl's mild laugh answered him. 'You know how persuasive Nina can be.'

'Moses on the mountain, I've seen her — but she can't persuade Rivka to spend money she doesn't have.'

'Not Rivka, no, Mrs Teitelbaum. The furrier's mother? She's a dressmaker, or she sews new from old, some thrifty trick like that. Nina will talk her into giving Rivka credit,' Karl said. Then, reassurance and goad: 'Nina didn't have to persuade Rivka of anything.'

'Except to pawn wages she hasn't earned yet. Nina should put her powers to better use and talk Rivka *out* of doing that.'

'At the moment it makes no difference to Rivka. She

doesn't have any wages any more. Her friend The Mayor gave her the sack. And the coffeehouse the same.'

Peter's brush stopped mid-stroke. He said, 'Can you help her?'

'Not this time. You mean with Shinebloom's? I can't.'

'No?' He pushed Karl a little harder. 'What about Clark's?'

'Peter, no. It's going around now the police picked her up. It's too soon. They're *shopkeepers*,' the word a repulsive taste in his mouth. 'Nina's looking out for her.' He gave a slight, equivocal shrug. 'We both are.'

Considerate as it was of Karl to seek Peter out to break the news of Rivka's ordeal, it came second to the visit's meatier business. He'd come by himself, by back street and alleyway, to comb through the details of his plan to rob the Houndsditch jewellery shop, then hear Peter's assessment of it. For The Painter's genuine talent was scrutiny: he saw *under* and *around*. You could count on Peter to shine a light on hidden obstacles, as long as his imagination was engaged. Karl didn't insult him by dangling crude promises of treasure, he invited Peter to jab holes in the strategy wherever it looked weak.

As a favour to Karl, Peter reviewed each step, but his observations — of the hazards to escape complicated by the cul-de-sac, the time needed to gain access to the office, then the safe, the nearness of other residents — were obvious and he dispensed them listlessly. 'Hammer and chisel? The noise from it echoes across the yard, which goes along the back of the building.'

'There's a door. That should muffle it enough.'

'Karl, he'll suffocate, whoever's inside there. Who *is* doing all your hammering for you?'

'Max Smoller, Jacob Peters. One hour on, one off.'

'For thirty-six hours,' a sceptical Peter said. 'Meantime what are you doing? Not lending a hand?'

'I'll be with Nina in Number 11. Drinking tea. Populating the place like an ordinary couple.' Karl risked a direct approach. 'It'd certainly narrow the odds if someone else was in the other flat. Populating it.'

'Why not Fritz and Luba?'

'You know why. With their screaming and yelling all the time? She throws plates at him. *You* told me so.'

'Luba has a right to scream at him. We're lucky she doesn't throw plates at us.'

'They'd bring the police down on us in five minutes.'

'Fritz has his wooden sword for protection.'

'He's not so dependable these days.' Karl nudged again with a lighter touch. 'Come on, Peter. We can play cards all night. Nina and Rivka will cook for us, breakfast, lunch and dinner. And breakfast again.'

Without betraying a reason Peter handed his paint brush to Karl, saying, 'Finish it for me. The road needs more yellow.'

'Wait. I don't know how to paint.'

As Peter stepped off the stage, he heard his name called after him as a complaint. 'Do what you can,' he called back.

He found Harry managing the theatre's affairs from the back row of the stalls. Formal as an usher, standing in the aisle, Peter cleared up the mystery of Rivka's absence from the Saturday night performance. As he piled detail upon detail Harry's face flushed; he bit his lower lip, he nodded his head, his anger doubled at each revelation. 'Tell her—' Harry said, '—you're going to see her? Tell Rivka she can sing at the Pavilion any time, soon as her voice is better. Also tell her...' Now Harry's anger dissolved in a bath of subversive pleasure. 'I thought of a good English stage name for her. Look.' Harry flourished the playbill from Saturday and underlined the moniker with his finger. 'Show her this. It suits her, no?'

So Peter arrived at Rivka's door the bearer of cheering news. When she recovered she'd have her debut at the Pavilion Theatre. Not just her debut, her *renaissance* – as 'Anna Southam the Stepney Songbird.'

A second before Peter knocked, Carlusha opened the door to him. Actually, the little boy opened it to let his father out. Perelman, his cape, broad brimmed hat, two bulky pieces of luggage, and bulkier Russian laugh blocked the doorway.

'Photographic equipment,' identifying his burden for Peter. 'You're walking by Montague Street, come see me. I'll take your picture.'

'Can't afford any luxuries. Will you tell Rivka I'm here?'

Perelman assigned the task to his son, who fled upstairs with it. 'Listen, I'll make you a special price. Make you look beautiful, like your friend Karl. Wait, not 'Karl' – he still calls himself Gardstein, doesn't he.'

'No.'

'Gratis.'

'No, but thanks.'

'Peter, you'd be doing me a favour. Making portraits, I need the practice. This size.' Perelman cut a square of air with his hands, thumbtip to thumbtip. 'In a handsome frame.' 'I can't think of anybody I'd give it to.'

'Not Rivka?'

'What for? She doesn't need a photograph of me.'

'For a token.'

At the turn of the landing above, Rivka saw the splash of pearl-coloured light bleaching the entrance hall floor

165

to the foot of the stairs. As much as it was Wednesday noon let in through the front door, it was the visible breath of her emergence. Her flesh felt it as a physical impulse, her bones were magnetised by it. She'd been touched by the sensation just days before, when she emerged from Holloway's subterranean shadows back into the law-abiding world, likewise when she emerged from the backstage clutter of the Pavilion onto the bright stage to sing her audition. A stir of air strengthened into a flow that gathered Rivka towards the men's voices, Peter's and Perelman's. Those two would see at a glance why she wasn't annihilated by catastrophe.

First they'd take in the sight of her in new clothes, the dove gray skirt and dark olive jacket, her high-collared white blouse, buttoned shoes, black velvet hat. Not a shell to hide inside or a costume prettying up any mental damage, just the opposite — they'd see an expression of the clear-sighted resistance brought to birth inside her. Underneath Rivka's clothes her body could tell the same story. Skin scrubbed clean, hungry stomach fed, panicked heart tranquilised, health returned. *Look at me*. She wore her hair unpinned at the back, combed down the way Nina coiffed it, even though her shirt collar covered the purpling, yellowing bruise on her neck. Would Peter see the difference in her? The art gallery visit was less than a week ago. A continent of time. *Look at me*.

She heard Perelman say to Peter, 'Here she is,' and in Peter's quick smile Rivka read relief and pleasure. Was it only two days before on the street outside the Caledonian Road Underground station that she'd seen her misery reflected in her landlord's expression, the good hope in her crushed and crippled? Men's faces are better than mirrors.

Giddy confidence pushed her along into their

company, into the afternoon's pearly air, wholehearted, learning her passions. 'Can we take a long walk?'

'How about a short walk and some food?' Here she is, Peter said to himself, materialised from the pain, time and dignity they stole from her. Somebody must have given Rivka's dignity back. Not the authorities, her release didn't come wrapped in clemency. The obvious guess was Nina. Or did Rivka grab it back with her own two hands at the prison gate?

One of those hands looped Peter's arm and her other hand clasped it, arms locked together crook to crook. They sidestepped Perelman while he lingered in front of the house — opened one of his bags, resettled its contents, opened the second bag, checked its order, innocent inconveniences that delayed his departure. He squinted up at Peter, 'So you're going to eat?'

'Probably. After we walk a little.'

'Good. Make her eat some meat,' Good Uncle Perelman commanded. 'What restaurant? The Warsaw?'

'We'll see where we are when we're hungry,' was all Peter said.

Loitering there any longer to fiddle with his photographic equipment would have made it blatant he was stalling, so Perelman took his time giving instructions to Carlusha before he shut and locked the door. Rivka's self-appointed watchdog, he retreated to the windows, but the rattling of nearby coach wheels, the wheezing percussions from motor cars, clouds and sprays of street noise, made it impossible for him to hear their conversation as Peter and Rivka strolled down Wellesley Street. She talked, energetic, animated, and he listened — to what confidences?

Perelman noted the time and place of her rendezvous with Peter, and their likely destination. He made a few educated guesses about the nature of their reunion. Later he'd sit down with her, Perelman figured, and winkle out the particulars. If they added up to serious problems, he was right there on hand with avuncular advice. Was Rivka in cahoots with Nina Vassilleva? And now with Peter the Painter? A hundred yards behind them, from the turning into Stepney Way, he gauged how closely they walked together, Rivka's head leaning toward Peter, his body loose and secure.

Are they lovers so soon? Where did it happen? Not in my house, I hope! Perelman asked himself, *How could it, with any of us around, Carlusha's curiosity, I'd hear a whisper. Ergo, therefore, cancel out the obvious, they must have been in Peter's bed while his friends played cards in the next room. Fritz and Luba. Jacob and Gardstein. Yoska. All the others, a third my age, a tenth of my experience. I juggle threats and promises and they juggle stolen silverware. Okhrana behind me, Special Branch in front, underground, above ground, then back under again, still light on my feet, dear girl, Rivka, I dance them a dance. While those Pan godlings of yours dance each other off the edge of a cliff!*

Peter and Rivka walked along to the quiet music of their conversation. Neither one led the other, they agreed on a direction without choosing a destination. He admired her (Peter told Rivka in his mildest language) for meeting the loss of both her 'situations' (he used the English word) so calmly, without crushing herself flat under a useless fit of desperation. 'Do you want me to ask Karl if he can talk things over with The Mayor?'

'Shinebloom's is finished for me,' Rivka said, though she sounded undefeated 'Nina gave me good advice. 'Do something else.' It's my own advice too.'

'Better opportunities, that's right.' He slipped the Pavilion playbill from his coat pocket, unfolded it for her and stopped so Rivka could read it. 'My assignment from Harry is to tell him if you like your name on there, or if you don't. Anyway, tell him one way or the other before the next one goes to the printer's.'

In Hebrew and English, from the well-known to the obscure, *tummlers* to escape artists, twenty acts decorated the little poster. 'Mine isn't on it.' Peter pressed his thumbnail underneath the last name on the bill. Through the underbrush of her accent Rivka pronounced her stage name. 'Anna Sout-ham d' Step-eny Song Bird. Songbird?'

'Anna Sou*th*'m, *the* Stepney Songbird.'

In those last two syllables, Rivka thought, rested all the alias's beauty. She knew 'song' and 'bird' but this was the first time she'd heard the two English words tethered together to name a third thing. It magicked an exotic picture into her mind, of a bird whose lifelong activity and sole purpose on earth was to perch in full sight of humanity and cry out its song. 'I don't know when I'll use it. Please, Peter, tell your friend it's a good name for me.'

'Yes? Good. I will.'

'It's beautiful.'

And so are you, he thought. The trick of her hair nearly brought that sweetness into his mouth. So primly brushed down, a schoolgirl's style, but somehow she made it look womanly. A beautiful transformation. *But remind yourself*, he thought, *beauty isn't the prize*. What is, then? To see her as she is. *Because I slept with a French whore and made believe her face was the face of the girl in Manet's painting.* He fell asleep curled around the ache that his room was not the bar of the Follies-Bergère. To hell with make-believe and the fictions you use to smash uncertainty. Do what you've

169

always done: name the thing when it shows itself. Yes, then. What do you call this? Peter felt the throb slide through his lungs, down his arms, into his palms. He left its thick emotion unvoiced, escorting Rivka past the Warsaw and on down Brick Lane.

Call it The Brink. Because that throb he felt had a jolt of fear mixed in it. Fear of dreaminess. Rhapsodic hope, love song of the anarchists he hated, who lived outside their bodies in a future always pure and perfect and remote. Here's the name of this fear: dreaming Rivka into a woman who never arrives. Peter imagined a future twenty-four hours away and its one real possibility. *I'd wake up with her in my cold room*. With that thought for company he was careful how he touched her. Careful not to communicate any particular feeling. Women are supernaturally sensitive to vibrations created by concealed emotions. Or by the concealing. *What do you call this?* Peter calmed himself with the thought, *Let it show itself in a simple action*. His hand found the small of her back and he guided Rivka around the tall wheels of a peddler's stall.

The cloudy tangle of ideas about her dissolved in his saying her name. 'Rivka... '

'Peter,' her echo. She teased him, 'Yoska's friend.'

'Yes.'

'Where are we going?'

'Shinebloom's,' he decided.

Rivka stopped to say, 'Not there. I don't want you to beg for me.'

'I'm taking you to Shinebloom's to eat lunch,' he smiled back. 'Let them serve you for a change.'

Rivka's excited laugh fired out of her like the shot of a starting gun. Her legs wanted to race and she tugged Peter's arm to hurry him towards Sclater Street.

Shinebloom's for lunch, after The Mayor sacked her, *because* he sacked her — she'd seen it now: a sample of Peter's easy genius. Karl bragged to her about it and Nina didn't disagree. For strategy and tactics, they said, *Go to Peter, he is a luminary.* 'I'm hungry!'

'That's a healthy sign,' he complimented her. 'We'll order all the side dishes.'

'Chew each bite twenty times.'

'Stay there for dinner, too, and we won't give up our table. We can talk for hours.'

'Will you tell me what you did that time in Kiev?'

He turned his face away from her and let go of a sharp sigh. 'What time?'

'The post office... No—' concentrating to get it right, '—a customs house.'

'So you heard the story from Karl. Why do you need it twice?'

'It's not just a story. You did something.'

'Not very much. We didn't grow wings or anything.'

'But you did it—'

'Did what?'

'Whatever you did, it was for a reason.' Rivka let the implied question hang in the air.

So did Peter. 'It's all just roaring,' he said, then clamped his lips.

'Sorry.' She let her hand drop away from his arm. 'I thought you felt easy enough with me.'

A few slow steps in a vacuum of silence took them to the corner of Sclater Street. Peter said, 'Did Karl also tell you I'm not a Jew?'

'He didn't say anything about it.' Rivka wondered how the question mattered. 'Are you?'

'No.' To let her in on something true about himself, that was his reason, and to stand there and make sure she

171

believed it. To see Rivka believing the truth about him. Beginning with this. 'My life isn't settled, you understand? I make money any way I can. Any place I can find work. They chased me out of Latvia. I'm through with Russia, too. So for the sake of survival, mine, not anybody else's, not Liesma's, in Germany I'm a German. In Marseille I'm a Frenchman. In Paris, or here, with Jews all around me I'm a Jew. It's my freedom, you understand? It means I'm free to run for cover. Things aren't right in this city? Good. I'll go to that one. Also it's a trap, how I live, Rivka, my life is a permanent *offence*. A day doesn't go by I don't worry, *Do they know I'm hiding, pretending I'm harmless, the bastards who want to finish me?* I know how they think — there it is, I'm hiding from them so their suspicions about me must be right. Round and around.'

Rivka thought, *He's a Jew who doesn't know he is*. She said, 'It was a good thing, what happened to me. Until last week I was a baby. Stupid. Blind in both eyes. No, I knew about dangers in the world. Was sure I did. Russians, God knows. They came out of the ground one at a time: there's no *crop* of dangers. What I say now is, *Thank you, Englishmen*. Before last Friday I didn't know, yes, it *is* a crop, something bigger is underneath them- they're the part of it you can *see*. I didn't know what goes on.'

The teenage Russian soldier, his commanding officer Orlov, the Russian gendarmes, the policeman by Big Ben, her interrogators, her torturers, the Tsar, the King, the Kaiser — all of them the same malicious crop. The correct terms escaped her, the political language Karl and Nina used, Peter's language; she groped to describe a grand revelation and it crudely shrank into a picture of her world, *the* world, divided into sides white and black. Eager and stammering Rivka started, started again and kept trying to tell him she'd faced the reality that he'd been

172

facing for years: this struggle between sides deals you opportunities to declare your loyalty and morality. And hatreds. Before her days in prison and talk with Nina, she didn't realise these were political feelings. Political *ideas*.

'I don't know how to say it.' Then she tried again. 'Here's the side my feet are on.'

'Here? 'Here'?'

'With you and Karl and Nina.'

'To do what?'

'What I can.'

'Karl doesn't need you to sing or wipe tables.'

'He thinks I can help him. And Nina. She thinks so.' Underneath the grain, a simple, human force. 'They helped me. I want to help them.'

The door to Shinebloom's opened. Two customers ambled into the street, lit their cigars and for a few seconds brought the rumble of the room outside with them. Peter's touch on her shoulder kept Rivka from going inside. 'How? Did he say?'

'Nina will tell me tomorrow. She's taking me to meet somebody.'

'You should turn them down.'

'I already promised them yes.'

'Whatever it is, it won't make a difference. It's a mosquito bite.' By now Peter didn't care if what he said was an insult to her intentions or trustworthiness. 'Do something to help yourself — keep out of trouble.'

'Too late for your help, but thanks for it,' a jet of anger in her publicly hushed voice. 'I've got a father and one's enough for me.'

'You're not the kind who listens to her father,' Peter joked, lightly serious.

From Nina's ear to his. Common property. 'Even when he's right,' she admitted. 'I made a mistake. It taught me.'

173

'Tomorrow you can add one more to learn from. Rivka, think for a minute. It's better to be a singer once a week than a criminal from now on, no?'

If that was true then the calamities she'd survived weren't much more than portions of bad luck. Her long talk with Karl and Nina armed her with a reply. 'I'm not a criminal. I'm a fighter.'

Straight from the manual, Peter almost said out loud. A criminal is a counter-revolutionary who wants to join the established order. A criminal is a professional who robs, steals and swindles to make a bourgeois life for himself. A revolutionary fighter is the enemy of every criminal. A revolutionary fighter breaks any law to overthrow the old world and punish its supporters... He dropped the subject, held the door open for Rivka and both of them were swamped by the steamy kitchen odours of Shinebloom's. At their table Peter looked at Rivka from a great distance.

As expected, The Mayor bounced over to them wringing his hands, overflowing with apology. 'Of course you can come back after things have cooled down', he told Rivka, 'Pray God it's soon. If anybody does, you know what can happen to a business in the district if the police want to make trouble. No charge for your meal today. You're welcome here, both of you, both of you.' He'd interpreted Peter's quiet attendance there with Rivka as a warning, or a gentle reminder of what the Liesma gang thinks of ex-friends.

'Do you know what you want to eat?' Peter said.

'Wednesday's a bad day for fish. Probably the brisket.'

'Brisket.'

'You?'

'Cabbage and apples is good here. Maybe some soup. Potato soup.'

174

A moment or two and Rivka said, 'Did you ask him for bread and margarine?'

'He'll bring it.'

'I'll ask him.'

The Mayor himself served the food to them. Peter watched Rivka eat. She chewed big bites, mouth open, a farm girl underneath. Peter ate his cabbage in fastidious, even dainty, forkfuls while the distance across the table widened. A familiar feeling, a good one that saved his skin more than once. Let any affection for Rivka grow and as sure as salt is salty it's going to be a weight around his neck, anchoring him there, dragging him backwards.

Rivka waved at someone Peter couldn't see through the hedge of other diners. Then Yoska stood up like a buried man shaking the earth off his legs, and Peter saw: it was Jacob Peters — still sitting at the table, slouched back in his chair — who returned Rivka's hello with a kind of salute. Three fingers drawn downward, roughened by old scars, his thumb and forefinger stiff, in the shape of a pistol.

II

THE CRIME

One

'Friends on every side,' Karl's words, Gardstein's guarantee in that East End neighbourhood, and he added for Peter's further peace of mind, 'You couldn't be safer in Grove Street.' But Peter didn't feel safe anymore in Fritz and Luba's first-floor flat. Or, come to that, within ten miles of an action in the making. Where are you safe if life and limb depends on the quick thinking of careless people, the attention of the absent-minded, the comradeship of the selfish, the judgment of the fallible? *Leave London*, he thought. For where? Back to France? North, then. Manchester. In Manchester he could get by. Right now staying in a safe house in London was a dangerous arrangement. There were cracks in Liesma under Karl, this Peter knew — he saw them walking, talking, eating in Shinebloom's, and at the moment he was playing gin rummy with one of them.

'Fritz,' Peter had to prod him. 'Staring at it won't turn that six of hearts into a jack.'

'It's my go?'

'Yours.'

'How do you know I want a jack?'

Peter didn't say, *How does anybody know anything? By watching.*

'I'll throw down,' Fritz decided. But he sat still, reading the cards in his hand, his other hand stuttering toward the face-down deck.

Peter lit a cigarette. 'You want me to decide for you?'

'Sorry.' He threw down a card, plucked at random,

grabbed up a replacement from the deck, stuffed it in the sloppy fan of nine others he was holding.

Peter drew from the deck and folded his hand. It was the tenth or eleventh game in a row he'd won. 'Glad we're not playing for money?'

'Aren't we?' Fritz didn't know whether he should feel relieved. On a good day he was a rotten card player and today wasn't a good day. His attention wandered back and forth between the game and the back bedroom where he'd left Luba still in bed, grim, sulky, close to tears. A few hands of rummy with Peter was a good enough reason to free himself from Luba's festering mood.

'We don't have to play any more if your mind's not on it.'

'My mind's not on card games,' Fritz agreed.

'Talk to her.'

'Let her stew. Deal another one.' Fritz watched the fresh ten cards blow toward him like dead leaves then swept them into the heap he gathered in his hand. Then he proposed the motion, 'Karl should trust me more.'

'More than what? Or who?' Peter glanced at his cards, moved them more than he had to, gave nothing away.

'Peter, you think he trusts me, that's what I'm asking. His opinion of me. If he thinks I'm a good man, that's my best hope.'

'I'm sure he does,' Peter confirmed it. 'You picked up the three. You have to discard.'

Fritz threw down the card he'd just added to his hand. 'I want to help him with his "dance"' — he spoke the word softly, with a glance over his shoulder — 'in Houndsditch. Did he talk to you about it?'

'I'm not in it this time. What could he get from me?'

Fritz sluggishly raised and lowered his shoulders. 'He's

a genius, I think, Karl's a real brainstormer. He's a master, in my opinion.'

Peter folded his hand for the eleventh or twelfth time. 'Sorry, my friend.'

The loss doubled him inward, this jittery man with the booming voice he usually failed to keep a lid on, his wide square back hunched forward, all his nervousness packed inside it. 'You're a master too. At cards.'

Peter said, 'If there's something you can say to help it, you should go say it to her. Pinch the fuse.'

Fritz nodded, sighed. 'Deal one more.'

'In my experience if you ignore it,' Peter said, dabbing ash from his cigarette, 'it gets worse.'

Fritz grinned. His mouth refused to do anything else. 'I go in there, I want to be out here playing rummy. I don't know what I want. Not so strong up here—' he tapped his forehead '—in my belfry. Not like before.'

'Before Luba?'

'Her? No!'

Fritz pushed himself to his feet without explaining what 'before' he meant, and strayed back to his bedroom. Peter heard him say Luba's name and tilt the door half-closed. *Do what you can.* Uncomfortable thoughts nagged at Peter. Morally summoned, he thought about Rivka. What could he do? Try to talk her out of whatever it was that Nina and Karl had talked her into doing for them.

Luba's mood fouled the shut-in air of the back bedroom. She'd kept it up, this 'persecution' of Fritz, for two days, without an obvious reason. 'Worse than the Russian secret police' — that's what he told her before tramping off to play cards in the other room, 'You're worse than the Okhrana.'

Luba had uncovered the pistol when she was looking for a place to store Fritz's clean undershirt. It wasn't there

181

the day before, sandwiched between his second pair of socks and the two boat tickets to Australia. Luba convinced herself that Fritz had bought one of those tickets for her, even if it was in an envelope with his wife's name written on it.

Her lover was a married man, his wife waited for him in Russia, this she knew from the start. Now she'd found out something about him, about the kind of man Fritz might be, that wasn't so clear-cut. *What was this gentle man doing with a gun?* So Luba stayed in bed, under the blanket, pillow over her head, on into the afternoon. Fritz's weight on the edge of the mattress rolled her a little towards him, unavoidably.

She pulled the pillow aside and said, 'You were gone a long time.'

'He's a good card-player. It took me six hands to win one.'

Luba propped herself on her elbows, brought her need closer to him, in her relaxed mouth and unrested eyes. He gave her the same steady look he gave a hand of shuffled cards, trying hard to read some order and pattern into the uncrackable combinations dealt to him. She helped his trouble by saying, 'Do you want to kiss me?'

'I like kissing you. I thought you didn't like it anymore.'

'Kiss me, then.'

Fritz twirled his hands, a speechless complaint, *You say one thing and mean the opposite.*

Until the begging in her eyes seeped downward into her voice. 'Kiss me, will you, Fritz, please, please, don't you want to?'

He plunged into Luba and she spread under him like a bath of warm water. Frantic fingers, hers, his, peeled back Fritz's clothes down to the porridge whiteness of his skin. His passive flesh made Luba want to bite it, tear at it with her fingernails, to bring warm redness to the surface.

Fury whirled inside them both. Luba slapped at him and Fritz bore down with his bulky strength; he locked her arms, bit her cheek when she bit his, he thrashed around on top of her, the blind throes of a landed fish. Limbs pounded the bed, which squealed underneath them, a noise hard to separate from the human gasps, sighs and dying whines, easily heard through the wall, not so easy to tell if it was love play or a fist fight going on in there. A mercy, Peter thought, it was over in a hurry.

In the aftermath — rather than afterglow — they were separate again. Luba kept her face turned away from Fritz, who sat up and, twirled his hands, speechless again. 'Wasn't that what you wanted?' She nodded her head. 'What's *wrong*, then? Look at me. Luba.'

If this was the moment when she might open him up she could be Obliging Luba — why not? She showed Fritz her unsmiling face. He was the one begging now. He asked her again what was wrong.

'You don't tell me the truth,' Luba told him, fearlessly.

Insulted, practically dumbfounded: 'Always! I *always* tell you —'

'Uh!' she cut in. 'Here comes another lie.'

'You don't know what you're talking about.'

'I know, Fritz, I *do* know. I've got two eyes in my head and they both work.' She took those heavy-lidded dark blue lanterns off of Fritz and aimed them at the low dresser at the foot of the bed.

'What is it?' agitated now, baited. 'You want to start a fight about my wife? No. Why? What lie did I tell you? Judith told you I was married our first time together. When I say different?'

Luba sprang. She sat up, let the blanket fall from her. 'Where do you get your money, Fritz?'

'You don't have to worry about it,' the flat reply.

183

'How do you make money?'

'I told you ten times.'

'Never. Where?' Luba prodded his arm. 'Tell me again.'

'Locksmith,' he said.

'A locksmith who doesn't go to work. You never have a job!' She thought of the bits of jewellery he brought to her now and then, romantic little presents, some Belgian lace, dinners at Shinebloom's.

'I hear your brothers talking. They don't like it because I'm not a Jew. They don't know anything. Less than *you* know.'

'You can't talk about them! They're in *business*, Fritz! My brothers know how men earn a living every day.'

'Yes? Do they know how much a locksmith makes on a job? Do you? How much?'

'More than nothing.'

'*Much* more! Enough to live for a while.'

'Then why do I have to pay our rent? And without a key of my own to the front door!'

'You don't pay, I pay.'

'Liar! Three times out of my pocket, seven shillings and six pence, three weeks I paid! You can't even tell the truth to yourself.'

'Be quiet.'

'Not about this.'

'About what? You're crazy, Luba. Let go of me.'

'No.'

Fritz yanked his arm from her and pulled his shirt on. 'Craziness. Go back to sleep. Wake up different.'

'What do you do? Where do you go?' Luba's strength held through the soggy trembling in her throat. 'I don't know what you do!'

'Good. You don't have to worry. Me neither.' Buttoning his trousers, buttoning up the argument. He tilted his head to listen to men's voices in the other room. Peter talking with Karl. Then he felt Luba's small hand on his arm again.

'We live as husband and wife,' she said softly. 'I know something. I saw what you keep in there.'

Fritz moved to the dresser drawer, pushed by an instinct for self-protection. He opened it and with relief he saw his Browning pistol was right where he'd left it. 'Did you touch anything? The bullets?' Luba shook her head. 'This is none of your business.' Then he said, glancing out the window, 'This place. There are crooks around here. Street robbers. A man can't go outside unprotected.' Fritz twitched away from her, eager to be part of the conversation in the other room. 'I'm good to you,' he said. As he stepped away, he caught a a glimpse of Luba covering herself up with the blanket. 'I'll come back in a minute. I have to say hello to Karl.'

A sincere smile from Karl could be as promising as any from a chorus girl. Fritz found Peter playing solitaire, Karl quietly restless. 'Karl,' he said with a boyish wave as he shuffled over to explain with raised eyebrows and hushed voice, 'Luba, she's, you know how, she—'

'Giving Fritz his marching orders,' Peter finished Fritz's apology.

'You're wrong, Peter.' Fritz took the teasing seriously. 'She needed handling.'

'Trouble's settled now?' Karl asked him.

'No trouble.'

Peter anted, 'Just a lot of noise.'

'Noise.' Fritz shrugged it off. 'Yoska says you've got a thing going.'

'You want to help?' Karl said in Lettish.

'Anything,' Fritz answered in the same language. 'Whatever I can. It's an action?'

Peter heard the fractured, unreliable soul shuffle under Fritz's eagerness, just as Karl did; but if it worried Liesma's boss, he didn't show it. 'We need some equipment. Malatesta is organising it for us.'

'What kind?'

'Also some money.'

'From Malatesta?'

'How much cash do you have, Fritz?'

'Some. A little.'

'We need a hundred roubles. It's for Malatesta. You have to meet him in Islington, his workshop. All right?'

'Sure, Karl. That's what you want me for?'

Karl heard Fritz's disappointment, flicked it into the air. 'No, no. Can you collect these things from him, oxygen tanks, some rubber hose, pay him ten pounds?' Into Fritz's nodding Yes, Yes, Karl went on, 'And then do something else.' He unfolded a scrap of paper and showed Fritz the address on it. 'Rent this place for us. Flat 9, Exchange Buildings. It's in Houndsditch. You can find it all right?'

'Houndsditch, sure.'

'You have to use your own money. Only a few shillings. Five or six, that's all.'

'Six shillings,' Fritz repeated, another item of inventory. 'What is it? A safe?' Fritz caught the insider's glance Peter traded with Karl and concluded, 'Who's your locksmith?'

'What do we need a locksmith for? With a cutting torch.'

'In case something goes wrong with it,' Fritz suggested.

'We'll have Yourka Dubof with us.'

'Yourka, with the young fingers.'

'I want you for the second team. If we're still working after thirty-six hours. Yes? That's three weights on your back.'

Fritz soberly recited the duties he'd accepted. 'Get the

186

cylinders from Malatesta, rent the flat, wait thirty-six hours. Good. All right, Karl. Yes. When?'

'Three weeks from Friday. Between you and me if we're out of that place by Saturday night I'll light a candle in St Basil's.'

Solitaire played out, Peter said, 'I'll sing *Sanctus Agnus Dei* in the choir.'

Karl ignored the scepticism and asked Fritz, 'Luba's here usually, isn't she? Saturdays? Sundays?'

'I can send her away. She can go to her brother's.'

'No, she's usually here, she should be here. She's here?'

'Today, yes.'

Karl called her name. Then Fritz did, and added, 'Bring the watches from the box. *All* of them.' Luba slumped into the room, barefoot, loosely dressed, hair unpinned. She handed over three gold watches to Fritz. 'Where's the other one?'

'Mine?' she said.

'It's not yours, I gave it to you. Go get it.'

When she brought back the small rose gold pocket watch, engraved with a cottage on one side and a bluebird in flight on the other, Fritz gestured for her to show it to Karl. As he examined it Fritz said, 'Yoska can talk three or four pounds out of Beron.' Karl handed it back to Fritz, who promised Luba, 'You'll get it back.'

Innocence mixed with crookedness. *Fritz probably believes what he told her*, Peter considered. No serious change. Everything serene, life as normal. There's safety for you, the appearance of normality, safety in remaining undiscovered, disappearing beneath the surface by mirroring the surface. Peter didn't ask his friend about how Rivka fit into the Houndsditch plan. Three weeks. Enough time, with the right kind of dedication, to dig that out for himself.

Two

Rivka carried herself on quiet, not stealthy, but careful footsteps along the front hallway toward the living-room door. A song from the ancient days of childhood chirped in her mind's ear, a Lettish folk song about a brave little row boat stroking away from the calm harbour on its first voyage into the wildness of the open sea. Mid-afternoon Rivka expected the room to be fireless and vacant; she saw Perelman before he saw her and would have ducked back into the hallway if he hadn't glanced up from his newspaper.

Apology for the intrusion, finger aimed at the black marble clock on the mantelshelf, she said, 'It's so late?'

Perelman boyishly kicked his heels in front of the coal fire that fought back the chill from the window onto the street. 'Where are you going on such a rotten day?'

'To an appointment,' Rivka said.

'For work?'

'Yes, I hope.'

'Good, very good. Where?'

'And visiting a friend,' thinking quickly, speaking calmly.

'You need something warm inside you,' he said, 'before you go out in that mucky weather. Do you have time to drink some tea?'

Trapped here, twenty minutes to wait. 'One cup. Thank you, yes.'

'Deborah brought English tea cakes home yesterday. You be the lady,' swivelling the teapot's handle Rivka's way, 'I'll be the lord.' She refilled his teacup and poured her own, he served her a freshly warmed teacake from a tray above the fire and with mild interest asked Rivka how far she had to travel to her appointment.

'I don't know,' she said truthfully. 'It's some place I don't know.'

'Can you find it all right? Tell me where you have to go.'

She gave him the first name that came into her head, 'Aldgate Pump.' *Owled Gade Poomp.*

Perelman corrected her pronunciation then made an offer. 'I'm free for—' quick scrutiny of the clock, 'two hours and twenty minutes. I can take you there.'

'No, please, my friend's brother, he's waiting for me at two o'clock. He'll walk with me over there.'

The sincerity in Perelman's eyes spread into his soft words. 'I don't want you to get lost, sweetheart. Where would I get another lodger who sings so beautiful?'

'I know I owe you two weeks' rent—'

'Ssh, ssh.'

'—I keep a record. I'll pay it soon, Mr Perelman.'

'We know each other long enough you can call me Charles.'

'In three weeks,' she promised him. 'I'll have money then. By the new year.'

'Ssh, ssh. If you're working again, if you're well enough, that's what counts.' Then he wondered out loud, 'I thought Nina was going to help you. Don't they have money these days?'

'They did help. They are.'

'You're a respectful child,' he said. 'Do you know Peter very well?'

'Karl's friend?'

'Piatkow. Your Peter.'

'Not mine,' she smiled.

190

Perelman mirrored back the smile, raked his fingers through his thick brown hair, a mild flirtation. 'He doesn't like to talk, does he? Not to me. Maybe not to *men* very much.'

'He likes to talk about paintings. He took me to see some.'

'Talked about them. Lectured you.. Showed off how much he knows about painting because he was in Paris, am I right? This man's got geography in his heart where romance should be!'

Through their laughter, Rivka said, 'Did Peter have a woman the last time he was here?'

Perelman showed her his empty hands, ignorant or discreet. 'So he doesn't have a word to say to you on *that* subject. He didn't treat you bad, did he?'

'You think he's a cold fish.'

'No — Peter? Definitely no. But men act different with other men. I should ask you how he acts with a woman, with you.'

'Not cold.'

This smile Perelman didn't return, his voice suddenly intimate and serious. 'You and Fanny, you two are good friends.' Rivka heard this as a question and she answered with a nod. 'She gossips.' Perelman said. 'So you probably know from her how my wife goes with other men.'

'No,' Rivka fibbed.

'She does. It's all right with me. A younger woman needs excitement, doesn't she? Also comfort, which she doesn't want from me, one thing I can give her, give a woman. Nothing to do with how old a man is.' The roomy silence he left for some encouraging reply from Rivka was broken soon enough by an accidental knock on the wall. Perelman put a stiff finger to his lips then jabbed it towards a child's stockinged foot jutting from its hiding

191

place behind the armchair in the corner near the door. Theatrically obvious, Perelman stood up saying, 'Rivka, did you see Carlusha upstairs? Poor boy's bedridden.'

'Oh no. Is he very ill?' Dripping worry, 'You want me to look in on him?'

'Terrible congestion in the chest, so I kept him home from school today...' Perelman dropped heavily into the armchair, swooped his hand downward, grabbed his son's ankle and hauled him out. 'Little piglet! What are you doing?'

A giggling squeal, then one of pain when Perelman gave Carlusha's foot a twist. 'Spying on you,' the boy confessed.

'You're a terrible spy,' his father's judgment.

'I found out things.'

'And I found *you*. If I was the Okhrana I could drag you back to Russia.' Without letting go of Carlusha's flailing leg, Perelman said to Rivka, 'I'll have to teach him.'

Whether he meant a lesson in morality or in the basics of espionage, Rivka wasn't sure. Carlusha in tow, still squealing, Perelman escorted Rivka out the front door. He remained there with the purpose, apparently, of punishing the boy with public humiliation, but he kept an eye on Rivka long enough to see her meet a man at the turning of Stepney Way, somebody whose identity Perelman couldn't completely make out.

If he'd disguised himself as a tree, Perelman would have heard Max Smoller identify himself to Rivka by saying, 'Yoska told me how you looked. The freckles.' True, persistent flecks across her forehead and the bridge of her nose, undefeated by English winter.

'You're Max?' Rivka said. 'My husband for today.' He wouldn't be her husband in a thousand years, this man who for one thing, looked twice her age.

192

'I didn't give my real name where we're going. Never do that. The one we're going to see, Millard, I told him my name is Levi. I'm Joe Levi. So remember, don't call me Max. And you should pick a different name too.'

'Gerte, then.'

'Why "Gerte"?' Max asked as they strolled.

'Gerte worked in the bakery where I worked.'

'Here?'

'At home. Sasmacken.'

'That's all right, then. In front of Millard I'll call you Gertie. But you don't have to open your mouth. Are you good at acting? Yoska says you're a singer.'

Rivka saw a flash of rigidity in his brush-cut hair and crudity in his thick nose and heavy lips, and a hair-trigger tension in his eyes that wasn't calming. The undeniable *scent* coming off him was of a man who wasn't born with enough subtlety to see her in her true light. So he'd overpower her instead.

Yes, she could act. To play Mrs Joe Levi she needed a story to explain the circumstances to herself. As they walked to Houndsditch Rivka invented their history: *Joe is my distant cousin, his family took me in when I was a child, after the Russians murdered my parents in a pogrom, I looked up to Joe as a protector, he was going to be married but the girl changed her mind, 'I love you, Gerte,' he gave his love to me, three years ago, I was sixteen...*

'Don't make him suspicious. He thinks Jews are worse than gypsies,' Max advised her. 'You speak any English?'

'Not as much as I think I do,' Rivka admitted.

'Well, don't say anything. If he asks you something, look at me and I'll answer for you.'

Where it comes to foreigners, what kind of behaviour don't Englishmen find suspicious? For the next hour or two, she figured, she'd act as if she knew They were watching her, and gave herself that one guiding advantage, something They didn't credit her with the brains to know.

Except for a brisk nod of welcome, Mr Millard, the landlord, ignored Rivka's presence in his office. As she stood invisibly in front of him he made a demonstration of general respect for Max, or Joe, as head of the Levi household. Rivka trailed a step behind them and was left out of the small talk on the short walk down Cutler Street to No. 11 Exchange Buildings. She heard Mr Millard ask Max if his wife spoke English.

'Not much,' Max said. 'Not much of anything else, either,' he joked, reminding Rivka to keep quiet.

'Your present home must be a blessedly quiet place,' Mr Millard joked back, 'It's quiet here, you're a good distance away from the street.'

Deaf and dumb Mrs Levi's first view of Exchange Buildings wasn't of a place but of a secret event, an approaching event that her own visit to No. 11 brought closer. From the foot of the narrow staircase that led to the bedroom above, she looked outside at the two storeys of soot shadowed brick walls, the green wooden shutters sealed against the street level windows, the cul-de-sac off Cutler Street, and found herself mulling tactical thoughts. *Where could we run if the policemen raid us? Will it be suspicious to leave the shutters closed? Dangerous to leave them open?*

Max called to her. 'Gertie, come up.' Rivka answered him in weary Yiddish on her way up the stairs and overheard Joe Levi say to their new landlord, 'No children, no. Somewhere for me and my wife. The same price as the other one?'

'Ten a week. Shillings, not pounds, don't worry,' his landlordly joke. 'The good thing here Mr Levi is we can have this ready for you by the end of the week. You don't have to wait for No. 9.' Deal done, a half-turn toward Rivka to add, 'And it's so handy for the West End.'

The rooms were bare, poky and dim, the dull light the grimy windows let through greyed the place even more. Rivka tried to look like a wife eyeing up the living space. *A bed here, a chiffonier in the corner, a chair over there,* unsuspicious appraisals she hoped showed on her face. Believing the fiction, her defence against being unmasked. 'Joe, *vu is der kloset?*'

Max translated the question. Mr Millard pointed to the yard below, then slid aside so Max and Rivka could see the narrow alleyway where the lavatory stood — a small brick hut in a row of others between Exchange Buildings and the backs of the shops in Houndsditch. Rivka frowned her satisfaction and un-asked for approval. Max and Mr Millard shook hands, money emptied out of one pocket and folded into another, the curtain came down on Rivka's first and last turn as Gerte Levi.

Out in the street again, their new landlord left them with a signed-and-sealed wave, as they window-shopped in front of H.S. Harris Jewellers.

Three

That *schvantz* changed his mind, said meet him here, *thought Perelman.* To get under my skin. Make me wait. Show me who's on top. Ten more minutes and that's all, that's me, the end.

He angled the brim of his wide hat against the drizzle that began to fall as he stood alone in the lea of Bevis Marks. Inconspicuous as a parade, he tucked himself into his cape, stamped his feet on cold rusty flagstones, then paced away from the synagogue entrance. A reluctant Jew exposed to the weather. From inside, the hum of Friday night services reached Charles Perelman through the bright arched windows. Socialist revolutionary or no, it took an effort not to feel affected by the Erev Shabbat gathering-in. Hebrew prayers and hymns ringed this orderly convention of Jews, and with his dark Ashkenazi looks, Perelman was one of them, by implication. Nobody asked him about it. He knew how Jews operated with Jews: claim you as a brother then they have the right, the *duty*, to tell you how to be a good Jew! Protest, object to them and you're a turncoat, worse than the *goyim*, than the Egyptians even!

A Good Jew can't be a socialist, a rabbi once lectured him, *let alone a revolutionary.* And revolutionaries of his acquaintance never stop telling him and each other how to be a Good Socialist. In Perelman they're up against somebody who fought with the burden of their *meschuga* claims; the Jews, revolutionists, police. Among them all, Charles Perelman was the only free man in London. He

197

stood in the middle of a bridge, Socialists ahead and Jews behind him. Or was that Russia behind him and England ahead? Or the Okhrana behind him and Special Branch ahead? Or Liesma ahead, maybe behind him too. What does that make the turbulent waters underneath his bridge? He stopped pacing, slightly confused now, the metaphor crumbling into nonsense. But, *but*, Perelman assured himself, he was free to be a Good Man as he reckoned it. For what other reason was he standing outside Bevis Marks on a wet Friday night freezing his *kishkas*?

The answer echoed back to him, performing a Charitable Act. Protecting Rivka with his loyalty and conscience and strength of spirit. Without her knowing she had a guardian angel at her shoulder. For Rivka's sake he'd lower himself to wait in the rain, in the shadow of the old synagogue, hang on to meet his contact, by now a quarter of an hour late. Strictly speaking this was not disrespect. Ten more minutes, *then* it would be disrespect and the *putznasher* might arrive with hot soup and a mouthful of apology to find Perelman gone.

'Charles?'

Perelman half-turned his head. 'Who else?'

Henry Wagner always looked overworked to Perelman. Worn thin even for a young man serving two masters: the Jewish community and the City of London Police. Beyond what he could see, Perelman knew next to nothing about his handler, an unfairness that rankled tonight more than usual.

'Not a comfortable place to meet,' Wagner offered, no soup in hand, 'Sorry.'

'This is cold? Try walking through a Russian field in January, my friend.'

Wagner strolled away from the lamp above the

synagogue door, an invitation for Perelman to do the same. 'I saw the big Rothschild here. High Holy Days. Top hats, very grand.'

The congregation voices answered the rabbi's in a sea swell of *Omain*. Perelman smiled back at the building. 'Jewish parliament. Baa-baa. I'm still a socialist.'

'What noise does a socialist make, then?'

'We talk like human beings.'

'Are we going to have a political discussion or is there something going on?'

The chivvying from him! Perelman thought, *Let him whistle for it.* 'Wagner. That's your real name? You only go by Wagner?'

'Of course.'

'Why "of course"? "Of course" you wouldn't lie to me.'

'I'm no liar.'

'How would I know?'

'Because in six months you haven't had any surprises,' Wagner said narrowly. 'No visits from the Okhrana.'

'I'm not sure.'

'They come to visit you, it isn't something you'd mistake for the milkman.'

'Russians or not, Okhrana are *secret* police, Mr Wagner.'

'They like to think so. Big boots. Nothing like us.'

'Who?'

The two men stood close enough for Wagner to flap his fingers between his chest and Perelman's. 'You and me.'

'Your inspector, he treats you equal? I mean,' Perelman professorially cleared his throat. 'In the police do they treat you the same as an Englishman?'

'Twice as good. I'm the Englishman who speaks Yiddish.'

'That's what they tell you. My friend, you think you're standing on solid ground –' he stamped the pavement under his boot — 'but take it from me, you're in the middle of a bridge.'

Drizzle fattened into a steady rain and underneath it, without an umbrella, Wagner lost whatever interest he'd had in Charles Perelman's philosophic ideas. 'Is something going on?'

'Definitely. Yes. Something.'

'What do you know about it? Where, when?'

Perelman raised his finger, advising patience. 'I've got somebody in place. With Liesma.'

'Who is he?'

'Somebody close to Peter the Painter.'

'So do we,' Wagner said. 'We haven't heard anything.'

'Who's your man in there?' Perelman bartered.

'Who's yours?' Keen silence from Wagner.

The same from Perelman. 'Then you should have the same information I do.'

'I don't pay for stale rumours. Something for something and he knows it. You know it too.'

'It's money,' Peter ventured, a money job, a robbery. Soon.'

'Nothing more definite?'

'Aldgate Pump. In around three weeks. My contact owes me money and promised to get it before January.'

'What's in Aldgate?' Wagner thought out loud. 'No factories. Banks? A bank? Is the Painter here for another Tottenham? That's no good for anybody.'

'You never met Salnish,' Perelman guessed. 'The wild-crazy Russian who ran Liesma before Karl.'

'No.'

'Here's something for nothing: Peter the Painter, he's worse. He'll shoot you if he doesn't like your shoes.'

'Get me good information, Charles, better than this. Where and when, who's involved.'

'As long as I can protect my informant.'

'Then you'd better tell me who he is. Otherwise if we lift the lot of them I can't help.'

'I'm her protector, you follow me?'

'If I'm not discreet what am I? Her name. Her alias,' Wagner urged him. 'Who is she?'

'No. She's my responsibility.' Then he casually recalled, 'Nina Vassilleva came to my house a week ago.'

Wagner said, 'She's no leaky bucket. When did she ever spill anything?'

'Not her. My girl's close to Piatkow, I said, the Painter.' Perelman wouldn't say any more and turned to listen to the singing in the temple. The cantor's clear tenor floated the Adon Olam above the clattering rain, a benediction.

Wagner heard it too and it made him eager to leave. He pocketed his pencil, closed his small black notebook. 'They're coming out any minute. Get her to give you real information, Charles, something that will help us stop them. The place, the date, accomplices.'

But Perelman's thoughts were in midair with the trailing notes of sacred song. 'An island,' he said to the synagogue's tall bright windows. 'An island on an island.'

A waste of fifteen minutes, Wagner almost said out loud before he dissolved into the foot traffic churning homeward. '*A meshugener zol men oyshraybn, un im araynshraybn.*' They should free a madman, and lock him up. Henry Wagner left there favouring a possibility lately tossed round H Division, that the Okhrana were chasing a different C. Perelman altogether.

Four

Fritz ripped the door back with such a burst of force the hinges rattled. Big feet planted, thick body braced, eyes exploding with the emergency, clowning around. 'Help me! I can't tune my mandolin!'

Nicholas Tomacoff grinned back at him. 'How did you know it was me?' Mild as a schoolboy, almost as young.

'You're the last one here! Everybody's waiting for music, come on.' Fritz corralled him inside, arm swung round Nicholas's shoulders.

'Who's waiting?'

Peeking through the front bedroom doorway, he saw Peter hunched in a chair, concentrating on a game of chess with the one they called the Barber, whose other name was John Rosen. The Painter and the Barber. George Gardstein, Fritz's cousin Jacob, four women and three more men, quietly talking together, drinking, smoking cigarettes, a music hall crowd waiting for the show to begin. Fritz pulled Nicholas into the back bedroom where the mandolin he'd been playing for all of three weeks lay on the bed beside his prop wooden sword.

'I can't tune it right,' Fritz accused the instrument. 'Maybe there's something wrong with the, the, the —'

'Tuning pegs?'

'The pegs, they don't keep the note.'

Nicholas tuned the mandolin by ear, strummed a quick run of chords and handed it back to Fritz. 'Have you been practising?'

'Sure, sure. All three songs.'

Nicholas cradled his own balalaika between his knees now. 'Which one do you play the best?'

'Last night we played 'Petersburg Road,' me and Peter. Violin sounds good with mandolin.'

'We'll start with that one, then. You think he'll play with us tonight?' Nicholas's fingers dashed up and down the balalaika's neck, skill of a higher order, a little flashy, stopped when he saw the guns and boxes of ammunition on top of the chest of drawers. The Browning automatic was disassembled for cleaning. The long barrelled Mauser, blocky and weighty, sat practically on display. As he looked them over Nicholas felt a rush of something like fascinated embarrassment, as if he'd accidentally opened a bedroom door and seen the lady of the house naked. (Since the squabble with Luba over the guns, Fritz was defiantly less careful about keeping his firearms out of sight.)

Fritz, Nicholas, mandolin and balalaika appeared in the fog bank of cigarette smoke. The air was even thicker in the living-room, a different season from the one settled stern and cold in the street. A different country: England outside, Russia and Latvia inside. Fritz waved Peter's violin case. 'We're playing 'Petersburg Road.' Little Tomacoff is homesick.'

Peter took the command for the invitation it was, tipped his king on its side, conceded the chess game with a nod and picked up his violin. Above the loud talking it was hard for Peter to hear if the three instruments were in tune. Which didn't matter much anyway, since they were drowned out by Fritz's barrack room howling. '*Vdol po Piterskoi, po darozhinkye, po Tverskoi-Yamskoi, s karakoltshikom . . .*'

Along the Petersburg Road,
along the small lane

A STORM IN THE BLOOD

to the Tverskoi-Yamskoi Quarter
with a little bell...

'How many different ways can you refuse to answer one question?' Peter said to Rivka over the noise in the room.

'As many ways as you can ask it.'

'Rivka, you think I'm an informer or something?' Peter kidded her, and her naïveté.

'You can ask me and ask me.'

'Because there's not much time left,' he said, turning serious. 'So tell me: What did you do for Nina and Karl?' He paused a moment, then gave her another push out of her silence. 'I'm not trying to make trouble for you. The opposite,'

'What do you make when you make the opposite of trouble?' she asked him.

'It's a riddle?'

'I'm counting to ten.'

'Then you know what the right answer is.'

'Do you? One ... two ...'

Peter scratched the beard on his chin, then his moustache, an exhibition of deep thinking. 'Security. Comfort.'

'... six ... Which?'

'Comfortable security. Secure comfort.'

'No.'

'You tell me.'

A shake of her head. 'Torture me the worst you can, I won't talk.'

Across the room, Luba, Nina and Rosie gathered around the boy who was strumming a heavyhearted melody on his balalaika. All the Russian melodies Rivka knew came out saturated with sorrow, even the dance songs. The boy dipped the swan neck of his balalaika

205

toward Rosie and she shyly tucked her face behind her hand. Maybe he pitied the deformity of her back, the hump she couldn't camouflage or prettify with a velvet scarf. 'I know that song,' Rivka said. 'Suliko.'

'Why won't you tell me what you did?'

'So we don't have an argument. Why do you want to know?'

Peter shook his head, took a draw on his cigarette, glanced away and repeated, 'I can sleep better if I know that Karl's looking out for you.'

'He is. Don't worry about me.'

'Who says I'm worried about you?'

A confidence bubbled out on the easy laughter between them. And Rivka gave in. 'I pretended I was Max's wife. For an hour, that's all. So he could rent the flat there and it looks normal, so it's safer.'

'A woman makes it safe and normal,' Peter considered. 'You think so?'

'Karl says.' She touched his hand so he'd look at her. 'I'm going back with them. For the exe. I want to be there with them.'

Three Graces at his feet flattered an encore from Nicholas. He sang the song again, pouring on the creamy anguish. Rosie, Luba and Rivka wondered how such soulfulness can pour from the mouth of a fresh-faced boy. Or from the flurry of his fingers that made the neck of his balalaika resemble a woman's spine. Rivka added a harmony just loud enough for Peter to hear. *Ya mogilu miloi iskal, no yeyo naiti mye lekho. Dolgo ya tomisja i stradal, Gdye zhe ty, may Suliko?*

> *I was looking for my lover's grave*
> *but it was hard to find.*
> *For a long time I worried and suffered,*
> *Where are you my Suliko?*

'Those Russians,' a loose laugh, confidentially for Peter. 'Misery is the only thing that makes them happy.

'Riga Prison is worse,' Fritz anted. 'You can believe it, because—'

'The one in Libau,' Jacob cut him off and made his case to Yoska. 'Fritz *broke out* of Central Prison. But Libau, they *walk* you out, the guards, a normal transfer, all right, rifles in front and behind you, then they shoot you in the neck for attempted escape!'

Fritz said, 'Maybe in '05, '06, '07, even. January I was in Riga and they beat my brains out...'

'Latvians in Riga, cousin, *Russians* in charge in Libau.'

'...then they hit me some more. Russian hammers, Russian pliers, Russian knuckles.'

Yoska had nothing to contribute to this comparative survey of Baltic penal regimes. But now he teased Jacob, 'You've got plenty of friends in Russia. Russian ones.'

'So I know what I'm talking about, don't I?'

Fritz brandished his hands at Jacob, by way of saying 'so do I,' fingertips shaking an inch or two under his cousin's eyes. A few of the nails had grown back crookedly; many showed the still-unhealed yellow and purple skin beneath, and white scars where the flesh of each finger had been sliced with a razor and torn back with pliers. 'This is how serious they think of anarchists.'

'Because Russians are stupid as a bowl of borscht,' Jacob replied. 'Anarchists are nothing to begin with, and Fritz, let me tell you, you're no anarchist.' To cap the point Jacob showed Fritz his own hands, scored with identical wounds: who had more authority in matters of political theory and physical torture? 'They do it to nationalist revolutionaries for a better reason.'

'Oh? What is it, then?' Fritz said and sat back, all ears.

'To show us how much they love the Tsar.'

The cousins stared each other down. Whether one was going to erupt in cackling contempt or fly at the other's throat — and who would do what — Yoska didn't want to bet. So he took the heat out of the moment by rolling up his right trouser leg and jabbing his finger at the long sickle shaped scar. 'I've got worse pain than both of you put together.'

Jacob said, 'From an accident, you told us.'

'No, no...'

'Jumping out of a bedroom window.' Fritz leered at him.

'I wish it was!' Yoska laughed back at Fritz. 'Ask Max Smoller. He was there. When we stole some furs. I'm telling you!'

'An accident, I thought so. You tripped over your own big feet.'

Jacob didn't laugh along. He grabbed Fritz's hand and pushed it in front of Yoska's face. 'This was deliberate. They hurt us because they wanted to, that was their only intention, to cripple us.' He let go of his cousin. 'Before they took out their tools we sat in a cell very sure of what was coming. Our friends were screaming on the other side of the door. One of them they gave back to us with his ear drums burst and his private parts torn to shreds, like a dog chewed him there. But they didn't have any dogs, it was just the Russian guards.'

'You sit in the chair and believe them,' Fritz said quietly. Tears glossed his eyes, unhidden from Jacob and Yoska. 'I believed them. 'Your life is worthless.' I'm nothing to them, so I'm nothing.' He glanced up. 'Not now. I feel better.'

'You're right about that. Our lives don't mean anything,' Jacob said, 'except when we resist.'

'Jacob, can you be quiet for five minutes?' Yoska said,

his hands open, shoved toward Nicholas, Peter and Rivka, a plea on their behalf. Rivka's dark head was bowed as she conferred with her musicians, choosing a song they could play and she could sing.

Jacob tabled the discussion in favour of the music. Peter's violin, Nicholas's balalaika, Rivka's soprano silenced him. The silence of good manners. Silence as strength. Endurance. No, both false.

Two guards came for him in his Libau Prison cell. Here comes the start of it. They tied him to a hard wooden chair. The same kind of chair he knew from the schoolroom. In place of a desk though, a plain wooden plank strapped across its arms. Wet with blood and saliva; not his, not yet. Four guards stood around him. A stinking cloud of sweat and vodka rolled over him whenever they moved. A fifth one, the officer who stood behind the chair, the Guiding Force, smelled of other things. Shaving soap. Hair oil. It was early in the morning. 'Ten questions,' he said to Jacob. His friendly hand patted Jacob's shoulder. The Guiding Force knew this man wouldn't say one helpful word and anything he did say was a lie. No answer Jacob could give would satisfy him.

'What do you do for a living?' A toss of his head, a sincere smile that wouldn't look out of place on a bandstand, coming from a singer devoted to pleasing the spectators.

'Dock worker,' Jacob said. One guard gripped Jacob's left wrist: then he felt the nipping pressure of the pliers' rodent jaws bite the rim of his thumbnail. Lines of pain flashed back into his arm, liquid fire ran down his thumb, through his palm, the nail split lengthwise in two pieces, sheared from the pulp of his flesh. Jacob screamed.

'What whore are you fucking?'

'No whore.'

Pressure on his right wrist. The Fat Guard leaned the weight of his whole body on Jacob's arm, and one of the others had to

209

pry Jacob's fist apart. When its nail came away his little finger burned, blowtorch fire, buried under his screaming.

'You nationalists. You want Latvia for yourselves. Tell me something. Is there a difference between Latvians and Jews?'

'All the same,' Jacob answered.

'Index finger, left hand.' The Guiding Force leaned down over Jacob's shoulder to clarify: 'That wasn't a question.' It was the only time he saw the profile of his torturer's unremarkable face.

Jacob knew this man. To him, Jacob wasn't an enemy, not at that moment; he was a task to perform, a broken machine that could be repaired with simple tools. A mechanical problem: nothing more complicated than how to remove the next fingernail – to give rest or pain, a slow peeling or an abrupt pull, a predictable rhythm or jagged, unexpected. For this little time everyone inhabits the same clear world. And for everyone's benefit the Guiding Force will change a man in front of his own eyes. Look quickly and you see a perverse act of mutilation and destruction, but stare at it, if you're strong enough, and you'll see how creative it is...

He looked at the guards' hands. All of them bloody. Jacob's mouth hung open, dripping blood. Without moving he could see his ten fingernails scattered on the stone floor. Behind him Jacob heard the officer say, 'One more question...'

Rivka's singing reached Jacob then, and the warmth of Peter's room, the closeness of his friends. Fritz whispered to him, guessing, admiring, 'So you didn't scream?'

'Loud enough to break his glasses!' Jacob said. 'Looked him in the face every time. Strong screams.'

'I screamed too.' Fritz felt Jacob's hand reach for his and he clutched it. Shyly, behind his downturned eyes, he was glad of that intimacy. Better than cousins, like Jacob said once – brothers. Persuasive enough for him to throw anarchism over and return to the nationalists.

Jacob put words to the one thought ringing in Fritz's mind. 'We have to show them we're strong. Weakness provokes them.'

Inside the room, a few feet away from the chance privacy of the landing where Peter and Karl huddled, Nicholas played a few bars of melody on his balalaika, slowly singing the Russian lyrics. Rivka sang them back in her peppery soprano. One or two refrains and she'd mastered the new song, even improvised a harmony for the chorus. Peter pretended not to be listening and spoke intensely to Karl. 'Tell her you don't need her.'

'It wouldn't be the truth,' Karl said.

'She doesn't have to be there.'

'It's a help. It's only what the girl wants to do.'

'Rivka shouldn't be doing this, Karl. I don't care *what* she thinks of herself, she's no recruit.'

'Who recruited her? *I* did? No. What the Russians squatting in Latvia did to her father. What the English did to her.'

'And you'll protect her from the English police...' Peter doubted, his voice sharp. 'Not in the middle of an action.'

'The girl will be sitting in a flat for a few hours, Peter. Drinking cups of tea.'

'I'll have to talk her out of going to Houndsditch.'

'Good luck. Nobody talked her into it.'

Peter sidestepped the argument. He rattled the geometry of Poolka's plan. 'Give me a reason. Why do you need somebody in the other flat while you're digging?'

'You know why.'

'A lamp burning that the neighbours can see from the street, that's enough.'

'And Mrs Levi in the window ironing her husband's shirt. Which isn't enough, either.'

They collected in the back bedroom, the Sisterhood (as Rivka nicknamed them tonight, herself included). Luba's blankets sprawled over the mattress, a skirt and jacket lay strewn on the floor next to a pair of Fritz's boots, his overcoat and a shirt bunched together. Rosie, Luba, Nina and Rivka lounged in their salon. Rosie and Luba had the bed, Rivka camped on the floor and pushed Fritz's clothes against the wall to pillow her back, Nina stood and seemed to have one ear on the men's conversations stirring in the other room. Out there Fritz on his mandolin plink-plunked his way through 'Along the Petersburg Road' for the ninth time. Rosie said, 'The Russian boy plays it better.'

'He's *teaching* him. Fritz is learning.' Luba said, defending the stumbling and cracked notes Fritz was bullying into a melody.

'Nicholas was a musician the day he was born,' Rivka said. 'The music is in his fingers. He doesn't think about it, he just plays it.'

'He can strum me!' Luba, naughty, arms stretched above her head, slim as a balalaika's neck, not really meaning it.

Rosie's monotone muffled the pity that crouched inside her words 'His wife is somewhere,' she said.

Luba sparked, 'How do you know?'

Nina said, 'He only got here in the summer. Fritz brought him home from the theatre.'

'Little chickadee,' Luba said sympathetically.

'He's married, Rosie?'

Rosie continued on her own track. 'Every man has a wife. She could—'

'Every pot has a lid,' Rivka chipped in.

'— or it doesn't mean he's married to her yet. Maybe she isn't born yet.' She said to Luba, 'Fritz has one.'

'Maybe Nicholas is your husband but he doesn't know it,' Luba snapped back, thinking *I'm Fritz's true wife.*

'No, Nicholas is probably Rivka's husband. The way they play music together.'

'Nice to meet you, Mrs Tomacoff!' Luba kidded her.

'My name's Mrs Levi, please,' Rivka set her right. Then she protested, 'He looks like a boy.'

'He's older than you,' Luba said.

'Anybody can sing. All the best musicians are men, I'm telling you.'

'You sing so beautiful. Everybody listens. Men look at you. They stop and —'

'Just now?' Rivka said. 'They talked the whole time.'

'Not Peter.'

'That's true. Peter didn't,' Rosie agreed.

'Music isn't serious,' Nina said. She stood at the dresser now, tidying away the boxes of ammunition in their drawer. She covered the pistols with one of Luba's underskirts. 'I can't sit still and listen to it. Karl, either.'

Was it that he'd heard Nina say his name? On his way past the doorway just then with a bottle of beer in his hand, Karl glanced in on the Sisterhood. He raised the brown bottle in gentlemanly salute and vanished again. Cowled in her silence, Rosie kept her eyes on the empty doorway and saw his shape in the air looking back at her. She thought, *Everything outside the square of floor with him on it is a madhouse.*

In the corner of the room by the bedstead, Yourka Duboff approached Peter with the humility a young apprentice shows a venerable master. Six years difference

213

between them, that was all, both men in their twenties. 'Can I show you my painting?'

Peter dug through his jacket pockets, gave up and said, 'No more cigarettes.'

'I've got one. You want a cigarette?' Yourka grabbed the chance to be of some use.

'Is it your last one?'

'I smoked all the rest. Enough cigarettes for one night.'

Yourka pulled out the flat rectangular package from behind a chair, where it had waited all night. Without fumbling, he untied the string, scraped away the brown paper, stepped back and held the unframed painting for Peter to view, a watercolour landscape of scrubby countryside, slender wind-blasted trees and grassland in the foreground that led the eye back to dense green woodland and signs of habitation.

'Is it a real place?'

'Near home,' Yourka said. 'From my memory. You can criticise it. I want you to.'

Peter didn't say it was a beginner's study, a talented beginner's. He mulled over the obvious composition, earnestly realistic colours, the movement in it halted by the thick masses of forest left and right. He said Yourka had a 'sharp eye for details' and congratulated him on the delicacy of his brushwork. Yourka's clean, long fingers were as delicate, and his face, open and broad, wanted to hear the answer to every obvious question.

'Keep it for a while. Keep it. We don't have to talk about it now,' Yourka said. 'Give it back to me later. After Sunday. Or keep it, keep it.'

'Good. I can see how it looks in daylight.'

Along with the landscape Yourka handed Peter his address on a torn corner of paper. 'Come to me. I'll give

214

you coffee and cake. You can tell me where I'm going
wrong with my painting.'
    'Where's this?'
    'Shepherd's Bush. West from Piccadilly.'

From the table where she stacked the casserole dish and
dirty plates Rivka saw Max Smoller and his wife by the door,
leaving the party early. Max fluttered his hand good-bye
to Karl. Standing there the couple could have been empty-
pocket immigrants boarding the gangway of a steamship,
Max's wife more oppressed and fearful than Max. Nobody
had introduced Rivka to her so she couldn't tell Mrs Smoller
*Don't worry, it isn't a crime Max is doing, it's an enterprise, for
the sake of balance, so he's not defenceless, he'll get away with it.*
Also, *it's just a role I'm playing*. She couldn't think of herself
as Max's woman for a single moment.

Fritz wasn't drunk. Angry, though, anybody would take
him for a drunk. He paced the landing in front of the
food, waving his arms around. Every word out of him was
an injured shout, his legs uncontrollable, marching him
two steps in one direction then off the other way, eyes
blinking between fear and hate, tied by rope to his
tormentor. 'You paid *too much*.'
    'How do you know what a chicken costs?' Luba faced
him down.
    'I walk in the street, I see the plucked *'ennas* hanging
and the *prices*.'
    'Where? Brick Lane?'
    'Brick Lane.'
    'This one I got from Reuben who charged me tuppence
more than last time.'

Fritz laughed it off. 'Tuppence.'

'Of my money — *mine.*'

'Here it comes!'

'You ate more of it than anybody else.'

'Counted how many bites I took?'

'Two legs and two wings. I saw you.'

'Was it a good show, watching me eat?'

'No, disgusting. *You're* disgusting.'

'Tomorrow you can measure how much I ate when it comes out. Meet me in the shitter with a tape measure!'

Both of them shouting now, squalling in public, naked as babies, clawing bits out of each other in front of friends close as family. For everybody besides Fritz and Luba the flare-up quickly turned into something like a sporting event. Yourka Duboff and Yoska cheered and clapped every point Fritz scored. Nina and Rivka egged Luba on with little barks of solidarity. Embarrassed and unsure, Nicholas asked Peter, 'Does he mistreat her all the time?' Peter had no answer for him: he merely looked Luba's way as if to say, *Just watch.*

'Always the most!' Luba said. 'More than anybody!'

'My share, that's all.'

'More than anybody. Always the biggest piece.'

Fritz wore a look of the slandered and persecuted. 'You're lying.'

'No.'

'Don't lie about me.' Fingers tucked into a fist, arm cocked to land the punch that wipes out the lie. Luba braced herself for it but it didn't come. Fritz opened his hand and patted Luba's head. 'All right,' he said. 'I won't eat dinner tomorrow.'

Everyone laughed, except Luba, who stood her ground, trembling. 'It's not such a joke. Nothing's funny.'

Fritz followed her out of the room. Before the sharp

slam of the door, the others heard Luba threaten, 'I'll stop paying and he'll throw you out. Peter, too!' Nicholas dived into the fun, picked up his balalaika, strummed a high-spirited introduction and sang, *'Pust' gitara zvutshit nye-ustanaya, pust' rýdayet struna za strunoi! Mozg durmanyet glaza tvoyi pyanýe, tvoy napyev i tvoy smekh rokovoi...'*

> *Let the guitar ring out, let it not tire*
> *Let it cry, string by string,*
> *I see your drunken eyes through a fog,*
> *And through the song I hear your fateful laughter...*

He stamped his feet to keep time, called out for them all to join in clapping, stomping and singing along, to muffle the crying, blustering and wheedling going on in the back bedroom.

Fritz had been gone from the party for an hour, tramping through the streets to sweat the fever out of his steaming blood, and '... come back with calm nerves,' he said.

He dropped a small packet into Peter's lap. 'Also, look — cigarettes.' Then he folded himself on to the floor in the corner of the room Rivka and Peter had colonised with two chairs, no apology for crashing in on their conversation. He'd made up his mind somewhere on his midnight stroll to bare his breast to Peter; now Fritz had returned to divulge disturbing information. Passing it along to Peter was the same as telling Karl himself, free of the Adonis's scalding judgment. 'Don't repeat this to my cousin,' he said.

Peter could assure him, 'Jacob isn't interested in hearing anything from me.'

Fritz spoke to him as if Rivka wasn't there at all. 'I didn't

217

want to go with them to Houndsditch. It's a weight off me, I'm telling you, that Karl didn't say "Go in on Friday with him and Jacob."' He clutched his wooden sword, bouncing its tip against his shoe. Ten feet behind him (Fritz took in with a snatched glance) his cousin was busy drumming away at Karl. 'Because something's wrong with me. Up here.' Fritz patted his forehead. 'Russian police, you know? You know how they do it. They mashed me soft. Here, touch.' He bowed towards Rivka now, took her hand and helped her find the teaspoon sized dent on the side of his head. 'I get headaches from it in the morning. It's true. I'm scared of myself. If they grab me I'm scared I'll get interrogated again.'

'Russians can't touch you here.'

'No, English, *English*. They arrest me, put me in their torture room and...' His guilty plea and apology, 'I can't stand up to them, Peter, I'm not so strong any more. I won't keep quiet.'

Pity moved Rivka's hand as she stroked Fritz's hair. And Peter damped down the fear bristling in his own gut. He said, 'If you're not going in you don't have to worry. None of us do.'

Fritz brightened up. 'Going to Australia in January.'

'Maybe I'll go with you,' Peter said.

'Yes?'

'Why not?'

'You have to find eighty roubles. That's for one ticket.' Fritz slid his eyes from Rivka to Peter. 'I'm taking my wife there.'

'... Damage we can do if we're smart. To their fucking *city*. We *are* smart. Don't doubt it. You should be calm. You *are* calm, I know it. Nina's feeding you, you're eating?

218

I don't want to be your mother, I'm just making sure. Friday. Money is all right. It's a necessity, I'm not fighting you on it. We'll get it. *How* we get it, that's going to hurt them. A bit. But I say to keep going, after Saturday. Saturday, Sunday, whenever we're out of there. Hit them again, quick, bigger. A bank...'

Karl nodded his head to show serious consideration of each new point Jacob made. He scratched at a smear of food on his lapel. Yellowish-brown against the black, an arc shaped like a comet. If it was in silver it would be a decoration, effeminate, a frippery. How long had it been there, a gob of — what is it? horseradish? chicken fat? Dried now. Better — it would come off easier that way. He felt the grit build up under his fingernail as he scraped at the dry layer. Still the ghost of the stain stuck to the lapel arching towards his buttonhole.

'... every action. Two years, five years. Street warfare and executions, mobs running wild — when the government can't protect them anymore, they'll call the army. Don't let them rest or prepare, show them it's out of their hands. Really it's out of ours, too, we're a necessity of history: it's necessary for us to be here at this moment. You're doing what you need to do, same for all of us. It's a terrible time. Why am I excited, then, tell me that! *I'll* tell *you*. We're lucky it's us. This generation. Ours. We'll be the ones with enough money and then, finally, we won't have to lose time on robberies. Aim at clear targets. Make them feel the loss! I know how. Listen. Attack them with a bomb next time. On a train or blow up the Tilbury docks, a warehouse. Or the British Museum. Fortnum and Mason's. Bang, bang, bang. They recover from the first one — *bang!* — we hit with the next one, people in the streets, I promise you, the government can't protect them they'll be yelling, 'Fuck the King! And

219

his dead mother!' and the Archbishop of Canterbury with cherries on his tits for dessert...'

The smear looked more like mustard than chicken fat. There was one way Karl could find out: taste what he'd scratched up under his fingernail. No, that's ugly. Mistake, mistake. The first mistake was allowing Nina to talk him in to buying a jacket with velvet lapels. Any dirt, greasy dirt especially, locks in. Velvet never goes back to how it was even after you clean it with a cloth. Can you use a damp cloth on it? Water's no good, it ruins the material. Now there's a permanent smudge and every time he wears this jacket he'll look like a pig-man, sloppy, careless.

The balalaika music jangled into Karl's ears, congealing and hardening into a headache. With a friendly grip of Jacob's biceps, he said, 'How are your arms? I'm counting on you and Max digging one-hour shifts. Thirty-six hours, I want to be out.'

She framed herself in the doorway, Luba did, reached both arms around Fritz's neck and pulled him into view. That was her intention, for the others to see what he did when she offered her mouth to him. Fritz kissed her with a growl of sexual power, but the force in it wasn't his — no, the show of strength belonged to Luba, her kiss blood-hot defiance. The pull of destiny (she'd used that dizzy word) wrapped her body around his; Fritz's assaulted, stupefied mouth sucked at the passing opportunity. All for an audience of one, as Rivka alone watched them. And Peter alone watched Rivka.

Chto mnye gorye, v zhizni morye nado vypit' nam do dna! Sertse tishe! Vyshe, vyshe kubki starovo vina! Nicolas encored. Yoska danced around in a circle by himself, wiggling a bottle of beer over his head, singing along on the chorus.

> *What do I care! In our lifetime a whole sea*
> *we have to drink to the ground!*
> *My heart, be still!*
> *Higher, higher, raise the glasses*
> *with old wine!*

On the landing, where Peter failed to get through to Karl, he also failed to talk Rivka out of the Houndsditch escapade. Her steady resistance forced him to see her the way she wanted to be seen: as a woman whose strong heart decided things for its own settled reasons. That same spirit of hers would keep Rivka from hardening into a moll like Nina; this Peter understood. Let her find out for herself what the robbery costs against what it brings in, and after it her passion to live will take her the other way, in the direction these actions took Peter — away from never ending revolution.

'You're the youngest,' Peter said, mentalist's fingers tented on his forehead. 'I'm saying the youngest daughter.'

'I'm not impressed,' Rivka smiled.

'Not the baby. Everybody's favourite, though.'

'I'm the only one who's got freckles all over.'

'The *strange* one. So Mama and Papa worry about you more.'

'They know it's useless. I hope they don't.'

'We're not such favourites outside the family.'

She swept a look over Peter, haircut to shoes. A shake of her head. 'You're the strange one in your family? I don't think so.'

'Ask my uncle, the colonel.'

'Does he have medals and a sword?'

'Presented to him by the Tsar.'

'*This* impresses me.'

'Then I'm sorry I didn't mention it sooner.'

'When?'

'Before you came to the art gallery with me.'

'I went anyway,' she said.

Peter replied, 'You did.'

'Can we go again?'

He dipped his head and felt Rivka's hand cradle his cheek. Peter leaned down further and breathed in the aroma of her hair, kissed her forehead, then her mouth. He surrounded her in his arms and felt her body shiver faintly against his. From Rivka's lips an aching stillness reached him, reached into him, tender and undeniable as a fall of snow.

'We know how Peter is thinking,' Nina said. Her words, her *tone*, battered Karl's exhausted ears. But he was the only one left in the flat. And after all, he was in charge. 'You said he wanted to keep her out of it, so now that's what he's doing. With his prick!'

What is it her business! Why do they aggravate her? Karl considered Nina's profile, puzzling out her condemnation of Peter and Rivka. Twenty minutes ago they left together. Since then every noise outside gave Nina a twitch. *She's sitting here waiting for them to snap out of their trance and come back.* At last he said, 'Why shouldn't they? Three of us still camping in Peter's bedroom.'

Nina went on bunching and rebunching the

handkerchief she'd balled up in her hand. Rosie kept clear of the spat, helpfully stoking the coal fire. Then Nina hinted at the nub of her anger. 'They can't go to her room. Think of Perelman finding him with her under his roof! He'd chase Peter out with a gun.'

'Maybe he took a room at the Ritz.'

'No, Karl,' she disagreed, as if that guess of his had been serious. 'Houndsditch. She took him there. Our furniture's moved in there. There's a *bed*.'

'She did, all right. So what? He won't stay longer than he has to. Don't expect to find Peter eating breakfast there tomorrow.'

'Birds flying around her head,' Nina said under her breath. 'Come down to it, it's just sex. Men are so *grateful*.'

He teased her, '*Who* are you talking about?'

'In particular?'

Playing along, 'Give me names.'

'Yoska's like a cow who needs milking.'

'How do you know?'

'How do you think? Fritz, the same.' Even in the dim light she saw Karl's face go the colour of cold wax, drained, mutely appalled. 'It's nothing. A few strokes, a touch, nothing.' She gestured with her hand, the one clutching the handkerchief. 'Like a doctor. I touched them a few times, over, finished.' She buzzed her lips.

He tried to show her nothing, he'd stopped playing. 'Who else?'

'Here? People you know?' He nodded. Frankness was her virtue, So Nina told him and the telling pardoned every act and drew the borders around her love for him. 'Three days I carried Fritz's piss in a bottle to the toilet when he came back from prison. When he was sick in bed, in Great Garden Street, remember that? A comrade needs a favour, you do it for him.'

223

Different men, other times, they're gasping and groaning in her, breathing my air. Nina was a stranger, as she was before he entered her life, how she is when he's absent. Gently, she asked him if he wanted to know about any of the others. He gave her silence for an answer, make of it what she wanted. The only sound in the room came from the roasting coal which tinkled and cracked like melting ice. Behind his closed eyes Karl watched a blonde woman bend over him, his friend's mother — old, he'd thought at the time, though she couldn't have been thirty. She planted kisses on his hairless chest, licked his nipples, dragged her tongue over his ribs, kissed his belly, the tops of his hips. He didn't know what she meant by it, he thought she was going crazy right there in her own kitchen. 'Beautiful boy. My beautiful boy...'

Late, early, did the exact hour matter? Karl's bed waited for him somewhere else. He moved his mind towards it but his body refused to lift itself out of Peter's chair and follow. For his body, here was warmth and quiet. No reason to concentrate, listen or elaborate. Nina also waited for him somewhere else. It's the middle of the night down in Houndsditch too; by now she's found whatever she's found there. Made them stop or didn't. So be it. Inside this blessed solitude Karl felt the winds that all night were battering his ears drop to nothing. Behind them not even a tattered breeze, only vacant stillness that let him drain into sleep.

Rosie could keep herself awake feeding coal to the fire till sunrise if need be. *He knows I'm nearby...* She inspired herself with that thought. And she went on thinking—

He can rest and be peaceful because he's not alone.
This is love.
Every good thing Karl is in his heart Nina ignores and
* neglects.*
I see the whole way down. Under his beauty under his
* perfect bones.*
Once you admit you're less than him it's plain and clear.
Big as a building. Karl is golden.
I'm less than him. I'm lower in looks and health,
I'm lower in brains.
But when God tied a knot in my spine
He gave me special powers. A mound of bone and bad
* meat*
on top of my shoulder. A lump of ugliness you can't hide
in an overcoat.
A piece of luck.
To remember every time you're naked in a mirror
good or bad doesn't show on anyone's body
so you must look under.
Pray God (Elohim hear my prayer) give Karl something
that shows him where to look.
Let him look under.
If he opened his eyes this minute
he'd love me.

Five

Not the fear of being found or found out and not a last-minute dread of the crime going on downstairs. Not the worry she'd be abandoned by them without warning, and not the dull throb of boredom. Rivka couldn't put a name to the restlessness jittering through her, a sensation so physical it made her arms itch.

'If I had a deck of cards I could play solitaire,' she said to nobody. 'If I knew how to play solitaire.' They'd left her alone in the flat, part of the plan all along, so why was she kicking? She had her pot of tea, loaf of bread, bowl of jam, a fire to keep her warm. In her half-furnished rooms 'Mrs Levi' was uneasy for other reasons. Table and chairs, a day bed planted in the downstairs room, Rivka looked around her and saw the seeds of a home — as long as she ignored the safe-cracking drill, sacks of sand and mortar, squares of asbestos, sixty feet of red rubber tubing...

It was Peter who had done this to her. His gentle attentions. His joy with her. His absence, now. The salty clean smell of his skin clung to the blankets on the daybed. Rivka wrapped herself in them and inhaled. She took Peter's remnant inside her, a breath of him. Which soothed her one second, then agitated her the next. It gave the uneasiness in her chest and empty arms a reason besides lonesome foreboding.

Rip away these wooden walls, replace them with iron ones and she would be back inside the metal belly, Rivka of *The Comet* wallowing across the North Sea. Strange noises reached her from the ship and the sea, phantom sounds a person never hears on land. Moans from the hull, thumps on the deck, draggings and scrapings, screeches and growls let out by things invisible and unimaginable to her. Here in the flat, she knew the sounds that echoed in from the street: horse hooves, the creak and knock of a cart's hard wheels, a door slammed shut, a shout in Yiddish answered in English, hurrying footsteps. Outside it was Friday night, the Sabbath.

Yourka Duboff believed that lookout was the perfect job for him. He was an *observer*. Hadn't Peter said as much at the party? *An eye for details.* A good artist has to be an observer, and that was the reason Karl chose an artist as his lookout. Yourka's footsteps mixed with the straggling others in Houndsditch. His were unhurried, though, and not synagogue-bound; they rested in front of the jewellery shop long enough for him to light a cigarette. Precious little for a window shopper to see in there — empty velvet shelves, a clock in the shape of the Eiffel Tower, a single electric light burning in the office behind the display counter, the safe tucked in the corner.

How long before they could get him inside? At the earliest, three or four a.m. Sunday, Yourka estimated, an early hour when they could count on thirty minutes of privacy. That was all he needed. What was Karl doing with acids and oxygen torches? The time it took, the messy violence, but nobody said, *Dubof, what's your opinion*? After twenty-four hours Karl will give up on the tunnelling and burning, watch, he'll come to his senses and call in the fingertip artist.

It was hard for Yourka to imagine the streets much emptier than they already were. He watched the cold wind lift a sheet of newspaper and sweep it along the pavement, away from the parade of closed shops. *The wind is a good thief*, he thought. Yourka patrolled back to the turning into Cutler Street and cocked his ear to hear how far noise carried from the digging. At the cul-de-sac's entrance just a remote tapping, the innocent sound of a plumber, say, repairing a sink. Closer to the flat's front door it became muffled knocking, yard work in back, nothing to alarm the neighbourhood or the thieves, either.

Thump-scrape. Thump-thump-scrape. One of them, Jacob or Max, was shouldering into the job of hammering through bricks and cement to break an entryway. For Karl's welding torch? No, for Yourka, his talent. Sunday morning Karl can watch him gentle the tumblers of Mr Harris's safe and scoop the Tsar's gold into a bag. The revolution in miniature: muscle first and then finesse.

The revolution in miniature: muscle first and then finesse, he paused to think again. *That's the kind of subtle observation that occurs to Karl.* Yourka paced to the end of the narrow street, repeating the epigram to himself, sealing it in his memory so he could make the remark later to Liesma's boss as if he'd thought of it on the spot.

Thump-scrape. Thump. Thump. Jacob drove his crowbar into the wall with steep downward strokes. In the privy's cramped box his swing had to be short and hard. Each jab hacked out another chip of brick and spray of mortar dust, and he felt the sharp force of every strike, an abrupt vibration that jolted the muscles in his arms, back and neck. Body heat and the candlelight kept the shithouse hot as a kiln. One thought returned with the curl and splash of waves on the shore, stroke after stroke: *Do the work*.

That's it, isn't it? Of course in a toilet! Perfection! Up

from the lowest, filthiest place in the civilised world, here we come to take your gold. Soldiers of the latrine! Karl must be chuckling at that. An artistic part of his plan, sheer poetry. That's right, it was *his* plan: after Beron fences the stuff it would be Karl's say, what happens to the money. Seven shares. *Send it all*, that's what I'll tell him, *Arm our friends*. This should be going on all over London. Berlin. Vienna. Paris. Chicago. Fuck them. We hit and hide! In *toilets*. How long can they hold out against that, tell me? We can keep going for years. Until all the good men are on our side. And the rest of them are fucked.

You think we should execute them? Round up the bastards and shoot them against a wall? *Thump. Thump.* They call us barbarians. We'll show the world how civilised we are. Arrest our enemies, yes. Confiscate their property, yes. Then be generous in victory. We'll educate them. Bring them to a place, an arena, and one by one return the tools of their trade. To a judge, his gavel. To a professor, his text book. A priest, his sensor. A banker, his fountain pen. Give them a fresh chance to use their tools for the benefit of the people. Use them to beat each other to death, two by two, in public, around the clock. Let it take years. That's the right way to fuck them. Without wasting a single one of the people's bullets. Contend with us and see what happens.

Closer. Closer. With each slam of the crowbar we're a fraction of a fraction of an inch closer, one less chip of brickwork between us and their gold. This work makes it our gold. Honest work, it satisfies me. George Gardstein's plan in motion! That's why they call it an *action*. The motion of it is here, in my arms and back: *I'm* the motion. I slam the point of this crowbar into the brick and what used to be a wall is a hole we can climb through. He says it's sixty feet to the safe. Through the storeroom, then a door, then another wall, then the safe. Then and then and then and then. Do the work.

Thump. Thump-scrape. Thump. Fuck them.

Rivka appeared downstairs (for no good reason, it crossed Max's mind.) When he looked up, she thought he had his squinted eye on the tea pot she was carrying, but he was looking at her.

'You come down for hot water?' he said, not so friendly.

'Tea's gone. Sorry, I don't know what to do with ...' She opened the lid to show him the dregs inside.

Max tapped his wrench on the edge of the sink. 'We don't have to leave it clean.'

'What's that, a clock?'

The mechanism fit in the palm of Max's hand. He wiped its brass threads with a rag. 'Regulator.'

'What's it for?' While Max decided how or whether to answer her, Rivka studied the slim black cylinders that leaned against the sink. 'You put it on one of those?'

'Tells me how much gas is left.'

'For burning.'

'That's right.'

'How long does it burn?'

Max turned back to his work. 'About forty-five minutes.'

'Is it long enough?' No reply. 'Who's going to use it, you or Jacob?'

'All right, I get it. It's boring for you,' he said sharply. 'You're up there by yourself. Just you and your pot of tea.'

'No more tea,' she whispered. Then, 'I'm sitting like a lump.'

'That's the job you got from Karl: you sit upstairs till we finish, lump or no lump.' Uneasiness tightened Max's throat. 'Go next door, then. Sit with Karl and Nina.'

'No, you're right. He said stay here.'

'We aren't in the army. They won't mind, go sit next door,' he recommended. 'It's better.'

Minutes later, Rivka sat sharing a late night supper with 'the Gardsteins,' as (for some misbegotten, daughterly reason) she thought of them tonight. Boiled eggs, black rye bread, sardines, paté, jam, noodle *kugel*. Nina poured dark tea into glasses, set each glass on its saucer, a sugar cube on the side, Russian style. 'Let's say it's an early breakfast,' Karl said.

From Nina, 'Twelve hours early. Thirteen, fourteen.' Then, for Rivka's benefit, 'He's a championship sleeper.'

Without fuss, he slid his Mauser from the table and holstered it inside his overcoat. 'For your breakfasts I always get out of bed.' A meal like this, in a quiet home with Nina, tucked indoors beside the heat of a fire with the night-cold and street-cold shut out by secure wooden shutters — *this is peace.*

The peacefulness of kinship, Rivka would have told him, because the throb she felt rise and fall in her chest carried her home to Sasmacken. So, all right, they were only few years older than Rivka, but Nina's spry taunts and goads were Mama's, Karl's beleaguered, sighing, everlasting patience belonged to Papa, and for Rivka it was easy as drifting into sleep to relax into the illusion of this family life. Banished from her first home to find her second.

Apart from the single question he asked Rivka about Max and Jacob's progress, Karl devoted himself to enjoyment of the food and the companionship of two doting women. For the mastermind of a jewel robbery, that he was many shaky hours if not days from bringing off, Karl seemed unburdened. Passive as a passenger on a train. The great machine has hauled itself away from the station, with you inside it; you are a captive of its velocity, a parcel of its momentum now, travelling in *its* direction to *its* destination, nothing for you to do but stay in your seat and ride along...

'By colour,' Nina insisted. The subject of tonight's squabble was how to judge when to pour the first cup of tea from a fresh pot.

'No, by minutes,' Karl repeated for the third or fourth time. 'Colour isn't science, it's art.'

'Brewing a pot of tea isn't science, either.'

'Five minutes in Petersburg is five minutes here. Your tea will taste exactly the same.'

'China tea or Indian?'

They'd kept the merrily brittle to-and-fro going for longer than Rivka thought possible, which made her suspect the performance, at least partly, was staged for her entertainment. This became more likely when Karl appealed to her for a deciding vote.

'She'll tell you colour,' Nina said.

'Why don't you close your mouth and listen to what Rivka says.' Karl didn't want to listen, either, but to grumble. 'Rivka, you know how Nina acts. She has to disagree with me on every point.'

Rivka raised a neutral hand and there the lunacy ended in stalemate. Karl softly hummed a song from the other night, and underneath it, the muffled pounding at the back of the flat, continued, almost keeping time. Karl said, 'That's Jacob's bashing. You can tell.'

Nina listened for a second. 'It's Max.'

'You can tell by the style. Jacob's a locomotive — *oomph, oomph, oomph*. Smoller, he's...' Karl curled his hands into paws and imitated a mole scraping through the dirt.

'It's Max.'

'Who is it,' Karl asked Rivka. 'Jacob or Max?'

The plates rattled out of Nina's hands back onto the

233

table. 'You can't ask her! She was just down there. She *knows* who's digging.'

Karl frisked his pockets for coins. 'It's Jacob. Want to bet me?'

'I'll write you my IOU,' Nina said. 'It's Max digging.'

All three listened again. And, along with the pounding down below heard footsteps approaching the back door. The door opened, the footsteps waited and in a soft voice someone inquired, 'Hello?'

Karl waited a second to reply. 'Max?'

With a weak grin Max answered the laughter and hand claps they gave him when he entered the room. 'What's funny?' From his waistband he freed his Browning revolver then, perhaps as a courtesy, placed it on the mantelpiece. 'Any food left? I need something in my belly before I work.'

For two frightened women in another Exchange Buildings flat, one door along from Family Gardstein, the night-time hours of phantom hammering, thumps, scrapes, comings and goings chilled into a mystery that drove spikes of ice into their stomachs. The innocent explanations the settled on at seven o'clock had by ten o'clock become fears so crude and tormenting that Miss Weil and her maid, Miss Chard, stood clutching each other for comfort and safety by the front door, poised to make a night-gowned run for it if any attacker broke in through the back door.

Mr Weil's key rattling the lock downstairs gave their hearts another jolt. The man of the house didn't even get a chance to take off his hat and coat — the sight of his friendly bearded face uncorked the women's nightmares. 'Listen,' his sister said, 'You hear those noises?'

'Noises?'

Finger to her lips, she hushed him. 'You hear it? Down.'
'Down? Where?'

'In the back,' said Miss Chard.

Miss Weil shushed her. Mr Weil concentrated on the silence. No, they weren't crazy, he heard the noises too. *Thump. Thump-scrape.* 'What is it?'

'We don't know, sir. Deliveries, or...'

Miss Weil babbled over Miss Chard, 'I don't know! It's something.'

'...something, somebody we don't *know* who...'

'Stock deliveries, we thought maybe. But it's night.'

'It's Friday night, sir.'

'It's no delivery,' Mr Weil said. 'I just locked up. I'm the last one.'

'Then we thought furniture movers.'

'You said furniture, I said builders,' Miss Weil agreed with Miss Chard.

Thump. Thump. Thump-scrape.

Strange, definitely strange. Mr Weil said, 'There's nobody outside. That's not furniture. Could be building work.'

'Who does building work on Shabbas?'

'Irishmen?' he suggested.

'Oh no, sir, I don't think so,' Miss Chard said. 'Not at night.'

'Nobody's Irish next door.'

'What are they?' Mr Weil asked his sister.

Miss Chard said, 'They look like you, sir. And they talk to each other in Jew.'

Miss Weil, even more bedevilled, 'Who does *building work* on *Shabbas*?'

Good thing he was still wearing his hat and warm coat. 'Stay here,' Mr Weil told them. 'I'll get to the bottom of it.'

235

'Not by yourself,' though Miss Weil didn't intend her prudence to stop him.

'Go back inside. I'll get a policeman.'

Six

To Mr Weil, he looked young for a police constable, with slight shoulders holding up his brass-buttoned tunic. Its collar, he noticed, floated loosely around the PC's neck. Not enough meat on him to support the towering authority of the law. *If this is the one I've found*, thought Mr Weil, *that's my luck, and his*. The policeman he'd stopped just near the corner in Houndsditch listened with nods of concern and tried his best to separate useful information from the looping melody of Mr Weil's foreign accent.

'My sister is very scared. Can you help me, Constable?'

That plea came through clear enough. PC Piper couldn't think what he'd accomplish by telling a distressed citizen that in spite of walking this City beat alone he was still a probationer. So, demonstrably in command of procedure, he took out his pocket notebook, made a note of Mr Weil's name and asked him, 'Can you take me to the place you heard these noises?'

'Our flat, the other flat, behind right here. It's why she's worried scared.' He stopped in front of No. 119, the dark doorway of Mr Harris's jewellery shop.

Piper rattled the spear-topped iron gate that was stretched and secured across the shop's entryway, then leaned in for a look through the window. Empty shelves, empty counter, an office beyond, a constant light burning above the stout safe in back. Still and undisturbed.

'Can you hear? That building noise, we don't know what it is, hammering. But who builds on Shabbas?'

'Sorry, can you let me listen, please?' Piper heard the

237

wind buffeting the mouth of Culter Street. 'Round there, your flat?'

'By the corner, yes. Next door to us. You'll hear it.'

'Would you mind waiting here for me? Just in front of the shop, sir, all right?'

A stiff, unhappy smile from Mr Weil, an abrupt wave of the hand. 'Number 11,' he said to the constable. 'Those new neighbours.'

At the first tap of the knock Rivka saw the men's relaxed mood slip from their faces and from the room. Karl and Max made her think of startled cats who stiffen, shrink themselves into their eyes and ears, reflexes quickened, balanced on the verge of a jump. From her chair by the fireplace Rivka had a view of the dimly lit lobby between the stairs and front door, but no longer of Karl. She heard the voice of a stranger, an Englishman.

'Is the missus in?'

Karl replied, 'She's gone out.'

Rivka teased Nina with raised eyebrows and whispered to her, 'A gentleman for you.'

Nothing from Nina gave Rivka permission, or heart, to joke any more about the situation, or to speak one more word.

They heard the Englishman say, 'Right, then. I'll call back.'

For safety, in control of himself, Karl kept his voice low. 'Stay in the bedroom for now,' he said to Nina and Rivka, then retrieved his Mauser from the floor, holstered it in his long coat, pulled his coat on. Max checked his Browning's chamber and quietly followed the others upstairs.

Karl's gentlemanly style didn't help PC Piper's

uneasiness. He paced back towards Houndsditch, if anything, more nervous than when he'd left there, not content at all that he'd disguised his bolt-from-the-blue investigation from the foreigner in No. 11. *Is the missus in?* Oh, that was sure to put any criminal off the scent. Done is done, he decided.

Up the narrow length of Cutler Street, in the gaslight haze and patchy shadows, Piper saw a figure who was not Mr Weil. He didn't risk calling out (do you shout at a rabbit you want to trap?), he didn't hasten his step, only watched as the man retreated as if attached to the opposite end of a steel rod that pushed him away at the same speed Piper approached.

Yourka whisked himself around the corner and through a back alley. His safecracking skills wouldn't be much use to Karl on this action. As a lookout, however, Yourka was about to earn highest marks. He carried his warning about the lone policeman around the back of Exchange Buildings, through the dusty yard and into Karl's flat. The living-room looked deserted. He walked into the silence, past the table with its abandoned cups of tea, and stopped in the little hallway. He caught the sound of feet shuffling above him. Into the thick darkness on the staircase he whispered Karl's name. Then Nina's.

More shuffling on the stairs, then Karl answered him. 'Yourka?'

'I saw a policeman,' Yourka said.

'Up here.'

As he headed towards Bishopsgate on the lookout for reinforcements, PC Piper calmed his twitching nerves with the thought that there was no shame in a probationer leaving a possible crime in progress to fetch help. On the contrary, it demonstrated clear thinking and initiative. And in Piper's case on that December night, luck. Inside five minutes, his path crossed the beat of two constables, Walter Choate and Thomas Woodhams. He was especially glad it was Choate he'd met, a strong, broad-chested six-footer — a Goliath to Piper, who arrived with close experience of East End types. Before Piper stammered out a word, Choate asked, 'What's turning, lad?'

'Disturbance round Cutler Street. Back of 119 Houndsditch.'

'Cutler's Arms, you mean?' Woodhams asked him.

Piper shook his head, caught his breath, helpless to offer anything more.

'Show me,' said Choate. Something besides his calm grip spread calmness around him. You could see the boy he used to be still alive in his face, his round, open forehead and in the innocence, unpurged by crimes and the aftermath of crimes he'd seen, that softened his light eyes. The handlebar moustache, groomed and thick, the wisps of sandy hair, had the look of obvious disguises, tokens of manhood that somehow failed to mask his boyish soul.

Mr Weil stood waiting for them at Harris's jewellery shop. Piper let him give the other policemen a full account of the strange noises, and when he'd finished the short history he said to PC Choate, 'I went back two minutes ago. It's still with the noises.'

PC Piper frowned at Mr Weil. 'Didn't I ask you to keep your eye on the shop?'

'Half a minute I was inside.'

'Did you see anybody come out?' Choate asked him.

'Nobody come out. He's inside. Making noise.'

'We would have seen 'em,' Choate assured Piper. 'Tom,

put yourself over there.' Like a field marshal, he pointed out a position at the entrance to the cul-de-sac.

'They're foreigners,' Piper remembered to mention.

'Are they, now? Noisy buggers. You don't know what it might be,' Choate said, then, more heavily, 'It's these days, ain't it? Diabolical.'

If Rivka had heard what Choate said in the street below, she would have agreed. She, for one, could testify to the presence in the room of the devil. Not Satan himself, maybe, but junior demons sweating menace into the air. First Karl then Max rattled Yourka with questions he couldn't answer: Only one policeman? Is he coming back? What brought him snooping around here? Or who did?

'I don't know, I don't know, *I don't know!*'

'Oh,' said Max, sarcastically accepting the answer. He shook his pistol at Yourka with no sarcasm.

Who got the message. 'Good, yes! Now I'm an informer?'

'Oh. That's interesting,' Max said. '*Informer.* I didn't say the word. You did, Yourka.'

'Look out for coppers *and* inform on you at the same time! You're too clever for me, Max, you figured it out, I surrender.' Yourka ended with a snort of contempt laced with disgust.

Max leaned back on the edge of the brass bed as though he had all night to prove his case. He ignored Yourka, spoke directly to Karl. 'It's perfect. He gets paid twice — first by them, then by us.'

'Nobody's paid me *once* yet. When I get money I send half of everything to Russia,' Yourka shouted. 'What do you do with yours, Max?'

'I've got two kids and a wife! What've you got?'

'My clothes ... and Liesma!'

Rivka rasped at them, 'Stop fighting! What are you doing?'

Max ferociously turned on her. 'I'm asking you the same. I don't know you so good. You aren't Liesma. Somebody who fucks one of us, that's who you are. Maybe you've fucked us all now, Rivka, is that what you did? Fuck us with the police?'

Absolutely silent, Karl watched them go at each other, no idea how to stop them. In truth, he hardly heard what they were saying; they bickered because they were scared, filling the silence until he spoke, with an answer to the only question that mattered: Do they stay or go? 'Be quiet,' he said. 'Let me think.'

Max lay back on the bed. He used a corner of the plaid duvet to wipe the muzzle and grip of his Browning, then he released the clip. Thin light from the gas jet was enough for a look down the barrel and a close check of the mechanism. His thumb snapped the cartridges from the clip onto the bed. Lips moving as he counted, sure pressure on each round, Max reloaded then slid the clip home inside the gun's square handle.

'They will come back,' Karl said. 'We'll get out.'

Yourka lifted the curtain edge and watched through the window, his first duty. 'Can't see anything. Nobody in the street.'

Concentration drove out the smoothness of Karl's face, hardened it. Nina said to him, 'Somebody has to go down and tell Jacob.'

Rivka volunteered, 'I will.'

'No. I will,' Max said.

'Wait.' Karl stood with Yourka, looked down from the window. 'It might be all right.' On this side, a cautious flit; on that side, the prize. Is it retreat or desertion? 'We

242

could go out the back way and get Jacob. Let Rivka come here tomorrow.' Karl said to her, 'Tell us if it's still safe.'

A proposal from Yourka. 'Send her outside now and see if it's safe. If we can get on with it . . .'

'What should we tell Jacob?' Nina said.

Karl listened to the cold, concealing night. 'They don't know how many we are.'

'Or there might be twenty of them at the end of the street right now,' Max said.

'If they want to come in,' Karl said, 'you know they will.'

Rivka had felt this same vibration in her bones before, on the Talsen Road. The galloping danger of horse hooves stamped into the earth, each dull beat reaching into her through the soles of her feet. Here in this bedroom dread collected like humidity, absorbed all the breathable air; the heat of it raked her skin, even if the room was chilly enough for each breath to betray its fever in a puff of fog.

A few strands of hair drooped across Karl's forehead, twigs from a bough. He neatened them and said to Rivka, 'Do you hear anything?'

Conversation in the alleyway down below. A woman's voice. A door across the way clicked open, quietly shut. The pictures combined in Rivka's mind; she saw figures moving with serious purpose, towards this flat, against them. She looked Karl straight in his eyes to ask him, without uttering a word, *Do I hold still? When do I run?*

PC Piper gathered reinforcements on his trot back to Bishopsgate, a sergeant and two plainclothes constables. On duty and off, Sergeant Robert Bentley carried himself with the flair of a leading man. Nothing as frivolous as the stage, though, would ever blur his picture of the world or his place in it. His feet were planted on the side of order, a high vantage point that gave him an unobstructed view of human weakness — the material weaknesses of victims, the moral weakness of criminals. As a result, his attitude was unjoking and his manner with the public and junior officers alike cordially steam-rollered trivial distractions.

Mr Weil led Robert Bentley directly to the downstairs room closest to the source of the hammering noises. Bird-watchers in a forest hide would settle in as soundlessly, as engrossed in observation. *Thump. Thump.* The steady beat went on. *Thump. Thump-scrape.* The sergeant kept his voice low and gestured that he'd heard enough. 'What time did it start?'

'My sister informed me since seven o'clock.'

'Tonight.'

'Not the morning, in the night, yes.'

Miss Weil's voice rattled down the stairs. 'Is that you, Max? Don't scare me.'

'Ssh! Ssh! Keep quiet!' He shuffled past Robert Bentley to answer his sister in a whisper loud enough to carry up a flight of stairs. 'I've got the police! He's down here listening!'

And the muffled thumps behind the wall stopped dead.

The police ranks on the street grew to seven with the arrival of two more sergeants, William Bryant and Charles 'Daddy' Tucker. The blue engine of state authority, seven strong in this place tonight, occupied both corners of Houndsditch and Cutler Street, the turning into Exchange Buildings, the jewellery shop entrance, every likely path of escape. Cut off without a chance or doubt. Look at Charles Tucker's face and you see the authority of a protector, fixed as granite.

Everyone's Daddy — not by seniority but steady, abiding temper and City of London Police folklore, famous among plainclothes and uniformed officers — Daddy was the one who watched out.

Charles Tucker cast a glance down the cul-de-sac. 'Not sure Mr Piper is best placed where he is.'

Sergeant Bryant took the point. 'Trip over his own bootlaces.'

'Hey-ho. Hear what Bob's got to say.'

On his way back from Mr Weil's, Sgt. Robert Bentley entertained exactly the same thought. Piper could stand guard at the jewellery shop, close to the other constables, and bring PC Choate to join the experienced hands. You could always count on him to discourage troublemakers. With William Bryant at his back, Walter Choate and Daddy Tucker within hailing distance, Sergeant Bentley knocked on the door to No. 11. Karl inched it open.

Seven

Business-brisk, the officer asked him, 'Have you been working or knocking about inside?'

Out of sight on the steep staircase, Rivka huddled with the others. Crouched on the landing behind Max, she saw Karl standing in the gap of the half-open door. Rivka wondered what kind of heat lay throbbing inside his silence.

'Don't you understand English?'

Karl's empty stare communicated nothing.

In case somebody inside might hear, Robert Bentley raised his voice a little. 'Have you got anybody in the house who can?'

Karl filled his stare with a desire to understand.

'Fetch them down, will you.'

The door inched shut again, not solidly; the tongue of its mortise lock didn't click into its niche. Robert Bentley sniffed, tossed the others a sidelong glance that said the time for playing silly buggers was up. 'Open the door or we're going to smash it in!' With his fingers splayed against the door it opened with a nudge.

Through the doorless doorway, in the living-room on his right he saw traces of a home life. Genuine as sin. A good fire burned in the fireplace; scraps of an evening meal littered the table; the furniture looked worn but homey. Tilting his head to look further into that vacant room, Sergeant Bentley saw traces of a different sort of life: the pressure gauge next to coils of rubber tubing on the floor, next to the welder's blowpipe.

One pace behind him William Bryant spotted the man on the stairs, or no more than the bottom half of his long unbuttoned overcoat; from the waist up Karl was a mute figure swallowed by the dark. 'Wondered where you'd got to,' the bobby said.

Robert Bentley challenged the man, 'Is anybody working here?'

An answer came from the figure on stairs. 'No.'

'Anyone in the back?'

'No.'

'Can I look in the back?'

'Yes.'

'Will you show us the way?'

Karl held still. 'In there.'

At Robert Bentley's first step into the living-room, the back door blasted open. Out of the rattling shock, a dust-covered man burst towards him. Jacob's long strides closed the distance and the pistol came down on his enemy. Arm straight and stiff, he held the Dreyse automatic shoulder high, squeezed off two shots, then a quick three more. On the stairs Karl unslung his Mauser and let loose a spread of rounds at the crumpling policeman.

Gunfire drummed at Robert Bentley and William Bryant from two directions. Their reflexes were spasmodic and useless. With naked hands, Sergeant Bryant moved to fend off the Dreyse's muzzle flash, as if he were batting away a swarm of wasps. Too many, too fast and vicious for him to escape. In front of him Sergeant Bentley made a better target.

The roar of each gunshot buffeted the air. Rivka felt the thunderclaps explode in her ears, the blind bullets' concussion, she tasted burnt cloth. Somewhere in the cloud of noise she howled, hoarse, rhythmic screams, the kind you'd hear pour from the mouths of women giving birth. But she screamed for God to carry her out of the slaughterhouse.

Robert Bentley shouted, too, in shock and pain. The first bullet split his shoulder and twisted him square onto Jacob. The pistol fired again. His second bullet ploughed deep into the sergeant's neck. *Drop! Drop!* Jacob willed him to the floor with emotion no different from his feeling ten minutes before when he was hammering through the toilet wall. *What I want is on the other side of this.* The seep of blood wet Robert Bentley's collar, then spread inside his tunic, down his chest, as he fell backward.

Which left William Bryant still standing. Bullets lashed into his arm and chest. Their rushing force flattened him against the doorjamb, where he dragged breath back into his empty lungs, lurched to escape and fell face-first across Robert Bentley's sprawled body. His attackers didn't let him go; he didn't move faster than they did. It was chance that got him, staggering, wounded, out of No. 11, dazed chance that pitched William Bryant towards Cutler Street and salvation.

The liquid in Robert Bentley's mouth tasted of sea water. *Bloody fool. Fight fair and I can beat you without a gun. Oh, Father, what I've seen. This body's no bloody use to them. The men what killed me they're alive and no use. Do this to them. Somebody. Daddy or God. Point me to the skies. I'll get myself out of this. Gone half eleven when. Because he wasn't inside nobody heard the revolver click. Ain't it, Bill?* If he'd used the last of his strength to open his eyes the dying sergeant would have caught sight of plainclothesman Woodhams scurrying down the cul-de-sac to his rescue, and heard the snap of Thomas Woodhams' thighbone when a bullet from Karl's Mauser blew it to splinters.

A long sprint from the door, Daddy Tucker watched the same gun and the arm aiming it reach through the doorway. He half crouched, ready to rush the murderer, PC Strongman beside him, when another gunman sloped into the street from No. 11. Jacob walked towards the two policemen, raised his gun without a tremor and shot twice. The bullet that struck Daddy Tucker in the hip twirled him into the wall, the wound in his heart dropped him. *'We're no danger to you!'* Arthur Strongman said with an electrified stare. He bent down to drag Daddy Tucker out of the killer's range, his eyes still fixed on Jacob, who bore down on him, firing into the dark, clearing the way with bullets, crushing them with his ecstasy. Under the streetlamp, before he fled back, the pistol stopped and gave the constable a silent answer. *Look at me. You can't stop this. I'm your terror.*

Daddy Tucker died on the pavement of Cutler Street, propped against a wall. Two boys, Harry and Solomon Jacobs, knelt close to him. The last sensation he knew was Solomon's hand shaking his shoulder. So Daddy Tucker's last thought was of that comfort, *A good stranger's Christian mercy.*

'What is it outside?' Rivka clutched the sleeve of Nina's dress.

Rebuke flashed across Nina's face. 'Stay here, then. You can't make it?'

'Tell me what to do.'

'Run. When he says.'

Karl waved them downstairs. Nina's nimble plunge down to him showed Rivka how quick she had to be. Already by the door Yourka slipped out behind Karl. *Go!* Max yelled at Rivka. His urgency hit her like a slap on a horse's flank. She took two stairs in a jump, lost a shoe, fell against the banister.

'Bastard cunt!' Max shouted behind her. His curse wasn't at Rivka. The clear doorway stood blocked now by Walter Choate, big enough to fill it top to bottom and side to side. He tackled Karl and stopped him getting away. Max's boot heel clipped Rivka's chin as he bounded over her to hurl himself into the fight to free Karl from the policeman's grip.

In their wrestling dance they fought close enough for one to smell the steam of the other's breath. Walter Choate grabbed hold of Karl's wrist, forced the Mauser's barrel off him, and Karl fired once, again, again, again. Four loud eruptions froze Rivka to the stairs and a shallow arc of wounds riveted Constable Choate's left side — his thigh, his calf, his foot — but he refused to drop. Then Jacob was on him. Precise as a craftsman he punched two bullets into Walter Choate's spine — but he refused to let go, leaking strength, melting into the pavement, dragging Karl down with him. Jacob jabbed the constable's face with the butt of his revolver. Max shot at him, a single blast that found flesh but missed its target.

Karl's body bucked forward and with a moan he crumpled on top of Walter Choate. Mad-eyed, listening hard to follow the sound of running footfalls in Cutler Street, Yourka added his fists to the downpour pummelling the half-conscious policeman, who lay deaf and sinking into his small corner of oblivion. 'Let go, you shit!' Jacob screamed in English at Walter Choate. 'Your fucking hand! *Let go!*'

As if balancing on a high ledge, her back flattened against the green shutters, Rivka edged around the entwined dying men. At the far end of the narrow carriageway Nina waved at her, frantic, angry — *hurry! don't stop!* – but Nina's summons was blotted out by the blankness paralysing Max. He read his own desolate fright in the mirror of Rivka's face. At first she thought he was offering his hand to give her courage and take the same from her. Then she saw the gun in it, the obscenity of its muzzle levelled at her stomach.

A sharp prod from Jacob roused Max. Yourka helped hoist Karl to his dangling feet and with Jacob propping him up on the other side they carried Liesma's leader slung between them like a drunk. The six of them made it to Cutler Street, Jacob loosing off shots at pursuers, Max and the two women hustling along at his back. Rivka alone thought, *Here it is: all the truth of it in the flesh. Torn open and red wet on the ground. That policeman with the boy's face. Our cruelty's accomplishment. From the side of good...* Nina barked at her to keep up. Rivka followed into the refuge of an alleyway... *My good brutal friends. Help me escape here and stay alive. Tell me rest easy, they deserve the slaughter we dish out. We're cruel and good...*

'You can't go back to Perelman's,' Nina said to her.

Where, then? The scorched hole in the back of Karl's coat floated ahead of Rivka, its red stain bloomed around it. *Nina, don't call me your sister after this. No more. I won't love suave violent men.*

252

Eight

What substance of his life does a man own? His choices. At each step, each choice is his possession, solely. Anarchist or Social Democrat, street fighter, stay-at-home, whatever name anyone calls him or he calls himself, look for the substance of a man in the history of his choices. It's a waste of breath and brain power to debate friend or enemy out of choices his nature made for him. Try to and you're a dirty thief... So Peter wasn't about to ruin a peaceful Friday night by preaching his own choices at Fritz and Yoska. They chose what they chose and that was the end of it. By keeping his talk clear of subjects like safecracking and the expropriation of bourgeois wealth Peter discovered he had quite a lot to say on the comparison of afternoon beverages — coffee in Paris versus four-o'clock tea in London. (And he screened off any worry about Rivka, who at that minute was probably sitting bored out of her freckly skin in Houndsditch, by herself, utterly ignored by Karl, Nina and the rest of them.)

In Peter's history, twenty-seven years of it so far, when his nature said fight, he fought; it was telling him now to pull back. He noticed something: the need to have opinions had drained from him. In place of them there was patience. Which made him a radical among radicals, freer to enjoy the card games in the restaurant with his friends and the midnight stroll with them afterwards to the boulevard, where Fritz and Yoska turned towards Houndsditch and Peter went the other way, back to his digs.

Or he would have if Fritz hadn't stopped him by

pointing to a party of men lurching towards them further down the street. From that distance, the usual early-hours Commercial Road sight, straggling drunks. Then he saw the woman. 'Is that Rivka?'

Yoska made out the faces of the two men carrying the third. 'Jabob and Yourka. They've got... who is it?'

'Karl,' Peter said.

Exhausted and sweating from the half hour trek lugging Karl home through the back streets, first Jacob then Yourka stammered out fragments of the disaster they'd left behind them. 'Nobody can tell me how they found us,' Jacob said.

Yourka shouldered the limp weight of Karl's body, lowered him to the ground. 'Max says an informer.'

Fritz, flabbergasted. 'Who?'

'He says me!'

'Where's Max and Nina?' Yoska knelt beside Karl, touched his knuckles to the unconscious man's forehead.

'They went to find a doctor,' Rivka said. She gripped Peter's arm then repeated the information to Yoska, who wasn't listening.

He said, 'Blue fuckers shot him in the back.'

'No, Max did,' Yourka said. Then, maybe not so quickly, 'By accident.'

'This bogie had him and didn't let go,' Jacob said. 'We shot that shit. And four more.'

'How many killed?' Peter asked Jacob.

'Two for sure,' Yourka said. 'They bottled us in—'

Jacob silenced him with a look. 'Three. Definite, for sure. The one in the street,' he informed Yourka, 'he's dead, believe me.'

'We can't stay here,' Fritz laid it out to Peter.

A piece of news he didn't need to hear from Fritz. 'Get Karl off the street.'

'Get him to that doctor, the German. Fritz, what's his name? Berons goes to him sometimes,' Yoska said.

Fritz cried out, 'Leave him here! He's gone!'

'No!' Rivka slumped to Karl's side.

'Help me lift him,' Peter said to her, calm as he could.

The slight pressure of their hands on his shoulders twisted a scream of pain out of Karl.

And Fritz, too, a tortured complaint. 'You *see*.'

'*You* see?' Peter stood up to him. 'Should I explain it to you, Fritz?' He nodded to Rivka and together they lifted Karl to his feet, but she was too short to hold him upright and steady. 'Don't let him fall. Good, Rivvie. Let Fritz take him.'

'Where are we going?' Fritz demanded from Peter.

'To your place. Nina's bringing a doctor.'

Rivka felt Peter's hand reach for hers, squeeze it and then let go. For the second time that night she marched behind the black-red stain on Karl's coat. At every street corner between Houndsditch and there, she'd held herself back from running off alone, abandoning Nina and the others, because they knew the safest route home.

The further from the horror, the closer to Peter. If she had to go on the run again she'd hide with him. She'd moulded her naked body around his, lay in bed in his arms — one night ago? A different lifetime? — there and then Peter spoke to her in a careless voice he never used with anyone else. *A touch from you is stronger than any argument Karl makes*, he told her and, *I want to live in a smaller world*. This nightmare threw him back in with the gang of them. It changed everything.

'He goes out from the house, Rosie, every time I think, *this is when Fritz doesn't come back*. He says it's some errand but really he's on the boat.'

'You know he's going to Australia. He didn't trick you about it. Fritz showed you the tickets. Two tickets, he bought. One for him and one for his wife.'

'No. For me.' Luba's flat statement of the facts, a barrier to argument, as if conviction was undeniable truth.

In the bed beside her Rosie nestled deeper under the blanket. 'Then why do you say he's on a boat?'

'I know he isn't, I just think it.'

'No, that's being simpleminded.'

Luba snipped back, 'You'd know about that. If you ever had a man you'd know how it felt and you wouldn't call worrying about him simpleminded.'

Rosie didn't speak her unkind thoughts. Namely, that Luba's stupid wailing was over her own unhappiness. For Fritz's happiness she wouldn't surrender the smallest portion of hers. She's a little girl. Luba had no clue how a woman feels when she forgets herself, body and soul, contemplating the perfect beauty of a man. Luba frets and swoons for Fritz when he's away for a few hours, even though when he's with her their fights about his wife are as terrible as the ones over who let ants swarm into the sugar bowl. She suffers over the daydream of her future as Mrs Svaars and loves Fritz most when she attracts him with her body. Love isn't conquering, it's surrender. That was the thing Rosie knew from experience. To quiet her, she said to Luba, 'He's with Peter and Yoska, not on a boat.'

'Fritz told me a lie last night. Right in this bed.'

'Why? What?'

'Something with Yoska. I don't know. Whispering. He told me go in Peter's room because Yoska brought something and I shouldn't see.'

'Did you go?'

'What else? Yoska barged in here and Karl, too... He said he'd explain to me later, so, yes, I went, what else?'

'What did Yoska bring him?'

Downtrodden Luba groaned under the burden of a shrug. 'He didn't tell me. Lie, lie, lie.'

'La, la, la...' Rosie's singsong medicine for the heavy of heart teased a smile to the corners of Luba's mouth. It flickered to life there, fluttered and died.

They could have camped at Rosie's a ten minute walk away, but the room there was drafty and damp. Also, waking on Saturday in Settle Street would deprive Luba of the pleasure of one of Fritz's hangdog morning-after apologies. For the vacant hours till Friday midnight and after, Luba's shared bed was a haven, momentarily separate from men's existence which came banging and crashing in with what sounded like a grand piano cart wheeling down the stairs outside Luba's door. Or up them. Fritz's enemies, strangers he kept secret from her - was it them breaking in? Would hoodlums shut the door behind them? Would the police? In her nightgown Luba stood by the door, stiffly listening.

'It's Fritz. I hear him.'

'Stay here,' Rosie whispered from the bed.

The low voices and confusion of footsteps collected in the front room. Luba heard the door pulled shut. 'I'm going to see.'

Rosie's frantic signalling didn't hold Luba back or stop her eavesdropping, ear pressed to Peter's door. Was it Fritz's moan she heard? 'Fritz?'

'Don't come in,' he ordered her through the door. Shoulder first Fritz leaned his weight against it. 'Go back to bed.'

Behind him, Yourka lifted Karl by the heels, Jacob by

257

the shoulders, and together the two men hefted him onto the bed. Yourka said, 'I'm going to get a doctor.'

Jacob forbade it. 'Nina went ten minutes ago.'

'Then I'd better find Nina. He won't last much longer.'

'She's bringing the doctor.'

'I'll hurry.' The cold pressure Yourka felt at the side of his head was the barrel of a pistol. 'Jacob, wait. Wait. Listen to me. What are you thinking?'

'You're in a hurry to leave here.'

'To get Karl help! Where else?'

Jacob's quick answer, 'Turn yourself in. You want to do that, Yourka?'

'I don't!'

'Help yourself?'

'Wait. Where's Max? Where did *he* go?'

'You tell me.'

'He told Rivka where.'

She couldn't see a thing except Jacob's thumb as it clicked back the hammer. Mouth dry, Rivka said what she knew. 'Max went with Nina.'

'Maybe.' Jacob twisted his gun against Yourka's forehead.

'He did or he didn't,' Yourka put to him 'but he isn't here, is he?'

'Where do you think Max went?' Jacob asked Rivka.

'With Nina. For a doctor,' she said.

Jacob replied by easing the Dreyse's hammer down. He slipped the gun under Karl's pillow, a precaution not wasted on Fritz, who shouted at Jacob, 'Yourka wants to get away fast, then he's smarter than you! They're coming here. Tonight — now!' In uproar he pleaded, 'I'm *innocent* but the police, they'll take *me*!'

'Innocent, sure.' Jacob matched his contempt for the word to his estimation of the weakling who spoke it.

258

'I wasn't there! But I'm still fucked because I can't prove it!'

'Fucked in a barrel,' agreed Yoska.

'All right, so what?' Peter told Fritz.

'I'll vouch for you,' Yoska's dark joke. He rehearsed his testimony. 'Fritz Svaars was with me and Peter the Painter all night. We drank coffee. I beat him at gin rummy.'

'Listen to Peter,' Jacob said.

And Peter spoke to them all. 'They know our names. How long before they come looking? We can't be here when Nina gets back with the doctor.'

'I said so,' Yourka reminded everybody.

'She'll think of something to tell him. It can give us half an hour, if we're lucky, an hour. If he doesn't know about the gun fight yet.' Gently, Peter moved Jacob aside and stood over the bed. He looked down at his friend who lay on it suffering. 'Still with us, comrade?'·

Karl opened his eyes. 'I heard every word. Do you have a place to go?' Only Karl saw his quick nod. 'Where's Nina?'

'Looking for a doctor.'

'No doctor.'

Behind Peter, Rivka said, 'For his pain.'

'Morphine, Karl,' Peter said.

'No,' his reply. Then, faint crescent of a smile, 'What's the matter? Can't you take it?'

Fritz demonstrated the hour's seriousness — his intentions too — by pulling the Browning automatic from his trouser pocket and flamboyantly double-checking its clip. Yoska did the same with his heavy pistol. 'Fritz, you have bullets for me? I need more.'

'In my room.'

'Mauser shells?'

'Boxes. Plenty.' Fritz's glance landed on Peter. 'Where's

259

yours?' Before he got a reply, he said, 'You take my Mauser.'

Karl's groan contorted his face; it rose and fell on a crackling billow of pain and ended in a cry for Nina. It stopped the breath Rivka drew to speak to Peter. It choked off her natural kindness and made her fear for her fate. As if she'd become suddenly aware of a stink on her clothes or skin, a nauseating odour that soaked into her on her walk through the slaughterhouse. Unless her body itself was the source of this vileness, a stench so powerful it warned people away. Except the ones who carried the same smell.

Untouchable.

Peter's scent. The hazy distance in him even in bed, even with her, no mystery to Rivka anymore. Always judging (she thought before tonight), lowering his judgment on all humanity. No. Peter is touchable to her at last. Do you see judgment harden his eyes? No. It's knowledge of himself. He's breathed these fumes for such a long time, the sick vapours around dying bodies and killers. *I'm one of them*, Rivka thought, *a limb of the creature that rampaged and murdered*. Revolutionary. Fighter. Our Common Cause. Words, alibis. There's nothing in a human language for the thing she is now; find a name for it in the low grunts of animals, in screeches, barks and howls. She said to Peter, 'What should I do?'

'You want to help? Wait for me in Luba's room. Keep her inside, and Rosie too, if she's still there.'

Rivka wasn't quick enough on her feet. Luba pushed through the door, Rosie following close. 'My God, my God...' Luba cried out. In two breaths shock turned to accusation. 'Fritz, my God!'

'I didn't *do* anything!'

'Liar!'

Jacob barked, 'Fritz wasn't there.'

'It doesn't matter where I was. I was with Yoska and Peter.' He threw them a look. 'It won't matter for you, either.'

Luba slapped Fritz's face. Before he managed to get a grip on her wrists, she slapped him again and scratched his cheek. 'I'll tell the police you didn't go, you stayed with me all night!'

'You think they won't arrest me? On your word? They'll beat me until I confess to everything,' Fritz said. 'They'll make me confess I assassinated the Tsar and deport me to Russia!'

'Don't say that! Not if I tell them you were here.'

'Luba, don't talk crazy. You're not going to the police.'

Almost unnoticed, Rosie shamed them all. She knelt next to Karl and spoke his name. With a handkerchief she wiped the slick of sweat from his face. 'Nobody looks after you.' Tenderly, she removed his boots, then opened his coat, and didn't flinch at the sight of blood leaking onto the coverlet from the bullet hole in Karl's back. 'I'm going to get you something.'

'No doctor.'

'Nobody's coming.' Nina reported from the landing as she hurried inside.

Jacob sprang over to ask her, 'Where's Max?'

Echoed by Yourka, 'Where did he go?'

'To Perelman,' Nina said. 'Is Karl worse?'

'You can see,' Jacob said.

Nina looked without budging an inch. 'That doctor, I begged him to come here, he said no. I don't trust him.' Then she said, 'He might go to the police.'

'Or he might not?' Jacob taunted, ready to run.

'I think he will,' Nina said.

'If he will, then he did,' Fritz figured. He said to Luba, 'How much money have you got?'

'What you gave me.'

'That's all? Look in jewellery box. Bring me the money. You get out of the house. Go to your brother's.'

Luba shook her head. 'Jack won't help me. Nathan, either.'

Rosie came back carrying a wet towel, which she handed to Luba and said, 'I'll stay,' she said. 'You go to mine.' From around her neck, Rosie freed the loop of brown string tied to the Settle Street key. She traded it to Luba for the wet towel.

Fritz stopped Rosie and whispered, 'When he dies, there's kerosene. Let the whole house burn.'

Downstairs, the door slammed. Fritz's stomach jumped. At the window Yoska pawed back the curtain's edge in time to see Jacob and Yourka run down Grove Street in opposite directions, to take their chances alone.

Peter had retreated, too, with Rivka, into the back bedroom, door shut against Fritz and Luba's howling at each other. 'I don't know how long we've got, so listen.'

'It's good for Karl that Nina's with him.'

He shook Rivka by her shoulders. 'Listen to me. She won't stay here. You can't, either.'

'Where can we go? I don't have any money.'

'At Shinebloom's, try your manager friend. He likes you,' Peter said, as quick as he thought it.

'Should I go to the restaurant?'

'His house is better. You know where he lives?'

Rivka closed her eyes to remember. 'Club Row.'

'You go there.'

'If you won't be here where will I meet you? When?'

He told her, 'We can't stay together. It's not safe.'

'Peter, no! Why? No, if we —'

'What happened in Houndsditch tonight decided things. I can't stay here.'

'Wait. I'm going with you. We'll help each other.' She coiled her arms around his waist. 'We can choose what we do.'

He twisted free of Rivka, this anchor. 'You're talking like a real anarchist.'

'I won't give you up.'

'You'll fight.'

'Yes.'

'Against the Enemies of Freedom.'

'Who?'

'To overthrow the ruling class? For your comrades in the revolutionary struggle?'

'For us.'

'"Us"?'

'You.'

'I'm not Liesma.'

Peter's sharpness, his anger, baffled her. 'For us. To be together. How we were two nights ago. I want to be with you tonight, tomorrow. By tomorrow we can be safe together, in a different city.'

'Please, Rivka, don't think about the future! *This* is the future — of an hour ago! Policemen are hunting for you, understand? For Nina and Karl, for me, all of us, tonight. People saw you, Rivka, somebody can describe you. You think the police went home after? What matters is how smart we are *this minute.*'

'It's smart for me to stay with you.'

'From your experience of actions,' Peter said, mordant and lucid. 'No, it's stupid. I have to get out of this by myself.'

'What happens to me?' The shudder in her chest began in terror and ended in trembling courage. On tiptoe she

263

reached up to hold Peter's face between her hands and she said, 'You're inside me.'

'You'll have a better chance alone.' The fragrance from her palms and hair, its nearness, its memory, quieted Peter. 'Don't go to Perelman's.'

'There's nowhere else for me.'

'You have to keep away from there,' he said with grim strength to make sure she took it in.

Rivka's kiss on his mouth drew Peter's arms around her. Her breath in his ear, 'Promise you'll find me in a few days.'

As he pulled free of her he pressed Rivka's hand to his cheek. 'Don't expect anybody to help you. Actions never finish. Not exes like this one, when there's blood.'

'After this we're going to be together. Promise me, Peter.'

'What good is any promise with insanity crashing down all around? You don't know. I don't know what's going to happen to us.'

Lovers' language, if roses grew with petals of human skin.

Nine

Poor Nettie Perelman, rousted out of bed by her father in the wee darkling hours. Loosely clutched by sleep, she still knew it wasn't a school morning, it was Saturday and she had the right to stay in bed until her mother called her downstairs for breakfast. Nettie whined her complaint. 'Ssh, ssh,' Papa Perelman quietly comforted her. The light in Nettie's room confused her. 'Don't wake Mama, little dollie.'

Some part of Nettie was still dreaming as she let her papa sit her on the edge of the bed and replace her flannel nightgown with the blouse, stockings and skirt she'd worn to school on Friday morning. From inside a cave somewhere Nettie heard her father say she was going on a journey to visit her Aunt Hannah. 'Where's your case, Nettie? The wicker one.' One eye open, Nettie's hand, finger pointing, flopped to her side. 'Under here?'

'I want my sailor dress,' she said to the top of his head.

'You can take whatever you want, puppy dog,' a kiss on her knee.

'Don't call me that.'

'No, I'm bad. Sorry, puppy dog.'

'*Boys* are puppy dogs,' Nettie groaned at her dumb bad papa and threw herself backwards onto her pillow.

Perelman twisted round to say to the man standing in the hallway, 'She's a good actress.' To this the man said nothing. 'I'll talk to your wife. Tell her you're all right. You want me to say where you are?'

Max shifted on his tired feet. 'No. I'll get a message to her.'

'Are you coming back?' Max had no reply for him. 'I wouldn't, either.' Days before, Perelman suspected that Rivka also was mixed up in whatever action George Gardstein had on the boil. Max confirmed it, along with the number of dead. Perelman said, 'Nina's her friend, so all right. But Piatkow...' He spat the name. 'Bastard house painter should've kept her out of trouble.'

'What's a bastard, Papa?'

Max enlightened Nettie. 'A dog.'

'You think so? Him?' However low Perelman's opinion of Peter sank, it never reached the depths of informer.

'Somebody spilled. You ask me.'

'Piatkow?' He considered the perverse possibility, shook it out of his head. 'Cold-hearted selfish bastard, yes; a dog, no.' To Nettie he said, 'You can put your shoes on downstairs.'

'Are we going now?'

'Yes, doll. On the night-boat. Do you remember Papa's friend Max?' Perelman waved Max in from the hallway.

His clothes, hands and face were powdered with black brick dust, his short hair pomaded with sweat. 'Hello, Nettie.'

'Max is taking you to Aunt Hannah's.'

'Are you and Mama coming tomorrow?'

'Soon, soon.'

'And Fanny? And Carlusha?'

'Sunday, all of us. First show Max how good you are at play acting. Show me your terrible illness face.' The ten-year-old let her cheeks and lower jaw sag, her dull eyes half close. 'Cough.' Nettie's cough racked her shoulders, caved in her bony chest. 'You don't feel so good, do you.'

'No... Papa,' in her ravaged, orphan frail whisper.

266

Aglow, Perelman bragged to Max, 'Quite an actress, no?'

'I'm going to be an actress in the theatre,' Nettie almost sang, miraculously recovered.

'I give you permission. Something else. For tonight you pretend Max is your papa. On the train and night-boat, Nettie, you call him Papa and make your ill face.'

'Why do I have to?'

'Because when you can do your friend a kindness, my darling, you must do it. Max's own little girl can't go to Paris with him. She feels so poorly she can't go out from the house.' In the gentlest confidence a father ever gave a daughter, he said, 'I want you to keep Max company so he doesn't feel sad.' Then Perelman advised Max, 'At Customs tell them she's got diphtheria. Everybody will leave you alone.'

Daubed with a lather of shaving soap, in a washstand mirror in a comrade's bedroom, at the other end of Commercial Road, Peter's face reflected a numbing fact: escape was just the start. Always, always. Today's goal was more than just to disappear — it was to avoid ending up like those hotheads in Tottenham last year, Hefeld and the other one, both with bullets in the head. 'I must want to live some more,' he said to the mirror.

So far, success. He'd counted on his friend Pavell for sanctuary, with Fritz and Yoska clinging to his back pockets, and they'd got their temporary roost. Safety at Pavell's till first light, five hours to catch their breath and make a plan. Together or separate? Somewhere in London or outside? Think for yourself. Choose for yourself. Act for yourself. On every other flit, Peter got away alone, with secrecy to protect him instead of numbers. Look at these numbers! Fritz may be calm for the minute, but he's a jar of nitro-glycerine tipped to explode. Yoska, with his bad leg, moves slow as a wounded elephant. Two more targets, two chances out of three something will tilt the wrong way.

At each stroke of the razor, an irreversible cut. Inward from the untwisted ends of his moustache, left then right, shallow arcs uncovered his smooth upper lip. Then he scythed clean the neat triangular beard, the angled ruff of hairs under his jaw first, left side then right, and finally Peter erased the point that sat so elegantly barbered on his chin. A dozen strokes, a few more? He'd shed a skin and no twinge of nostalgia pained him. Looking back at him was an unfashionable face Peter hadn't seen in years – his pre-revolutionary face.

He joined his friends in the unlit front room and said, 'I'm getting myself to Poplar. Out of the city.'

'Meeting the girl?' Yoska said.

'Am I the only one with an idea?'

Fritz brooded, 'They won't try to arrest us. If they see us they'll gun us down.'

'No,' Yoska shakily laughed it off. 'They'll capture us, Fritz. So they can torture us all day. *Then* they'll shoot us in the back.' The laugh went, not the shakiness. 'For what we know about Karl, the exe, the whole thing.'

'They have to murder us.' Of this Fritz was convinced. 'To prove it to the Englanders they've got power over foreigners.'

'Tame us. Put us back in our cages,' Yoska caught on.

'We don't know anything, do we? We weren't there. In Houndsditch.'

'No, no.'

'What do they care? We're anarchists, *auslanders* –'

'Thieves, Jews, yes...'

'— we'll do.'

'Police want a prize. Our hides nailed on the King's wall.'

'Our heads hanging on the, the, in the ...'

'Trophy room,' Yoska supplied.

'The King of England's trophy room. They're coming after us with a meat axe.'

'One for each of us.'

Fritz hoisted himself off the sofa to declare, 'Our people! Get word to them — I don't mean people like Pavell or Hoffman, not Liesma — I mean *citizens*, people around here. They'd make an uprising.'

'Uprising,' echoed Yoska. 'Because of us?'

'In the streets, why not? Barricades in Brick Lane. We didn't do anything against anybody.' He polled Yoska, 'Did you shoot any policemen tonight?' Then Peter, 'Did you?'

Until this deranged notion was aimed at him Peter had kept his distance, happy to let Fritz shoot off sparks. Now, though, survival was at stake. Someone had to douse the firebrand with a bucket of cold water. 'Ring a bell and see who comes running. Why don't you do? Walk down the street, Fritz, ring your bell. 'Save your brothers from the bastard English police!' You'll die of loneliness. Or a brick in the head. Krauts, Polacks, Russos, Letts, Wops and Yids — the Yids more than any of them. What do you think? They want to *be* Englishmen! They want people to leave them alone, that's all. To forget about them. It's the reason they *came* here. They'll come running to help like your house is on fire? You really think so? You're lucky if nobody turns you in.'

'Englanders don't want them! It's the funniest English *joke*. We'll always be Wops and Yids,' Fritz said, finger pointing. 'English are English. Everybody else is — you

269

know it's true what I'm saying — everybody else is down in the dirt. If Yids and whoever around here don't believe today, tomorrow they'll see for sure. When the children walk around thinking they're English. They'll act like Englanders, learn how to talk like them, drink tea and put on English clothes. Then we can have a big laugh. Listen to Englanders talking behind Yids' backs. And not just behind, either — sometimes right to their darling faces.'

'Let's sit here and wait twenty years, all right? For the Great Uprising,' Peter said.

'You have to educate the people.'

'Tonight? Why don't we educate them tonight, Fritz, so they'll make a revolution in Brick Lane and save our skins?'

'When they look outside their windows and see how the English are persecuting us they'll get educated.'

'Too late for you and me.' Peter made a curse of the word *uprising*, turned away from Fritz and called himself a fool for not borrowing money from Pavell to buy a train ticket out of London.

'He's your friend, so he must be all right,' Yoska said to Peter. 'You trust Pavell, then I do too.'

'Good. What do you mean?'

'Nobody wants the police on them.'

'We can't stay with Pavell,' Peter said. 'Before first light, if he's back or not, we leave.'

'Where?' Fritz, throwing down a dare.

'I'm heading for Poplar.'

'I'll go to Betsy, then,' Yoska decided. 'She'll hide me.' Then, a thought. 'All of us.'

'How far?' Peter said, suddenly interested.

'Ten minutes. Sidney Street. By her flat you can get to the roof.'

Peter figured the odds. 'A yard? A back door?'

'It's a quiet place. Normal,' Yoska said. 'Quiet people live there.'

'Where is it in the street?'

'Middle. On a little road. Also there's a yard behind there, a good alley.'

'Middle house.' Peter considered it. 'Who knows you know Betsy?'

'Mr Gershon does.'

'Who's he?'

'Betsy's husband! A whole year and he doesn't know about me and Betsy. She can keep a secret, perfect.' Yoska massaged his leg. 'Don't worry about Gershon. He won't be around.'

'It's good,' Fritz joined in. 'We should go by Cable Street, stay off the big road.'

'Twenty minutes,' Peter guessed. 'Yoska, you have a key to the street door?'

Yoska took a pebble out of his jacket pocket, showed it to Peter. 'Sure.'

A melody plinked in a corner of the room, glassy, leisurely, as if, arguments and decisions settled, the balalaika player understood he had permission to play. Friend to them all, to Peter and Fritz, Yoska and Pavell, who used his brains and tracked the persecuted men here to offer what he could, to comfort, to sympathise, to help. Fritz swayed to each strum, limp as sea grass, overwhelmed by a nostalgic mood. Nostalgia for his peaceful life before the calamity in Houndsditch galloped down on him and mangled him under its hooves, taken over by the homely memory of a few nights ago. 'Petersburg Road,' he requested.

Nicholas Tomacoff plinked the steel strings, sang the first few words of Fritz's favourite song. '*Vdol po Piterskoi, po darozhinkye,* and Fritz joined in, *po Tverskoi-Yamskoi, s karakoltshikom* . . .' the two men's two voices, balalaika simpering underneath, and Peter in a strangled hush, 'Are you crazy? Stop it! Hang a sign on Pavell's window and tell the whole neighbourhood we're in here!'

'Sorry, Peter.' Nicholas laid the silenced balalaika across his knees. 'I'll keep quiet.'

Ten

Do something. When they can't do anything else, people go.
Going is something they can do. She shut the door behind her
and it's the same to Luba as finishing. On this side of the door
it isn't finished. I still help him. We're not dead and gone. This
is dying. This is my home. Forget Settle Street, all of this city,
nowhere outside is in the world. This room. This floor. This
fire. This man. With him is the last place I live...

Rosie's memory of Luba shutting the door behind her
flickered in her mind. An hour ago, it could have
happened a hundred years ago — when together they
trailed around Stepney to bring a doctor who'd come out
before dawn to tend to a suffering man. 'He doesn't want
to go to hospital. So this is all I can do.' Medicine to quiet
the pain, for ten shillings dug out of Karl's trouser
pocket. 'Can you hear me? What name do you want me to
write on the certificate?' Karl dredged the strength to
answer, 'George Gardstein.'

The doctor said it to Luba; Luba said the same to Rosie:
'I did what I could.' Then, 'I can't think about it anymore.
I'm going to my brother's.'

Rosie stopped herself from replying, *Somebody to do your*
thinking for you. Luba abandoned her in the room with
Karl, who was leaving her too. Blood-soaked sheets
underneath him, towels wet and red on the floor,
butcher's flowers, more blood on Karl's pillow, his
clothes. Gray light chilled the window's edges, unhaltable
day pushing in, the last of Karl's life. Forsaken.

Not by Rosie. *Not by me. This is our home today. We're one*

273

body. Rough or tender, no one touches us anymore. Is this how it feels when you're finally a ghost? A Presence watching, like the medium told me. I'm a Presence for you. You be one for me. A ghost can't touch the world. You can't be helped any more or hurt. You're a memory. While they're alive. Then you're forgotten, same as if you never lived.

'Rosie?'

She crawled over to the side of the bed. 'I'm here.'

'You don't have to wait. Go home.'

'What do you need?' Rosie poured some water into a glass and found the small brown bottle the doctor left on the table.

'Do something for me.'

We aren't dead yet. I'm not a ghost or a memory yet. I can do this. For Karl. My Karl. If it's my last act in the world it will be this act of love. Help him remember it for an hour.

Strong instructions in a weak voice from the bed. Rosie emptied the drawers and shelves of papers and photographs, moved stacks of Karl's notebooks and pamphlets from corners of the room into a bigger heap next to the fireplace. The bullets she found she collected into a flat cap, which she laid on Karl's bedside table. Then one by one she fed papers from the heap into the fire. She stirred them with the poker to do a thorough job. Now and again she glanced back at Karl to persuade herself he was awake and watching.

Eleven

Karl's eyes stayed open because he lacked the strength to close them. Strength of will. A minute before, Rosie asked him if he wanted her to give his hair a brushing. He failed to make a reply. So she neatened the damp flattened nest with Nina's hairbrush. Silence taken for acceptance. The strong beauty of Karl's face had slipped, sunk back, like the concavity of a cliff weakened by brute winds. Second by second becoming less of what it was.

Now comes this: Nina is smart to get out quick. She knows the police will come tonight, tomorrow, to lift her. She knows good ways out of the district. It's best for her. And me. Tell me the use of it, Nina standing over me, bunching her handkerchief between her hands. 'What a rotten terrible thing got done to you!' My boy. My love. Nothing can be done about it. She knows what I know. Thinks my thoughts. My girl. My comrade of the flame. I'm thinking of you in the streets, safe. Friends in Poplar. There by now on the trolley bus. I don't care. Even if she isn't thinking this she's doing it, which is better than the same thing. Together, escaping them, split apart.

He worked to concentrate on the few things he could see from the bed: his bootless feet, the bedside lamp, buttons on his coat, the gentle peaks of red-orange fire bobbing across the coal in the grate. Rosie's back, her unkind hump, a shadow between him and the heat. He wanted to ask her to move aside a little but the first word his breath started to form ended as a pocket of air in his mouth. His body shivered, cold and wet, overture to the next round of pain that rolled down from his neck and

275

shoulders, crested in his back and side, surged downward and deeper into his stomach.

Cold as a Russian icehouse in here. My legs are frozen solid. My body won't let me make decisions any more. When I mess myself, who will clean me? Nina got out quick. Selfish quick. I know who she is. Whose daughter. Abandon the helpless. But: no. She'll look after Rosie. Nina cares for her more than she likes to show. This is worse than old age. Dribbling out of my back. So I won't be an old man with her in America. Nina or some other one. In Penn-sylvan-ia. She was my last woman. My lifetime of twenty-four years. I killed men (I confess it!) so a man killed me. He changed me into meat on a slab. I changed what happened in a day. More than one time. I decided and ordinary days broke apart. Measure by fractions. They're pouring out of me – things I did, my habits, my decisions, my names – now they have a number. I don't know where my legs are. I'm not here.

'Karl? I'll give you some medicine. Yes? It's morning. You can have some. Lean your head a little more. Karl?'

Did you touch me in the back? Did someone punch me? I remember a metal rod. The burner, the ... what? From the tanks. Blowpipe. Tip of the flame. Did we pull his money from inside? The prize, we exed it, no? Good piece of asbestos. Max burned me in the back. You can't say it was luck. We did it. I did something. Some action that ended me here. I always thought I'd get a bullet, but quick to the brain. Executed. In a jail or on the street. I remember fighting. Friends carried me and put me in this box. Who did? Jacob and Nina. The other one. She left the window open so the moths came in. Light keeps powder on their wings dry. A column of heated air rises. Updraft. Per ounce per volume of. Pushes them in the air. Am I in my coffin remembering this or am I in a dream of my future? Have I been born yet?

'Rosie?'

'I'm here.'

'You can't do anything.'

Lead weights tipped down the well of Rosie's heart. Her sadness doubled, hearing those words; they opened a wound as old as she was. Lumbered with that knotted hump on her back, what could she do? All her life the same refusal over and over again. Sara Rosa, who couldn't play schoolgirl games. Rosie the red-faced maiden, who couldn't attract a man. Sara the Seamstress, who could hardly feed herself, employment the charity of Luba's brothers. Never completely trusted to do anything. She knew what she could accomplish; as much as Nina and Luba could, those two together. Those cripples.

She went back to her station on the floor in front of the grate, to the haystack heap of photographs, charts and tables, pamphlets, post cards and letters, and fed the fire. Cared for the fire, helped it burn. When a curled sheet of ash threatened to smother the coals she swatted it to pieces, stirred it away. She kept an eye on the burning and added coal when it was needed to keep the flame even. *Do it and it is done.* Rosie's face and hands, the front of her, roasted in the constant heat; her back absorbed the cold that was in possession of the other side of the room. Half dead, half living.

Peter had fled. Jacob, Yourka and Max. Yoska and Fritz. All the men were gone when Rivka shook herself out of her numb trance and, wrapped in Nina's shawl, drifted back into the room. The third time she repeated Rosie's name, Rivka touched her on the shoulder and got this reply: a reluctant and brief turn of her head away from the fire. Did Rosie know?

Did she refuse to know? Until you stood close to him, Karl looked to be alive. His sleepwalker's eyes were open,

277

distantly engaged, his lips were slightly parted as if in conversation, paused by the interruption of a further thought. Rivka brushed the wetness from her face, then bent down next to Rosie and said, without much hope, 'Do you know where Fritz went? Did he say? Or Yoska?' In the blackness swaddled around her Rosie didn't hear Rivka's voice. She only rocked forward on her knees to lay a pale blue envelope on the fire. Help for Rivka had to come from somebody else. A reliable friend. No one was left at Grove Street who cared if Peter was safe or not.

Twelve

STORY OF HOUNDSDITCH MURDERS.

CONSTABLE'S GRAPHIC NARRATIVE

'A MAN'S HAND.'

LEVI — THE OPENER OF THE DOOR.

THE FIRST SHOT

In the very heart of London three good officers were shot fatally, and two seriously wounded by burglars who were interrupted in tunnelling their way to the safe of a Houndsditch jeweller.

In the ordinary contest of police against thieves the position would have been dead against the criminals.

But here they shot their way to liberty — in the criminal foreigner's characteristic way. And though the police, searching in scores, have what are supposed to be descriptions of their appearance, they are still at large.

Once more it is proved that the warrens of London slums are excellent grounds for concealment, and the fact that the men know little English emphasizes the truth of that old maxim of the criminal.

The chase is continued to-day by over a hundred detectives, every man eager for the avengement of the death of his three comrades.

'WANTED'

Police Descriptions of Three Men and a Woman
Following is the description issued by the police of the three men and one woman wanted in connection with the murders—

1.

'FRITZ': Aged twenty-four or twenty-five; height about 5ft. 8in. or 5ft. 9in.

Complexion sallow, eyes grey, medium moustache turned up at the ends, colour of hair on head fair, nose rather small, slightly turned up, chin a little rounded, a few pimples on face, cheekbones prominent, shoulders square but slightly bent forward.

Dressed brown tweed suit, thin light stripes; dark melton overcoat, velvet collar, nearly new; usually wears grey crush tweed cap, red spots; sometimes a trilby hat.

A native of Russia, speaks English and German imperfectly.

2.

'PETER': Surname unknown; known as 'Peter the Painter'; aged twenty-eight to thirty; height 5ft. 9in. or 5ft. 10in.

Complexion sallow, skin clear, eyes dark, hair medium, moustache black, medium build.

Very reserved manner.

Usually dressed in brown tweed suit, large dark stripes; black overcoat, velvet collar rather large; rather old large felt hat; shabby black lace boots.

Believed to be Russian Anarchist, frequents club and institute, Jubilee-street. Resides Grove-street.

3.

'YOURKA': A Russian; age twenty-one; 5ft. 8 in. in height. Heavy moustache; dark brown hair; sallow complexion. Dressed in blue jacket suit and grey cap.

4.

A WOMAN: Aged twenty-six to thirty; 5ft. 4in. in height. Slim build; drawn face; brown hair; blue eyes.

Wearing a dark blue three-quarter jacket and skirt, with white blouse, light coloured shoes, and large black hat trimmed with black silk.

DEAD ASSASSIN

ACCIDENTALLY KILLED BY HIS COMRADE

A remarkable discovery was made by the City Police Saturday. One of the murderers was found dead in a house at 59, Grove-street, Commercial-road. He was identified as the 'Mr Levi' who rented No. 11 Exchange-buildings, and there seems to be no doubt that he was killed by his comrade.

He was taken to the house in Grove-street in a cab by two men early on Saturday morning. He was bleeding from a wound in the head and wore a bandage. Medical advice was sought, and some suspicion being aroused the police were summoned. Before they arrived the man was dead.

It is believed that Levi is not the dead man's name. It has

281

been established that he is not a Jew, and the police believe that neither of his companions was a Jew.

THE ALIEN CRIMINAL

HOW THE DOOR IS OPEN TO HIM

This is the third crime of this particular type for which alien criminals in Britain are responsible. The first was the unsuccessful attempt on the Motherwell (Glasgow) branch of the Royal Bank of Scotland by three Poles armed with revolvers.

The second crime was that at Tottenham on January 23 1909, when two Poles, Hefeld and Jacob Lapidus, snatched a bag of money from a clerk who was carrying the week's wages to Messrs. Schnurmann's works. They were instantly pursued, and fired on their pursuers repeatedly, killing Police Constable Tyler and a boy and wounding eighteen persons. Finally both shot themselves.

To such an extent has the Aliens Act been relaxed that in 1906 a Russian Pole who had shot a policeman was admitted as a political refugee. But most of the Russian criminals who leave their country for its own good and come to England find the door opened to them by that provision of the Aliens Act regulations which exempts from scrutiny small vessels carrying fewer than twenty passengers.

THE HOUNDSDITCH MURDERS

⟶══◉◉══⟵

NEW DESCRIPTIONS OF THE WANTED MEN.

'FRITZ' & 'PETER.'

---

30 ARMED POLICE SEARCH FOR ASSASSINS

THE INQUEST.

THE MURDERER'S DYING STATEMENT.

'SHOT BY MISTAKE.'

With energy and hard determination that have never been surpassed in the elucidation of a great London crime the police of every department are hunting for the Houndsditch assassins — the burglars who, interrupted in their work, shot and killed three City policemen and seriously wounded two others.

Every detective trained to expertness in ransacking the East End dens of suspected aliens is in the pursuit. Every railway station and all Continental passenger steamers are being watched.

No fewer than thirty officers, each carrying a loaded revolver, were dispatched in one party in the dark early hours.

DEFENCELESS

Every Londoner must feel deeply angry that three brave members of the police force have been lost in a murderously unequal struggle.

Despite the tragedies of Tottenham and Houndsditch, are we to continue to send virtually unarmed men — socially valuable ones, too — against the pestilential foreign criminals that London and the world would be cleaner and happier without?

DOCTOR'S EVIDENCE

Murderer's Account of How He Sustained His Wounds

Dr John James Scanlon, temporarily assisting Dr Bernstein, a friend, in Commercial Road, was called:

Did you speak to him? — He was muttering. I spoke to him in English. I asked his name.

Before you examined him? — Yes.

'MY NAME IS GEORGE GARDSTEIN'

He said his name was George Gardstein. I asked him what had happened to him. He said — Three hours ago I was shot by a friend with a revolver in the back by a mistake.

I examined him and found a bullet hole in the left side of the back, and I found the bullet under the skin of the chest. It had not come out. It was about two inches from the middle line of the body.

The man was in a very weak condition. He vomited some blood while I examined him, and frequently asked me to give him a narcotic to relieve the pain.

He had great pain in the region of the stomach and abdomen[...]

I made up a mixture of belladonna, nux vomica, and opium.

THE INJURED

P.C WOODHAM'S STORY:
'WE RAN FORWARD — AND I KNEW NO MORE.'

The two officers — Sergeant Bryant and Constable Woodhouse — injured in the outrage are reported to-day to be progressing satisfactorily.

It is reported now as almost certain that Sergeant, who is in St Bartholomew's Hospital, will recover.

Constable Woodham, the more seriously injured, is at London Hospital. He is not allowed to see visitors.

He has, however, given the description of the outrage: —

heard the whistles go, and my sergeant and his mate tried to open the door. We saw a flash, and they fell into the road. We ran forward, and then I found myself rolling on the ground, and I knew no more.

He added that he saw nothing of the assailant, who apparently fired through the door.

JON STEPHEN FINK

THE HOUNDSDITCH AFFRAY

DEATH OF ANOTHER POLICEMAN

VIVID STORIES.

THE WOMAN WITH THE SHAWL.

A GANG OF SIX.

Another police officer — Constable Choate — died to-day as the result of the shooting outrage by burglars in the Houndsditch district last night.

The full list of the killed and wounded is as follows: —

KILLED

Sergeant Tucker
Constable Choate

INJURED

Sergeant Bentley (shot in the neck and shoulder), condition serious.

Sergeant Bryant (shot in the arm).

Constable Woodham (both legs broken by bullets).

THE COVERED FACE

Story of the Woman Companion of the Man who Looked like a Russian Jew

Miss Ada Parker, who lives exactly opposite the house where the burglars carried on their work, gave an *Evening News* representative some particulars about the occupants of No. 11.

'The first I saw of them,' she said, 'was about three weeks ago, when the gentleman came across the road and asked me if I could find him a servant to clear up the house before he took possession of it.

'He spoke in very broken English. From his appearance I should say he was certainly a Jew — perhaps a Russian Jew.

'The only people I ever saw in the house were this man and the woman I took to be his wife. She was a very smart-looking woman.

'Every morning about eight o'clock she used to come outside and take down two of the three shutters. Behind these two shutters were thick curtains through which nothing could be seen.

'Behind the middle shutter, which was never removed, was a lighter curtain.

'I said to my brother only yesterday, 'I do not know how these people get their food in; I never see the young lady go out for provisions the way we do. I suppose they must go out late at night.'

'The young woman always kept her face covered with a shawl, so that no one here knows what she is like.'

JON STEPHEN FINK

THE STEPNEY BOMB FACTORY

--><==⊙⊙==<--

TO-DAY'S IMPORTANT REVELATIONS.

MOROUNTZEFF.

THE ASSASSIN WITH THE BLACK BOX.

SOUNDS BY NIGHT.

CRIMINALS WITH A PARIS MEETING PLACE.

Today's inquiries show that the discovery made last night at a house, 44 Gold-street, Stepney, by detectives who are searching for the alien assassins of three City police officers [...] is one of the very greatest importance.

The discovery has established the fact that the murderer who died at a house in Grove-street, Whitechapel, was not named George Gardstein — as he told the doctor whom the two women summoned to him — but Poloski Morountzeff.

He it was who had occupied the rooms in Gold-street — rooms found to resemble nothing so much as an arsenal.

The landlord thought the man an artist. He appeared to be a dreamer; he had been seen painting at the window.

And whenever he went out he carried a black tin box — a box thought to contain painting materials, but was probably used to bring to the house the deadly explosives with which the man was surrounded.

THE DISCOVERY

LETTERS SAID TO REVEAL AN ANARCHIST PLOT OF SENSATIONAL CHARACTER

The police discovered at the house in Gold-street a complete process for the manufacture of bombs.

A number of mechanical appliances were found, and in glass bottles — used in order that the effective strength of the materials be preserved — were large quantities of

Nitric acid

Liquid mercury

Sulphuric acid

Potash, and

Nitro-glycerin phosphates

The police were able also to take possession of a magazine pistol, similar in pattern, it is believed, to that which was employed in the fusillade fired from the house in Exchange-buildings.

In addition a dagger was found, and a belt which is understood to have had placed within it 150 Mauser dum-dum bullets — bullets, that is, with soft heads, which upon striking a human body, would spread and inflict a wound of a grievous if not deadly character.

But even this does not exhaust the list of dangerous material.

JON STEPHEN FINK

MEETINGS IN PARIS.

FINGER-PRINTS SENT TO THE CONTINENTAL POLICE

MOROUNTZEFF.

The Story of the Man Who Painted at the Window

An *Evening News* representative says that the house [...]

It was obvious that the Lettish bandits and 'insurgents,' who at that time terrorised Riga and the adjacent country, had made the Russian Empire too hot to told them; go somewhere they must; and of course, some came to London, while no doubt others have gone as far as Canada and the United States.

Cornered, they fight like cats; the least chance of escape, however, and they are down on their knees begging for mercy. I have seen men imploring a Russian officer to spare their lives, but the moment the firing party was called out and hope abandoned, these same men struck up the 'Marseillaise' and died with that defiance in their mouths.

Feline in temperament, the Lett is also feline in his personal appearance. You can distinguish him at a glance, especially by the peculiar dead white pallor of his skin, the narrow cat-like eye and prominent cheek-bone.

And so the Anarchist degenerates into the common burglar, into Fritz or 'Peter the Painter.' That they should use magazine pistols against the London police is also quite natural; for they would have treated their own police to nothing less. Ideas of justice or mercy or a fair trial are as foreign to them as the streets wherein they pillaged and murdered. No immigration laws will keep them out; as long as the Russian system of government is what it is, men as desperate as these will be produced, and, if they find their way to England, so much the worse for us.

THE DEAD CONSTABLES

Sergeant Bentley Murdered on Anniversary of His Wedding

The shots of the Houndsditch desperadoes have killed three men of the finest type of the London police officer. They could not have laid low three men more popular with their companions or more respected by the general public.

The three officers were alike in their courage, their efficiency, their strength; they were also alike in their good humour, their kindliness, and the strong personal affection in which they were held.

Sergeant Robert Bentley, who died late on Saturday night from the effect of five bullet wounds to the neck and chest, would have been thirty-seven years of age on Boxing Day.

He was married nine years ago on the 16th of December, so that he was murdered on the anniversary of his wedding day.

His wife, although in delicate health, was able to be with him when he died. He leaves behind a little girl seven years of age.

Sergeant Charles Tucker, who was shot in the neck and died in a few minutes, was an older man. He had seen twenty-five years' service in the police force, and was already entitled to retire on a pension, but was retained owing to the heavy demands which will be made on the police during the Coronation.

Constable Choate, who died in the London Hospital on Saturday morning, had been in the City police force for fifteen years.

Only ten days ago he went down to Horsham for the burial of his mother. [...]

He was one of the best billiard players in the City police and spent much of his spare time practising the game on the table in the Bishopsgate station.

THE KING'S MESSAGE

Sympathy With the Relatives of the Dead Officers

The King has sent a message to the Commissioners of the City Police saying that he has heard with great concern of the murder of the three constables belonging to the City Police.

His Majesty has requested the Commissioners to express to the widows and families his sincere sympathy and the assurance that he feels most deeply for them in their sorrow.

He has also directed the Commissioners to express to the wounded constables his sympathy with them in the severe wounds they have received in the execution of their duty, and his hope that they will make a good progress towards a complete recovery.

His Majesty also asks to be informed of their present condition.

III

THE SIEGE

One

To push against opposition, even when oblivion itself is the enemy, to show courage and humanity, care for the reputation you enjoy among your neighbours — all beautiful ideals, let us agree, that are universally distributed around the world's population. It's reasonable to expect to find such qualities in abundance among doctors, human beings who swear an oath, in three small words, to the race's highest virtues: Do No Harm. This pledge had a special meaning for Dr John James Scanlon in the wake of that night's murders in Houndsditch.

During the desolate morning hours when Karl lay dying, pain blunted a little by the medicine Dr Scanlon made up for him, the medical man tussled with his own soul. On the one hand, his obligation to the Law bent him to notify the police of any wounding or death by gunshot; on the other hand, bending to that law meant courting the risk, when word got out, of denunciation by his neighbours in Whitechapel. He'd be shunned, blacklisted, branded an informer. Should things come to that, what good could he do?

Against his will Dr Scanlon found himself in motion, a cog in the strange clockwork of events ratcheting ahead on that mid-December weekend. Slow in contacting the police, quicker in alerting the newspapers, on Saturday morning he fired the starting gun on a race to Grove Street between an armed squad of detectives and a pack of reporters loping after the same rumoured survivors.

A contest bagged by DI Wensley's detectives, pistols

drawn, no more than minutes to spare. Shadow and quiet held the stairway. Wensley kept his voice low. 'Take care going up. No banister.' The file of men climbed to the first floor landing, where the door to the front bedroom was closed. Sergeant Leeson stepped forward and gave the doorknob a quarter of a turn. Unlocked. A nod from DI Wensley ordered him into the room, and the Sergeant's nod back brought in the others to meet a threat no greater than a woman half-asleep in front of the fire, destroying evidence. She didn't move an inch when the men tramped into the room behind her.

Sergeant Leeson clamped his fingers around Rosie's wrist to stop her adding the photograph of a young woman to the ash-choked fire. 'Who's that you want to get rid of, then?'

No protest from Rosie when he tugged it away from her and dropped it back onto the stack of unincinerated papers. Mechanically, exhausted, mesmerised, under his eyes, she slid Luba's photo off the pile again and toward the grate. The toe of the Sergeant's boot gently blocked it. Then she felt him reach under her arms and lift her off the floor. Rosie stayed quiet until she faced Karl's corpse. Past the four or five policemen elbowing around each other for a gander at the dead terrorist she saw where his blood blackened the sheet, saw his white shirt, Karl's rigid arm. And her cry, coiled inside Rosie for half the night, spiralled out of her lungs; her throat shook with it, a gull's shriek of earsplitting agony, the last sound to reach the world from a drowning soul, unbearable.

'Remove that woman,' Wensley said, and Sergeant Leeson bundled Rosie outside to the landing. 'What do you think this is?' he asked the detective standing next to him, handling the painted wooden sword by the foil belt attached to it.

'Looks like some kind of sword, Sir.'

'And their bullets are gum drops.' Wensley looked across to an object in the hands of his City Police colleague DI Thompson. 'Got something there?'

Thompson tilted the unframed watercolour into the light. 'Pretty scene.'

'Is it?' Wensley doubted, then examined it himself, front and back. He glanced at the signature: *Yourka 16/12/10*. 'Here's something prettier.' With his thumb he underlined the writing on a slip of paper stuck to the back of the painting, *G. Dubof* beside the address *20 Galloway Rd, Shepherd's Bush*.

The mixture of loose cartridges in the upturned tweed cap on the table next to the dead man interested the Detective-Inspector. Six Mauser pistol cartridges, older Mauser rifle cartridges, other bullets he counted in the jumble fit Morris-tube and small rook rifles. Next thing fished up, the Dreyse pistol, from its hiding place underneath Karl's pillow, plus two fully loaded clips. The Crown's barristers wouldn't lack for exhibits in court.

Clamour on the street from the wolf pack down there mooching 'round the door made Wensley think, *This work is difficult enough without outsiders mobbing us*. Their barked questions and complaints ruffled the air, not his concentration. Through the closer conversation in the dead man's room he heard booted footsteps hurrying upstairs, he heard his name spoken. 'Here, Constable.'

The young policeman said, 'It's a man, sir. Down at the door.'

'What about him?'

'He's asking to see Fritz.'

'Is he still there?' Wensley pressed him, made way for the PC to take a look from the window. 'Do you see him?'

'Yes. Little moustache. He's waiting very polite, sir.'

'What did you tell him?'

'Asked him to wait there till I spoke with you.'

'Did he give his name?'

The Constable read from his notebook. 'Not sure I got it spelt right, but the name he give me is Tom-a-coff. Nicholas, his Christian name, sir.'

'I say you: no. I do not go there help Fritz crime. Not other boys too.' Nicholas stumbled through an account of his visit to Grove Street, voluntarily offered, a proclamation of his good character. When he was stuck for the correct word he turned aside to the Russian interpreter, grudgingly, avoiding a direct look.

DI Wensley needed something more than veiny emotional assertion to convince him of this young man's value to the investigation, let alone Nicholas Tomacoff's moral goodness. At the table under the electric light, sitting as close to Nicholas as he would if they'd been enjoying a pint together in a pub, the Detective-Inspector frowned, rubbed his brow and with a short silence allowed everyone present to appreciate his seriousness of purpose. Then, 'You mentioned to the constable you're one of Fritz's friends. In what circumstances did you meet Mr Svaars?'

'Please?'

'Am I speaking too fast? I'm sorry, Mr Tomacoff. Again. You're a friend of Fritz Svaars?' He gestured toward the interpreter who repeated the last question in Nicholas's own language.

'I teach Fritz play mandolin.'

'You regard each other in a friendly way. You're friends. Nothing wrong about that,' Wensley said. 'It's perfectly natural for someone to help out a friend, perfectly understandable.'

'Not for make crime he hurt England. Good place in England,' Nicholas said, with feeling. 'Good men here.'

'Would you say more of your friends are English or foreigners?'

'No. Please again?'

'Plain and simple, Mr Tomacoff, the majority of your friends, are they English or are they Russians? Or Letts, Jews, or what?'

'All kinds, all. Yes. English boys jolly good, same.'

The Russian, who stood at DI Wensley's elbow, offered to put the question; Wensley moved on with a curt wave. 'Who else do you know at Grove Street? The man who was shot dead, the gentleman we know as George Gardstein?'

For this answer Nicholas sought from the Russian an unambiguous translation. He had met Karl for the first time at the party in Grove Street less than a week before. He could not, would not, say he was a friend of his.

'Who else was at this party? Besides Svaars and Gardstein.'

'Luba. Nina...'

Discreet as a butler, the constable cribbed from his notebook and refreshed Wensley's memory. 'Luba Milstein, Svaar's mistress. Nina Vassilleva, she's Gardstein's.'

'And the man we know as Peter the Painter?'

'Him, yes. His woman also.'

'The Painter's got a mistress, too, like 'em all,' Wensley noted to himself. 'And what's she called?'

'She is call Rivka.'

'Know her second name?'

Nicholas shook his head, apologetically, more aware than he'd seemed until then that this record-straightening chat was taking place within the confines of

299

an interrogation room inside Leman Street police station, and he needed to ask for permission if he suddenly wanted to leave. DI Wensley pushed a blank piece of paper and a sharpened pencil across the table. 'Nicholas, I'd like you to write down the names of everybody who came to that party. Do that for me now, yes?' In precise English lettering, solid as notes on a stave, he'd written three names and started on a fourth when Wensley asked him, 'This celebration, the night before they went to Houndsditch, was it?'

'Two, three day.'

'What went on?'

'What was party? Play song, much,' Nicholas said softly, hearing them again. 'Music from balalaika, violin. Sing. Talk.'

'What did you talk about? With who?'

'I? I teach Fritz play mandolin song. Other boys talk. What I hear them, not so much. They talk on jail. Home.'

Nicholas volunteered this information with the thought, *In any jail in Russia a police interrogator wouldn't be so polite; by now he'd be listening to me yelp and beg for the beating to stop.* A stone-hearted tormentor? Not this fellow! Even Fritz would see this Englishman wasn't born with the stomach for torture. Besides that, what kind of man was he? Nicholas plucked clues from the two hours he'd been sitting at that small table across from DI Wensley: the man's patience, the firm hint of its limits, mature assurance in the stillness of his voice and face, traits Nicholas took to be as English as the rain. His walrus moustache, fatherly; his broad chin, of the people; his wag of the head, his homely jowls, sincere. No Jew-hater peeped out at Nicholas from his questioner's pinprick eyes — the bigot that Peter said lived inside every Englander — no contempt in them for a foreigner 'lower

300

than the dirt', no, the opposite. DI Wensley's eyes compressed under the consideration he gave to every word Nicholas uttered, and to keep any judgment from leaking out. Here was a man whose respect, when he ceased to withhold it, was awarded to you with the force of vindication.

His estimation was not wildly off the mark, although the sincerity and fatherly assurance the young Russian poeticised out of Frederick Wensley's moustache, chin and jowls were, in truth, on show to pass along a practical message: *Make no mistake, puppy, I'm a stayer.* He was the Somerset outsider who'd waded through his years of insult and near-invisibility in the Met, diligent and keen and thus mistrusted, passed over, and he stayed. Probationer to constable to detective to DI at forty-five, a sluggish climb, but without a misstep.

The foreigners he'd known in the district for more than twenty years, all with the same fault in their language – total incomprehension of the letter W – called him 'Vensel'. Which migrated into an H Division joke and almost affectionate nickname: 'Weasel'. Never mind, it's been no harm, not to me. The Weasel's on 'em, so harm to them. Street robbers. Pickpockets. Burglars. Murderers. Anarchists. Enemies of good people. We've got enough to battle against in our lives without *this* deliberate muck. *Look at me and listen* (Wensley said to Nicholas in every word he didn't say), you're trying to figure me and reckon your chances? *Here, I'll tell you, pup. I'm the bastard who's going to arrest your friends.*

'You haven't been in England for very long, I understand.'

'June I am here. Seven month.' A long time, by Nicholas's calendar. 'Stay London is good with me.'

'Mr Tomacoff, are you an anarchist?'

Nicholas slapped the table. 'I say you no! Not of Liesma!'

'All your friends, the men you've named...' Wensley pointed at the page between them on the table. 'They're members of Liesma. Anarchists. Criminals who murder English policemen.'

'I teach Fritz play mandolin. He ask me go his house for make party.' For a few seconds Nicholas met Wensley's strategic silence with intensity of his own. As if the taut string that held his spine had been cut, his shoulders dropped and he said, 'I take you where they hide.'

'Who? Fritz, you mean? Peter?'

'Also Yoska.'

DI Wensley turned around to ask the Constable, 'Which one's Yoska?' While the PC thumbed through his notes Wensley pushed Nicholas, 'When did you see them?'

'Three o'clock. Fritz Svaars, Yoska Sokoloff, Peter Piatkow.'

'Write down the address.' On the page of names Nicholas added the address, and Wensley read it aloud for the Constable to copy into his notebook. 'Havering Street. Number thirty-six.' Then, to Nicholas, 'How do I know you're not leading us into an ambush?'

An appeal to the interpreter, and after Nicholas took in the meaning of the question he slumped back in his chair, bruised and bewildered. 'Take guns. Fritz and other boys take guns.'

'You'd better pray they don't use them.' What Wensley said next had the sound of an afterthought, a question from the private man, not the detective. 'Do you pray?'

'Pray?'

'To God. You believe in God? Reigns over us like the King in England, the Tsar in Russia?'

'Sir, I believe same God like you.'

They left Nicholas in the room, in the unofficial custody of the Russian interpreter. Let him catch his breath, reminiscing with his countryman about samovars and balalaikas, moonlight on the Don. In the corridor outside DI Thompson more than hinted at his doubt that Nicholas Tomacoff's word could be trusted. 'You don't think they give up their comrades, do you, Wensley?'

'We'll find out when we call upon Havering Street.'

The Constable felt relaxed enough to remark, 'Seen it in Whitechapel, right, sir? Give a Jew an inch and he'll put a bed in it. Give him two, he'll take in lodgers.'

It was slander and Wensley did the Constable a favour by letting it pass without rebuke. Business of the day was with his partner in this manhunt, the City Detective-Inspector. Wensley thought back, and said to DI Thompson, 'I do believe him. Question the authority of God, you question every other kind of authority. He really does want to stay in England. Got that from him free and clear.'

'Yes, well?'

'You can't be any kind of a citizen and question authority, can you?' He wagged his hand confidentially between his chest and Thompson's. Finally, another reflection. 'I should have said that in there. Might've pinched the address out of him quicker.'

Peter blamed his sharply plummeting spirits on the rotten joke Yoska made as they walked past the doctor's surgery two doors along from their hideout. It spooked Peter's mind with the regret that he was not on his way to Poplar, alone and unburdened by one man ready to fling himself like a grenade against anybody in a uniform and another one skipping — or limping — here to there like an infant playing hide-and-seek with his wee friends in Special Branch. 'That's the alley you're talking about?' He led Yoska the few steps back to the turning, to the iron gate at the mouth of what looked to Peter like an unbroken passageway stretching the length of the row of brick houses.

'It cuts through the yards. This street' — Yoska jabbed his thumb over his shoulder '—to that one.' He pointed vaguely ahead of them, to the opposite side of the square enclosed by two- and three-storey buildings. Maybe a hundred windows looked down on doors to the yards and alley, Peter guessed. A route back to the mundane chaos of Commercial Road. 'Let's get inside,' Yoska said.

Sleet glossed the cobbles and pavement of a thoroughfare as ordinary as any in Stepney. At the far end a dray cart loaded with beer barrels rattled out of a brewery yard, and at this early hour, it was the only movement besides the three fugitives huddled at a front door, a fifteen-second dash from either corner. Peter trusted Yoska to bring them to a safe place and when he vouched for the tameness of 'my Betsy' Peter trusted him on that score, too. Not irrevocably.

For sure, he couldn't count on Yoska's powers of stealth. 'Watch. It'll just take one throw,' the Limper said. He'd got the pebble in his hand and hurled it, with a sportsman's accuracy, at the second floor window. It hit with force enough to spin off at a skewed angle and vanish. 'Betsy!' Yoska's hoarse cry of love reached her as the nightgowned, nightcapped figure slid the window open and peeked down. 'Take us in, dear.'

At that distance Peter couldn't make out her face; he heard her voice, claggy with sleep, reply, 'Who's with you, Yoskele?'

'The sooner you let me in the sooner you'll find out.'

Betsy dropped the street door key to him, which missed Yoska's head by half an inch and bounced to the kerb. 'I see it,' he said, grabbing Fritz's arm to balance himself as he craned down to fetch it, and in triumph Yoska twirled the key 'round his finger by its lilac ribbon.

'Come on, I'm cold,' Fritz said. 'I smell snow.'

A whipcrack of sleety wind stung the back of Peter's neck; a solid enough reason to follow Yoska and Fritz through the door, he thought.

Two

Rivka imagined Peter's voice in her ear — she had the feeling he was still close — and so by the third day, Peter's howling absence wore itself down to a whimper. A blessing he wasn't standing beside her to see how hiding in alleys and doorways, fighting off drunkards, lechers and other devils had mangled Rivka inside and out, turned her into a beggar who couldn't beg, nameless and puny. Grainy muck stained her fingernails, gutter sludge scraped up with the potato peelings she fought over with a starving whore twice her age. Lonely necessity made Rivka selfish. She covered herself in Nina's shawl without thinking once if its rightful owner lay hunched and frozen to death in the same razoring wind, protection gone. Flesh shrunk to wreckage, diseased by anarchy. As Anna Southam, the Stepney Songbird is *song*, Rivka Bermansfelt is *want*.

The same desolate trance that wafted her back to Shinebloom's stopped her from going any closer than the pavement across the street. From there, screened by traffic, Rivka caught brief views of The Mayor through the restaurant's window; pudgy arms flapping, he directed waitresses and plates to and from the kitchen while he carried on energetic conversations with his customers. A man she could trust? Rely upon to feed her, hide her from the police? For dishes she broke, he let Rivka repay him with a song — and for his own safety he sacked her after he'd heard she was in Holloway Prison. It's possible the Mayor didn't recognise the black-shawled woman planted in the hurly-burly of Sclater Street, he may not even have noticed her. If he did, he made no sign.

Another man did see Rivka behind the linen stall. He stopped at Shinebloom's, held the door halfway open and noticed whoever and whatever was in motion behind him. Leon Beron, the heavy-bellied, astrakhan-collared broker, who always made Rivka think of a badger, the one who decorated his watch chain with a £5 gold coin; Yoska traded his prizes with the Badger, trusted him that far. The gold from Houndsditch would have gone to Mr Beron. Badly camouflaged, this badger's reconnaissance. Rivka tugged the shawl closer around her head and face, bare cloth between her and the grim weather, then ducked away into the hurly-burly of pedestrians.

Lunchtime in Shinebloom's, the political knockabout was quieter than usual. Diners shared gossip about Karl's *real* murderer, the size of the haul they *got away with*, where he stashed the gold and gems before he died. And what reprisals from the English were on the cards. Leon Beron said to The Mayor, 'More snitches and policemen than customers at the Warsaw. Somebody told them it was Karl's regular place. This is an oasis, compared.'

'Police haven't visited us. Not yet,' he added, then let the matter drop. 'By the way, Hannah made applesauce for the brisket today.'

A tall, thin man came in and invited himself to Beron's table. 'Can't get a table at the Warsaw, it's full of Special Branch and their squealers.'

'Steinie,' Beron's greeting. 'Order the brisket.'

'So I figured you'd be here.'

'Very smart. My congratulations.'

From the next table, a voice in Russian. 'They're biding their time. Feeding their horses.'

Steinie agreed with him. 'Rifles and bayonets, after last

308

Friday. We should build barricades. The sooner the better. You've got all those market stalls.'

'Sit down,' Beron begged him. 'The bayonets aren't coming today. What did you bring me?'

The Mayor sympathised. 'Your regular nonsense, Lev,' he told the Russian.

Lev paid no attention. 'They'll plan something. They've got all the time in the world. Then they'll ride down on us like a typhoon, same as at home.'

'Usual nonsense.'

'What Gardstein did...'

'Did to *them*, to England,' someone said.

'...is their excuse for a pogrom.'

'Three bogies got killed,' Steinie reminded them with a show of three fingers. 'For sure they'll come down here. Any place it's easy to find us.' He put to the Mayor, 'Why's it nonsense, a pogrom in Brick Lane?'

'The innocent with the guilty...' one of Lev's friends began.

A contribution winged in from another table. 'They won't start it in Brick Lane. Jubilee Street first. They'll burn down Rocker's club to make a point. Then they'll come to us.'

'Brick Lane runs straight down. Easy for horses,' Steinie said.

'You think Englanders want to burn down their own city?' The Mayor's parting shot.

'Sure! To take it away from us!' said Lev.

'Police or no,' Beron said, 'I'm going back to the Warsaw. At least informers talk quiet.' He didn't budge, though, and repeated his first question to Steinie.

Steinie finally sat down. 'I'll have something beautiful for you in a couple of weeks. Special. You'll have to be careful with it, break it up.'

309

Beron leaned in close, to wonder, 'In the newspaper it says they didn't get to the safe. Did Gardstein bring something out?'

Steinie's reply was no reply. He turned around to the Russians, pointed at the Mayor and joked, 'He doesn't think Brick Lane is a shetl.'

The coarse laughing didn't annoy Beron so much, and neither did the debate beginning to boil around him about the strategy and methods the police will employ in the coming attack. The voices he heard weren't Social Democrats or Anarchists, Latvian Nationalists or Syndicalists, Communists, Christian Socialists, Individualists or Socialist Revolutionaries. Most of them Jews, like him. He said to Steinie, 'Whatever they want to do, it's going to be bad for everybody.'

Two nights ago, she slept on the frigid ground behind a pile of ash and kitchen slops, and the night before she didn't sleep through a single hour. Wherever she stopped walking to rest her feet Rivka attracted men who pestered her, with an offering in each hand — coins clutched in one, cock in the other. On her third morning dumbly tramping the back streets of Whitechapel and Stepney, when the next turning led her past the Pavilion Theatre, Rivka got her first piece of good luck. The blistered dark green stage door was unlocked.

She slipped into the building and found a place to conceal herself among the props and costumes, where she slept like a dead thing until early evening. The chatter of performers and stagehands jarred Rivka awake in time for her to clear out of there and stumble across other nooks, unlit, unvisited, above and beneath the stage. The secret was to choose the right moment to move. After the curtain came down on the final encore, shoeless, quiet as smoke, she sneaked back upstairs to rebuild her nest of drapery and tweed coats. For another two days her luck held.

The fate Rivka feared was stalking her had already netted two of the Sisterhood. Better for her nerves she didn't know that Rosie was under arrest, and Luba too. Days before, Luba's brothers chased her down and marched their delinquent, pregnant, sister to the police. First to Jack and Nathan, then to DI Thompson, Luba confessed her affair with one of the anarchists behind the Houndsditch crimes. Both women were spilling what they could — names, descriptions, addresses — and if Rivka had known how the odds were shrinking out there she wouldn't have risked being seen in the street, much less gambled her freedom by stealing food off market barrows.

Revolution? Social justice? Revenge? Any need outside of Rivka's body — and she felt the ghostly pain of Peter's absence cold as an amputated limb — simply disappeared from the world. Today she found shelter, and today she stole food she could eat without cooking. A bread roll, a piece of fruit, a handful of boiled sweets. Rivka had real talent as a thief. Her grab was as quick as her eye, her eye as quick as the judgment to take a thing or pass it up; in a snap the prize was gone under the hem of her shawl. What did people see if they looked at Rivka? Flawless calm. No guilt or fear heated her cheeks, she didn't abscond. Rivka watched herself. *What do they see?* A woman strolling past, who has no reason to hurry, another one like us — you can see it in her, our morality and motives, our bland innocence.

It wouldn't be luck if it didn't run out, and Rivka's deserted her on account of a runaway carrot. From the landing above she listened for the clunk of the stage door and the clack of its bolt. *Clunk-clack*, she was locked in for a second night, so Rivka could breathe easy and make up her bed behind the magician's cabinet. She tipped the wardrobe room door closed behind her without noticing the uneaten leftover from her supper fall out of her pocket and wedge itself between door and doorframe.

Footsteps on the stairs stopped at the landing. An electric light switched off, then on again, Rivka heard the footsteps reach the door. 'A carrot, for God's sake,' Harry the manager complained, 'they treat it like a pig sty.' More topsy-turvy inside, a spilled cup of water, curtain and costumes on the floor, the human shape underneath them. 'Who's there?' He saw Rivka's face and said her name.

'You remember me.'

'Peter?' Harry half-called, half-inquired.

'He's not here. I don't know where he is.'

'They're saying he's mixed up in that Houndsditch business.'

'He wasn't.'

'You know for sure?'

'For sure.'

'He was with you?'

'No.'

Rivka's certainty unsettled Harry. 'The woman the police want,' he said, opening his satchel, retrieving his copy of the *Evening News*, 'is it you? They put in a description.'

She took the newspaper from him and read. 'It could be me.'

'It could be.'

'Yes,' Rivka told him. 'Why are they looking for Peter? He didn't go there. He didn't do anything against the law.'

'Not last Friday, maybe.' Harry knelt to bring his face level with Rivka's. 'Did Max let you in here?'

312

'Nobody did. I got in.'

'What a way to live,' he said and shook his head. 'Your name's on the playbill. See?' With his thumb he underlined the name *Anna Southam the Stepney Songbird*.

'Peter told me. It's a beautiful name.'

'Your name. Look at the date. Week of the twelfth. Anybody asks me I'll tell him Friday night you were singing at the Pavilion.'

'No. I can't. I'll go.'

'Where?'

'If they look for me here you'll get trouble from the police.'

'So you'll go where?'

'To Peter. Where he is.'

'He wants to know you're some place safe. Am I right? Good. All right,' Harry nodded with her, they were in agreement. 'I can even arrange a hot bath. All the comforts.'

He carted the tin bath from the storeroom. The coal stove in his office heated the bath water. Harry took the curtain that Rivka used for a mattress and strung it across the room to trap the heat long enough for Rivka to wash herself. On the other side of the curtain, Harry stood guard. 'Do you know any of Peter's friends?'

'You're his friend.'

'His patron! Still, he doesn't talk to me. In the Pavilion, about painting my scenery, he talks my ear off; but what goes on outside?' Harry puffed his cheeks and shook his head. 'Where he could go?'

'Somewhere with Yoska and Fritz.'

'Fritz,' Harry placed the name. 'The shaky actor, with the sword.'

Fritz hovered in her mind, stiffly declaiming his lines as Gamba, the Russian policeman. 'The police tortured him.

313

I heard him talk about it. When they got him in Russia. Or back home, in...' Rivka's whole body shivered, bath water lapped out of the tub; she wept as if it Fritz's memory of prison was hers too. 'They tore his fingernails off.'

'I won't tell anybody you're here.' Harry coupled his promise to a caution. 'But I won't go out looking for Peter, either.'

Wreckage stretched ahead of Nina as far as she could see; its trail reached behind her from Houndsditch to the very threshold of her rented room. Curled against the wall, she burrowed under stale-smelling pillows and blankets, where, unforgotten, Karl moaned inside her moan, 'Why did you leave me?' All of us on the stairs in the smoky frenzy, explosions and shouting. Didn't Karl put himself between Nina and the bullets? It was no accident. *Why did you leave me?* Max Smoller's blood clot of a jealous heart, hungry for the attention Karl saved for Nina, lover-comrade, who had his confidence, devotion, protection. Max was gunning for another prize. *Why did you leave me?* To bring a doctor, who refused me to my face. The dying body on the bed, you know, it wasn't Karl any more. Not you! To stay was no comfort for either of us. Only for Rosie. *Is that why?*

Nina went on talking to herself in a waking dream, out of bed now, on her knees on the floor with a knife, brown paper and string and a scrabbled pyramid of her valuables. 'I left there before they went in to do the robbery,' she repeated a dozen times, rehearsed the words until they came out of her mouth as the convincing truth.

The parcel looked anonymous enough not to need

hiding, but Nina buried it first in a dresser drawer. Which was too obvious. Next, she slid it under the washstand, where it was too visibly out of place. Then she abandoned that task for a more important one. Off came her jacket and white blouse, off came her skirt. Dust in the wash basin greyed the painted rose at the bottom and darkened under the first splash of spirit vinegar. The acid odour burned Nina's nostrils, teared her eyes. Like a farm girl tugs and squeezes the udder of a cow she tugged at handfuls of her hair to milk the black dye from it. Her fingers were painted with it, trickles of the melting colour smudged her face, collected around her eyes.

As a courtesy the knock on her door was really an announcement that took for granted Nina's permission to come in. Especially since her landlord, Isaac Gordon, had a plate of food for her, cooked by his daughter. 'Polly's worried about you, Nina. We don't see you eat. In a day or two you're going to starve to death.' One look at the wild-haired, sunken eyed, miserable mess hunched over the wash stand gave Isaac the feeling Nina was much closer to death than that.

'My stomach's no good,' she said, and stopped what she was doing. The strength that was holding her up drained out of her legs and Nina crumpled to the floor. Her hands covered her face: it looked to Isaac, through her fingers, as if she were crying black tears. 'He was my best friend.'

'What can you do with this? You can't bring him back.' Isaac set the plate on the floor next to Nina. 'Will you eat?'

'He cared for me. Without him I'd be *dead*.' Her hands went limp. 'Without him I *am* dead.'

'No, no. Don't punish yourself.'

Nina grabbed the brown paper package from under

the wash stand. 'Keep this for me. Tell Polly to hide it under her bed.'

'Is it valuable?'

'It's everything. All of my...' she trailed off.

'Are you going away again?'

'I don't know. I think so. If I do.'

A clammy mist of awareness crept over Isaac. Days of gossip in the neighbourhood, the talk he had with every shopkeeper, every edition of the newspaper he read carried a description of the woman seen with the murderers escaping from Houndsditch. Carefully, he said to Nina, 'The one who passed away, he wasn't your friend in the countryside?'

Nina floated back to her bed. Her reply wasn't to Isaac. 'It would've been better if he'd shot me.'

Rest and food cleared Rivka's thoughts. With Peter hiding God knows where, in God knows what shape, her own safety felt worthless, almost an act of greed. Hour by hour, kindness by kindness, the sanctuary Harry made for her in his office wedged more distance between Rivka and any chance of seeing Peter's face again. When Harry ferried a hot meal to his 'princess in the tower,' she worried about Peter going hungry; in her bed behind Harry's desk and a locked door, she lay awake, electrified by visions of Peter hunched in the chill and wet filth of an open yard or derelict building, on the run, human prey in the sights of strangers who took the fever hidden inside him for fanaticism.

To them his largeness was the largeness of a glacier; no one except Rivka knew how Peter's warmth waited to be finagled out of him, chased, *found*. He'd try to hold you at a distance with stiff lectures about the realities of combat and crime, tactics of escape; he'd give you examples of his superhuman realism and run off without leaving a trace, burrow deep, bow to the necessity of severing all human ties and force *you* to accept that we don't live in a magic world where a man and woman remain knotted to each other with fiery strands of love. Rivka knew different.

In less than a day exhaustion and gratitude drained out of her and left Rivka was possessed by the urgency to find Peter. At an early hour, before sunup, Rivka raided the wardrobe room and dressed herself from the rack of costumes. A clean white blouse, dark jacket and dress, a black silk-trimmed hat to cover her hair, Nina's unfancy shawl — who'd recognise Rivka Bermansfelt under all of that? In a race to Peter's hiding place she was one up on the police: these were her people, they spoke her language, in East End streets she wasn't a stranger any more. More than that, Rivka had a place to start her detective work. Did she know anyone who could name the men in Peter's circle better than Charles Perelman?

Scorched odour of soot, a mouldy smell from canvass and damp pallets, coal smoke, sour residue of beer, the breath of the street. Through those early morning absences, Rivka followed the track she used to walk between Shinebloom's and Wellesley Street, her mind racing, at work on the problem of contacting her landlord without dangerously exposing either of them. A glimpse of that danger froze Rivka at the turning into Commercial Road; the sight of that wanted poster tilted the ground under her feet.

The City of London Police offered a reward of five hundred pounds for the murderer of the three good men Rivka had watched Jacob shoot dead in Houndsditch. Somehow, they had photographs of the criminal, and his name, and neither was Jacob Peters. The man they wanted to arrest and convict, jail and hang was Peter Piatkow, alias Schtern, alias Peter the Painter. In the first photo, a debonair anarchist murderer, his hand jauntily tucked into the small of his back, a straw boater hanging off his fingers. It is clear that Peter has composed himself to present a mood of refined distraction, staring into the wings from a stage-set outdoor balcony. He'd struck the same pose in the art gallery, haranguing that man who'd laughed at the beautiful paintings.

In the second picture, Peter's expression isn't so certain. He's trying to relax and stand a little more naturally. What the camera captures is his soberly determined impersonation of a relaxed man leaning against the back of a chair. Under the ledge of the intellectual brow, Peter is gravely occupied. It's how he'd be at a country house party, Rivka thought, exiling himself to the balcony, staring through the French doors. His eyes follow the spectacle inside. He observes the dance of Frivolous Beauty in the arms of Hollow Charm, the graveside waltz in a world he knows is ruled by tyrants. The photograph catches what Rivka calls Peter's revolutionist stare, and she can tease him out of it with a kiss from her freckled lips.

If it could secure his salvation, she'd pull down and set fire to every copy of the poster in the East End. Tacked by three corners to the wooden hording this one came away whole. Rivka folded it in neat quarters, printed side in, and scratched on it with a pencil, *Fun mir tzu P. Vie? Avek.* From me to P. Where? Away. Then she picked up her pace and carried the secret appeal to Charles Perelman's door.

Now, in his wide overcoat that gave him the bulk of a bear, he came out to see who had rung his doorbell, who had stuffed a wanted poster underneath a brick on his stoop and then skittered off. A flick of his eyes caught Rivka unhidden on the pavement opposite his house and after another quick look up and down the street, Perelman approached her, showing no expression she could interpret. Peter's advice to her was, 'Don't go back to Wellesley Street.' Maybe this was why — the fear she'd raise in Perelman just by seeking him out, and no telling what he'd do if he was afraid of her.

He didn't speak to Rivka until he was standing so close to her she could smell breakfast on his breath. 'For a minute I thought you were Nina.'

'Would you yell at her to clear off?'

'It's better it's you, Rivka.'

'So you won't yell.'

'Are you in trouble again?'

'I don't know where Peter is.'

'The police, either.' He rustled the wanted poster without completely unfolding it.

'Peter gets the blame for what somebody else did,' Rivka said.

'The police have it all wrong,' Perelman's sarcastic reply. 'They usually do! Who shot them, then? Do you know for sure?' Rivka glanced away. 'Where are you sleeping? I guessed you stayed at Nina's, or — where?' As she refused again to say, Perelman stopped prospecting. 'All right. You shouldn't tell me. If he knows you're looking and the bogies are watching you, what do you think? He'll make it easy for you to find him?'

Jumpy, Rivka said, 'You told me to be careful if I'm living in your house. Go inside, Mr Perelman, please.'

A touch on her elbow kept Rivka there. 'The police talked to me. Asked me what you're asking. What could I tell them?' Master of the situation, stage comedian, he reprised his immigrant excuse, 'My Eng-litch no *gudt*!' Perelman laughed at how simple it was to trick the authorities and protect his friends. 'You were gone.'

At that she decided to tell him, 'He went somewhere with Yoska and Fritz.'

'The Liesma bunch.'

'You know some of them? Other ones besides Karl and Nina? Friends?'

'I haven't been in with them for years,' he said truthfully. 'Did you hear Peter or anyone mention John Rosen? Or Federoff — Osip Federoff?'

She shook her head.

'Hoffman?'

'Nobody. Who are they, Rosen and...'

'I'll try to find out something,' he said. His hand still gripped Rivka's elbow. 'Peter ordered you to keep away, yes? Don't follow him?' Perelman, her guardian, stroked her face. 'Out of love, that's all. Does he say he loves you?'

Better he should ask if she loved Peter. Let Peter be the thinker; she would love for both of them. His mind, her body, pressed so close together under the goose down cover they made one human creature. Whatever his words to her, the flame Rivka felt warming him wasn't Liesma, it was her.

Rivka's lips curled inward to keep the secret from escaping her mouth, but it found a way out through her reddened cheeks and damp eyes. They had each other, these lovers, their love like belief in witches or ghosts. 'It's a sacrifice to be alone', Perelman said, his eyes damp' Honesty for honesty, he felt the truth of it in his groin.

'You'll send me a message? You can bring it to me at the Pavilion,' Rivka said.

'That's where you've been sleeping?'

'A friend let me. He leaves the door open.'

320

'Do I know him?'

'He's the . . . He works there sometimes.'

'The Pavilion, sure, I know it. It's not a good idea to meet there. It wouldn't be safe for you. Me, either. Rivka, listen. I don't know how long before I hear something. I'll leave the poster outside the stage door. Someplace you can't miss it. Look for it around ten or eleven in the morning. If it's not there when you look, it means I don't have news. When I put it there, I've got a plan. You and he should be together.'

Wisely, or shrewdly, Nina's landlord washed his hands of the brown paper package she'd left in his safekeeping. Two or three times on their slow walk to Arbour Square, his son assured him that the instinct to turn the package in, unopened, showed everybody he was a man of unflinching morals who put his faith in the law. And Mr Gordon junior's Yiddish conveyed to Mr Gordon senior the personal and official gratitude expressed in frank English by Detective-Inspector Wensley, along with a reassurance that without being spoken, warmed all three men: whatever they did they did on the side of common good.

Even uncommon good. Their transaction was a compact between allies in a rational fight against irrationality. Whose friends were these malcontents, anyway? Radicals who lived by nobody's rules except their own, outsiders, no part of the Jewish community, never mind the English. Under the black flag they don't care who they rob, maim or kill. To oppose these criminals was a principle of citizenship for Isaac Gordon, and one of service for DI Wensley.

They opened the package together. Books and

revolutionary tracts, personal papers, a dozen or so photographs acquainted the Detective-Inspector with 'Minna,' daughter of Indrik Gristis, the lodger and cigarette-maker the Gordon family called Nina Vassilleva, whom they now met as the lover of the dead anarchist George Gardstein. DI Wensley was no believer in the spirit world or destiny, but watching Mr Gordon & Son leave his office cradling the rewrapped package as if they'd been handed back a fizzing bomb, he was left with the feeling that some kind of clairvoyant channel had peeped open between him and Nina. She was cut off from the rest of the Liesma gang, her lord and master lay in the police morgue, her old gang scattered — what could she do? Nina's fear twitched inside Wensley and her lonely thought came through to him, *Find somebody who can get me out of London.*

At that moment in her room at the Gordons' Nina grabbed relics from Houndsditch — her blouse and black hat, skirt and jacket — then set about burning them. A suicide will shed her belongings, the traces of her life, and for Nina this was a kind of killing. Her life in London with Karl, gone, finished, her heart clawed out of her chest, she buried her face in what was left of him, his blood on her coat, and rocked herself into nothing like sleep. *His blood won't dry, won't burn... it's my blood on this coat...* If she kept it with her or shredded it with scissors, what difference would it make? *Run from what will happen or towards it or do nothing, wait for it to catch up, in this deep trouble it's all the same thing. They'll make me suffer for it. The end is the end, anything else is impossible: do nothing, stay put, not a murmur, don't put money in the meter, they won't hear the coin rub the slot or the dial twist and click, I'm not here anymore, not anywhere.*

By evening she'd circled the city by bus and

Underground, even queued at Victoria Station clutching money for the boat-train to Calais, without luggage, to start from nothing. But Nina came back badly scared, limp, as undefended as a sleepwalker. Polly Gordon sat next to her on the floor. For many minutes neither spoke. In the company of a sweet-natured twelve-year-old girl, Nina could only think, *All her mistakes are ahead of her*, remembering herself at that age, ignorant, stiffnecked, hopeful. She was hardly aware she said out loud, 'You want it, you can have it.'

Polly took the blue dress lining from the pile of rags on by the fireplace. 'What are those feathers?

'You want them? They came off my hat. Take them.'

'I can sew them on again,' Polly said.

'Everywhere I went there were detectives. Following me.'

'How do you know?'

'Men follow me. You're right, it's true,' Nina said, with faded boldness. 'Not like these men. When I looked at them they hid from me. Behind newspapers.'

Polly concentrated. 'So did you see them or didn't you?'

'If I go to Russia they'll shoot me, darling, if I stay here they'll hang me,' Nina cried, abducted by grief. She didn't feel Polly's small hand rubbing her shoulder.

'I'll sew the feathers back. So it can be as good as a new hat.'

For Polly's sake, with a small shudder, Nina stopped crying. 'What's going to happen will happen,' she said, and surrendered herself body and spirit to her agonies — which settled Nina's fate as sure as chutzpah settled Rivka's.

Three

Not in his seven months in England, and never in Russia, did the balalaika player rub elbows with such luxury. Stretched on his back in his hotel bed, he breathed the clean incense of linen brought cool and pressed from the laundry that morning. Englishmen asked him what he wanted, then delivered to his room whatever he said — new clothes, boots, food — and they gave him money. Nicholas floated in a pool of luck, composing the letter he planned to write home after the killers were locked tight in their jail cells. *Dear Mama, your son is a success in London. The Authorities have given me a great responsibility. My value to them is beyond question because I know things about* certain people. *I am under the protection of the police and they are in my debt! Your little Nicky is the one with answers for them. The fine carpet in my hotel room would make you swoon, not to mention the* respect *they show me at every...*

A daydream ruptured by DI Wensley's blunt knock on the door. Abrupt as a rock face, he stood over Nicholas and informed him that the time to make good on his promises had arrived. Today, armed and braced for resistance, they'd accompany him to Jacob Peters' address. Arriving there after a cramped and solemn journey by motorcar Wensley delivered his instructions to Nicholas in a fresh burst of bluntness. 'We don't need you inside.' His hand, pressed flat against Nicholas's chest, made the meaning of his words doubly clear, even before the Russian interpreter's translation. 'Wait for us over there. Don't interfere.' He pointed to a fruit seller's barrow across the street.

Narrow shoulders slumped, feet not yet ready to move, Nicholas stood by and watched the four police officers until they reached the building's street door. They took with them the virtuous moment he'd imagined for himself, when he'd step forward to touch the wanted man on the shoulder, formally identify him, and declare himself England's friend. 'What if they don't recognise Jacob when they see him?' he said to the interpreter, whose name was Casimir.

'Little man!' Casimir twisted around to chuckle at Nicholas, then hustled along the pavement to catch Wensley and the others before they shut the door behind them.

Housebreakers didn't hunt in packs. A quick look at his clothes and knickknacks littered across the floor, his mattress upturned against the wall and gutted like a fish, told Jacob that he wasn't walking in on a burglary. Not to mention the two men picking through the debris and the two others suddenly clamped to his arms.

'Is your name Jacob Peters?'

He heard the question twice, first in brittle English, then in Russian. He might wrestle free of the grip they had on him and make it to the street, but on a raid like this Jacob could count on there being more police outside, so it was no good to run. His brotherly appeal to Casimir came out in a greener's Russian, too ignorant to even know the English word for England.

I didn't do anything. Why are you in my room?

Casimir said to Wensley, 'He says he don't know why you come to him.'

'Inform Mr Peters he's under arrest.'

At the sound of the Russian words *pod arestom* Jacob's outrage flared. His upper body thrashed in the constables' grip. One of them punched Jacob in the neck. They bent back his arms, trying to restrain a maniac. *I didn't do anything! Do I have a bad reputation? Who told them my name? What crime? What crime? Who accuses me? Casimir struggled to keep up with the angry stream – a translation of phrases, not whole sentences – and his confusion only magnified Jacob's thrashing bewilderment. Any innocent man would fight like this.*

'Calm down,' Wensley said to Jacob, without effect. 'Get him to quiet himself, Casimir.'

I didn't do anything.

'We know your friends. George Gardstein, Nina Vassilleva, Luba Milstein, Fritz Svaars, Peter Piatkow. You've visited them at 59 Grove Street.'

Fritz, he's my cousin.

'Peter Piatkow. Peter the Painter. Where is he?'

I don't know him.

'He was at Houndsditch. With you and the others. Where the three policemen were shot.'

Not me.

'Where's your cousin Fritz now?'

Jacob stopped struggling to show them that this assault on him, this slander and false arrest, was something he could withstand. *My cousin did wrong. Not me. What can I do if Fritz shoots a policeman?*

Wensley gave a shallow nod to the constables and they started for the door, Jacob in tow. 'Wait. Casimir, ask him if he knows what happens tomorrow.'

Jacob shrugged, innocently.

'What happens tomorrow?'

Nothing.

327

Jacob's arm got a stiff shake from one of the constables. 'Guv'nor wants to know what's tomorrow.'

Nothing. I don't know.

As he'd guessed, Jacob found more policemen outside. Through the sheen of blanched daylight, there was the balalaika player, flanked by bogies. He shouted Nicholas, 'Got you too? Same as Russia. They arrest innocent men here!'

DI Wensley didn't bother to listen to Casimir's translation. With a leaden softness, as a private thought, he repeated the question he wanted to hear the foreigner answer. 'What happens tomorrow?'

The young man standing closest to the Detective-Inspector thought the question was for him. Nicholas used the opportunity to practice his English. 'Excuse me, sir. Yes. What is tomorrow. Yes.'

'I'm going to find the others. Bring in the bloody lot of them.'

'Fritz, Yoska,' Nicholas struggled. 'Two. Two.' He pressed his first fingers together. 'With.'

Now Wensley listened to Casimir say, 'He means they're together.'

Nicholas had more to say. 'Peter and his woman,' Casimir spoke for Nicholas, who showed Wensley his two snug fingers again.

'What about them?'

I remember her name.

'Yes?'

We sang duets at Fritz's party. Rivka.

'You know her second name?'

Maybe I can find out.

'Doesn't matter,' Wensley said. 'They're all dead dogs.'

FUNERAL OF THE POLICE HEROES

❖═●◐═❖

IMPRESSIVE SCENES AT ST. PAUL'S

STREET CROWDS

CITY SHOPS CLOSED DURING THE SERVICE

THE WREATHS

Amid universal sympathy and sorrow a funeral service was held today for the three City policemen: —

Sergeant Tucker

Sergeant Bentley, and

Constable Choate

who were murdered on Friday at Houndsditch, the assassins being a gang of alien burglars, whom the dead officers were about to arrest.

There were a good many people waiting outside St Paul's at ten a.m., and by half-past eleven the crowd had become dense.

When the rite was over a procession was formed in St Paul's Churchyard, and the three hearses of the murdered constables moved slowly past a crowd of several thousand people, who reverently bared their heads.

Both the three hearses and six carriages in attendance were covered with crosses and wreaths of white purple and scarlet flowers.

The bodies of Sergeant Tucker and Sergeant Bentley were taken to Ilford Cemetery; the body of Sergeant Choate was conveyed to Waterloo Station, as this officer is to be buried in Surrey.

Four

It wasn't a week in this flat with Fritz and Yoska, it was a ditch-digger's lifetime. It wasn't refuge, it was incarceration. It was being locked inside a freight wagon on a train running night and day without ever pulling into a station. To Peter's ears their inane discussions weren't made out of words; the sounds coming from their mouths were monotonous metallic hiccoughs of wheels grinding over tired rails, bearing him down tracks that stretched away into the distance, without end. Peter lifted his head out of his hands. He caught Yoska's answer to Fritz's question (whatever it was), a sleepy lob aimed to antagonise.

'. . . then you don't have to. I can go to the dog fights by myself. Go to Pitsea and rest my nerves, which is what you need to do.'

The blockheaded idea thudded home. Mouth gone slack, Fritz gave him a look of frozen disbelief, and then he said, 'How much rest do you get, please, watching two poor animals tear each other to bloody pieces?'

'It's entertainment.'

'Blood and fur all over the floor. Poor dogs yelping in pain. Idiot bastards betting money on which pup dies! Very entertaining and relaxing for you, Yoska. Why dogs, anyway? Why not *orphans*?'

'You like horse racing.'

'So what?'

'They're animals. So are dogs. Dog fighting is a sport.'

'Dog *racing* is a sport. At a horse race I don't bet on which one's going to get whipped to death by the jockey.

Or,' Fritz added, 'get his brains smashed out by another horse.'

'Sometimes a horse dies.'

'By accident!'

'In a steeplechase,' Yoska said. 'They *make* the horses jump. I've seen it. It's torture of horses.'

'You've never been to a steeplechase. Neither have I. If I haven't, then, for sure, you haven't.'

'In Scotland.'

'When were you *one day* in Scotland?'

'Tell me where was it, then.'

'It wasn't any steeplechase. For sure, my friend.'

Yoska conceded nothing. 'Anyway,' a fresh lob, 'we can always come back to Betsy's. No reason to stay in Pitsea.'

'Try not to talk like an idiot. It makes me nervous.'

'My opinion's different. Does that mean I'm an idiot? No. It doesn't. So forget I said anything.'

'I wish I could.' Followed by three seconds of silence. Followed by Fritz standing up to shout at Yoska, 'You can't leave here!'

Yoska slowly lifted his heavy shoulders, let them drop again and said to Peter, 'What do you think?'

'Me?' Peter replied.

'Did you hear what we were talking about?'

Peter nodded. 'Every word.'

'All right,' Yoska said behind a shrug of his eyebrows. 'In your opinion, is dog fighting a sport?'

Doom gathered in a single cloud directly above him as Peter lowered his head into his hands again and thought, *Either they'll murder each other or do something to get all three of us killed.* What saved him from turning his groan into an articulate answer was Betsy Gershon's coded knock — *three quick, three quick.* She arrived home with food, drink

332

and newspapers, and on her skin the temperature and smell of the street.

'I saw him,' she said. 'It's good.'

'How? In particular?' Peter said.

Yoska's chief concern was Betsy's straw bag. 'Did you get a piece of whitefish?'

'Underneath the potatoes,' she directed him. 'Fishmonger's was the first place I went.'

'What are the police doing?' Fritz asked her.

'Betsy,' Peter grabbed her arm. 'How is it *good*?'

Betsy pulled away and threw up her arms in self-defence against the questions from all sides. 'You can read everything, so stop asking me. They put in something about it.' She dropped a copy of *The Evening News* on the table.

'Three men charged,' Peter read. 'Tobacconist identified aliens as armed fugitives...'

'Who's the tobacconist?' Fritz leaned in to see the headline.

'Somebody else you're going to mark for death?' Peter teased him, without a smile.

'They charged them? How many?' Yoska said.

Peter read the report to himself. 'It's more than a week old, this paper.'

Betsy said, 'I took it from the fishmonger before he wrapped Yoska's whitefish with it.'

The questions, frets, complaints came pelting in on her again.

From Fritz, 'Every day we ask you.'

From Yoska, 'You can't go to the corner and buy today's newspaper?'

Her explanation was simple. 'You know I don't read it.'

From Peter, 'You don't have to read it, just bring it here.'

333

From Fritz, 'How else do we know what's going on?'

'I hear the news,' she said, 'from people. They know more than what's in the papers.'

'Jacob's charged with murder. Yourka also with murder,' Peter read. 'Nina, conspiracy. Luba, too. And Rosie.' He read the single column twice over, the almost mocking descriptions of the prisoners, their shabby clothes and dirty unkempt hair, their ignorance of English court proceedings. 'Nothing about Rivka.'

'They're still looking for her,' Fritz nudged Peter. 'They think she's with us.'

'Good thing you're going, then. They won't come here for you.' Betsy squeezed Yoska's arm then quickly let go. 'He's coming tomorrow. His cousin has a room.'

'It won't be for free,' Yoska said.

'Extortion,' Fritz called it. 'Did Perelman say how much?'

'Twenty pounds.'

'Extortion,' Peter calmly agreed.

'How much do you have, Betsy?' Yoska went to the sugar bowl on the kitchen shelf. 'What can you give me?'

She grabbed the bowl and the coins Yoska took. 'My money got spent on your whitefish!'

'We can't go together.' Possibilities and risks were braiding into a plan as Fritz spoke. 'One at a time.'

Yoska protested by slumping back onto the sofa. 'Five minutes ago you said we can't leave here at all. Why can't we go to Pitsea, then? Nobody's looking for us there.'

Fritz had to puncture the hope. 'No, only at every train station.'

'Too bad we can't take a train to America.'

'Australia's better.'

'No.'

'It's cleaner.'

'You can't take a train to Australia, either,' Yoska argued. 'You have to go on a boat.'

'That's how to get to America. By boat.'

'But you got tickets to Australia.'

Still inside this freight wagon, skull rattling on this doom-bound train. Where is the necessity here? In three or one? Stand with Fritz and Yoska and face what's coming or leave them to it? With no credo to anchor him and separate a necessity from an opportunity, Peter carried on an imaginary conversation with his dead friend Karl, a familiar debate. The subject, Peter supposed all along, was political, fundamental to why they fought to tear down empires. Though the truth of it glistened now like a crystal in the sand: not political, no — sentimental. *What is the necessity here? What's necessary, Peter, is the good we do together, because we* are *together. A man who fights for himself is an exile. He exiles himself. No connections, no mutual joys or any chance of freeing himself from the pain of life by easing another's pain. Providing. Defending. A name in common. We fight to be in each other's care. How else does a man survive? Why should he?*

Peter's comrades in Sidney Street were in the grips of a debate that wasn't so imaginary. 'Ropes from a window in the back,' Yoska was proposing.

'With your rotten leg? And fat behind? Push you through a window, you'll take the window with you.' Fritz went on, 'That's if they're polite and they knock on the front door.'

'I'm not worried,' Yoska said. 'We can shoot our way out.'

The elongated, umbrella-shaped contraption sheathed in its waxy cloth cocoon and tenderly supported under the gent's arm must have been his camera and wooden stand, though what use Betsy Gershon had for a photographer, her landlady couldn't figure. She let him in at Besty's shouted request and studied his neatly tailored outfit, the Chester coat, the tweed leggings, and kept her eye on him until he trundled himself and his photographic paraphernalia around the first-floor landing.

Another flight up, at the second-floor landing, where Fritz and Yoska waited for him, Charles Perelman arrived out of breath. 'Salvation,' he coughed, patting his chest.

'He's going to take our photo,' Yoska joked. 'For the wanted posters.'

'You didn't say that. Don't give us bad luck.' Fritz wasn't in a joking mood.

A limp wave from Perelman. 'They already know how ugly you are.'

In the warm kitchen Betsy poured boiling water from an iron kettle to make tea, set out plates of bread and jam. 'It's cold outside today,' she sympathised.

'Second day of the year. Colder than the first. It keeps on that way you'll see ig-a-loos in Commercial Road by February.' Perelman spread out in his chair. 'No tea. Coffee. You have coffee?'

'Deduct it from the twenty pounds,' Peter said from the kitchen doorway.

Perelman welcomed the sight of him with a broad smile. 'There you are. The Scarlet Pimpernel. Red, anyway.' No one laughed at the *bon mot*, so Perelman drably went on, 'Twenty pounds isn't a fortune, especially for what you're getting.'

'In Dalston?' Fritz asked him.

'Fifteen minutes from here. It's a back room. It belongs to my cousin.' He leaned back, made room for Yoska to pour coffee from the saucepan into the saucered cup in front of him. 'Careful of the grounds. Some went in.' A magnanimous second thought. 'Doesn't matter.'

'For how long?' Yoska said.

'As long as you want it. Is money a problem?' A plea from Perelman, honesty for honesty.

'Ask Fritz,' Yoska replied.

Fritz flourished the quartet of five pound notes without handing them over. 'Your cousin. Does he know who he's renting to?'

'To me. As far as he knows. Or cares. Are you worried about supplies? I'll bring them to you.'

A proposition that jerked a laugh out of Yoska. 'How much extra, you old gouger?'

'No delivery charge. Special arrangement for customers hiding from the police.'

'Comrade landlord,' delivered with a pat on Perelman's shoulder.

'Incidentally, Yoska, I wouldn't count on doing any more trade with your friend Beron.' Perelman had the floor. 'Police found him in Clapham yesterday.'

'They lifted him?' Peter said, taking a chair at the table.

'Found him. On the Common, in the bushes,' each revelation accented with a dramatic widening of his eyes. 'Somebody beat his head in. And gave him two handsome duelling scars.'

'Duelling scars. All right.' Yoska's laugh was weaker now.

'Like holes in a violin.' Perelman's finger sketched an S shape in the air. 'One in each cheek.'

Fritz called it by name. '*Spiccan.*'

'Who says he was a spy?' Peter challenged Perelman. 'Where did you hear it?'

'It's all they're talking about in the Warsaw. Don't you read the newspapers?'

337

'What else are they saying? Are they talking about us?' Fritz was breathing hard, pacing out of the kitchen and back in.

'Sure,' Perelman said, relaxed, stretching his arms. 'Nobody knows anything.'

Fritz stopped pacing. He kicked over a chair. 'We're not leaving here.'

Betsy rushed to the upended chair as if it was her child Fritz knocked over. 'My furniture! Think about somebody else! You're not staying here! None of you! No more, no more!'

'Apologise to her,' Yoska ordered.

'Her furniture? Her fucking *chair*?' Fritz stalked over to Betsy. 'My *life*, you cow!'

Yoska fell forward, off balance on his bad leg, and crashed into Fritz with the force of his demand. 'Shut your mouth. Apologise to her.'

'He's crazy! Keep him off me!' Betsy shrank from Fritz's outstretched hand. He held his Mauser in it.

'Nobody's leaving,' Fritz said.

'Keep him away from me, Yoskele!' She raced for the sanctuary of the storeroom, Fritz behind her with his gun, Yoska behind him with his.

The tilt of Perelman's head, into conspiracy, invited Peter to agree that the two of them were the only sane people in the house. 'I can't stay,' Peter whispered.

'You're the one with enough brains to understand.' Another tilt of his head. 'What will you do?'

Peter leaned away from him, saying, 'Is anybody talking about Rivka at the Warsaw?'

'I know something about her.'

'Tell me.'

'She didn't come home. She was in Houndsditch, wasn't she.' An exaggerated frown. 'I could've helped her.

338

I got Max out, but...' Perelman barred his lips with his finger. Then, another confidence. 'Don't worry about him. He's safe. In France.'

'I don't care about Max.'

Perelman held the silence between them to show he was reading the single thought in Peter's mind. 'I know where she is.'

'There's nothing in the newspapers, the ones I've seen. Did they arrest her?'

'No. Not yet. Not if I have anything to say about it.'

'Rivka doesn't know the streets.' Peter's hand went to his brow, as if shading his eyes from the light. 'Or who she can trust.'

'That girl of yours is plenty smart. She wants me to find out where you are. If you're all right. I can tell her. We have a way to pass messages to each other.'

'Where is she, Charles?'

The shouting between Fritz and Yoska, and Betsy's wailing in the storeroom, had died down to a low rumble. On guard, Perelman listened for a second, then quickly said, 'At the Pavilion Theatre.'

Perelman wore the veneer of a liar, a trickster. He might have been born with it. Like the oil coating of a duck's feathers, it was the lubricant that allowed him to glide in and out of complications, led lazily by the promise of whatever benefited Charles Perelman. Underneath this slippery veneer lay what? Motives more despicable than selfishness? Or far less... His thin covering of bravado, possessor of secret information, fixer, obscured a depth of sincerity. An old player's last throw. *Not if I have anything to say about it.* The two possibilities melted one into the other during the long moment before Peter let out a breath and said, 'I'm not staying with them.'

339

'Bravo.' Perelman said, a fatherly congratulation for the sensible, the moral, decision.

'Tonight. They fall asleep around midnight.'

'Judge for yourself. Stay away till twelve noon. I have to make arrangements with her. Can you manage not to get arrested for twelve hours?'

Betsy dragged in ahead of Fritz and Yoska, the same parade that had marched off ten minutes earlier. Both men had put up their guns, Yoska's moustache was frothed in shaving cream, and Betsy, stripped of her skirt, blouse and shoes, stood barefoot in her bloomers. Fritz, panicky and grave, dealt out the explanation. 'We're all staying.'

Perelman objected, 'You can't. My cousin's room, Fritz. I made arrangements.'

'We've been here too long already,' Peter said, still a comrade in this.

Fritz turned on him. 'I listened to you and let you bring Karl back to my flat! If *you* listened to *me* we wouldn't *have* this trouble!' His Mauser was unholstered and pointed, for sharp emphasis, at Peter's chest.

'You're losing the chance to move. It has to be soon,' Perelman's levelheaded advice.

But Fritz tore off in a different direction. He grabbed an envelope out of his jacket pocket and closed Perelman's hand around it. 'You don't have to stay here. I want you to go and post this letter. Can you read the address?'

Perelman glanced at the envelope and tucked it inside his coat. 'I don't have to read anything. The clerk will tell me the postage and I'll pay what he says for a stamp.'

'Betsy doesn't want us in her house anymore,' Yoska said, with a throb of sympathy.

Fritz's agitation was a windstorm that all of a sudden had blown itself out. 'Where's the room?' He meant the question for Perelman but he asked it haplessly to the empty air.

'Fifteen minutes to walk there. Nelson Street,' Perelman said.

'Not until it's dark outside. Five or six...' Fritz concentrated his mental powers on the shifting uncertainties of those fifteen minutes of broken cover. 'Not tonight. Tomorrow. Later. Nine or ten is better.' Other dangers reared in his mind. 'Or tonight. One at a time. When everybody is off the streets.'

'I'm not going until you're in there safe,' Yoska decided.

Agreeing, Fritz said, 'We need a code.'

'Three knocks, then three again.'

'Who knocks? Yoska, you? On Nelson Street?' Fritz said. 'What if they lifted me and it's the bogies inside?'

'Nobody knows you're going there!' The idea was an insult to Perleman. 'Decide when you're going. Or do you want me to bring the key here?'

'Three-knocks-three-knocks is Betsy. It's confusing,' Yoska said. 'Send somebody here to knock two-knocks-two-knocks if Fritz is there safe.'

Fritz looked at him. 'Send who?'

'I don't know. A boy. You can pay a boy.'

'What boy?'

'A boy, I don't know, in the street. Give him a shilling and tell him to come and knock.'

'Are you crazy?' Scrawled in choking frustration across Fritz's face was the flabbergasting insanity of plucking a stranger out of the street, a nipper to entrust with their secret whereabouts and to despatch on an errand whose success or failure would mean the difference between getting out alive and hanging dead by the neck at the end of an English rope. 'A *shilling*, Yoska? To knock on a door?'

The bickering went on. Behind his hand, Perelman whispered to Peter: 'They won't know *what* happened to you.'

What's the meaning of this? People wonder it to themselves and out loud to each other, sometimes to the empty air. Bewildered. Rattled. Disgusted. Crossed. Charles Perelman shouted it at his wife when she told him the details of her first adultery: Deborah's 'young gentleman' in the manager's office, a ram so good at ramming, in the storage cupboard, the nook under the stairs. Pleasure at the tip of her beckoning finger. *What's the meaning of this?* The shameless 'clean breast' (her pornographic *mea culpa*), not the fornication. It meant a sunken truth about his marriage had breached the surface. Perelman's life as Deborah's husband lost its enchantment, they both shed the wormy delusion at its core, everybody knew where everybody stood and so the family rubbed along, together.

As Perelman walked toward City Police headquarters the refrain played in his ear. *What's the meaning of this?* A consideration that didn't slow his step. No clammy tide sloshed in his stomach, though he did feel a trailing presence; another Charles Perelman who walked behind him and couldn't keep up. 'Carolis Perlmanis' who'd spat at Russian army officers and hectored the lower ranks to fight for themselves, not the decadent Tsar. When he could throw rocks and run fast. Young limbs turned into an old cask of a body. Well. Agile enough to accomplish subtler things. At the door, too rushed to fish for his handkerchief, he wiped his forehead with the cuff of his coat sleeve, and then, not really aware he'd moved indoors Perelman heard himself tell the desk sergeant

342

that the wanted men no one could find, he, Charles Perelman, had found and he'd come in to speak to the man in charge.

'Wait over there.' The Sergeant gestured with his pencil at a wooden bench by the wall.

It's too easy to mistake consequences for meaning. What will come out of this is Carlusha will grow up knowing his father didn't cower under the threat of anarchist revenge. And Deborah will know her husband's seventy-year-old balls still swung with some heft. What treatment is coming from Detective-Inspector Wensley, the man in charge? There's a sickish scent around deception and no matter how used they are to smelling it on an informant, policemen let you know it stinks in their nose. Perelman, you're in their house. They'll punish you for this betrayal with a £500 reward...

In the corridor on his way to DI Wensley's office, the gray floor under Perelman's shoes was a ribbon of ocean. As it flowed underneath him he thought, *It's how a tall ship must feel riding a swell, if a ship had feelings.*

'I'm not here.'

The Detective-Inspector asked Perelman to repeat what he'd said. When he did, Wensley replied with a nod of agreement. 'Tell us,' — the DI, Henry Wagner, there to help with Perelman's Russian Yiddish, the constable pencilling notes — 'how you knew where they were?'

A hinted accusation. Perelman sat stiff-backed in his chair. He didn't look at Henry Wagner when he answered, forced to rely upon another man to represent him honestly. 'She came to my house today. Betsy Gershon. 'Help me, help me.' Frightened.'

'Gershaw?' the Constable asked without looking up.

Wensley ignored him. 'Afraid of the men?' he said to Perelman.

'Especially Fritz.'

'Sokoloff, he's there with Fritz too?'

'Both of them.'

'What about Piatkow? The Painter, is he in there?'

Perelman took a sip from the cup of tea they'd brought for him, the only one on the table. 'He was with Fritz and Yoska an hour ago.'

'He's the worst of the lot,' Wensley said.

The Constable thought the remark was to him. 'Yes, sir. Murdering scum, is all.'

'They're relying on me. I arranged them a room. They don't want to stay in Sidney Street.'

'Oh? Why's that?'

Perelman answered in English, as if the fact was staring them in the face, 'Police will find them.'

'Quite,' Wensley allowed, with a dryness that passed for drollery. 'How much time have we got?'

'Fritz wants to go tonight. Then he wants tomorrow. Yoska wants to stay with Betsy, unless Fritz goes. Tonight. Tomorrow. Probably tomorrow,' Perelman obliged. 'They're moving across to Nelson Street. One at a time.'

'These men are brawlers,' Wensley thought aloud. Then he asked Perelman to give an opinion. 'Are Svaars and Sokoloff as excitable as their friend?' The question stymied Perelman, so the Detective-Inspector simplified it. 'Did you see any guns?'

'Mausers.'

'How many?'

'Fritz and Yoska, two pistols, definite. Maybe Yoska's wasn't a Mauser. I don't know this gun, that gun.'

'Piatkow is armed, too?'

'The Painter... Well, him.' Perelman retreated. 'I don't know him so good.'

Wensley's fingers tapped a little rhythm on the table,

helping him tabulate Perelman's information. 'If I were those men I'd be eager to get out. Desperate. So...' In the mixed company of police and civilian he left the next thought unspoken. 'What else can you tell us about the arrangements at Number 100?' Fingers clasped, Wensley sat back and absorbed his informant's description of the narrow staircase, the second-floor room, his observation of other residents in the building, which rooms they occupied, whether any of them spoke English. Wensley's attention and brisk handshake communicated an unmistakable impression to Charles Perelman: in that hour, man to man, they'd forged a pact.

He met Wensley's directness with a clubbable helping of his own. 'How soon before I can come back for the reward money?'

'First we have to catch them.'

'Soon, then.'

'Apply for it, Mr Perelman. I'll support your application.'

One thing Perelman didn't stop to doubt: his visit to the City Police had tipped a mechanism into motion. He carried that private knowledge with him through the foyer where he passed the desk sergeant with a courtly, almost military, salute. He'd given the spinning world a little push, sped events on their way. For the pleasure of it. There's your what's-the-meaning-of-this. He felt the blood in his arteries flowing clean and strong, his legs lightly carrying his weight, his stomach as relaxed as a cat on a sunny windowsill and hungry for a large supper — brisket and potatoes, apple sauce and *lockshen* pudding. Perelman followed his feet toward Brick Lane, the Warsaw's menu floating in front of him.

The difference in temperature between the radiator heat of Wensley's office and the glassy slice of January air outside brought out a ridge of sweat on his forehead. He reached into his coat pocket for a handkerchief and his fingers brushed the folded edge of Fritz's letter. Back Perelman marched to hand over this bonus to the man in charge.

Ignorant of the important business Perelman finished with DI Wensley only a few minutes before, the desk sergeant welcomed him with a tight frown as if the old Jewish gentleman had wandered in to report his pocket watch stolen. 'Mr Wensley can't be interrupted at the minute.'

Perelman showed him the letter. 'For him. Important. You know?'

'Give it here, I'll see he gets it.'

Before the sergeant could take it from him, Perelman slid the letter back into his pocket. 'No. I must.'

'Suit yourself. Wait over there.'

Not ushered in — the bench again. Five minutes. Ten. After a quarter of an hour, other chores took the Sergeant away from his post, leaving a Constable in charge. Perelman was still sitting there when he returned, a fact the policeman barely registered. The Detective-Inspector probably hadn't found a moment to mention to the Sergeant (amongst other colleagues) that Charles Perelman came to the police at risk to his own safety to offer them fresh intelligence about the most dangerous fugitives in London. Critical information, rare enough for him to be treated like a dignitary, even rewarded. He presented the envelope to the Sergeant again and pointed to the foreign address. 'Fritz give it to me,' he pressed.

'DI Wensley's still busy. I just passed his office. He's speaking on the telephone. I expect him to be a while. Either you can leave that envelope with me or sit down where you were and wait.'

346

Perelman let the sergeant sweep Fritz's letter an arm's length along the desk where the plump, pig eyed constable glanced at it. 'From me. Charles Perelman. You tell him,' he said, against the grain of what it meant: it didn't mean anything.

Fritz grunted his thanks. 'You're generous,' he said as Peter vacated the chair next to the stove.

'I'm warm enough,' Peter answered, lit a cigarette and stood in a corner of the next room, where the night's chill seeped in through the wall. In the sharper air he'd stay awake and outlast Fritz, who drowsily finished cleaning his pistol in the fat warmth of the kitchen. At one in the morning, Yoska had bowed out of their nightcap argument (this one over the superior recipe for pickling herring — Polish or Russian) to huddle with Betsy on a mattress in the storeroom. A few minutes before two o'clock, sleep finally pushed Fritz under, gun in hand.

Either his footsteps rattled the stillness or it was some excitement in a dream that shook Fritz. Drooped forward at the little square table, his head resting on the ledge made by his crossed arms, he twisted left and right to shake free of some discomfort but didn't open his eyes. Peter watched Fritz for any sign of waking and with the door to the landing open he bent round towards the storeroom. No sound from there but Yoska's muffled snoring. *How does Betsy sleep through such a racket? A pillow over her head, her blanket on top, her affection for him on top of that . . .*

Peter took the first flight of stairs slowly, two at a time, with a firm grip of the banister that tilted down through narrow shadows. At each landing, past each tenant's

347

door, he moved on the balls of his feet. *A child on tiptoes outside his father's bedroom. Not a sneak thief, I'm no burglar. Yoska manages it. With his clump of a foot and whale's body. Pay attention . . .* to the tin he felt his boot send skittering down the hallway. Peter stopped dead, crouched down.

They stayed asleep or in their beds, whoever lived in the ground floor flat. Tucked safe. *No ghosts or bad men stalking your house. So hush, babies, in your cots, sleep . . .* Wind as brittle as frost sifted in around the door to the yard at the back. The doorknob stuck halfway through its rotation and when Peter forced it the complaint it let out cracked through him like a gunshot. *Hush, my babies.*

Then, he stood drenched in dark air.

In the four-storey square dozens of windows looked down on the courtyard, at this dead hour all of them blind. The passageway that stretched a hundred feet in both directions, fogged in thicker darkness at each end, marked the border of Peter's self-reliance. Across it he was tethered to Perelman's word that Rivka was in the Pavilion Theatre where he said she was, and it was Perelman's glad duty protect her. And with her — or because of her — Peter. Under Perelman's protection. No credo but the tether between two men. Somewhere in the street, a horse whinnied and scuffed at the cobbles with a restless hoof. A wheel creaked on a freezing axel. *Poorest of the poor*. For no reason except the one that chained him to the anchor of a woman's heart, Peter sprinted into the wind-shredded, sleet-spiked dark. It parted ahead of him and closed behind him, he drew it around him as he ran.

Unblanketed in the vile cold, the horse lurched forward, tried to shift his flank into the wind, furiously jangled his bridle and kicked at the closed wooden wagon harnessed to him. A bedevilment to the gelding and no

shield against the weather for the detectives sitting inside.
'Where's our gloves, then?'

'They don't care if our fingers drop off from frostbite.'

'I care.'

'Thank you, Sergeant. Most considerate.'

'Two of you, and you two, Hawkins Street. You others,
you're with me. We're going into Number 102.'

'Indoors. Splendid.'

'Pity the other buggers.' The two hundred policemen
soaked by the wet snow as they fanned out through
Hawkins Street and Richardson Street, Lindley Street and
Sidney Street, who ringed the Stepney square to bottle in
any foreign desperadoes until first light, when more guns
would arrive. 'Those anarchist buggers, too.'

Five

In her dream, Rivka walked alone, in bare feet and nightgown, along the Talsen Road. High daylight washed farmland and forest at her back, but everything in front of her lay swamped in night. From this reach of darkness her father emerged with his unmistakable knee-sprung gait, smiling at Rivka, much older than he should be, white-haired, and loonily unaware of the danger just seconds away from overtaking him. A mob of men, some on foot, others in motorcars, hurried down the dirt road behind him. In the places where moonlight splintered the shadows Rivka saw who they were: English policemen. Next thing, a tumbling wave of uniforms, truncheons, guns and machinery curled over Mordechai, fell on him and dragged him under.

Barehanded, Rivka dived into the swirling disaster to fight off not policemen — they were gone — but a swarm of insects. A thick chaos of them blinded her, thousands of tiny wings and soft bodies matted in her hair. As fast as her fingers combed out mashed, sticky black strings of them, more attacked her face and head, flew into her mouth and ears. Furiously she raked her scalp, spun around, shocked, gasping, because the sticky black strings she pulled out were clumps of her hair. They collected at Rivka's feet and mixed with the litter of damp straw there. She'd brought a broom with her to sweep the stone floor clean.

The cubicle she stood in could be part of a stable block or laundry. In the past it might have had some unremarkable

351

use, but Rivka knew it to be her father's jail cell. He was gone. The authorities had sent for her, to clean it, to prepare it for its next guest. Her first job was the sheet. Like the straw, the stone floor and wooden walls, it was damp and crusted with human filth. It waited for her in the middle of the stall, loosely bunched at both ends, the length of a man. For a second she thought it was Mordechai's corpse she'd been summoned to wash and clear away, but his bedding was all that was left of him.

With a winding motion, Rivka folded it over her forearms. Through the half-opened door she could see the new prisoner waiting for her to leave. He was clothed in a sheet, which he gripped tightly against the cold. His head was bowed, and, she saw, wounded, cracked into three pieces crudely held together with loops of twine. The raw, unknit edges of bone sawed against each other. 'I'm finished,' Rivka said to him, eager to be gone. Peter didn't reply or seem to recognise her. As she passed him in the doorway he begged, with a defeated heave, 'They won't give me a light for my cigarette.'

Rivka startled herself awake. A taste of brine dissolved on her tongue as she came to. The shocking sight of Peter's broken skull was the lone scrap of the dream that followed her back to her bed in Harry's office. That, and a grim mood – the shadow of the certainty that she lived in a world arranged by troubled men, men wronged by other men and governments and empires of men. It's a true thing. It wouldn't change; this she had learned in London.

Dread hardened into a premonition. Cold iron stairs, cold stone stairs, then the stinging chill of the pavement outside, numbed Rivka's bare feet. Under the gray gloom and threat of snow, she picked through the rubbish blown around the Pavilion's stage door for a message from Charles Perelman, frightened by the chance that she'd missed finding one, if he'd left it, last night. By looking in the wrong place. By looking too late, after the wind scattered it into the street or the rain chewed it to pulp. Empty-handed in the humming stillness, Rivka turned back at the mouth of the alley to stand inside the door and abide.

No need for any philosophic discussion of the subject; as men, Frederick Wensley and Henry Wagner agreed that good order in the world is fragile, even unnatural. At best, they'd say, it's a waning truce between belligerents compelled by their own moral purpose, the ones who can muster enough virile strength to demonstrate it. We net wild beasts and stake them to the ground. It's what civilised men need to do to keep from being brought down themselves. Today's seething menace occupies the front room on the second floor of No. 100 Sidney Street, E1. DI Wensley will meet it as a practical clash, not a political one; anarchy to a policeman is what an inferno is to the fire brigade.

Under orders, Henry Wagner helped in the chicanery, sharpened the threats, magnified the authority, used his Yiddish persuasiveness to empty the building of its good citizens. Betsy Gershon had to be tricked into coming downstairs, and then hauled next door and then browbeaten for half an hour before she gave what sounded like an honest report of the fugitives she harboured in her room. Neither the Detective-Inspector nor his interpreter completely trusted Betsy's word. In the open gates of the wood yard across from No. 100 Henry stood watching for any movement in the upstairs windows. Was it one gunman in there, two or three?

353

Beside him by the gate, Wensley also stared upward at the tenement, its windows, its attic roof and then, a brief blink, further above into the answerless sky.

Henry recognised in the officer's face the passing of cogitation into decision. The Weasel had finished measuring his opponents' tactical advantages and vulnerabilities, and turning aside from Henry set himself on a course. 'That's all we'll need from you, Mr Wagner,' he said over his shoulder with deliberate courtesy. 'Thank you for helping with your people.'

'*Rikhtik, mayn folk,*' his reply to Wensley's back, lost in the wind. The Jews, did he mean? The Russians, the Poles? Foreigners? Right. The interpreter's people. A remark came echoing home to Henry, in Charles Perelman's voice, from that sodden quarter of an hour he'd wasted tapping the old conniver for information outside Bevis Marks. Where Rabbi Perelman attempted to educate him. 'You're standing in the middle of a bridge.' Though he, Perelman, was no more Henry's people than the frightened, mulish occupants of No. 100 he'd spent the last hour talking out of their beds and rooms; and no more than the local gawkers collecting behind the line of policemen, the nuisance of Cockneys and Jews shouldering each other aside for a better view; and no more than the bullheaded imbeciles inside the building, too stupid to guess they were surrounded or too crazed to worry.

And no more than the divisional superintendents, detective-superintendents, superintendents and detective-inspectors, bowler-hatted decision makers who post a cordon around the English they speak, officer to officer. Henry couldn't be completely sure, but he thought he heard one of them ask Wensley, 'Who are the hounds?'

Who are the hounds? The question of the day. While

Henry interrogated himself with it, DI Wensley spoke to Sergeant Leeson. 'Throw something at their window. Give 'em a tickle.' Here was one of Henry's people, the sergeant, down in the ranks.

Benjamin Leeson took a moment to choose pebbles heavy enough to fly the twenty yards or so and stay on target. He scraped up a handful of gravel with the same gentleness that muffled the strength he'd called upon to lift Rosie Trassjonsky, inert as a sack of pebbles, from the floor of her dead friend's room, carry her down two flights of stairs, then past the pack of newspapermen. His boots kicked through mud and slush on his way out of the wood yard, puddles sealed with thin panes of ice splintered to shards under his heels. Dull flecks of snow caromed off gusts of wind above the empty pavements. Sidney Street had the skeletal look of a place evacuated for demolition. The Sergeant found a comfortable angle, took quick aim and splashed his handful of pebbles across the second floor window with a strong over-arm throw. The rattle of them falling back to earth and skittering over the cobblestones was the only reply from the building, the only sound anyone heard.

Before the window exploded.

Behind the shower of glass, a concussing burst from a Mauser. Fritz sent a few more rounds stuttering in a line right across Sidney Street from pavement to pavement, following the Sergeant's a headlong dash for the yard where he fell backwards, tripping over his heels. From where he lay Benjamin Leeson's cry carried upward to the gunmen and behind him to his brother officers by the twin gates. 'Jack, I'm hit!' To Yoska, the narrow-faced plainclothesman who knelt over the one Fritz wounded wasn't a man with a name, he was another target.

One who moved commandingly, got the gates pulled

shut too quickly for Yoska to steady his revolver. Furious blows, bullets hammered at the entryway as Wensley knelt over Sergeant Leeson, tore back the man's coat and shirt and grimaced at the pooling blood.

Fritz and Yoska fired again, wild shots into the first-floor rooms in the building across the street where Fritz said he'd seen men with rifles. 'Sweet dreams! Sweet dreams, darlings!' he hollered, humiliating the English Tsar's police with another Mauser burst and the laugh of a heroic lunatic. 'Hear what I told them, Yoska? That's showmanship!'

'We're running things!' Yoska laughed along. They could appear with the suddenness of ghosts in any window. 'Hurt them enough and they'll bargain with us.'

'No bargaining. What for?'

There was no truer thing Fritz knew. In a feverish rhapsody he thought, *No politics or history here, no philosophy, no geography that isn't a conversation between armed men. Us in here, them out there. Right where we woke up this morning, this thing that's happening is proof of what the world is before politicians and philosophers get their hands on it. Simple. What you have, they want to take. Your food, your money, your house, your country, your manhood, your body, your life, your dead bones.*

One time I saw a twelve-year-old boy standing in a brown field. Late summer, in the middle of a drought. A cow was in the field with him. The boy picked up a rock and threw it, hit the cow in her eye. She didn't know what it was, what was wrong, she tried to shake the pain away. It nearly broke my heart to watch her. The boy went over to her, picked up the rock, took a few steps back and threw the rock again. She went down on her front legs. The boy hit her again. I couldn't watch any more. Jesu, the pity of it. He was older than me by five years and a stronger fighter. This house is ours. Mine. I'll struggle for it.

356

You come to take it from me, now you're notified. I'm no cow in a field.

His sleep was so narcotic that Peter woke from it in confusion. He'd been captured and nailed into a crate. For deportation. They'd loaded the crate into the cargo hold of a ship bound for Riga. *All right, then, somebody tell me who this woman is with her head tucked against my shoulder, her arm hugging me. Another prisoner?* Fragments drifted back to colour a picture of the night just gone. He'd left Fritz and Yoska in Sidney Street. He'd been shunted by the wind and rain from doorway to alleyway, shaking in the unstoppable cold, down turnings that led away to God knows where. At the dead end of one of these alleys, he'd crawled through a hole in a fence. The wooden shed he'd found there with its jutting, coffin-shaped addition, Peter guessed was a chicken coop. More shelter than a doorway, a better hideout than the stray tarpaulin he'd given up for the alley.

Inside, the crust of bird droppings on the floor didn't surprise him; that he could see it, did. A ragged spill of light spread from a wood fire in the middle of the shack where somebody had squared a few bricks together to make a pit. The haven of another street tramp. Too weak to fight anybody for it, or drag himself outside again to face the freezing unknown streets, Peter sat down to wait for its owner to come back.

Two potatoes and an onion baked in a pan of ashes. Famished as he was, Peter left them alone, as a token of his harmlessness. His integrity. He was in someone's home. The coffin-shaped structure turned out to be an enclosed bedroom; inside, a quilt lay scrambled atop straw-cushioned bedding. On a narrow shelf, a row of

357

homely belongings — pewter jug, china bowl and plate, teacup, spoon, fork and knife. The planks of the wall were sealed (and by the look of them held together) with strips of newspaper pasted in neat vertical rows. For many minutes, Peter kept his eye on the flap of felt and tar paper draped across the entrance. When a gloved hand lifted a corner of it he got to his feet — or tried to. Bright pain flashed in his ankle and seated him again.

'Lor', look at you! A man!'

Lor', look at you! A woman! Peter might have answered, if he'd been sharp enough for farce.

Not a flicker of fear in her. She set down the armload of strangely dry firewood and apologised to Peter for not being in when he'd arrived. 'Since I was by the bucket I stopped for a piss,' she added, 'It kept up for a great while.'

Her name was Roma. She didn't ask Peter his or anything else about him; his troubles, his human connections, the mysterious coincidences that brought him in from the night. Whatever she needed to know about her visitor was somehow obvious to her. Roma's one-sided chatter made things easier. Her voice was girlish and came lisping from a mouth that was missing half a dozen teeth. The bundle of her hair that Peter could see (most of it she'd twisted under a headscarf) was coloured with henna. Judging by her rough hands, and the stiff shuffle that moved her from the fire to the shelf, then over to Peter, she might have been his mother's age. She handed him the plate and, from the end of a carving knife, served him one of the potatoes.

'I won't hurt you,' he said.

'No, 'course you won't.' Roma skewered the other potato for herself, took a bite and leaned across Peter's legs. From the wall above her bed she took down a crucifix to show him the guarantor of her protection. 'I prayed to 'im twice a day. Three times today.' Guarantor of tonight's expected unexpected happiness.

It was long in coming, Peter heard. Roma's bad luck bloodline was Didicai, she told him, gypsy, and in 1887 she'd made the mistake of marrying an Englishman, who gambled away the horses and wagon passed down to them with song and ceremony by her Romany family. The scrap of ground under her shack belonged, like the row house at the end of the cinder path, to her absconded husband's family. 'You live for the good souls. It betters 'em an' betters you,' Roma concluded, as though reciting a learned lesson to an angel of the Lord. Then she asked Peter, 'How'd you hurt your foot?'

Another blade of pain seared his ankle when he slid it towards the firelight. 'I can't remember. Twisted it. Not broken.'

'I'll give you medicine for it.'

A fragrance of rosemary and lavender and herbs Peter couldn't name enveloped him from the steam warmed cloth Roma used for a bandage. Enveloped by the warmth, the earthy perfume, the unsought kindness, he let himself fall asleep.

He awoke snagged in Roma's unconscious embrace, lost in the morning. A V-shaped crack across the crystal of his pocket watch, its stationary second hand and the other hands stopped at 3:35, told Peter what time he'd probably hurt his ankle, but not the present hour.

His whispered *thank-you* and *good-bye* to Roma, and gave her a soft push, but they didn't budge her. She snuggled deeper under his neck, tightened her hug. Then he felt the wetness of her mouth on his collar, again on his neck, his chin, her stagnant breath clouded his nostrils; her face dipped to kiss Peter's throat as her sleepy hips rocked against his leg, happy prisoner of a dream, Roma tried to climb onto him. Peter gripped both of her arms and twisted her down to the floor.

'Are you awake or asleep?'

'Awake,' she said, drowsy, crawling back to him, eyes and mouth half open.

'Good-bye, good-bye. My jacket. What did you do with it?'

'Wait. Stay with me. In my bed. Lay back down. Look...' With one frantic hand Roma shook out the jacket she'd folded to pillow his head, with the other she fumbled along the shelf to get hold of a small tin box. 'You can have money.'

Peter lifted himself on his good ankle and lunged forward on his bandaged one. He swiped Roma's tar paper door out of his way and didn't stop to clamber through the gap in the fence: he fell against it and shouldered the rotten pales apart. As he walked length of the alley and met the street to mix into its unremarkable business Peter reminded himself to mask his limp. A few supple paces made him realize his ankle pained him less. Was it a few hours of rest or the healing power of her gypsy remedy? Whichever he decided to believe.

Ten thousand pedestrian errands threaded through Spitalfields. Peter slipped in among them as neatly as a swimmer arcs under a swell. On business that would mark him out if it were unhidden. He passed by in the market, as noticeable to strangers as any other stranger, a man down on his luck, looking for a tailor to sew the ripped collar of his jacket and a cobbler to mend the heel of his boot and a watchmaker to repair his pocket watch. Unremarkable business. Follow this track along the stations of an unmemorable day, ten thousand of them, follow the trail of those days into an untroubled life.

A porter pushes a hand-truck. A merchant unrolls a bolt of cloth. A customer buys two bags of salt. Peter could do any of those things, and after a hundred repetitions or a hundred thousand reach the bottom of an uncomplicated existence sustained by the grace of a philosophy good for nothing better than to pilot you safely on to the next errand: Hope For No Great Change.

At the market's exit, a clock on a cast iron stanchion told Peter the time was 9:45, more than two hours before Perelman's 'arrangements' (with Harry? the local constabulary?) opened a way back to Rivka at the Pavilion Theatre. At the next corner Peter recognised the turning into Cheshire Street. Harry's theatre was behind him, the same as Sidney Street. People fluttered past him, excited faces, rushing steps, men, women and children fired up by a rumour of some spectacle. Fritz and Yoska, what else? Last midnight, praise God in the highest, Peter had the good sense to obey his instincts and get out. Good or bad, their fate was their judgment.

The relief of being in the free air lasted as long as it took Peter to step off the kerb and walk into Sclater Street. He'd gambled on finding a haven till noon in Shinebloom's restaurant; instead he was gripped by the fear that encircles a young child in a blind dark room, cold, trapped, asphyxiating in a tank of rising water. Under the words MURDER OF POLICE OFFICERS and in larger, bolder lettering £500 REWARD, Peter saw two photographs of himself.

The first: 'Peter the Painter,' debonair anarchist/murderer, his hand jauntily tucked into the small of his back, a straw hat hanging off his fingers. He's composed himself to present a mood of refined distraction or

361

nonchalant self-certainty, staring into the wings from a stage-set outdoor balcony. Modelling the profile bound to decorate a stamp.

In the second picture, his face concealed less. His expression wasn't so certain. That Parisian photographer, Peter remembered, suggested he should relax, stand a little more naturally; in an expert's hands, Peter had obliged. The camera recorded his determined impression of a relaxed man leaning against the back of a chair. Under the ledge of his brow he looked gravely occupied, contemplating the deep realities of a world he knew, when he was a twenty-six-year-old in Paris, was ruled by tyrants and spineless complicity. It was a political stare. He didn't look at anything from such a height any more.

Unrecoverable truth.

'*In Germany I'm a German. In Marseille I'm a Frenchman. In Paris, or here, with Jews all around me I'm a Jew...*' Peter remembered what he'd said to Rivka outside Shinebloom's, his stomach shuddering, his future in the smell of her hair, the smell of her hair an anchor chain around his neck. Five hundred pounds the price on his attachment to Rivka. Also a few shillings for the hangman's rope.

He left the wanted poster, his stomach shuddering again, bent over the brink. Here. Outside Shinebloom's door, the reality of it, not the memory — The Mayor calmly invited Peter to come in off the street. 'I wasn't sure it was you,' he said, loosely circling his own face with a finger, remarking the change to Peter's. 'Your beard.'

'Gave it to the razor.'

'It's good. From here I wasn't sure it was you. You look —'

'I look like a vagrant,' Peter said. 'Do I smell?'

The Mayor sniffed Peter's jacket. 'Onions. Not so bad.' He offered his hand. 'Come inside.'

For a small man, The Mayor's grip was bone-crunching and harsh. The handshake he gave Peter was the kind a father gives a son miraculously returned home, a solemn pumping of the arm before the loveable neck is embraced and the weeping starts. His thick fingers worked Peter's hand until their warmth turned humid. To hold off any face-kissing and neck- hugging, Peter took a step into the restaurant. In a blink, the Mayor had a grip of Peter's right wrist, and with a darting move he snatched his left one. Then he shoved Peter against the door jamb. The Mayor was short, but compact and muscular; he handled himself like a wrestler. Legs braced, he twisted from the waist and dug his shoulder into Peter's chest, winded him, pinned him hard to the door.

'Help over here! Somebody help!' The Mayor shouted into the street as Peter twisted himself half free. 'Peter the Painter! It's Piatkow, the anarchist!'

A grandmother, headshawled and gowned for a funeral, trotted in to cane Peter with her walking stick. Frail blows skidded off the side of his head. One hand loose, he grabbed the stick and swung it across his body. The silver handle crushed The Mayor's nose, yet he clung on, sputtering blood. 'Somebody help!' Peter coshed him and broke free. He brandished the bloody stick as he ran, in what direction he didn't know, out of the district.

'Rifles over there.' Fritz tipped his Mauser's long muzzle against the window frame, at the upper floor of the brewery beyond. 'Shotguns in those windows.' The muzzle slid an inch to the side, pointed at the building directly across Sidney Street. 'Something in the doors too. That's how I'd do it.'

'Write your plan on a piece of paper, I'll take it over to

them.' Yoska straightened his bad leg as far as he could and lowered himself to floor next to Fritz. 'What — you don't think I'd come back?'

A tolerant sigh. 'I'm saying it's an obvious strategy.'

'To make us come out?' Nothing, not even tolerance from Fritz, who turned his head away. With a nudge to Fritz's shoulder Yoska apologised for his own slowness. 'Fritz, you've got the right idea. Figure their tactics. They want to scare us with all the guns they've got.'

'They don't want us to surrender.' Fritz angled a look at the brewery. No movement, nothing to see, but his breath was short and he felt dryness in his mouth. Then he saw the long double barrel of a shotgun dip into the light from a shop doorway below. He crawled back from the window and tilted his head to get Yoska to do the same.

Yoska leaned forward to see for himself. He grinned. 'They can't hit us with one of those.'

His grin twitched at the corners of his mouth: he reminded Fritz of a weightlifter quivering under a barbell he was no longer strong enough to hold. He reached over and patted Yoska's back to steady him.

His grin sank. 'Damn Peter,' Yoska said.

'He surprised you?' Now Fritz was the one wearing the plaster smile. 'Peter always looks out for himself. I'm his friend and I never know what he's thinking.'

'He doesn't talk. Or, when he does, he doesn't say anything clear.'

'It sounds like he means something else, even when he doesn't.' Arms crooked on his knees, Fritz recalled, ' "Ignore her, she'll get worse." That's what Peter advised me about Luba!'

'Another runner.'

In silence Fritz agreed. Then he said, 'Peter doesn't know how else to be.'

364

'Anyway, he's a good fighter.'

'Listen, Yoska. The way things are, we wouldn't be better off if Peter was in this room.'

'Another gun...'

'We're together. This is *our* action. Yes?'

After a second's rumination, nodding his dark head, Yoska said, 'What happens to you happens to me.' A loud crack of a rifle shot made him twitch toward the window. 'Missed. They're just showing us.'

Fritz knew different. 'Did he say one word to you last night?'

'About going? No. Oh,' Yoska remembered. 'He said I should shave off my moustache.' He presented his face to the light. 'How does it look?'

'Pale.'

'Shows off more of my rotten skin.'

Another rifle shot. Another miss. Fritz checked his Mauser's clip. 'From that brewery. I told you.'

The noise of cheers outside at the end of the street tempted Yoska to peep over the windowsill. He saw mounted police and a police cordon, seven or eight constables with their arms linked, capes flapping in the snowy wind, holding back a hundred-strong crowd of sightseers. To protect them from the terrorist assassins. 'Is that the uprising, you think?' Yoska joked sourly.

Another rifle shot. On the roof above them, a chimney pot shattered, blown apart by a perfectly aimed high-calibre round. 'Found us,' Fritz said, and dived for the floor.

A hailstorm of bullets pelted through the second-floor window, opened jagged holes in the furniture, the walls, exploded dishes in the kitchen, porcelain ornaments on the table, sent shrapnel spinning through the air. Flat on the carpet, Yoska followed Fritz out the door and down the stairs.

From the landing outside the first-floor room Yoska saw Fritz kneeling at the blown-in window, squeezing off shots *one-two-three* into the brewery, *one-two-three* toward the wood yard. 'Go down! Down!' Fritz shouted to him, finger jabbing to send Yoska to the ground floor.

The door to the Fleishmans' flat hung open. Abandoned in secret at some ungodly hour, bequeathed to Yoska, everything in it. Preserved. A silver pocket watch. A jewellery box on a night-stand. They must have seen Yoska's large body move behind the window. A shotgun blast took out the frame, the glass, and sprayed stinging fragments into the side of his face. He crouched behind the bed, protecting his eyes with a cushion. Shots from Bulldog revolvers rattled into the wall behind him. *A man pulls a trigger and a bead of lead comes hurtling at me out of his gun. How many men? How many guns? How many bullets in each gun? So many they hardly have to aim! Sokoloff, you stupid clown, get out of this place...*

From the doorsill, Yoska loosed off a few bursts at targets he couldn't see. Shotgun fire answered him from half a dozen guns — loud enough, it sounded, to push down the brick wall. *In the haven of this building Betsy waited for me at the top landing. Late at night. In her nightgown. I went inside to the kitchen and there was a bowl of soup, some bread, some beer and a woman who didn't care about my rotten skin or crooked leg. Sleep beside her in her bed and I'd be a thousand miles from England. Or anywhere. These stairs took me up, up, up...*

But the voice calling him upstairs wasn't Betsy's; it was Fritz's. 'Go to the top window! Shoot from there!'

Yoska hung at the door to Betsy's flat where he stopped Fritz with a touch of his sleeve. 'If Peter could do it, we can. There's probably not as many of them watching the back way.'

'Use your brains! And your stinking *gun*, Yoska! Keep them off!'

From his position across the street Detective-Inspector Wensley saw the muzzle flash in the garret window before the man-shaped shadow loomed behind it. He said to the Superintendent, 'The Gershon woman's lying to us about how many are inside. For my money there's more than two.' They watched Yoska lean a little way out of the upper window, empty his gun — ten shots furiously whistling through the air, aimed at nothing. Shouts and gasps went up from the crowd, as if they'd just witnessed an acrobatic feat by a circus daredevil.

'Keep those people back!' Wensley hollered down to one of his sergeants.

His order was buried under a deafening volley from the Scots Guards marksmen at the end of the street and the barrage from police shotguns which ploughed the brickwork, scoured glass from every window, tore splinters from the street door. In Betsy's kitchen, Fritz hugged the floor, holding the stove door open for a shield against bullets that raked the shelves and dug furrows in the ceiling. Then, raggedly, the gunfire ceased. *They think we're dead. Storm the building, why don't you, clear us out, charge straight into my pistol barrel.*

Fritz raised himself to the window, where he counted the men ordered to fight against him, the ones he could see. He risked getting his head blown off to have a look at their faces. A commander, the man gesturing toward the police line, his narrow face busy, looking here, looking there, fixing the battle plan. They called in the army! Five snipers in position, on their bellies in the street, four more in peaked caps with the red-and-white chequered ribbon. Some excitement for the young experts with their Lee-Enfield rifles. One of them, hatless, blonde, propped on his elbows and smoked a cigarette. *He wants to get indoors, out of the sleet. They don't want us to surrender.*

'What's there?' Yoska crouched in the alcove behind Fritz.

'Street lamps. Look, daylight and they leave them burning.' Fritz rested his back against the wall. 'Dangerous place for lamplighters.'

'If we shoot the lamps you think it'll make an explosion?'

As Fritz fed a ten-shell clip into his Mauser he answered the question poor Yoska was really asking him. 'We can get away from here.'

'Yes, good. Tonight?'

'If we do one thing.'

'What, tell me. I'll do it.'

'Kill them all.'

Harry encouraged Rivka to borrow a 'good-looking dress' and whatever else she needed from the costume rack, a set of clean clothes that would be comfortable for her and inconspicuous at a family luncheon. 'I'm inviting you for a home-cooked meal,' Harry announced. By one thirty, they had to be in Esher at his sister's house, a bus and train journey that was going to take almost two hours. With these nuggets of news, Harry meant to gee Rivka along, but they'd slowed her instead. Something besides his worry over her daily diet spurred this urge to shunt her miles outside of London.

To reach the less operatic fashions Rivka had to tunnel through half a roomful of Russian peasant wardrobe, the sack-shaped skirts and billow sleeved blouses that would have raised questions around the dining table in Esher, never mind on her way to the bus in Commercial Road. That is, if she'd intended to leave the Pavilion at all. No signal from Charles Perelman yesterday didn't mean no signal today, so for thirty minutes Rivka dragged out her wardrobe search. When he knocked for the second time, she confessed that she'd only just pulled out a blue skirt and jacket and a lace trimmed cream blouse that fit her. 'Why do you want me to go?' she challenged him through the closed door.

From Harry she heard a fractured version of the story agitating everybody else in London; the showdown that had been boiling since dawn in Sidney Street. Most of it was rumours, he told her: *The police trapped the Houndsditch murder gang in a house there; the notorious Peter the Painter is one of them; another policeman lies dead at his hand; the foul anarchists are encircled...* 'Nobody's saying they caught him. If they catch him, Rivka — if Peter gets arrested — we can't do anything until he's on trial. We'll do something. You hear me? We got to think about you first. There's a wig on the shelf, you see it? Goldish-coloured. Rivka?'

Wrong as he could be, Harry took her silence for emotional collapse. As she robed herself in the skirt and blouse and jacket, Rivka was weighing every word Harry had said. *The police are on the lookout for the Liesma anarchists, their friends and associates, accomplices. It's all right, it's fair. Harry's afraid for himself.*

'Look who it is!' he said when Rivka stepped from the wardrobe room, costumed. 'Anna Southam, the Stepney Song Bird! Your debut!' He added, 'Not as a singer today. Next year.' An impresario's sweep of his arm ushered Rivka past him and to the staircase.

Uncage a zoo animal in the wild and its senses would be as keen as Rivka's in the alleyway behind the Pavilion

Theatre. Above the scatter of rubbish and city dirt, a sweetness flavoured the air; the sharp edge of the cold had scraped it clean. A blanched disc of sun turned the cloud over Whitechapel to gray pearl. The scaling dark green paint on the stage door, the rusted gooseflesh of the iron railing, the glossed black cobblestones under Rivka's feet — they were all insistently present, vibrant physical realities, so close to being forced away from them. Everything she saw was exceptional.

Under the corner of a dumped carpet, the white sludge of yesterday's newspaper. Beside it a single shoe. The mossy stack of laths, bound with rope at one end, the other end sprung apart, tucked against the wall. A strip of rose-coloured cloth fluttered, snagged on the end of a lath. That was new. Not snagged, Rivka saw: tied there. She lifted the splayed slats; underneath them, not fallen but placed with care, was the brick she'd left on Charles Perelman's front step. Wrapped in wax paper under the brick, she found the twice-folded wanted poster that carried her prayer to him. *Fun mir tzu P. Vie? Avek.*

Harry called to her from the stage door, 'Sorry, sorry. Wanted to tidy away your bed things.'

She didn't give him a chance to shut her out. Rivka tucked the paper under her jacket and flew at Harry, shrieking, 'No! I want to go back in!'

'What's wrong? What's happened?' Harry expected to see a squad of armed detectives charging after her, but they were alone behind his theatre, Harry and this terrified woman flailing at him to get back inside. He touched Rivka's arm to calm her. 'We're going to my sister's — it's fine. You'll be all right in Esher.'

She cried louder, from the deep pit of a pain he couldn't fathom. 'No! No, no, no, *no*! Let me in! I don't want to go, Harry!' Panicked tears wet her face and his

370

coat. 'No! They'll get me! I want to go in!' What was Harry going to do? Fight her off? Carry her to the train like a sack of potatoes? She fell through the door, choking, desperate for breath, under control enough to repeat, 'They'll take me!'

'All right, you'll be fine here. Stay inside.' From the other side of the door Harry said, 'I have to go.'

Harry's key clicking the mortise lock home also broke the grip of Rivka's hysteria, leaving her with a dizzy head and pounding heart. To keep from fainting, she rested on a props crate and unfolded the wanted poster. Her bold plea slanted down one margin.

> *Fun mir tzu P. Vie? Avek.*
> From me to P. Where? Away.

In reply, along the crease at right angles to Rivka's message, was Charles Perelman's smudgy Arabic-looking handwriting.

> *Naben di greener tir. Vart. Haynt.*
> By the green door. Wait. Today.

Skill or talent? — this ability Peter possessed to materialise in a different building, country, identity. Or had it become a habit, a necessity of life? The oily water in the canal reflected brown-green shadows, nothing else. What would it take for him to jump in and drown? One more step, a last push. The last decision he'd make. Later on this afternoon Peter's body would bob up in some other pocket of West India Docks — unless he was as adroit dead as alive and it washed by unnoticed to the Thames and out to sea. *Let it float.*

Consider this: he'd made it past the guards at the

arched gate to the freedom of the wharf, riding on the feeling that he belonged there as much as anywhere. No one challenged his right, scruffy as he looked, to trawl for day labourer's work. Peter looked up at a featureless lid of gray sky, which minutes ago showed him the sun adrift behind it, flat as a silver coin. *Gone again.* Blame this island weather. On the ground, meanwhile, dray carts hauled crates and bales, dock workers shifted cargo, gangplank and crane fed hundreds of ships' holds at crowded moorings and attracted Peter with the force of an occult power. A one-word spell invoked it: *Away.*

Peter's mind ached, his heart and body too, disconnected parts of him held together by the single yearning for a reason to be anywhere. On the quayside, ships supplied a reason to be at the West India Docks. And after, to hire on as a deck hand, as an apprentice from Alsace named Probst. And after, to work that job to its port of call. And after, to start again. *The things I did that put me here, let them float.*

'Late for the call-on.' No suspicion, accusation or threat in the gang master's voice. 'You're looking to ship?'

'Is there work, do you know?' Peter straightened his posture.

'Depends dock or ship, today or tomorrow.'

'Today.'

'Nothing on the dock. You want to ship, talk to Mr Beek. He'll be hiring for the *Evangeline Tay* bound for Caracas. Not till tomorrow, though.'

'Mr Beek. Thank you,' his best English accent, edges smoothed by the quayside clatter.

'No, I ain't Beek. He's short and ugly. Get here early for the call-on, lad, case you lose out on the *Evangeline*. Best of luck,' the gang master wished him.

After that, Peter scoured the sky for a reason to double

372

back to the Pavilion. A second's thought flung up a dozen reasons not to. Trust the word of that scoundrel Charles Perelman. And after, find out Rivka isn't where he said she was. And after, prowl the district looking for her. And after, pay for it. Trust the word of an agitated girl; find out Rivka couldn't keep Perelman's arrangements or she misunderstood them or didn't trust him and she wasn't waiting where he said she'd be. And after, miss her in the street. And after, keep going, unanchored.

As Peter looked back at the docks through the imperial arch of their gate, as if he'd left his settled mind on the wharf, another reason maddened him. *Trust Perelman's word*, he told himself, *trust Rivka's, and you'll shed a skin.* He fought his garbled instincts. And after, he buried his revolutionist history. And after, not alone under the London sky, he decided to be a man who trusts.

Every obstacle complicating Peter's life until then fell away. What remained was a practical problem: find a route to the Pavilion Theatre that circled clear of Brick Lane.

The elation that carried Charles Perelman on light feet from the Pavilion's back alley was not his own, he realised happily. It was a bubble of joy borrowed from Rivka. As he went on his way, he pictured her opening the wax paper, unfolding the poster and reading the message she was hungriest to hear: today she'd be with her missing lover. Never mind he's a criminal running from the police, violent, deep dyed in red, forget for a moment that from today onward, any life she'd have with him would be precarious and persecuted. If finding Peter gave her happiness that was good enough for Charles Perelman.

She'll be happy because of what I did.

Good enough, but not enough. The population of the world, he philosophized, walking along, is nine-tenths composed of deluded types. From naked savages in the jungle who eat their enemy's brains to George Gardstein lying dead in the morgue. An undeluded man sees the truth of things clear. You learn this by living seventy years with your eyes open. You observe other lives. Not just in your circle, my friend, but a variety — revolutionists and monarchists, English, Russian, Letts, Jews and the rest. The trick is don't let politics influence you; it's deluded men telling you how the world is exactly as brutal as it needs to be. Laws, too, though sometimes your independent thoughts will agree with them.

As he approached the solid stone front of the City Police Headquarters, Charles imagined a different conversation from the brief one he had. For a start he expected to be speaking with a higher ranking officer. Not DI Wensley, who (courtesy of yesterday's tip-off) must be handling things in Sidney Street. A respectful welcome wasn't too much for Charles to expect. Not fawning, only a sign the desk sergeant and the plump constable remembered and regarded him. Be fair, until he told them the reason for his second visit in two days how could they guess its importance?

"Ere's Mr Wensley's bad penny turned up again, George,' the desk sergeant quipped. Charles missed it.

The constable looked up. 'Yes, sir.'

And the sergeant took over. 'Mr Perelman, again, is it?'

'Perelman, yes,' Charles said.

'Detective-Inspector Wensley's grateful for the information you supplied 'im. Very handy. He's not here at the moment, you understand.'

'Yes. His boss? Somebody more?'

374

'Tell me whatever it is and I'll do what needs doing.'

'Other information for him.' Charles noticed the wanted poster on display beside the desk. He tapped his finger next to the words 'Portrait of the said Peter Piatkow.'

'You've got information about this man?' The desk sergeant tapped on the poster too. 'Him?'

'I know where is he.'

George said to the sergeant, 'Thought they had 'im in Sidney Street with his friends.'

'Not there,' corrected Charles. 'I am together him before. Not Sidney Street no more.'

'You know where he is, you say?'

Charles checked the time on his pocket watch. 'Soon. Pavilion Theatre.'

'How d'you spell it?'

'I know the one, Sergeant,' George said. 'The Yid music hall in Vallance Road.'

'Vallance.' Charles confirmed it with a sharp nod. 'Soon, soon. Today. With girl. She's good girl. Not anything of Liesma men.'

'Piatkow's meeting a girl ... at the Pavilion Theatre ... today.' The sergeant wrote the details on a note pad as he spoke. 'Do you know this woman's name? Can you describe her?'

'Her name Rivka. Is lodger. Only good girl, Rivka, best good.'

The elation that settled in Perelman's chest on his walk home belonged to him alone. Wasn't he the Matador, who'd swept his cape over the horns and brutal haunches of another bull? He outsmarted them and he'll outlive them, too. *Because of what I did. The only honest revolutionist in the bunch!* A revolutionary act comes down from the conscience of an independent man. *Do What You Will.*

375

His broad stomach rumbled, his mouth puckered at the delicious thought of comforts waiting for him in his kitchen. Chicken broth and Russian rye bread. Strong cheese. Dark beer. Warmth from the stove. As he ate and drank, warmed his frigid bones and opened his newspaper, a flea bite of doubt pricked the surface of Charles Perelman's contentment. *I know there must be something wrong with giving Peter to the police. But I don't know what it is.*

One thing the Home Secretary knew: rank by itself doesn't command, not a troop or battalion, a man or mob. *Presence* does. His motorcar nudged into the crowd that for five hours had been massing around Sidney Street, but among those members of the public, Winston Churchill's arrival didn't command much besides the curled lip and irate thumbs-down. Any patriotic cheer for the minister fell under barracking that started when he stepped into the street with his top hat and walking stick. "Oo let 'em in?' From one voice, then ten, then fifty, who took up the taunt as a slogan. "Oo let 'em in?'

He did, Winnie and his softhearted soft-headed, chums did, he pushed the Tories into it in '05, his government did it and *Look, Winnie, look what you done bein' humane and open-handed towards the poor sods dyin' in their thousands, Jews kep' down an' Rooshians praclickly slaves! Come on to England, lads, here's your asylum and new temple!* 'Oo let 'em in?' These hovel-dwelling parasites who shelter inside British freedoms and tolerance like ticks inside a horse blanket, to huddle together and plot blood-thirsty revolution. No respecters of sovereign borders, who did they think they were, bringing their feuds, guns, savage temperaments and bomb factories to England?

Who let them in, with their peasant culture, tribal god and satanic lust for control of the world masquerading as high morality and religious devotion?

A punch to an old rabbi's face earned two punches back, not from him. English roughs laid into Yiddishers, attacked them for the insult of putting up a fight. Over here the crowd boiled, over there it churned. Fists jabbed, boots kicked, women cried out, men cursed each other. Somebody raised an iron bar over his head but didn't smash it down — a policeman snapped it out of his hand, another one grabbed the brawler in a headlock, tackled him to the ground. Some poison in the cordite you could see bluing the mist across Sidney Street infected the people; it corroded the buildings, gnawed pieces out of the bricks, liquefied the mortar, showed everyone the augury of a ruined city.

Three rifle bullets had blown holes in the ebony back rest of Betsy's favourite chair. Yoska fit a finger through each one, lifted the chair back onto its legs and placed it where it belonged at the end of the sofa. He did the same for the little round mahogany table, which he also brushed clean of plaster dust. Then Yoska sat in the chair and rested his elbow on the table as if the destroyed room around him were a boulevard cafe and his waiter had just gone to fetch him a glass beer. 'What?' he said in reply to a look from Fritz that begged him to recognise the ridiculousness. Yoska twisted in his seat to examine the three bullet holes. 'You think they can hit the identical place twice?'

'No, I was just thinking — if you're going to tidy the place before Betsy comes back you should start in the kitchen.'

They both heard the shouts in the street and looked towards the glassless windows. Yoska made the same joke

377

about a partisan uprising in Stepney. This time Fritz granted it soft laugh and then he said, 'I'm tired. You?'

'Sleepy, you mean? I don't want to sleep.' Yoska listened again. 'What if they're waiting to see if we come out?'

'They'll be disappointed. You have more ammunition?'

Yoska felt in his jacket pockets. 'Eight clips. We can stay in here for a month. Plenty of food in the other rooms. If nothing bad happens.'

A flick of his eyes. ' "Bad"?'

'Worse.'

'Don't make my head hurt, Yoska. I depend on you.'

'You don't want to have a conversation. I understand.'

'We don't have time to talk about nonsense, that's all.'

'Can I ask you a question?'

Fritz held out his hand and jiggled his fingers at Yoska's revolver. 'Let me look at it.'

'How come?'

'Make sure you've got it loaded.'

While Fritz reloaded the Browning, Yoska leaned close and asked him, 'Is this a leap year?'

'No. Yes. How do I know?' He passed the gun back. 'The safety's off.'

'Because I can't remember if a leap year is when you add a day or lose one.'

'Add one,' Fritz said, with authority. 'At the end of February. Every leap year there's a February twenty-ninth.'

'That's where I'm not sure. If leap years are the ones that go three in a row, then you'd lose a day when it isn't a leap year and end up on February twenty-eighth.'

'You've got it backwards.'

Yoska puzzled, 'Divide by four ... add one to the month...'

'The year. If you can divide it by four.'

378

'Four into nineteen-eleven ... Do you have a pencil?'

'Please forget about it.'

'Sure.'

'You want to stay here or go to the ground floor?'

'Because I was wondering,' Yoska said, 'where I'll be at the end of February. If I'll get an extra day.'

As though Fritz had finally reached a conclusion about his friend, he said, 'You're a humble man, Yoska. Don't let them see it.'

From the people outside, a chorused cheer — or jeer — flared into the air. On hands and knees Yoska crawled to the window and peeked over the sill. 'What are they screaming about?'

Fritz listened a second. 'It's English. I don't know enough words. 'Long live the king'?'

'Can't see them very good.' Gun hand on the windowsill Yoska lifted himself to his knees and leaned out. 'Some gent's come down here in a taxi.'

In a heaven where severed souls go on through an eternity of their last moment before death, Yoska hears English voices and thinks, *What's the name of that song I know?*

The concussion of thirty rifles, the yellow flash and burst, the red plume and spray of dust: none of these drove Fritz back, they rushed him to the window. He retrieved Yoska's revolver and fired quick rounds against the bombardment, his Mauser in his other hand firing too, until both guns clicked empty. He slipped down against the kitchen wall to reload. Spare clips for the Browning were in Yoska's pockets, so Fritz couldn't look away from the pitiful sight of Yoska's body sprawled backwards on the floor. Arms flung up, bad leg bent under him, a black-edged bullet hole in his forehead, the back of his skull gone, curds of Yoska's brain in the splashed stew of his blood and hair on the carpet. And in his face a heavy-lidded expression of mild surprise and absence.

'You're not a dead animal,' Fritz prayed over Yoska's corpse.

Rifle shots sparked through the windows, cracked, ricocheted off the bricks outside. *Kill them all.* Fritz stood and fired again, every pull of the trigger, every bullet blessed with a shout. 'You can't kill me!'

I'm absolutely innocent... I told Peter don't carry Karl home. This from that... I'm clean. My darling I can't write to you... Two weeks on the run I don't know how much longer I can go... This from that... They were guarding the roads... If they catch me they'll hang me for sure for spite... I want to say this for sake of my reputation. The good that somebody like me can bring to Humanity isn't worth a penny... If we were on the ship going to Australia... Be peaceful... We'll be ashes the same as everyone...

Threads of smoke wound out between the wallpaper's curling seams. Fritz watched brown patches bloom in the pattern of pomegranates, leaves and vines. Then finger-sized flames blistered shreds from the paper and waft them through the windows. Flakes of paper, smoke scarves, hungrier fire explored the ceiling.

'You can't kill me.'

In the kitchen, three walls crawled with flames. A thundering wave of dark smoke drenched the outer room, then surged in around Fritz. Blind in this furnace, for as long as he could he held onto a memory — of cool water, a cooling wind on a river bank, his wife's bare feet in the mud, the thin dress clinging to her hips in the stream, blue flowers on white, trailing like a water weed. A memory in her, the same.

'You can't kill me!'

And Fritz shouted it again into the squall of gunfire, barrage after barrage from police shotguns and snipers' rifles, against the eruptions of cinder wind and flames battering property back into dirt — what used to be an accordion, a chair, a carpet, gone to dirt, what used to be a house, the cremation pit for Fritz's body and Yoska's, anarchists no more, gone to dirt.

For three hours Rivka kept her eyes on the door, the solid rectangle transformed by her imagination into gauze lit by wildly spinning thoughts. Staged on its far side was everything Harry said was possible, and more. *The police trapped Peter in a house... He's under arrest, in jail... He's escaped from London... He's hiding in Brick Lane... He's on his way to find her... The police have shot him dead...* Each playlet whirled Rivka's thinking round to its aftermath: if Peter was arrested, she'd stay with Harry's sister... if he got out of London, she'd borrow money and follow him... if he was hiding somewhere close she would do what she had been doing for two weeks, she'd go on waiting for him ... if he was dead then she wouldn't allow another man to touch her for the rest of her life; her spinsterhood would be Peter's memorial. Rivka stared with such intensity at the back of the stage door that she almost believed she could reach Peter, alive or dead, with the power of her mind. Absurdly, she spoke his name.

The doorknob rattled; a force pressed from outside, a fist thumped the middle of the door, angry and dire. Here was a different possibility, one Harry was too delicate to name: a police raid on the Pavilion to take her. So Rivka didn't call out. The door shook against its deadbolt. She pressed her ear close and said, 'Is it you?'

'Let me inside.'

Rivka scrabbled at the lock, pounded on it, tore at the doorknob, but the door stood as solid as a headstone. 'Harry locked it. He went to his sister's house. I made him leave me here.' The only meaningful and obvious fact was the locked door; who locked it, why or when, thoughtfully, thoughtlessly or secretly, didn't make a difference.

'Do you see a key anywhere?' Peter controlled the anger in his voice to keep if from crumbling into desperation.

No hook on the wall, no cubbyhole, no time to ransack Harry's office. 'Peter, I can't find it. Tell me what to do.' Both of his fists answered her, drumming on the other side, a lunge with his shoulder, a parting grunt. 'Tell me what to do...' Rivka moaned to him and to herself. She hugged her stomach, doubled over, paced to the wings and back to the door, where her moaning rose to a wounded howl. Like a restless spirit haunting the staircase, Rivka climbed to Harry's office. Each small defeat brought on another moan — the desk drawer stuffed with papers, the locked drawer, the empty shelf, the promising china box — then the ghost of the Pavilion Theatre moaning for her lost lover drifted downstairs again to the keep her vigil at the stage door.

Another fierce slam against the other side of the door shook Rivka's bones. 'Peter?' No answer came back to her. She leaned close to the door and said his name again.

From somewhere deep in the theatre a soft cracking sound disturbed the air. Rivka stood where she was and stared into the silence and the backstage shadows until one patch of dark came loose from the rest. She saw the figure of a man.

'It's all right.' A sudden uncertainty tightened Peter's voice. 'Rivka?' Space collapsed between them. He pulled Rivka to him with one arm, Rivka bent him down to kiss

382

his mouth, his smooth face, his tall brow. 'Your hair,' he said. 'I thought it wasn't you.'

'Me,' she said, scraping the blond wig from her head.

He fumbled with a couple of the hairpins, plucked them free and buried his face in the scent of her red-brown hair. 'You,' he said. A squeeze from Rivka's hand shot a pain through his and he flinched it away. 'Not as bad as it looks.' He let her look at the sticky, still weeping, gash in his palm. 'Cut it on the window getting in. My knee, too.'

'But you're here.'

'Yes. Here I am. Look at me.' He sounded ashamed, not triumphant.

In front of her, Peter's torn trousers and ripped jacket, the mud spatters, bloodstains, trailing shoelaces, askew necktie. And his control disintegrating. 'Thank God for Charles Perelman,' she said.

'I wasn't sure you'd be here,' he said, looking at his rescuer: Rivka, not Charles Perelman. It was Rivka's hand pulling him from the suffocating wreckage of this earthquake. She was the one with the strength and sympathy to explain how catastrophes can be reversed, this long calamity that's ended by crushing the good out of everything he'd done. *Rivka waited for me here.* His cheek trembled, his shoulders softly shook. 'This time...'

'Peter, we're here. Together.'

'This time I knew I'd get caught.'

'But you didn't. You're here.'

'If they caught me, no, what I'm saying, the police...' Peter wept to her, sobs that broke his words and emptied the fragments into Rivka's hair. 'It would be a good thing if they caught me. Did I rob people because I'm a thief? Kill them because I'm a murderer?'

'You didn't kill anybody, I know you didn't. Jacob did.

Karl and Max did.' She tried to hang on to Peter's arm as he pushed away from her with a disgusted groan. He stalked the backstage corner, grabbed at the curtain ropes, brushed his wet eyes with the back of his hand. He wiped his brow and trailed a smear of blood across it. 'You did what you did. Then the next thing.' All she had was the throb that choked her throat (since she'd temporarily lost the power of speech) to tell Peter her dearest faith was in his goodness as a man.

'What did I do? Opposed them. Oppose, oppose, *worse* than Jacob or Karl. That's the truth. I was against the Romanovs in Courland, and imperialists *everywhere*. Social Democrats, too, because I was a nationalist. First! First I called myself a nationalist. *'Russia out of Latvia!'* Until I woke up, whenever it was, *et voilà* I was a socialist revolutionary.' Another pained, self-disgusted groan and an impotent swipe at the curtain ropes.

'Those Cossacks on the Talsen road,' began Rivka.

'With your father. You told me.'

She sat on the staircase, 'He tried to kill Russians, yes,' she said. 'A Russian tried to make him look weak in front of us. My mother, my sisters and brothers. That army colonel, Orlov, he smashed up my father's beautiful work. Well, Papa couldn't fight this bigshot officer, so he tried to get him a different way. He wanted to wreck something that belonged to Orlov and make *him* look small. Not because Orlov was a Russian. It was for Papa, to make himself equal.' Rivka laughed, in pity, at the memory. 'That rope across the road! To ambush the Russian army!' Her head-shaking had the look of palsy, uncontrollable, afflicted. 'When the Cossacks were chasing me across the field I thought, *Next get to the woods, Next get to the farm road, Next my cousin Jankel.* The next thing I went on a boat, and then I was here. Here I am. Not because of politics. To stay alive, that's all, because then I'll be with you.'

Peter sat on the step below hers. The colour of Rivka's eyes, the blue that captured particles of the unreachable high atmosphere, reflected the substance of his own sorrows. 'It's the same thing,' he said.

Upstairs the water was cold, the carbolic soap covered his skin with with the unlucky odour of a hospital, but for those moments, Peter sleepily bound himself over to Rivka's care. She bathed his body, washed the cuts in his hand and leg, and dressed them with strips of clean muslin. In the wardrobe room she had an easier time digging out a new suit for Peter. The collection of men's costumes was mercifully short on peasant shirts and sashes; male characters in the Yiddish operettas Harry put on seemed mainly to be landowners, burghers and comfortable city-dwelling bourgeoisie. The costume that happened to fit Peter was the apparel of an altogether higher-caste gentleman: dark woollen trousers, a morning coat, a pair of dove-gray gloves, a top hat and a walking stick from the prop box.

Peter and Rivka stood in front of the mirror, framed them like a couple in their wedding photo and saw two conspirators who had come through their disasters to conspire in each other's survival. Seeing him tricked out like a toff, Rivka said, 'We can leave by the front door.'

'Maybe, if it were night-time, after a performance.' Heading to the turning of the staircase, Peter grabbed the fire axe from its corner; he didn't stop until he was standing at the stage door in a woodsman's stance. 'Stand back,' he warned Rivka.

His first blow glanced off of the lock. His next one split

the door jamb above it. Again, Peter brought the axe down on the broken wood, and again, in a powerful arc. The fourth stroke cracked a hole twice the size of the axe head in the door, where the deadbolt used to be. Rivka and Peter exited the Pavilion like burglars and entered the jostle of Whitechapel Road like any couple on an afternoon promenade.

Down the hugger-mugger row of market stalls, barrows and shop fronts, their clothes attracted glances. Beggar boys held out their grimy caps, tin cans or just their hands, following Peter and Rivka along the pavement. Other youngsters noticed them too, with the fidgety loafing, keen eyes and nimbleness of veteran pickpockets. By the entrance of one shop, the owner deliberately blocked their path with a grinning invitation to be amazed by the beautiful quality of his rugs, and their even more beautiful prices. Without obvious hurry, Peter smiled his thanks and led Rivka around him.

The sluggish foot traffic stopped dead at a fabric stall, where a clutch of buyers and sellers jammed the pavement for ten yards on both sides. Peter's gloved hand pressed Rivka's elbow as he walked her to the street side. At the other end of the stall a plump, fair-haired police constable, dispatched by his sergeant into the wind and cold to patrol for fugitive anarchists, did likewise. Rivka saw him step from behind the barrow — half a second before she noticed the seep of blood staining Peter's glove. She took his arm, covered his injured hand with hers and stopped dead, staring into the constable's young face. Blocked on one side the barrow, on the other by motorcars, wagons, people on their blind business, and, between their shoetips and the policeman's, a muddy green-brown tower of horse manure.

What civil rulebook tells a person whose right it is to

go and whose duty it is to halt? It was one more conflict decided on the spot, down in the grains of a human being's passions. The PC's glance slid from Rivka to Peter and back again. Peter's grip choked the handle of his cane. Then the constable raised his finger to his helmet's brim, took a step back, and made room for the immaculately turned out English couple to pass.

'Thank you,' Rivka said quietly, her eyes lowered.

Peter accorded the policeman a genteel nod. 'You're most kind.'

'Keep an eye out for whizzers, I was you, sir,' he advised Peter with a dipping gesture of his hand. 'Pickpockets. Ten a penny 'round Little Jerusalem.'

Brown-tiled, begrimed, loud with public conversation and train-track clatter, Whitechapel Underground station opened to Peter and Rivka as bright and teeming as a Tahitian beach. Together there on the platform, someplace beyond it, they could hear the thrash of water on a boat's hull, see an edge of land divide the sea — the single prospect that filled their view, a fresh beginning in an unmade world.

Epilogue

To say nothing is known about the life Peter the Painter lived after the Stepney siege would be to deny a weight of heartfelt testimony. What can be said is that little is known for certain. After his supernatural disappearance, British newspapers, urgent for triumph, reported that the terrorist Peter Piatkow burned to death in the holocaust of 100 Sidney Street, but neither of the two bodies salvaged from the ruins belonged to him. Death-defying Peter, criminal mastermind, avatar of the anarchist underground, disappeared in a shimmer of heat and smoke. Will-o-the-wisp Peter, nemesis of immigration police, sighted in Australia in 1917, in New York the next year, the south of France in 1926, in Siberia after World War II. A Russian *apparatchik* turned loose from there in the Fifties testified that he was in prison with an Englishman who spoke perfect Russian, and this foreigner admitted, *confessed*, to him that he was Peter the Painter. Who died in the gulag in 1949. Nothing you could verify.

In July 2005 an eighty-nine-year-old retired stage manager (and locally notorious hoarder) named Bernard Burston died at home in Stoke Newington. His place in Osbaldeston Road was declared a health hazard by the Senior Environmental Officer of Hackney Council and a Court Order of Entry was enforced on the nearly derelict three-storey house. A crew of private contractors set about clearing out the decades of foraged rubbish Mr Burston had methodically assembled inside and outside his home.

The cleaning gang's archaeologically-minded foreman rescued a tea chest that was crammed with Burston family memorabilia. The accumulation was crowned with a long document written by Bernard Burston in which he made an eccentric claim: his father had lived his whole life falsely under the name Edward Burston, carrying on a middle-class suburban existence indistinguishable from thousands of others in their neck of north London. That his real name was Peter Piatkow, known to police as Peter the Painter, anarchist, armed robber and murderer. Bernard's chief evidence for this was a wanted poster, found in the tea chest nested amongst the Post-it notes, photographs, Xeroxed newspaper articles, theatre playbills, stapled jottings and other leafy jumble. Down one margin, in handwriting he recognised as his mother's, were the words *Fun mir tzu P. Vie? Avek*, and in another, not in her hand, the reply, *Naben dir greener tir. Vart. Haynt.*

A beguiling picture emerges from Bernard Burston's cranky forensic research into his parents' double history: Rivka's and Peter's history, if we're inclined to believe it.

Edward and Anna Burston lived in France before moving to England at the end of World War I. Edward taught French language and geography at a boys school in Highgate. Bernard describes him as a father he mocked for his shuffling conformity, his petty-bourgeois satisfaction and a vacancy in him where political consciousness and moral outrage should have been planted. Edward's fussy table manners were tokens of a restrained man, untroubled and untroublesome. Untroubled *because* he was untroublesome. A stickler at the dining room table, preparing his next day's lessons and nibbling his vegetarian suppers, who delivered the phrase 'please yourself' in his slight Talsen accent with a retreating shrug as he unhitched himself from any responsibility whenever his cocksure son demanded his way.

For instance, the time teenage Bernard trooped out of the house to hector Oswald Moseley and the British Union of Fascists. Jeering from the pavement, lobbing the odd brick, getting into dust-ups with Blackshirt roughs, Bernard writes, he 'notched up the hard experience' that gave him the right to slam the door on his father and brand Edward 'a physical and moral coward.'

Edward Burston's neighbours saw him as a good citizen. The right sort. A decent chap, considering — considering that he was a foreigner and Jewish to boot. Unambiguous evidence was out in the open. He was a professional man, industrious about getting and unostentatious about spending, a serious-minded gent and a stranger to outbursts, who harboured no particular grievance. Once, Bernard remembers, he was helping his father bury daffodil bulbs in the back garden, when Edward's eyes suddenly misted over, 'Look at the life I'm living now.' A teacher, taxpayer, honorary Englishman, settled down and bedded in, an orderly man, guided by the natural exercise of self-control. Bernard called his dressing-table a 'jeweller's showcase' of hairbrushes and combs, a silver tray under the bowl of cuff links, a French pocket watch always wound and accurately set.

Of his mother, Anna, the tea chest contained photograph upon photograph. Playing roll-the-ball on the lawn with her toddler daughter, Maisie. Performing a piano duet with Bernard. Then, forty years later, sunning her legs at the Brighton seaside. Where, in her collection of hundreds, Bernard wondered, were any snapshots of her husband? Edward the bridegroom? Mr Burston Sir, the French master with his Field House students? The New London Synagogue bridge champion? The weekend water-colourist? The enthusiastic amateur photographer? Well, exactly. His father was more at home behind his lecturer's gown, behind a hand of cards — behind the camera — than in front of it. To be there and not there in the same instant, that was Edward's way.

The lone photo of Edward Burston that Bernard possessed he'd clipped to the top of the wanted poster. It is a portrait of his mother and father together, snapped on their fiftieth wedding anniversary. They sit on two dining room chairs, pushed together for the purpose. A snatched memento for their children and grandchildren, a formal photograph, Edward and Anna, as husband and wife. She tilts towards him slightly, bent sideways at the waist, stiffly but fondly angled. Anna's near hand is clasped under Edward's, resting on his thigh, while her far hand clutches the arm of the chair — for safety, it seems, as if they were posing on the deck of a rolling ship. From behind the fancy eyeglasses, her look is direct, unapologetic.

Edward's nervy eyes are elsewhere, on the exit. Somebody (his daughter or one of his grandsons) has cornered him with a Kodak, trapped him in the spotlight. He's not a relaxed performer. The fidgety smile. Indulgence fading in the strained corners of his mouth. 'How much longer is this ridiculous nonsense going to take?' he seems to wonder. Behind them, on the sideboard, you can make out a small watercolour of a pond and water lilies. Edward inhabits a room and an existence of harmless comfort arranged by his wife. Not even fifty years of it can relieve him of the feeling that he has infiltrated some English gentleman's territory.

THE OTHERS

Late in January 1911, Jacob Peters and Yourka Dubof stood trial or the murder of Sergeant Charles Tucker, harbouring a felon guilty of murder (George Gardstein) and conspiring to break and enter H.S. Harris's jewellery shop intent on theft. Nina Vassilleva was charged with harbouring George Gardstein and conspiracy to break and enter. Luba Milstein and Sara Rosa Trassjonsky went to court on the conspiracy charge, a charge of 'assisting the escape from punishment of two others whose names are unknown' and as an accessory to the murders of Police Sergeants Charles Tucker and Robert Bentley and Police Constable Walter Choate. Within weeks everyone, except for Nina, had been released on grounds of insufficient evidence.

Found guilty of conspiracy, Nina was sentenced to two years in prison. At the start of her second month in Holloway the Court of Criminal Appeal quashed her conviction; the trial judge, Justice Grantham, was found to have misdirected the jury in his summing up. The appellate court decided that the probability of Nina's guilt could not be inferred, as Justice Grantham had emotively suggested it might, from her intimate association with George Gardstein. Freed from prison Nina returned to her work as a cigarette maker for Abdullah's.

Her political beliefs survived unshaken. Not long after the 1917 Revolution, Nina took work in London with the Soviet Trade Delegation, an organisation known to foster more espionage and promote more political and economic subversion in Great Britain than commercial trade. She lived alone and apart from the old community in Brick Lane, an exile among exiles, and died in St Bartholomew's hospital in 1963.

In the summer of 1911, Luba Milstein gave birth to Fritz's son. She named him Alfred, after Alfred Dzircol, who was known in East End revoluntionist circles by the alias Karl Hoffman. A friend of Fritz, who felt something deeper than a playful fondness for Luba, Alfred promised he'd look after her if ever Fritz could not. In January 1912, Luba and her son sailed for New York; a year later they were joined by Alfred, who landed in America as an illegal immigrant.

Together Luba and Alfred had a daughter and built modest lives for their family of four in New York City, where Alfred worked as a house painter and Luba as a seamstress. Marxists to the end of their days, they believed a better world could be shaped through socialist revolution, but turned their backs on terrorist action as an unacceptable danger to innocent people and a cloak that too easily protected naturally violent criminals. Alfred died in 1961. Luba died in a nursing home in 1973, where the last people to see her were two gentleman callers bearing bouquets.

Of the Sisterhood, Rosie fared worst. The mental shock of George Gardstein's death, her arrest and three months on remand in prison — followed by the hammering strain of a public trial — broke her already frail condition. By turns comatose and suicidal Rosie was confined as a 'pauper lunatic' in Colney Hatch Asylum until in May 1911, when even that poor haven for her fell under threat. London County Council, the municipal body footing the bill for Rosie's incarceration, initiated deportation proceedings against this 'alien in receipt of parochial relief'. Illness prevented her from answering the summons to appear at Bow Street Magistrates Court and in her absence the court granted an expulsion order. The Clerk of the Asylums Committee advised that Rosie remained suicidal, needed to be force-fed, and was not likely ever to be healthy enough to survive deporatation.

She remained an inmate of Colney Hatch Asylum until her death a few years later. At Christmas in 1912, Rosie received the anonymous gift of a perfumed sachet. It was from Nina. The note pinned to it read 'To the nurse who so kindly tended Carl Garstin (alias Gardstein) during his last hours.'

While Yourka Dubof drifted out of the city and into obscurity soon after his release, Jacob Peters stayed in London, politically active and, if anything, more visible. He founded the Latvian Social Democratic Bolshevik Foreign Bureau, an organisation dedicated to the task of raising money and manpower to support Lenin's faction in the communist struggle. A little more than six years after Houndsditch, the February revolution cleared a way for Jacob to join the Bolshevik ranks in Russia.

In Petrograd Lenin's officials recognised his accomplishments and devotion by enlisting him as an operative of the Bolshevik Military Organisation. They despatched Jacob home to Latvia where, as he'd done in 1905, he roused workers and soldiers to the revolutionary cause in marketplaces and cafes, at political meetings, demonstrations, even funerals. After Riga, he moved up the ladder from agitprop specialist to the Military Revolutionary Committee of the Petrograd Soviet, prime movers of the October *coup d'état* that slung out Trotsky's Mensheviks and elevated Lenin to supreme power. Inside two months of the October revolution, the Cheka was energetically in business, sniffing out and crushing the forces of counter-revolution. Jacob — 'courageous to the point of fanaticism', to borrow the description of his Houndsditch comrade George Gardstein — won the post of Deputy Chairman.

As a high official of the revolution's guardians, Jacob signed scores of death sentences and oversaw the judicial murders of hundreds of men and women. In 1930, now a senior member of the Central Control Committee of the Soviet Communist Party, honoured with the title Hero of October, Jacob presided over a tribunal assembled to purge (among others) 'disaffected elements' in the Red Army. Five years later, rumours began to circulate in the Kremlin that Jacob had roused Stalin's suspicion and fallen out of favour. In 1937 he was arrested. In 1938 Jacob Peters was purged from the Communist Party and executed by a Red Army firing squad.

Acknowledgements

My thanks to Roger Appleby, curator of the City of London Police Museum, for guiding me through material relating to the Houndsditch murders and the Sidney Street Siege. I'm also grateful to the staff at the Corporation of London Records Office for their help in locating and providing copies of photographs and police documents.

Among many books useful to my understanding of the era, locale and personalities dramatised in *A Storm in the Blood*, Donald Rumbelow's *The Houndsditch Murders and the Siege of Sidney Street*, through its crisp scholarship, rendered the complicated chronology of overlapping events and relationships with unparalleled clarity. I am also grateful to the Arts Council, East of England, for a grant during the early stages of this book's research and writing.

JSF